CHRISTMAS WITH THE EAST END ANGELS

It's the most wonderful time of the year — and the East End Angels are working hard to keep Londoners safe. Frankie is trying to keep everything together. She can count on the support of the East End Angels, even in the face of family trouble. Winnie's beloved husband, Mac, is putting himself at risk every day in the bomb disposal unit and she's finding it hard while he's away. Bella's friendship with Winnie's brother, James, is getting closer all the time.

Christmas on the Home Front is a hard time with loved ones far away — but the women of the Auxiliary Ambulance service are making do and mending.

CHRISTMAS WITH THE EAST END ANGELS

CHRISTMAS WITH THE EAST END ANGELS

by

ROSIE HENDRY

Magna Large Print Books
Leicestershire

British Libarary Cataloguing in Publication Data.

A catalogue record of this book is
available from the British Library

ISBN   978-0-7505-4719-2

First published in Great Britain by Sphere in 2018

Copyright © Rosie Hendry 2018

Cover illustration © Colin Thomas

Rosie Hendry has asserted her right to be identified as the
author of this work in accordance with the Copyright, Designs
and Patents Act 1988

Published in Large Print 2019 by arrangement with
Little, Brown Book Group

All rights reserved. No part of this publication may be
reproduced, stored in a retrieval system, or transmitted in any
form or by any means, electronic, mechanical, photocopying,
recording or otherwise without the prior permission of the
Copyright owner.

Magna Large Print is an imprint of Library Magna Books Ltd.

Printed and bound in Great Britain by
T. J. (International) Ltd., Padstow, Cornwall, PL28 8RW

For Isobel, with love.

1

'That makes twenty-three shillings and tuppence.' Frankie finished counting out the money on to the kitchen table. 'It's short again this week, Ivy! I need another shilling and ten pence from yer.'

'Well, you ain't getting it, 'cos I ain't got it.' Ivy folded her arms and sneered, her ice-blue eyes cold in her heavily made-up face. Frankie put her hands on her hips and glared at her step-grandmother. 'This is the third week running yer've left me short with your rent. I ain't going to keep topping it up out of my wages. If you can't pay your way, then we'll 'ave to give up this house, then you can go your way and I'll go mine.'

'Humph!' Ivy rummaged about inside her handbag and threw a sixpence on the table. 'There. Will that do yer?'

'It's still short. Perhaps you'd like to explain to the rent man why he ain't getting his full rent this week, since it's you that's making it short, not me,' Frankie suggested.

'I ain't staying 'ere listening to you; I've got to get to work.' Ivy snatched up her handbag. 'I don't know what your grandad would say if he could 'ear the way you speak to me.'

'I only asked yer to pay your fair share of the

1

rent each week, that's all. You should be able to afford it on your wages from the garment factory.'

Ivy sniffed. 'I 'ave things to buy to keep my spirits up now I'm a poor widow. They don't come cheap, you know.'

Frankie had seen some of the things Ivy chose to spend her wages on: the make-up, stockings and bottles of drink — sherry, whisky, whatever she could get — and all hard to come by in the shops these days; no doubt bought on the black market for an inflated price. 'I don't care what you spend your wages on as long as you pay your share of the rent. If you don't then we'll 'ave to leave 'ere 'cos the landlord'll kick us out. There's an 'ousing shortage, remember, so he'll soon find someone else who's willing to pay the rent.'

'All right, all right, but I ain't got any more to give you right now. I'll 'ave to owe it yer,' Ivy snapped and flounced out of the kitchen, slamming the front door loudly a few moments later.

Frankie sighed and sat down. She leant her elbows on the table and put her head in her hands, listening as the blood gradually stopped whooshing so hard in her ears. Life with Ivy was like living in a miniature war of her own, little battles flaring up between them regularly, always because of the older woman's selfishness or failure to pull her weight. Frankie was tired of having to pick up the pieces and do more than her fair share in the house or pay more than her portion of the rent. If her grandad had known how his widow would behave, would he have been so keen to ask Frankie to promise to look out for Ivy before he died? She'd never know the answer to that because he wasn't here to tell her any more.

Now, almost seven months since he'd been killed in the last huge raid on London, Frankie had been driven to the point of despair. She should stop picking up the slack and let the landlord throw them out for not paying the full rent, then she'd be able to go her own way and forget about that horrible woman. Ivy would get a huge shock if she ever had to stand on her own two feet again with no one to bolster up her selfish ways.

Only Frankie couldn't let them lose the house; she had to keep it going so that Stanley had a home to come back to at number 25 Matlock Street, after the war. He might not be a blood relative, but the eleven-year-old boy had become like a brother to her when her grandparents had taken him in after his mother had died. Now, with both her grandparents gone, she was the one responsible for him. He might be safely evacuated to the countryside for the moment, but one day he would return home and she'd promised him that it would still be here waiting for him.

Sitting up, she began to gather the money into the tin she used for the rent money, knowing full well that she had no choice but to make up the difference yet again. Did Ivy know that Frankie would never let them lose the house? Possibly. She'd never say as much to her, but her step-grandmother knew how much she loved

3

Stanley and the home she'd lived in all her life. Frankie would do whatever was necessary to keep it going. Ivy, like the plant she was named after, was hanging on to the comfortable home she'd married into. She wouldn't ever leave unless something better came along.

Frankie glanced at the clock on the mantelpiece. It was almost quarter past seven: if she didn't get a move on she'd be late for the start of her shift at Ambulance Station 75.

After she'd hidden the rent tin away in a safe place, she grabbed her sandwiches, stuffed them into her bag and pulled on her coat, wrapping herself up in her scarf and pulling her knitted green beret on over her auburn hair ready for her bicycle ride to work.

Outside in Matlock Street the air was icy cold, her breath spiralling out in plumes in the pale light, the sky lightening as the sun rose. Pushing off on her bicycle, she bumped over the cobbles just as her neighbour Josie emerged from the front door of number 5 and picked up her milk bottle from the doorstep.

'Morning, ducks,' Josie called, beaming a warm smile at her.

Frankie braked and came to a halt by her. 'Morning, Josie, 'ow are you?'

Josie rubbed her back, her swollen belly straining the front of her crossover apron, which didn't quite cross over any more, but draped to the sides like the curtains at a window. 'Not so bad, but I'll be a whole lot more comfortable when this one's born. All right for my old fella, he comes 'ome on leave and goes off back to the

4

army and leaves me in the family way.' She laughed and stroked her stomach with one hand. 'Still, it'll be lovely to 'ave a baby in the house again.'

'If you need any 'elp, you only 'ave to ask — you will, won't yer?' Frankie said.

'Course I will, thank yer, ducks.' Josie frowned. 'You all right? Only you look a bit peaky this morning.'

'I'm fine, just 'ad a bit of a run-in with Ivy over the rent again.'

Josie rolled her eyes. She knew how things were with Ivy as Frankie often talked to the older woman, seeking advice from her and glad of someone to turn to who understood just how difficult Ivy could be. 'She oughta count 'erself lucky she's got you there to keep the 'ouse going. If it were left to her she'd have been kicked out months ago.' She shook her head. 'I don't know what your grandad would have said; she's got worse since he died.'

Frankie shrugged. 'We live separately as much as we can. She deals with her own rations and I do mine; we don't cook together, do our own washin', more like lodgers in the same 'ouse, only she don't pay her way or do her fair share of the cleaning.' She'd had plenty of arguments with Ivy over not washing up her used plates and cups. It wasn't as if Ivy did much cooking; she seemed to survive on fish and chips or go to the pie and mash shop or a cafe. It was no wonder she didn't have any money left from her wages. 'You're a saint to put up with 'er, I don't think I could.' Josie shivered. 'It's cold out 'ere. Drop in

5

on your way 'ome tonight if you fancy a cuppa.'

'Will do, thanks, Josie. See yer later.' Frankie pedalled on in the direction of Station 75, glad of her neighbour's friendly support; without it Matlock Street would seem a much lonelier place.

2

'You don't need to wait until my train goes,' Mac said as he and Winnie walked into Liverpool Street station, their arms around each other. 'You should go or you'll be late for your shift.'

Winnie shook her head. 'I don't care. I'm spending every last second I can with you, and if that makes me late for work, then so be it. I can make up the time later, or forgo my breaks.'

Mac grinned. 'Aren't Deputy Station Officers supposed to set a good example? Keep to the rules.'

She laughed. 'Rules should have a little bit of bend in them, don't you think?'

'You are quite incorrigible; did you know that?'

'I know, but you love me all the same.'

'You know I do, very much.' Mac stopped walking and kissed her, then pulled her into a tight embrace.

Winnie closed her eyes and leaned her head against his chest, breathing in the scent of him: soap and essence of Mac. She squeezed her eyes tightly shut to dam the tears that were threatening to spill over. She didn't want to spoil what time they had left together by crying, she could do that in private later. Having Mac arrive home on a surprise forty-eight-hour leave had been absolutely wonderful, but it also had a bitter-sweet edge to it because he had to go away

7

again, and saying goodbye was utterly beastly. It never got any easier, even though they'd done it several times now since he'd joined the bomb squad. Each time it hurt and she was terrified that it could be the last time she ever saw him.

'Come on, I mustn't miss my train.' Mac loosened his arms, took hold of her hand and led her into the throng of people that were crowding the station: Londoners on their way to work, Winnie guessed, and service people in uniform, their heavy kit bags in tow.

So many people on the move to who knows where, she thought, leaving people at home waiting for them, missing them and worrying about them. This horrid war had torn up the lives of so many people, tossing them to different places far from their homes and families, those lives now governed by the services. She wished it was over and done with so that she and Mac could settle down into their married life and not be forced to live it in a few snatched hours of leave, with always the worry that it could be their last hanging over her like some dark cloud.

She'd got it bad, Winnie thought, she really was down in the dumps and now was most definitely not the time for feeling that way. She shouldn't waste this precious time with Mac, so giving herself a mental shake, she pasted a smile on her face and worked on her chin-up and stiff-upper-lip attitude so that she'd be able to send him off with a smile and not tears.

Standing on platform ten beside the train that would take Mac back to his bomb disposal depot in Colchester, Winnie looked at her husband, trying to drink in every detail of him to last her until the next time she saw him: his beautiful blue eyes which were shot through with amber streaks; his dark blond hair, and the tall, solid, gentleness of him. Seeing him dressed in his khaki army uniform still gave her a jolt — it didn't seem right after knowing him for so long in the navy-blue boiler suit he'd worn when he worked as an ambulance driver with her at Station 75. She would never be happy that he now worked digging up bombs instead, would never stop worrying about him, but she'd had to accept that it was what he wanted to do.

Winnie reached out and touched the red sleeve flash sewn on to his uniform, her fingers tracing the bomb embroidered in gold thread with royal blue detailing. 'You will be careful, won't you?' Mac put his hands on her shoulders. 'I always am. We don't take unnecessary risks, so try not to worry about me.'

'Impossible, I'm afraid.'

'You be careful, too.'

'Life at Station 75 is rather tame these days compared with how it was during the Blitz; we haven't had a raid since May. If they hadn't brought in that ridiculous rule, I might have left to do something with a bit more action.' A new rule had been passed a few weeks before preventing ambulance crews from leaving the service now that the raids had stopped for the time being; there was always the possibility and fear that the bombers would return, and they needed the crews to be on standby if and when that happened.

Mac threw back his head and laughed. 'My dearest Winnie, if your mother could hear you saying that she'd be delighted, her wish to get you to leave the Ambulance Service would come true. But you can't and I'm glad, because if you did who knows where you'd be sent to. At least we're not that far away from each other and I know that your friends at Station 75 look out for you while I'm not here.'

'Well, it's out of my hands now, but it's frustrating sometimes to not have much to do other than keeping the station ticking over.' She sighed. 'I know that sounds awfully mad because in the thick of the Blitz we'd have liked nothing better than for the raids to stop.'

'All aboard,' a guard shouted.

Winnie's stomach clenched. This was the bit she hated.

'I've got to go.' Mac's eyes met hers and he kissed her, then pulled her into a tight embrace.

'When will I see you again?' she said as he released her. 'Will you be back for Christmas, do you think?'

'I don't know. I will if I can.' Mac put his hand on her cheek. 'I love you.'

Winnie grabbed hold of his hand and swallowed hard, her throat painful. 'I love you, too.'

Mac smiled at her and then turned and climbed into a nearby carriage, slamming the door behind him. He pulled the leather strap down to open the window, then leant out and took hold of her outstretched hand. 'Look after yourself.'

The guard blew his whistle and waved his green flag, and with loud chuffs of smoke that billowed from the engine up into the ornate ironwork roof of the station, the train began to move. Winnie walked with it, still holding on to Mac's hands, desperately eking out her last moments with him, but as the train picked up speed she had to let go. 'Goodbye, Mac.'

She could still see his face looking back at her out of the window, watched it as long as she could, imprinting it on to her mind until the next time she could see it. Then the train was gone, leaving nothing but a sooty taint in the air and the background hubbub of station noise. Winnie stood, still looking down the empty track. Wrapping her arms around herself, she closed her eyes and sent up a silent prayer that Mac would keep safe. Then she turned and walked back along the platform, dashing away her tears with the back of her hand as she headed for Station 75 where her shift was now about to start. She was going to be late getting there, but she really didn't care because being with Mac for as long as possible was far more important to her.

3

Bella read through what she'd written one last time. It was as polished as she could make it and she hoped that Mr Dawson, the journalist at *The War Illustrated*, and his editor would think so too.

'Are you happy with it?' Connie asked as she sat down at the kitchen table and poured a cup of tea out of the bone-china teapot. 'Yes. It's due in today so I'll deliver it on my way to work. It's getting much harder to find something interesting and new to write about now the Blitz is over and I've already written so many pieces.' Bella had been writing a fortnightly piece about life working at a London Auxiliary Ambulance station since the summer. Her brief had been to write about what it was really like doing the job, to show behind the scenes — all the things that a journalist couldn't see on a flying visit to the station. 'I mustn't complain about there being no air raids, though; we don't want the bombers coming back killing and injuring more people.'

'I expect they'll be back sometime, so enjoy the peace while you can.' Connie broke off a toast crust and fed it to Winnie's dog, Trixie, who was sitting patiently by her side, looking at her hopefully with her liquid brown eyes. 'Why don't you have a word with your journalist, see what he thinks?'

Bella shook her head. 'I can't do that. I don't want him to think I can't do the work.'

'Oh, Bella, there's no doubt that you can write beautifully; haven't you proven it many times over now?' Connie reached across the table and patted Bella's arm. 'Be proud of what you've achieved because it really is quite marvellous. Just think, your work has been read by thousands of people all over the country.'

Bella's cheeks grew warm. 'I know, but I don't want to lose this job, I love doing it.' She glanced at her watch. 'I'd better get going. Come on, Trixie, time to go.' She was taking the little dog into work with her this morning as Winnie had gone to see Mac off at the station.

'Have a good shift,' Connie said.

'I will, see you later.'

★ ★ ★

Holding Trixie tucked under one arm, Bella walked into the newspaper office where Mr Dawson worked. The clatter of typewriter keys permeated the air, which was thick with cigarette smoke.

'Ah, good morning to you,' Mr Dawson said, looking up from his desk where he'd been furiously scribbling in spidery writing on his notepad. 'And who's this with you?' He put out his hand and stroked Trixie's head, the little dog wagging her tail in response.

'This is Trixie; I wrote about her being dug out of a bombed-out building a few weeks back. She's coming into work with me this morning as

13

her owner's seeing her husband off at the station.'

'Ah, the famous ambulance station dog. Have you got this week's piece?'

'Here it is.' Bella handed it over and waited, her heart starting to pound as Mr Dawson read it through. This was always an anxious moment: waiting to see if her writing was accepted. All of it had been so far, but there was always a first time . . .

'That's a good piece of work,' he said, laying it down on his desk.

'But I'm afraid this is the last piece we'll run on the Ambulance Service; we won't be wanting another from you. The editor feels that although it's been very good and popular with our readers, it's time to move on.'

Bella stared at him for a few moments as what he'd said sank in, her chest tightening. 'Have I done something wrong?'

'No, not at all, every piece you've written has been excellent.' Mr Dawson ran a hand through his thinning hair. 'The thing in journalism is to know when enough is enough, if you keep on for too long with something then it can become stale and the reader won't like it. Knowing when to stop before that happens is the key, and the editor's decided that it's now. I'm sorry. Truly, I am, you've done a remarkable job.'

'Very well, if you don't want any more about the Ambulance Service then I'm willing to write something different. Anything.' Writing was too important to her to give it up without a fight. There had to be another way. 'I could write about . . . ' Her mind whirled through other possibilities but none of them seemed any good off the top of her head.

'I'm sorry, but there's nothing else for you at the moment. I'll keep you in mind if anything comes up that I think might be suitable for you, all right? I can't promise anything but if I need a good writer I know where to come.' He shrugged. 'That's the best I can do.'

What could she say? If she kicked up a fuss they'd never use her again. She just had to be professional and accept that they didn't want her to write her articles any more and she couldn't force them to take them. But it hurt. She'd doubted her ability to do it at first and writing each piece had been a challenge, but in spite of that she'd still loved doing it and not doing it any more would leave a huge hole in her life. 'I'm sorry, too, I've really enjoyed doing it.' Bella sighed. 'Thank you, Mr Dawson, for giving me the chance in the first place. I really hope you might find something else for me sometime.'

'I'll be in touch if there's something that's right for you, I promise.'

She nodded. 'Thank you, I appreciate that.'

★ ★ ★

Pedalling towards Station 75 with Trixie sitting in the basket at the front of her bicycle, the little dog's golden ears streaming back in the icy cold wind, Bella bit back the urge to cry. She was hurt and bitterly disappointed. Admittedly, she had been finding it harder and harder to find new and interesting things to write about, but the quality of her writing hadn't altered, the pieces were still good and entertaining, she could have written more. It seemed so unfair to have it suddenly cancelled on the whim of the editor because he felt like something different . . . She swallowed against the lump in her throat. She had no choice in the matter: the editor's word was final, all she could do now was hope that Mr Dawson found something else for her to write. But would he?

Reaching the entrance to Station 75, she turned in under the archway and bumped her way over the cobbles into the courtyard where the ambulance station was housed in flat-topped mews garages opposite a crescent of grand terraced houses. Hopping off, she scooped Trixie out of the basket and put her down on the ground and the little dog immediately dashed in through the open garage doors. Bella followed, pushing her bicycle past parked ambulances to the back where the staff left them.

'Mornin', Trixie.' Frankie had already parked her bicycle and Bella could see her crouching down and making a fuss of an ecstatic Trixie: the dog was wagging her tail so hard her whole body was wriggling from side to side.

'She must have known you were in here.' Bella leaned her bicycle against the wall. 'There's not much gets past Trixie.'

'She's a clever girl.' Frankie stood up and looked at Bella, her blue eyes suddenly looking concerned. 'Are you all right? Only you look a bit upset.'

16

Bella bit her bottom lip. 'They don't want any more articles from me for *The War Illustrated*. They think there's been enough on the Ambulance Service now, I — ' She stopped as her voice wavered.

Frankie put her arm around Bella's shoulder. 'I'm sorry to 'ear that; I know 'ow much you love doing it. Can't they give you somethin' else to write about instead?'

'I did ask, tried to think of something interesting on the spot but couldn't . . . Mr Dawson said he'd let me know if something else came up that was right for me.' She sighed. 'I'm going to miss it.' Frankie pulled her into a hug. 'I know you are; you're a good writer. It's a rotten shock for you and that ain't nice to have 'appen.'

'I never expected that when I went in there this morning.'

Frankie stood back and looked Bella straight in the eye. 'My gran used to say that when one door closes another opens. Keep thinkin' that and who knows what might come along next for you.'

Bella smiled at her. 'You are such a tonic, Frankie. I don't know what I'd do without you.'

'Keep your chin up, as Winnie says. And talking of our dear friend, 'ave you seen her this mornin'? Is she all right?'

'Only briefly before she and Mac left for the station. She looked fine then but you know her, stiff upper lip and all that, she'll be hiding what she's feeling. She hates it when Mac goes back.'

'We'll 'ave to keep an eye out for her today.' Frankie glanced at her watch. 'If she ain't here in

17

a few minutes she'll be late. We'd better keep the boss talking so she won't notice — the last thing Winnie needs today is a tellin'-off for being late. You can tell the boss about what's 'appened; that should keep her mind off the time for a bit.'

'Good idea.' Bella linked her arm through Frankie's and the two of them headed for the staff rooms above the garages.

4

It was Trixie who spotted her mistress first, waiting at her and Frankie's look-out post by the window of the common room where all the crew members had gathered as they always did at the start of a shift. At the sight of Winnie freewheeling in under the archway on her bicycle, the little dog responded with a yap and furious tail wagging. Frankie sighed with relief that her friend was finally here. So far, they'd managed to hide Winnie's late arrival from Station Officer Steele, but as the minutes ticked by, she was getting worried — she wasn't sure how much longer Bella could keep the boss talking.

As soon as Winnie disappeared from view, going into the garage to park her bicycle, Trixie dashed to the stairs and bumped down them, eager to get to her mistress. Following her, Frankie stopped at the doorway of Station Officer Steele's office and waited for a pause in the conversation.

'Frankie, is everything all right?' Station Officer Steele asked, her brown eyes warm behind her horn-rimmed glasses.

'Yes, everything's fine. I just wanted to let Bella know that I'm goin' down to start on our ambulance now.' Frankie looked at her friend and smiled.

Bella gave her a knowing look, understanding

that it was safe to stop distracting their boss. 'I'll come with you.'

'Don't be disheartened by what's happened, Bella. You've now got experience of publishing your writing and who knows what might happen next,' Station Officer Steele said. 'Be proud of what you've achieved.'

Bella stood up. 'Thank you.'

'And Winnie's very lucky to have such loyal and caring friends.' The boss looked at her watch. 'I'll overlook her being late on this occasion since she'll have been seeing Mac off, but tell her I may not be quite so understanding next time.'

Frankie felt her cheeks grown warm, embarrassed at being caught out. Looking at the pinkness blooming on Bella's cheeks, she clearly felt the same.

'But how . . . ?' Frankie began.

Station Officer Steele shook her head and laughed. 'There is very little that goes on at Station 75 that I don't know about. Trixie's never far away from her mistress, so seeing her bolt past my office door I knew exactly when Winnie arrived.'

'We didn't — ' Bella began.

The older woman held up her hand to stop her. 'Your friendship is strong and together you make a formidable team, which in turn contributes to making Station 75 such a magnificent and resilient ambulance station.' She paused and smiled. 'I'd have done the same for my friends in the last war.'

Frankie smiled at her boss, who could be strict

and ran their station like clockwork, but who also had a heart of gold and knew exactly what it was like for them, having driven ambulances herself in France during the Great War. 'We'll tell her and thank you for understanding.'

Station Officer Steele nodded. 'You do that, and I'll be down to check on the work in a while.'

'We should have known the boss would guess what was going on,' Bella said as they made their way down the stairs and out into the courtyard. 'I felt so guilty when she said she knew.'

'There's no 'arm done this time. I — ' Frankie stopped talking as Winnie came out of the garage doors with Trixie following close behind. She looked pale and her usual cheerful disposition was clearly lacking this morning, replaced by a look of mulish anger and upset.

'I'm afraid the boss knows you were late,' Bella said. 'We were doing a good job covering for you but Trixie's joy in seeing you arrive gave it away. She didn't mind, though, only said to tell you she might not be so understanding next time.'

Winnie shrugged. 'I appreciate you covering for me, but I'd do it again in a heartbeat.'

'Winnie!' Bella and Frankie chorused.

Winnie smiled, her pillar-box-red lipstick bright in her pale face. 'Mac is more important to me than being on time. If being with him for a few precious minutes more means that I'm late, then so be it. I'm prepared to work later to make up for it or forgo my breaks.'

Frankie linked her arm through one of Winnie's and Bella did the same on the other

21

side and they marched their friend back towards the garage.

'You are supposed to be a Deputy Station Officer,' Frankie said. 'So don't go lettin' on to the boss that you'd do it again. Let's just get on with our work and not give her anythin' to complain about today.'

'Perhaps you should be made a Deputy Station Officer instead,' Winnie said. 'I'm not sure I want to do it any more, actually.'

Bella let go of Winnie's arm and moved in front of her, blocking her way. 'Now look here, Winnie,' she said, standing with her hands on her hips. 'We know you're upset about Mac going back, but getting all huffy and awkward like you're brewing for a fight isn't going to help anyone, least of all you. You're not the only one who's upset this morning, you know!'

Winnie stared at Bella who stood silently in front of her, tears starting to glisten in her brown eyes. 'What's going on?'

Bella remained silent.

'Frankie, what's happened?' Winnie looked worried, all traces of the stubborn, angry lines in her face now gone. 'Tell me.'

'Bella, do you want me to explain, or should you?' Frankie asked.

'You do it.' Bella's voice was little more than a whisper.

'Bella lost her writin' job this morning,' she said and explained what had happened, watching as Winnie's grey eyes filled with sympathy.

'Oh, Bella, I'm so sorry that they've done

22

that.' Winnie threw her arm around Bella's shoulder and hugged her tightly. 'You are an absolutely superb writer and they are utter fools to let you go. Shall I go and see them and talk them out of it, make them see sense and reinstate your job?'

Bella's lips twitched and she started to laugh. 'They wouldn't know what had hit them if you did. I appreciate the offer, I really do, but the editor's word is final, apparently.' She shrugged: 'It's just that I'll miss it.'

'Of course you will, but you'll still keep writing for yourself, won't you?' Winnie asked.

Bella nodded.

'Good, because it would be an awful waste of talent if you didn't.' She held out her hands. 'And I'm most terribly sorry for being such a self-centred fool just now. I'm not the only wife whose husband is away and at least Mac isn't thousands of miles away like some men. I need to think of that and count myself lucky,' Winnie said. 'And thank you for covering for me and I'm sorry for being such a beastly grump.'

'Ain't you started work yet?' a voice called from behind them, making them all look round. 'I don't know, you women could stand around talkin' all day.'

'Indeed.' Winnie winked at Frankie and Bella and turned her attention back to Sparky who took the cigarette from behind his ear and lit it, blowing a plume of smoke up into the cold air. 'I've known many a time when you've talked so much no one could get a word in edgeways no matter how hard they might try.'

Frankie looked at Bella and smiled, nodding with her head to indicate they should leave them to it. Winnie and Sparky were sparring partners of old, the two of them thoroughly enjoying their spats.

'Thank goodness for that,' Bella whispered as they made their way over to their ambulance, ready to start the daily checks and cleaning. 'I thought for a minute that Winnie was going to throw away all she's achieved here because of feeling miserable.'

'It's understandable, but luckily for 'er she's got us here to sort her out. That's what she told us to do on her weddin' day, remember, when she got upset about Mac leaving to join the bomb squad.'

Bella smiled. 'I remember, and knowing Winnie I'm sure we'll have to do it again.'

5

Frankie was cleaning the windscreen of her and Bella's ambulance a short while later, her fingers wet and stinging with cold, as she listened to the general hubbub of conversation going on around her. She always enjoyed this part of the shift, with everyone busy preparing their vehicles, some crew members on top of them scrubbing the roof, others with their heads stuck in the engine doing the essential checks of oil and water. They were like a little army of ants, she thought, tending to the ambulances. Only today's conversation was one she wished wasn't happening, as the talk was about yesterday's attack by Japan on the American naval base at Pearl Harbor in Hawaii, and the fact that Japan had now declared war on Britain and America. Instead of getting nearer the end of the war, things had just become a great deal worse.

'The Americans are goin' to 'ave to join in now,' Sparky said. He'd spread this morning's newspaper out on the bonnet of his ambulance and was studying it intently, often reading out chunks of it aloud.

'Do you think they'll declare war on Germany too?' Winnie said, cleaning a wing mirror on her ambulance.

'Probably, though old 'itler might get in there quick and declare war on them first,' Sparky said. 'Whatever 'appens, if the Americans are

25

finally goin' to get involved it'll 'elp, 'cos they're a hell of a lot bigger than us.'

'Are you busy working or just holding court this morning, Sparky?' Station Officer Steele had come down from her office to check on the work, arriving unannounced, and silently in her well-polished shoes.

Sparky jumped at the sound of the boss's voice, making Frankie smile. She watched, along with the other crew members, as he deflected the boss's question in typical Sparky style. 'Just trying to make sense of all that's goin' on,' he said. 'Here, 'ave a look at this.' He waved their boss forward to look at the front page's headlines.

'Yes, I'm well aware of what's going on,' Station Officer Steele said, scanning the paper. 'It's shocking news.'

'God help the people in the Far East now the Japs are on the rampage,' Sparky went on. 'I wouldn't want to be out there now they've joined in.'

Station Officer Steele stared at him for a few moments, her face draining of colour, then she seemed to recover herself. 'Let's just focus on our work, shall we, Sparky? We have Hitler to deal with here and if he chooses to send his bombers over London today I shall need all my ambulances ready to go, including yours.' Her voice was crisp and for once Sparky just nodded in reply.

She started to walk away and stopped after a few steps, turning back and addressing the whole crew. 'We have a new crew member due to arrive this morning. Please look out for her and bring her up to my office when she arrives.' Then she turned and went back to her office as silently as she'd arrived.

'You'd better get some work done then, Sparky,' Winnie called to him, a smile on her face.

'All right, all right.' Sparky folded up his newspaper and tucked it inside his navy boiler suit. 'I'm gettin' to it.'

Once the windscreen was cleaned to her satisfaction, Frankie moved on to her engine checks, opening up the bonnet and pulling the dipstick out of the oil to see if it needed topping up. She cleaned the stick, wiping off the oil with a rag and then re-dipped it and pulled it out again, checking that the glistening coating of oil was exactly where it should be, and it was.

She'd just moved on to unscrew the cap of the radiator to look at the water level when a movement in the shadows under the archway leading out on to the road caught her eye. Frankie looked up and saw a young woman walk into the courtyard then stop suddenly at the sight of the ambulances with crew members working on them. The look of uncertainty on her face reminded Frankie of her first day here: she'd felt so nervous as she walked in, looking for someone to ask where to go, and then been hit with a jet of icy cold water from a stirrup pump aimed by Winnie who'd thought she was Sparky. Thankfully that wouldn't happen to this new recruit.

Quickly replacing the radiator cap, Frankie

walked over to the young woman. 'Hello, are you our new crew member?'

The young woman nodded, a look of relief washing over her face as she smiled nervously, her periwinkle-blue eyes meeting Frankie's. She was a couple of inches shorter than Frankie, slim with glossy, brown hair cut into a jaw-length bob.

'Welcome to Station 75. I'm Frankie.' She held out her hand and then noticed it was mucky with smears of oil. 'Sorry, I've been checkin' the engine.'

'It doesn't matter,' the young woman said, shaking Frankie's hand before she could pull it back. 'Thank you for the welcome.' She spoke with an accent, not quite saying her 'th' correctly. 'I am Erika Rosenberg, I have to report to Station Officer Steele?'

'That's our boss; she's waitin' to meet you in her office. I'll take you there, it's this way.' Frankie turned to lead the way up to the offices, aware that the other crew members had stopped what they were doing and were looking at them.

'Who's this, then?' Sparky called out.

'This is Erika Rosenberg,' Frankie said. 'That's Sparky, and over there is Winnie.' She pointed to where her friend was kneeling by her ambulance checking the tyre pressure.

'Hello, and welcome.' Winnie smiled warmly.

'And Hooky,' Frankie continued, pointing to Winnie's attendant, who had stuck her head out of the cab window to see what was going on.

'I'll introduce you to everyone properly when they're not up ladders or sweepin' out the back of ambulances,' Frankie said.

'How about callin' you Rose?' Sparky said. 'It's a nice name.'

The young woman looked puzzled. 'My name is Erika.'

'It's all right, we all go by nicknames 'ere, it's the way it is at ambulance stations,' Frankie explained. 'My name's Stella Franklin so I got called Frankie, nobody uses their real name. Rose is a lovely name and comes from your surname like my nickname.'

The young woman considered for a moment and then nodded. 'Very well, if that is how you do things then Rose I shall be.' She smiled. 'I like Rose.'

'Good. It's a good name to go by, much better than some of the ones that people get called 'ere. Let's get you up to the boss's office.' Frankie linked her arm through Rose's. 'You'll soon get used to how things are around 'ere.'

★　★　★

'Our new recruit has arrived,' Frankie said, knocking on Station Officer Steele's door.

'Jolly good,' the boss said, standing up and holding out her hand to Rose. 'Welcome to Station 75, Erika. I hope you'll be very happy here.'

'Thank you.' Rose shook her hand.

'Sparky's already renamed her Rose, on account of her surname,' Frankie said, standing in the doorway.

'Has he indeed?' Station Officer Steele smiled.

'Well, that's a rather lovely name to have. It might seem odd to call each other by nicknames, but that's the way it's always been here.'

'I like it. Roses are beautiful flowers; my mother likes to grow them in our garden she —' Rose suddenly stopped, a look of despair on her face.

Station Officer Steele put her hand on Rose's arm. 'Do sit down.' She looked at Frankie. 'Would you make some tea for us and a cup for yourself as well, then come and join us so you can get to know Rose as well?'

Frankie nodded and went to make the tea, aware that something had just happened there but not sure what. The boss had clearly picked up on it too and in true Station Officer Steele style was doing what was needed to help.

Returning to the office a few minutes later with a tray in her hands, Frankie was glad to see that Rose looked fine again.

'I'm going to make you Winnie's attendant, she's my Deputy Station Officer and will be able to help you learn the ways of Station 75. She's very experienced and a jolly good ambulance driver,' Station Officer Steele went on.

'Winnie will be delighted to hear that,' Frankie said, putting the tray down on top of a bookcase and handing out mugs of tea.

'She'll be free of Hooky at last.'

'Thank you,' Rose said, taking her mug from Frankie.

'Pull up a chair, Frankie,' Station Officer Steele said. 'Now, Rose, the letter I've been sent tells me you're originally from Austria and came to England in nineteen thirty-nine when you were just fifteen. Is that correct?'

Rose nodded. 'On a Kindertransport train.'

So that explains her accent, Frankie thought, and if she'd arrived on one of the Kindertransport trains she was Jewish and had been sent to safety by her family. Poor girl, what must it have been like to leave your family and all you're familiar with and come to a foreign country? Blasted Hitler and what he'd done to the world; he had a lot to answer for.

'Your English is very good,' Frankie said, warming her cold fingers around her mug of tea. 'I wouldn't be able to say a word if I went to Austria.'

'I learned English from when I was a little girl; my parents thought it was a good thing for me because they planned for us to go to live in America one day — my father's brother lives there. They left it too late to go . . . ' Rose shrugged.

'Are your family still in Austria?' Station Officer Steele gently probed.

'Yes . . . ' She paused for a moment. 'My parents didn't get out and I don't know where they are now, I haven't heard from them for months. I write to them but get no reply.'

'I'm sorry to hear that. I hope you get word from them soon.' The older woman patted Rose's arm. 'You are very welcome here and I'm sure you'll fit in very well. If there's anything you're unsure of do ask, either myself or any of the crew members, they were all new once upon a time.'

'Do you have any family here in London?' Frankie asked.

Rose shook her head. 'No, I just have my uncle and cousins in America but no one in England.'

'Where are you living?' Frankie said.

'In a hostel. It's fine but I don't like it very much.' Rose shrugged. 'I'm looking for something better.'

'Don't leave it before you have somewhere else to go, will you?' Station Officer Steele said. 'Housing's in short supply these days on account of so many homes having been lost because of the bombing.' She took a sip of her tea. 'Frankie, when we've finished our tea will you get Rose kitted out with our uniform, such as it is, steel helmet, coat and hat, please?' She smiled at Rose. 'We're hoping to have a proper uniform one day like the other Civil Defence services, but until then we have to manage with those.'

'And don't go wearing your best clothes for work either, Rose, it can get quite mucky at times.' Frankie smiled. 'We're all looking forward to the day we finally get our uniforms.'

6

'Are you all right?' Winnie asked as she drove the ambulance under the archway and out on to the Minories later that morning, her breath pluming in the cold air.

'A bit nervous,' Rose said, stroking Trixie's soft ears. The little dog had already made firm friends with Station 75's newest recruit and was sitting on her lap. 'I didn't expect to be sent out so soon.'

'Oh, Station Officer Steele's a firm believer in throwing new crew members in at the deep end because the sooner they get used to the job the better. I remember Frankie's first day — she went out with me to a rather ghastly call-out and had quite a shock, the poor thing.'

'What happened?' Rose asked.

'Some poor chap had fallen out of a window and speared himself on some railings — it killed him and wasn't a pleasant sight.' Winnie glanced at Rose, who was looking worried. 'But that was exceptionally bad; in fact, the worst first call-out I've ever heard of.'

'What did she think?'

'Well, she was very shocked and upset but she survived and has coped with plenty of tricky incidents since then. I do hope that hasn't put you off, it's not all like that. Frankie's was unusual.' Rose shook her head, making her glossy brown hair swing. 'No. I know I will see

people injured, it is to be expected. I will be fine.'
Winnie smiled at her. 'I'm sure you will be. At
least things are quieter now the bombing's
stopped. Life at Station 75's much less
nerve-racking than it was during the Blitz.'

'What was it like?'

Braking gently as they approached a junction,
Winnie checked for traffic and then turned the
ambulance to the left. 'Were you living in
London then?'

'No.'

'Once the bombing started we had air raids for
fifty-seven nights straight with no let-up, it was
exhausting. If I was working a night-time shift
then I'd be out in the middle of raids when the
bombs were falling and most sensible people
were tucked away in shelters.'

'Were you scared?' Rose asked.

Winnie looked at her and smiled. 'We all were,
but we had a job to do, and even though it was
utterly beastly at times I wouldn't have missed
doing it.' She laughed. 'That must sound
absolutely crazy, but in spite of being scared and
having to deal with awful sights and badly
injured people, I love my job and working at
Station 75, and I have made the most wonderful
friends and . . . ' She paused for a moment,
slowing as a heavily laden lorry turned off in
front of them. 'I met my husband there. I can
thoroughly recommend working for the Ambulance Service.'

'Is that Sparky?'

Winnie burst into laughter. 'Good gracious,
no! Sparky and I wouldn't last five minutes,

apart from the fact he's rather older than I am, we would argue too much. He's a fine one to spar with but he's most definitely, not the man for me — he's married, anyway.' She paused, a picture of her darling Mac flashing into her mind. 'My husband, Mac, was an ambulance driver but he doesn't work at Station 75 any more. He left to join bomb disposal.'

'He's a brave man.'

'Indeed, brave and rather crazy to do that job.' Winnie sighed. She was doing her best to accept Mac's decision but she still found it hard and wished he still worked at Station 75 where she could watch over him and know he was safe rather than off somewhere digging up unexploded bombs. 'Enough about me; tell me about yourself, Rose. Where have you been living since you arrived in England?'

'In Cambridge. I was sent to live there with a kind family.'

'Did you know them before you came to England?' Winnie asked.

Rose shook head. 'No, they volunteered to take in a Kindertransport child and I was lucky to be sent to live with them. I liked them very much and was happy living there and going to school until — ' She stopped talking for a few moments and then went on, 'Last year the police came for me and took me away.'

Winnie looked at Rose. The young woman's face had gone pale, her jaw held rigid as she stared straight out of the windscreen, her fingers rapidly stroking Trixie's ears.

'Why on earth did they do that?'

35

'Because I am an enemy alien.'

'But you fled to England to escape the Nazis!'

Rose shrugged. 'In my homeland I was reviled for being a Jew, and then here for being an enemy alien.' She sighed. 'I was just a seventeen-year-old schoolgirl, not a spy or a soldier.'

'What happened to you?'

'I was taken to Liverpool first with a lot of other enemy aliens, people jeered and spat at us there . . . they shouted terrible things, like they do now to Jews in Austria. I thought I had escaped that . . . ' Her voice wavered and she fell silent for a few moments while she composed herself. 'After that they took us to the Isle of Man.'

Winnie reached over and patted Rose's arm. 'I'm so very sorry that happened to you in this country. We're fighting a war to stop that sort of appalling behaviour.'

'It wasn't just non-British Jews who were rounded up, there were non-Jewish Italians, Germans and Austrians there, too. Anyone who might be a spy or might help the enemy.'

'You don't have to be an alien to want to do that, there are some British people who want to help the enemy; that beastly man Mosley, for a start.' Winnie sighed. 'The government panicked, thinking anyone from those countries might help the enemy if they invaded, but a lot of innocent people like yourself got caught up in it.'

'I understand why they did it but it was crushing because I thought I was safe here, that I wouldn't be imprisoned for being an Austrian Jew.'

36

'Did they put you behind bars?'

Rose shook her head. 'No, we were put in hotels and treated well, but we were kept behind barbed wire and had soldiers guarding us.'

'How long were you there?'

'Six weeks. They let me go when they finally realised I wasn't a threat to the country, then I went back to Cambridge and school to study for my Higher School Certificate.'

'I'm sorry they couldn't see that in the first place,' Winnie said. 'It must have been awful for you. It was hard enough having to flee your home and leave your family, without ending up being locked away for not being British. I'd have been bloody furious.' She took a deep breath. 'In fact, I am bloody furious on your behalf.'

'Don't be, Winnie,' Rose said. 'I am perfectly all right, I am free and no one is saying I can't do something because of my religion. There are plenty of people who are in a much worse situation now in Austria and Germany — anywhere where Hitler is in charge. I am not going to let it spoil my life.'

Winnie glanced at her. 'You are quite a remarkable young woman and I think Station 75 is very lucky to have you come and work for us.'

'I hope I can do a good job.'

'I'm sure you will — and I think you're about to find out.' Winnie turned the ambulance right off Cable Street and into Swedenborg Square. 'What number is it again?'

Rose checked the chit of paper that the boss had given her.

'Number eighteen.'

'There, that must be it.' Winnie spotted a boy who was waiting outside what must be number 18, waving at them. 'They're waiting for us.'

'It's me gran,' the boy said as Winnie and Rose climbed out of the ambulance. 'She's very poorly.'

'We'll soon get her to hospital where the doctors can help her,' Winnie said. 'Try not to worry. Just show us where to go.'

They took a stretcher out of the back of the ambulance and followed the boy inside the house, where they found his grandmother lying on a bed in a downstairs room, while his mother, with a grizzling baby balanced on one hip, was trying to get the old woman to take a drink from a cup.

'Hello, I'm Winnie and this is Rose, we've come to whisk you off to hospital.' Winnie smiled at her.

The old woman stared back at her with rheumy, brown eyes for a few moments and then smiled back with a toothless grin. 'Hello, ducks,' she said in a wavering voice before wincing and clutching at her stomach with her gnarled hands.

'She's been like this for a couple of days. We 'ad to have the doctor in,' the woman said, jiggling the baby to try to quieten it.

'He said she 'ad to go to hospital.'

'They'll get you sorted out in no time.' Winnie laid a hand on the old woman's shoulder. 'You just relax and don't worry about a thing.'

'She will be all right, won't she?' the woman asked.

'Yes, once we get her to hospital, the doctors

will work out what needs to be done,' Winnie reassured her. 'Right, let's lift her on to the stretcher — ready, Rose?'

Rose nodded and positioned herself, ready to lift.

'On the count of three . . . ' They quickly and smoothly transferred the old woman on to the stretcher and Rose tucked her up with blankets and hot-water bottles while Winnie filled in the label with her details for the hospital, glad to be helping someone who hadn't been injured by a bomb. After months of air raids she was relieved to be going to more gentle call-outs and this was a pleasant first one for Rose, too.

★   ★   ★

'How was that, then?' Winnie asked a short while later as they climbed back in to the ambulance after delivering the old woman to the London Hospital in Whitechapel. 'It was a good first call-out and you did very well.'

Rose smiled at her. 'It was fine. Do you think she will be all right?'

'I hope so; she's in the best place now, anyway.' Winnie started the engine and pulled away towards the hospital gates. She stopped to wait as a bus went past, then turned out into the road and they drove along in silence for a few minutes.

'It's shocking to see so much damage,' Rose said, staring out of the window at one of the many gaps where buildings had been reduced to piles of rubble by the bombing. 'It's terrible.'

'I know. There are places where nearly whole streets have been destroyed. Dear old London will never be quite the same again.'

'Have you always lived in London?' Rose asked.

'Oh no, I was born and grew up in India. I didn't set foot in England until I was eleven years old when my parents sent me here to go to boarding school. I was used to warm weather, so the cold and damp of an English winter was quite a shock.' Winnie glanced at Rose. 'I know what it's like to come and live in a strange country. My parents always called it home as they were born and grew up here, but India was home to me. It took me a while to get used to how things are done here, but I love it now.'

'I like it here most of the time, but I miss my parents and Austria.' Winnie nodded. 'If there's anything I can do to help you, please do ask me, won't you?'

'Thank you, Winnie, I appreciate that.'

'You're welcome and I do honestly mean it, we look out for each other at Station 75.'

7

The delicious smell of fish and chips combined with the sharp tang of vinegar hit Frankie as soon as she opened the door of number 25 Matlock Street. Her stomach growled with hunger as it was nearly half-past eight and she still hadn't had her tea, but Ivy had, and it had been fish and chips again. For someone who only this morning had claimed that she didn't have any more money to pay her share of the rent, she shouldn't have been able to afford them. It wasn't pay day, so where had she got the money from? Frankie thought. It was more likely the woman had lied and just not paid her fair share of the rent.

Closing the door behind her, she noticed an envelope lying on the mat, addressed to her and in handwriting she recognised; it was from her mother. She was still getting used to the idea of having a mother very much alive after having grown up believing that she'd died when she was a baby; getting a letter from her still felt like a novelty. She picked it up and put it in her pocket to read later.

Walking through to the kitchen, she saw the evidence of Ivy's tea — greasy newspaper — left on the table while her step-grandmother sat in an armchair, her feet propped up on the chair opposite and the *Picture Post* open on her lap.

'Oh, it's you,' the older woman said without looking up.

'Who else would it be?' Frankie's eyes strayed to the pile of Ivy's unwashed plates and cups that were still in the sink from this morning — and from yesterday, too. Frustration started to fizz through her blood, but she ignored it as she needed to deal with the gnawing hunger in her stomach first. She'd do battle better once she'd had something to eat.

Taking her torch out of her coat pocket, she went out to the garden and down to the far end where the chicken coop stood. The hens had long since gone inside to roost and as she opened up the nest-box lid, she could see them crouched on the perches, blinking at her in the dim light from her torch.

'Hello, girls; sorry to wake you up.' Frankie spotted two brown speckled eggs nestled in the straw. Carefully picking them up, she closed the lid and made her way back to the house with the makings of a meal in her hand.

Back inside, Frankie took off her outside clothes and got to work preparing some scrambled eggs.

'You 'aving all them eggs?' Ivy asked, watching as Frankie cracked the second egg into a bowl ready to whisk.

'There are only two and since I'm the one who looks after the 'ens I think I'm entitled to them.'

'You should share 'em.'

'Are you goin' to do your share of lookin' after them, then — the feeding and watering and cleaning out the coop?'

42

Ivy pulled a face. 'I ain't got time for any of that, I work.' 'And so do I! But I make time, so I'll 'ave the eggs.'

'Humph!' Ivy snorted and returned her gaze to the *Picture Post*.

Frankie lit a ring on the gas cooker, tipped the eggs into a pan and stirred them gently as they cooked, forcing her mind to focus on the task at hand rather than the anger she felt towards Ivy. She just needed to keep calm and eat her meal and then she would tackle her again about the rent and her so-called lack of money to pay it.

Ivy didn't say a word to Frankie as she ate her food. The eggs were delicious and combined with a slice of National wholemeal loaf with a scraping of margarine on top, they satisfied her hunger. Feeling full, Frankie put down her knife and fork and sat back in her chair, ready to do battle.

'I see you 'ad fish and chips again tonight, Ivy.'

Ivy looked up and narrowed her icy, blue eyes. 'So?'

'Well, you told me this mornin' that you didn't have any more money to pay your share of the rent — you're still a shilling and four pence short, remember? So 'ow did you pay for your fish and chips?'

'I found some more in my 'andbag.' Ivy sniffed. 'What I spend my money on has nothin' to do with you. If I fancy fish and chips for me tea then I shall 'ave 'em.'

'Look, Ivy, I really don't give a monkey's what you spend your money on as long you pay your share of the rent; otherwise we will lose the 'ouse. It's as simple as that. So, come on, you owe a shilling and four pence.'

'Well, I ain't got it.' Ivy folded her arms and sneered. 'You can want it all you like but you ain't gettin' it 'cos I ain't got it till pay day.'

Frankie shrugged. 'Very well, perhaps it's better if we did leave 'ere, the house is too big for just us two with an empty bedroom now. Someone else would be glad of the room, people are desperate for housin'.' The image of Rose suddenly flicked into Frankie's mind. She was looking for somewhere else to live. Could she come and live here as a lodger? Her rent would certainly cover the gap left by Ivy's spendthrift ways. Plus, it would be good to have someone nice living here, someone to share meals with and talk to instead of argue with. 'There's another way but I ain't sure it would work.'

'What?'

'Well, we could take in a lodger.'

'I don't want no stranger livin' 'ere.'

'But they would 'elp pay the rent, and then you wouldn't have to pay so much each week.'

Ivy considered her words for a few moments. 'Where would you get a lodger from? I ain't lookin' for one.'

'I might know someone already; one of the girls from work is lookin' for somewhere to live. I could ask her tomorrow.'

'All right, but don't expect me to cook or clean for her.'

Frankie cast her eye over Ivy's mess on the table and in the sink.

'I wouldn't expect you to; you've already got

enough to do for yourself.'

'Wotcha mean by that?' Ivy snapped.

'Your dirty plates have been sittin' there for the past few days; you need to wash them up 'cos I ain't goin' to.'

'I will when I'm ready.'

Frankie shrugged. She was tired and wasn't going to waste any more energy on this vile woman. She stood up and went to wash up her things, leaving Ivy with her *Picture Post*, and the Hollywood starlets she so loved.

Lying on her bed later, Frankie took out her mother's letter, staring at it for a few moments before she opened it. Her thoughts went back to the letter left to her by her grandad, opened after he'd been killed, which broke the shocking news that her mother was still living. Now, six months on from that discovery, she still didn't know quite how to feel about her mother. She was a nice woman, kind and caring, and yet . . . she'd let Frankie grow up thinking she was an orphan. That still stung. She wasn't sure that she could ever completely forgive her for that.

She'd met her mother twice since then — once in London and again at her home on a farm in Suffolk, where she'd met her two sisters and brother — but apart from that they stayed in touch by a weekly letter. She liked getting those letters, it was nice to have her mother writing to her, enquiring after her and saying that if she needed help she only had to ask. She'd never, ever, get that sense of caring and concern from Ivy, who was supposed to be family, but only a step-grandmother, and more like the wicked ones in fairy tales. Frankie had come to realise that her grandad had done her a favour leaving her that letter and revealing her mother was still alive, although she hadn't thought so at first.

Opening the envelope now, she took out two letters, one from her mother and the other from her youngest sister, Eve. She read her mother's first, which began, 'Dear Stella': her mother always called her by her proper name.

I hope you're well. We've had a shock here this week as Lizzie has gone and joined the WAAF and has to report for training next week. We didn't want her to, as you know, and she could have carried on working here at the farm, but she wouldn't listen to us and went off into Ipswich and signed up. I don't think she'll find taking orders very easy but that's something she'll have to learn to deal with; who knows, it might be the making of her.

Frankie hadn't hit it off well with Lizzie at all; her sister hadn't taken kindly to finding out that she had an older sister and had been very unwelcoming and unfriendly when she'd visited them in the summer. She'd come across as a stubborn, prickly girl who would without doubt find following orders difficult.

Frankie read on, enjoying her mother's descriptions of what she'd been doing, her life on the farm so different from Frankie's.

We're busy here getting ready for Christmas, the cockerels have fattened up nicely and they'll

46

make good Christmas dinners. *If you do get time off remember that you are very welcome to come and stay with us for Christmas, we would love you to come if you can.*
With my love
Mother

She turned her attention to the other letter. At fifteen years of age, her sister Eve was the total opposite of Lizzie and had been so welcoming and delightful that Frankie had quickly come to like her. Between Eve's weekly letters and the ones she wrote back to her, they had started to build up a good sisterly relationship, something that Frankie never dreamed she'd have but which she was enjoying very much.

Dear Frankie,

Eve had insisted on using Frankie's nickname as soon as she'd told her about it.

I expect Mother has told you about Lizzie signing up. I think I'm the only one who's glad she's going! I don't say that because I should be kind, but honestly, I won't miss her being grumpy with me and I won't have to share a room with her any more. I think she'll wish she was back home when they start shouting at her for not following orders quick enough.
I hope you're well and that there haven't been any more air raids. We've got some new prisoners of war working on the farm — they're Italian ones and like singing as they work. They

bring them every morning on a lorry that goes around delivering them to farms and then picks them up again in the evening.

Do you think you might be able to come here for Christmas? If you did you'd have a grand old time. Lizzie's going to miss that, she'll probably be stuck in some cold barracks somewhere.

Write soon.

Your loving sister,

Eve

Going to spend Christmas with her mother, Eve and the rest of the family was impossible, Frankie thought, she'd be on duty at Station 75, but it was nice to be asked and know that she was welcome there. Having her mother and family in Suffolk made her feel less alone, and that was comforting and was the complete opposite of what she had to deal with on a daily basis with Ivy — the woman she had so reluctantly promised to look out for.

8

'Here you are, it's Woolton Pie,' Connie said, putting plates of steaming food down in front of Bella and Winnie. 'I've adapted the recipe slightly, put some of our precious cheese ration on the top to give it a bit more taste. Tuck in!'

Bella breathed in the appetising smell rising up from the hot pie appreciatively; it was lovely to come home to a warming meal after their twelve-hour shift and the bicycle ride home through the freezing, dark night, which made her ears and fingers tingle despite wearing gloves and a hat.

'Thank you, Connie, this looks wonderful,' she said.

'You're most welcome.' Connie sat down at the table and began to eat her own portion of Woolton Pie. 'Mmm, not bad.'

'It's delicious, thank you,' Winnie said. 'You do look after us well.'

Connie smiled. 'I enjoy cooking and it makes sense to pool our rations — we can do more with them. I like having something ready for you, if I can.'

'Where did you learn to cook so well?' Bella asked.

'From our family cook, right here in this kitchen. I used to escape down here as often as I could; she let me help her and taught me how to cook. It was highly irregular and if my mother knew what I was doing she'd have been horrified.' She laughed. 'But that never stopped me.'

'Well, I'm jolly grateful that you did,' Winnie said. 'My cooking skills are extremely poor in comparison, I — ' She stopped as Trixie, who had been sitting by her mistress's feet, suddenly got up and started to bark at the door leading to the stairs up to the ground floor.

'I think we've got a visitor.' Connie got up, took a warmed plate from the oven and spooned out another portion of pie, which she set on the table.

'Are you expecting anyone?' Winnie asked.

Before Connie could answer, Bella heard footsteps coming down the stairs, the door opened and James, who was Winnie's brother and her young man, walked into the room, sending Trixie cavorting around his legs, her tail wagging happily.

'James!' Bella and Winnie chorused.

Bella rushed over to him, kissing his cheek and wrapping her arms around him, breathing in the essence of James combined with the smell of a cold winter's London night on his wool coat as he hugged her back.

'You knew James was coming,' Winnie said.

'He telephoned just before you got home — I thought it would be a lovely surprise for you,' Connie said. 'Come on, Bella, let the poor fellow get his coat off.'

'It's wonderful to see you,' Bella said as she loosened her arms and looked into James's grey eyes.

'And you,' he said, hooking a stray curl of her brown hair behind her ear. 'I had a meeting in London and grabbed the chance to come and see you before I get the train back to Bletchley.'

'Well, I'm delighted you did. Let me take your coat and you can eat.'

Sitting at the table opposite James, Bella thought the day was going to end a whole lot better than it had started. Seeing James was a real tonic, she thought, watching him tuck into Connie's Woolton Pie with great gusto.

'This is good,' James said. 'Thank you.'

'It's lovely to see you.' Connie speared a piece of pie crust with her fork. 'It's been too long since you came to London.'

'I know; it's been busier than ever at Bletchley — the war generates an enormous amount of paperwork and it all has to be dealt with. We've had to work extra to get through it and I'm sorry I haven't been able to escape to see you, even for a few hours.' James's eyes met Bella's and she smiled at him. 'So, when they said I had to come to a meeting here I was delighted, it gives me a few hours with you and I can get the last train back later.'

'I'm sure I would get thoroughly bored pushing paper around a desk all day,' Winnie said. 'Surely with your brain — you did go to Oxford, after all — you ought to be doing something more suited to your talents.'

James shrugged, looking slightly uncomfortable. 'Well, it's where the ministry put me; I have to trust that they know best.' He caught Bella's eye and winked at her before turning his

51

attention back to his meal. She watched him for a moment, considering what Winnie had said — for such a clever person it seemed odd that James's role in the war was office-bound. She'd tried asking him about it in an attempt to find out more about what he did, but he'd never given her any answer other than it was paperwork. At least it kept him in England instead of being sent off to fight on some foreign battlefield or digging up unexploded bombs like Mac and, even better, Bletchley was out of London and hadn't suffered in the Blitz, so there was much to be thankful for.

After they'd finished the meal, Connie and Winnie had volunteered to do the washing-up and had shooed Bella and James upstairs to spend some precious time together before he had to leave to get the last train back.

'Are you all right, Bella?' James asked as they snuggled up on the sofa together, one arm around her shoulders, his other hand holding hers. 'How are things at Station 75?'

'Station 75's fine, quiet and steady, as it's been since May. We had a new crew member start today, an Austrian refugee, Rose, she's lovely; the boss has teamed her up with Winnie.'

'Is that a good idea?'

Bella laughed. 'Your sister is actually a very fine member of Station 75; otherwise she'd never have been made Deputy Station Officer. Rose will do very well with her, I'm sure, and it will be good for Winnie to take someone under her wing, help her stop worrying about Mac so much — only don't tell her I said that!'

'I won't.' He smiled at her. 'What about you, Bella? Is everything as it should be in your world?'

She bit her bottom lip. 'I've lost my job working for *The War Illustrated*.'

'Since when?'

'This morning.' She told him what had happened.

James pulled her into an embrace. 'I'm so sorry, darling. I know how much you loved writing for them.' Loosening his arms, he looked deep into her eyes. 'You mustn't take it personally, it's the way the newspapers work; they might come back with something else to write. In the meantime, you've got to keep writing for yourself; why not write a book?'

Bella shook her head. 'I don't think I'm up to that, I've only been writing four or five hundred words not thousands. I wouldn't know what to write about and I don't have enough to say.'

'Then start writing a short story or an article or something different. Bella, you can do it, have faith in yourself.'

'I'll think about it.'

'Do. You have a talent and it would be a shame to waste it. Whatever you write is good, the letters you send me are works of art, the way you describe things and catch my interest. You mustn't give up.'

'What would I write about?'

'Your life, what you do, what you see. We are living through extraordinary times, Bella. The war won't last for ever — record it, write stories about it, anything as long as you enjoy doing it.'

He squeezed her hand. 'Have fun exploring your writing — try a detective story like *Sherlock Holmes*, or anything that takes your fancy — just write and send me a copy.'

Bella smiled at him. 'All right then. I couldn't stop writing anyway, even if I wanted to. I get all twitchy if I haven't written anything for a day or two, even if it's just my diary.'

'See, that proves you are born to write, Bella. So, do it.'

9

The frost-rimmed leaves of the Brussels sprout plants sparkled prettily in the low winter sunlight shining down on Station 75's allotment in the dry moat of the Tower of London. Frankie pinched a sprout budding on the stem between her finger and thumb, the cold from it seeping through the wool of her gloves.

'These should be perfect by the time Christmas is 'ere.'

'They might feel perfect, but they certainly won't taste it,' Winnie said. 'Nasty things, sprouts, even if these are off the ration; I won't be eating any.'

'You either love them or hate them.' Bella laughed. 'I'm in the love them camp; how about you, Frankie?

Frankie smiled. 'I'm with you, Bella. They're lovely.'

The three of them had been sent down to the allotment by Station Officer Steele to check everything was fine and to do a few jobs to keep it in perfect shape. Now it was the middle of winter there was much less growing there, just the sprouts, savoy cabbages, leeks, parsnips and swedes. All the other vegetables — the peas, beans, potatoes and salad crops — had long since been harvested and eaten by the crew of Station 75.

'I want to ask your opinion on somethin','

Frankie said, her breath pluming in the cold air. 'Ivy's not been paying her share of the rent and I keep havin' to make up the difference, I — '

'That blasted woman!' Winnie stopped raking over the soil and looked at Frankie, one hand on her hip. 'You should just leave her to it and come and live with me and Bella at Connie's house. There's plenty of room and it would be wonderful fun!'

'You know Frankie can't do that because of Stanley, she's got to keep the house for when he comes home,' Bella reminded her.

'What do you want our opinion on, Frankie?'

'Ivy's not going to change her ways — if anything, she's getting worse — so I 'ad the idea of taking in a lodger. I was wonderin' if Rose would be interested; she said she wanted to move out of the hostel where she's stayin'. Only I'm not sure if I should ask her.'

'Why not?' Bella asked.

'Ivy.' Frankie sighed. 'She ain't a joy to live with and I don't know if it's fair to ask someone like Rose to have to put up with 'er.'

'Is Ivy planning on looking for a lodger and looking after them, then?' Winnie asked.

Frankie laughed. 'God, no!' She's already made it quite clear that she ain't doing nothing for a lodger, just like she ain't doing nothing for me.'

'She'd be happy to pay less rent because of them, though,' Winnie said. 'Honestly, Frankie, I don't know how you can stand living with the beastly woman.'

Bella rolled her eyes. 'Don't go down that road

again, Winnie, we both know why Frankie's still there.' She paused. 'You know, Rose has already put up with plenty of tricky things in her life: the Nazis in Austria, coming to live in a strange country and being interned for being an enemy alien. I'm sure she could take Ivy in her stride.'

'Do you think so?' Frankie asked.

'Ask her and see what she says,' Winnie said, leaning on her rake.

'I think she'd be jolly pleased to come and live with you.'

Frankie nodded and smiled at her friends. 'All right, I will, and if she says yes it'll be lovely to have someone pleasant to live with again.'

Back at Station 75, Frankie found Rose helping Sparky sweep out the garages.

'Rose, can I ask you somethin'?' she said.

'Yes.' Rose stopped sweeping and smiled at Frankie.

'Have you found somewhere to move to yet? That's if you're still plannin' on leaving the hostel?'

'No, and yes I am still wanting to leave. It is too noisy in there and is not very home-like.'

'Well, I'm looking for a lodger to move in with my step-grandmother and me in Stepney, in Matlock Street. I wondered if you'd be interested — you'd 'ave a room of your own — you wouldn't 'ave to share,' Frankie explained.

Rose considered for a moment and then smiled at her. 'This is a good surprise; I like the idea of it very much.'

'The only thing is Ivy . . . She's not very friendly.'

'She's your grandmother?'

'*Step*-grandmother,' Frankie said. 'She was my grandad's second wife and she ain't at all grandmotherly. We live in the same house, but she looks after herself and I look after myself — we 'ave as little to do with each other as possible. You wouldn't have to see very much of her. She works in a garment factory sewin' uniforms, so on weeks when I'm workin' the night shift I don't hardly see her at all.'

'I understand. Yes, I would like to be your lodger, Frankie. I would like to live with you.' Rose smiled, her blue eyes shining happily.

'But don't you want to come and see the 'ouse first before you say yes?'

'No, I know that you're a good person and I trust you.'

Frankie stared at her. 'But you only met me yesterday!'

Rose shrugged. 'My instinct tells me you are, and you have been kind to me and all the people who work here like you and they have known you much longer.'

Frankie held out her hand for Rose to shake. 'In that case, we have a deal. When do you want to move in?'

'I have to tell them at the hostel so . . . ' Rose paused for a few moments. 'At the weekend?'

'We'll 'ave swapped around to the night shift then, so it'll give you the day to settle in and organise your things. I can make sure your room is ready for you. It's goin' to be lovely sharing a house with you, Rose. Matlock Street's a good place to live.'

10

Winnie tapped on the door frame of Station Officer Steele's office, a mug of steaming tea ready in her hand. 'Would you like a cup of tea?'

The boss didn't seem to have heard her; she was sitting quite still, her normally upright posture slumped down as she pored over something spread out on the desk in front of her.

Winnie cleared her throat and tried again, only louder this time. 'Tea's up, would you like a cup?'

This time her message got through and the older woman looked around and nodded, her normally pink face rather pale. 'Yes, thank you. Just put it here, please.' She indicated a space at the side of her neat desk.

'Is everything all right?' Winnie asked, putting the mug of tea down carefully, so it didn't slosh out. She peered over the boss's shoulder to see what she'd been looking at: it was today's *Daily Herald*. Sparky always left his copy in the common room for others to read when he'd finished with it. Today's headline declared 'Singapore key to Jap war plan' in large, bold type.

'My sister lives there.' Station Officer Steele pointed to the word 'Singapore' and kept her finger on it as if it gave her some connection with her distant sister. 'I was actually glad she lived out there and was away from all this . . . ' She shrugged. 'The bombing and rationing and air raids and . . . She was worried about me and the rest of our family in England and now . . . ' She shook her head.

Winnie sat down in the chair beside the boss's desk. 'Just because the Japs might have their eye on Singapore doesn't mean they're actually going to get it. We've got a lot of forces out there and Churchill won't let them get their hands on it. Try not to worry.'

Station Officer Steele looked at her, her brown eyes strained behind her tortoiseshell glasses. 'We never thought the Nazis would take France, Holland and Belgium and all the others, but they did.' She sighed. 'I hope you're right, Winnie, but I'm terribly worried for her. She's got two daughters with her out there and her husband's in the RAF. Perhaps they should leave just in case things get nasty, get out while they can.'

'Where would they go?' Winnie asked. 'It's a long way to come home and the seas aren't exactly safe with U-boats hunting down ships.'

'They could go to Australia, that's a lot nearer, but I doubt my sister would go without her husband and he couldn't leave.' The boss took her glasses off and rubbed the palms of her hands over her face. 'What a mess this world is in. We've been at war for over two years now and it's getting worse rather than better.'

'Now the Americans are at war against the Japs, surely it's only a matter of time before they declare war against the Nazis, too. The might of the Americans will make a big difference, they'll help us win.'

'But not before a lot more people have been injured and killed in the process. You'd think after what happened in the Great War that people would have learned that war helps no one — it just kills and causes so much destruction and chaos.'

Winnie put her hand on Station Officer Steele's arm. She'd never seen her boss looking so down and defeated before. She was the woman who kept Station 75's crews going even in the worst raids, staying calm and getting them through it with her strength and level-headedness. 'Do you want to go home? I can keep things going till the end of the shift. I could do my Deputy Station Officer bit.'

The older woman shook her head and managed a smile. 'Good heavens, no! I know I could trust you to do an excellent job but really . . . ' She paused and took a deep breath, sitting upright and returning to her normal composed self. 'I need to do my job here and keep my personal business to my own time, not indulge myself while I'm on duty.'

'Worrying about your family is hardly being indulgent. You're as human as the rest of Station 75's crew and we all have our moments when personal problems get to us at work. Remember when Mac and I parted ways? I didn't exactly keep my feelings about it to my personal time, as I recall, it made me utterly grumpy at times.' Winnie's stomach tightened at the memory of those awful weeks after Mac had told her he was joining bomb disposal; she'd been so furious with him that she'd broken off their relationship, leaving her desperately unhappy but unwilling to bend her views. Thankfully, her brother Harry had helped her see sense and she and Mac had got back together and had married in July, not long before he'd left for his training.

'Yes, I remember it well; you were both like bears with sore heads.' She smiled at Winnie. 'Everyone here was enormously relieved when you finally saw sense and got back together, but that was different and totally understandable, whereas I'm in charge and I should be professional at all times.'

Winnie shrugged. 'You know that you can always come to me if you need someone to talk to, it won't go any further.'

'Thank you, I appreciate that. I'm sure I will be fine. I shall write to my sister and encourage her to leave Singapore, even if it's just for a few months until we see how things are going to go. She can always go back again. I very much doubt she'll do what I say as she can be rather stubborn at times, but at least if I suggest it to her then I'll feel that I've done all I can to help from here.'

'Did she ever suggest that you leave London during the Blitz?' Winnie asked.

'Yes, of course she did, but I told her I couldn't possibly do that: I wouldn't dream of leaving Station 75.'

Winnie couldn't help laughing.

Station Officer Steele frowned. 'What's so funny?'

'You and your sister sound rather alike to me — both stubborn, if you don't mind me saying so.'

The older woman narrowed her eyes for a few moments and then smiled at Winnie. 'You're quite right, we're cut from the same stubborn cloth, only I don't have children to care for like my sister, so I hope that she'll take heed of my letter and get out for their sake.'

'I hope so too, but Singapore may never come to any harm; it's well defended, Churchill won't let it down.'

'I hope you're right, Winnie, because if you're not, there's nothing I can do to help them from here.'

11

By the end of her shift at eight o'clock on Sunday morning, Frankie's stomach felt as if a flock of Trafalgar Square pigeons were fluttering circuits around inside it. Rose was moving into 25 Matlock Street today, going straight there with her after work. Frankie was looking forward to having someone nice living with her, but she was worried about how Ivy would react when she met their new lodger because she hadn't told her everything about Rose: her step-grandmother had no idea that she was an Austrian refugee. It shouldn't matter at all, and to any decent person it wouldn't, but Ivy wasn't decent, or kind, or understanding. She was selfish and uncaring. Frankie was worried how she'd behave when she met Rose. She hoped she'd at least be polite, if not welcoming. Frankie needed to be on her guard, ready for one of Ivy's tantrums, because she didn't want Rose upset — the young woman had been through enough already.

'Is that everythin'?' Frankie asked, looking at Rose's luggage, which she'd brought to work with her at the start of the shift last night.

'Yes, I don't have much.' Rose held a battered leather suitcase in one hand and a violin case in the other. 'This is what I arrived in England with. I don't need a lot.'

'I'll strap the suitcase on to my bicycle; it'll be

easier to push it than carry it.' Frankie took Rose's case and secured it on to the carrier at the back of her bicycle. 'Ready?'

Rose nodded. 'Thank you for giving me a home.'

Frankie smiled at her. 'I'm glad you said yes, and I 'ope you'll like it.' *And that Ivy behaves herself*, she added silently as they walked out under the archway and headed for Stepney.

It was nearly nine o'clock by the time they reached Matlock Street.

'I'd get yourself a bicycle,' Frankie said as she pushed her own over the cobbles towards her home. 'It'll save you a lot of time and make gettin' to and from work quicker.' Stopping outside number 25, she smiled at Rose. 'Here we are, 'ome, sweet 'ome. I hope you'll be happy here.'

'It looks very nice,' Rose said, taking in the terraced house sandwiched between its neighbours like the others on the street. 'It's a proper home, much better than the hostel.'

Frankie looked at her home. From the outside it did indeed look like a proper home, although it hadn't felt that way inside since her grandad had died. She'd been living in the same house as Ivy, but it had lost all the warmth, security and comfort that her grandad had brought to it. Perhaps Rose's arrival would change the fortunes of the house and make number 25 Matlock Street feel more like a proper home again.

Leading the way inside, Frankie mentally braced herself for Ivy's introduction to Rose. With any luck, she'd be out so Rose could settle

65

in a bit before she had to face the unpleasant woman, but as she approached the kitchen, she knew she was out of luck. The wireless was switched on and she could hear Ivy humming tunelessly to a song.

'I'll leave your suitcase here for a minute before I show you your room,' Frankie said, trying to keep her voice steady and placing Rose's case down at the foot of the stairs where Rose propped her violin case against it.

Taking a deep breath, Frankie led the way into the kitchen where Ivy sat in her usual armchair, sipping a cup of tea.

'Mornin', Ivy. This is Rose, our new lodger.'

'Good morning.' Rose smiled at Ivy and walked over, holding out her hand for Ivy to shake. 'I am pleased to meet you, thank you for sharing your home with me.' Her accent sounded more pronounced than usual.

Ivy's eyes narrowed, looking the young woman up and down. She ignored Rose's outstretched hand. 'I ain't 'avin' no bleedin' Jerry livin' 'ere,' she spat, glaring at Frankie. 'You can take her right away again.'

Rose dropped her hand and looked at Frankie, her blue eyes wide with distress.

A surge of fury raced through Frankie. 'That's enough, Ivy. You don't know what you're sayin' and you're making yourself look like a bigoted fool.' Frankie stepped closer to Rose and slipped her hand through the crook of her arm, linking them together so they stood shoulder to shoulder. She could feel the young woman trembling.

'My husband was killed by bleedin' Jerries and

66

I ain't havin' one living under my roof!' Ivy jabbed her finger at Rose. 'So *you* can — ' But she was cut off.

'Coo-ee, only me!' a voice called from the hall, and Josie, their neighbour from number 5, appeared in the doorway. 'I saw you go past and thought I'd drop in to welcome your new lodger — ' Josie stopped talking as she took in the scene, evidently picking up on the strained atmosphere.

Thinking quickly, Frankie spun Rose around to meet Josie, suddenly very glad that she'd told her neighbour about Rose and shared her concerns about Ivy. Josie had arrived just in time to diffuse the tension and give Frankie a chance to rescue the situation.

'Rose, this is my good friend and neighbour Josie.'

'Pleased to meet yer, ducks!' Josie beamed at her.

'Josie, would you take Rose out to the garden? You could show 'er where the Anderson shelter is and introduce her to the hens.'

Josie's eyes met Frankie's, they exchanged a meaningful look, and Josie nodded. 'Course I will; come on then, Rose.' She linked her arm through Rose's and led her through the scullery and out of the back door, closing it firmly behind her.

Frankie closed her eyes for a moment, gathering herself together, acutely aware of the cheerful song playing on the wireless, which contrasted so sharply with the tension in the room.

'I ain't having no Jerry living here!' Ivy repeated, her voice shrill. 'I don't know how you could, either, after they killed your grandad. He'd be ashamed of you.'

Frankie snapped her eyes open and turned to face Ivy, who glared at her still, arms folded firmly over her ample chest.

'Well, that's all right then, 'cos Rose ain't a Jerry. She's Austrian.'

Ivy screwed up her nose as if she'd just caught the whiff of an unpleasant odour. 'Same thing.'

'No it ain't, Ivy!' Frankie threw her hands up in exasperation. 'Rose is an Austrian refugee who had to flee her 'ome and family because of how the Nazis treat Jewish people there. She is not the enemy!'

'Well, she sounds like a bleedin' German. She could be a spy, for all you know, pretendin' to be all innocent and all the while findin' out stuff for Hitler!'

'Well, she ain't! She came to England, knowin' no one here — she was only fifteen.'

'I still ain't havin' her live here, so you can just get rid of her,' Ivy insisted, picking up her latest copy of *Picture* Post and starting to flick through the pages, making it clear the conversation was over.

Frankie stared incredulously at Ivy, her dislike for the woman reaching new depths. She hadn't expected Ivy to be welcoming to Rose, but the woman had shown nothing but prejudice and not a single ounce of compassion. 'Very well then, Ivy. If that's 'ow you feel, then I'll tell the landlord we're leavin'. I've already been offered somewhere else to live and I'm sure they'll happily give Rose an 'ome, too,' she said, thinking of the many times Winnie had offered her a home at her godmother Connie's house. 'I told you I ain't prepared to keep paying your shortfall in rent — that's why a lodger was a good idea. So if you won't let Rose live 'ere you'd better start looking for a new place to live. Good luck; and you'll need it 'cos there's a housin' shortage.'

Ivy said nothing and kept looking at the *Picture Post*. Frankie waited for a moment but when the older woman didn't respond she turned away and walked into the scullery, her heart pounding hard in her chest. She'd done all she could to live with the vile woman, perhaps it was time to leave Matlock Street and start afresh. If she stayed, she'd only end up having to pay more than her fair share of rent and after Ivy's blatant display of prejudice today she wasn't prepared to do so any more. Frankie had promised her grandad that she'd look out for Ivy and she had for months, but the woman was so poisonous that Frankie simply couldn't continue. Her grandad would never have been so unkind to Rose; he would have shown compassion and welcomed her with open arms.

'Wait!' Ivy shouted from the kitchen.

Frankie stopped and turned around to see Ivy standing in the doorway. 'She can stay, but I ain't doin' anythin' for her.' Ivy pressed her mouth into a thin line.

Frankie ached to tell Ivy that it was too late,

she was leaving, but the image of Stanley flickered into her mind. This was his home too, he wanted to come back and live here when the war was over; if she let it go now, it would be gone for ever.

'All right; but only if you apologise to Rose — and I mean say sorry properly. And you must promise to treat her with politeness from now on. If you don't then you'll be looking for a new 'ome.' Ivy's cheeks grew pink and Frankie could see that she was struggling to agree. 'If I must,' she muttered begrudgingly.

'If you want to stay living 'ere, it's up to you.' Frankie shrugged and turned around to open the back door.

'Go on, ask her to come in so I can get it over with.'

Frankie went out into the garden where the ground was frozen hard under her feet, her breath coming out in plumes of mist. Rose and Josie were at the far end by the hen coop. Frankie could hear them laughing at the hens, who were pecking in vain at the frozen ground.

'Aye, aye, here she comes,' Josie said, noticing Frankie approach.

'You all, right, ducks?'

Frankie nodded. 'Me and Ivy 'ave had words, as you'd expect.'

She rested her hand on Rose's arm. 'I'm really sorry she was so rude to you, she — '

'It's all right, Frankie.' Rose smiled at her. 'I understand how people feel about the Nazis and how they've suffered because of what they do. Remember, they have hurt my family too.'

70

'I know, but there was no need for Ivy to be so vile to you.'

'You warned me that she can be difficult. It's fine, Josie's said I can stay with her until I find somewhere else to live,' Rose said.

'We'll squeeze her in,' added Josie.

'There's no need. Ivy's agreed that you can live 'ere — that's if you still want to?' Frankie said. 'I hope you'll stay; I've been looking forward to livin' with someone nice for a change. Ivy wants to apologise to you.'

'Wants' was a generous way to say it; 'forced' would be more accurate, Frankie thought, but as long as Ivy apologised and was true to her word, and Rose accepted her apology, things would be fine.

'She doesn't need to,' Rose said.

'Oh, yes she does,' Frankie and Josie said in unison, nodding their heads in agreement.

'Let her apologise, it'll do her good,' Josie added with a chuckle.

Back in the kitchen, Ivy stood looking more uncomfortable than Frankie had ever seen her.

'I'm sorry for what I said and for how I treated yer,' she said to Rose, her bottom jaw held so rigidly it was a wonder she could get the words out at all. 'I hope you'll stay 'ere.'

Rose smiled warmly at the older woman. 'Thank you, Ivy. Yes, I would like to stay here very much.'

Ivy nodded curtly and grabbed her handbag, making her way swiftly to the front door.

'Where are you going?' Frankie asked.

'Out,' Ivy said, her icy blue eyes meeting

71

Frankie's for a moment as she passed her.

'You'll want to wrap up warm; it's perishing out there!' Josie called after her.

There was no reply, just the loud slamming of the front door a few seconds later and the heavy silence that followed.

'Well, that's the first time I've ever heard Ivy apologise,' Frankie said, smiling at Rose and Josie. 'Miracles can happen!'

'I'm sorry if I caused trouble between you and Ivy,' Rose said.

'Oh, you didn't, honestly, Rose.' Frankie put her hand gently on Rose's arm. 'Ivy and I have never got on. It's a long story but she was a terrible second wife to my grandad and I didn't like seeing the way she treated 'im or Stanley.'

'Who's Stanley?' asked Rose.

'He's sort of like my brother. My grandparents took him in after his widowed mother died when he was little. He's been evacuated to the countryside. It's his room you'll be having.'

'Tell Rose about the promise you made your grandad,' Josie urged her. 'Then she'll understand why you've put up with Ivy for so long.'

'Before my grandad was killed, he asked me to look out for Ivy if anything ever 'appened to him. I promised him I would, but for his sake, not hers.'

'And you have, but Gawd knows she ain't made it easy for yer,' Josie said.

'And she doesn't know about it either,' Frankie added. 'So that's why I'm still living 'ere: that promise and keeping our house going for whenever Stanley comes home after the war.'

Rose looked at Frankie. 'You are a very kind person, Frankie. Everyone at Station 75 thinks so and I can see that's how you are at home, too.'

'And everyone at Matlock Street thinks so and all,' Josie said, throwing her arm around Frankie's shoulders. 'Now, I don't know about you, but all this excitement has left me parched; 'ow about we all have a cup of tea and toast to Rose living 'appily here at number twenty-five? I'll put the kettle on, shall I?'

★   ★   ★

'This is your room.' Frankie opened the door and stepped to the side, ushering Rose inside.

'It's lovely.' Rose stood in the middle of the room and looked around her, taking in the simply furnished, spotlessly clean room with its iron-framed bed covered with a pretty patchwork coverlet.

'I've packed Stanley's things away for now; didn't think you'd appreciate his shrapnel collection as much as he did.'

'Won't he want this room when he comes home?'

'Yes, but I ain't bringing him home until the war's over and it's safe for him to live here again. The bombing's stopped for now but that don't mean nothin', it could start again any time.'

'You must miss him,' Rose said.

'I do, but it's worth it to know that he's safe.'

'Do you have any other family? What about your parents?'

'My father died in the Great War and I

73

thought my mother was dead too until a few months ago.'

Rose frowned. 'What happened?'

'I'd grown up believin' that she was dead, that she died from Spanish flu when I was just a baby, but she didn't. She was very ill and left me in my grandparents' care to grow up 'ere in London while she lived in the countryside where she came from.'

'So why were you told she'd died?'

'Cos it's what my mother wanted at the time. She kept in touch with my grandparents, but I never knew about her until I got the letter my grandad left for me to 'ave if he was killed. In it he told me the truth about my mother and what 'appened.'

'That must have been such a shock for you,' Rose said sympathetically.

Frankie nodded. 'I'd 'ad no idea and I was so angry with them all for lying to me, letting me grow up thinkin' I was an orphan but — ' She stopped as the memory of discovering that life-altering secret played back in her mind like a film. 'She's told me why she did it and has regretted cuttin' herself off, but thought it was best for me, and her, at the time.'

'You've met her?'

'Yes, twice, and we write each week.'

'So, you've forgiven her?'

Frankie shrugged. 'I still feel angry, but not as much as I did. It'll take time to forgive her.' She paused. 'But I've got another family now, I 'ave two sisters and a brother so I'm not alone in the world apart from Ivy and Stanley any more.

That's what I think my grandad wanted, why he left me the letter.'

'He sounds like a good man,' Rose said.

'He was.' Frankie paused and then smiled at Rose. 'You must write to your parents and tell them you've moved, give them your new address so they can contact you here.'

'I will try — I haven't heard from them for months; I'm not sure where they are now.' Rose bit her bottom lip.

'Didn't your parents want to leave too?' Frankie asked.

Rose sighed. 'They applied for jobs in England but didn't get anything before the borders closed and it was too late to get out.'

'I'm sorry, you must worry a lot.'

'Yes.' Rose's eyes filled with tears and she went over to the window that looked out over the back garden.

Frankie followed her and put her arm through Rose's. 'Don't give up 'ope. It might be just that they're not allowed to send letters now, another stupid Nazi rule.'

Rose looked at her and managed a watery smile. 'I will never give up hope that we will be together again when all of this is over.'

'What a world we're living in. Try not to worry, Rose, take it a day at a time. If I can 'elp you in any way, you only have to ask.'

'Thank you, Frankie.'

'I'm glad you've come to live 'ere,' she said. 'I hope you'll come to think of it as your home for as long as you need it.'

12

The Red Cross packing centre was already a hive of activity when Bella arrived to do her voluntary shift that afternoon. She found a space at one of the long trestle tables and got to work, carefully packing the items that were already set out on the parcel lid into the box ready to be sent out to prisoners of war. Since she'd started working here in the summer she'd become adept at packing the tins and packets, fitting them snugly in to make maximum use of every available inch of space in the box.

'I think I'm going to need a lot more practice to become as quick as you,' the lady next to Bella said. 'I'm all fingers and thumbs and I don't think I'm going to be able to fit everything in.'

'I was like that at first, but you'll soon get used to it and get a feel for what goes where and fits best. Think of it as a puzzle.' Bella smiled at the woman who she'd not seen here before. 'Is this your first day?'

The woman nodded. 'The supervisor showed me what to do but she did it so quickly I didn't take it all in.'

'Here, let me show you.' Bella emptied out the woman's box. 'Let's start again. I find it works best for me if I fit similar shapes together, so I line up the tins like this.' She picked up a tin of corned beef and a tin of cocoa, which were both oblong shaped, and fitted them in the box side by side. 'They fit well together and then the bar of chocolate can go along the side of the box beside them.' Next, she selected some round tins — condensed milk, margarine, processed cheese — and put them in the box, some on top of each other, others on their sides, depending on their size. Bella worked her way through all the tins, packets and boxes of goods that needed to be fitted into the parcel, patiently showing the woman how to fit them in. 'Then I stuff paper shavings in the gaps so that they won't move around.' She wriggled her fingers under and around tins and packets to find gaps and then plugged them up with handfuls of small paper strips. 'And finally, a layer of paper shavings goes on top, then the lid goes down and it's ready for the stringers to tie up before it's sent out.' She smiled at the woman. 'That's how I do it; I think each packer fits everything in slightly differently but as long as you can get everything in and pack it securely so the contents won't move about while the box is in transit, then it's fine. You'll soon get the hang of it.'

'That's made me feel better, thank you for showing me.' The woman held out her hand. 'I'm Maude.'

Bella shook her hand. 'I'm Bella. I'm happy to help you any time.'

'I'm just glad to being doing something for the POWs. I found out last week that my son's a POW in Germany, his plane was shot down and they said he was missing . . . ' Her voice wavered for a moment. 'Then came the news that he was a prisoner and I wanted to do something to help

77

him and others like him as well as doing my WVS work.'

'Well, you're very welcome here; there's always plenty to do.' Bella picked up a tin of condensed milk and slotted it into place alongside the packet of tea she'd already put into the box she was working on. 'My brother's a POW in Italy, he says in his letters how much he and the other men look forward to getting these parcels. I like to think that perhaps he'll get one that I packed one day.'

'You never know, but whoever it goes to will be glad of it,' Maude said, putting some tins into her box the way Bella had showed her. 'How often do you come here?'

'At least once a week when my shifts allow. I can't come if I'm working the day shift,' Bella said.

'What do you do?' Maude asked.

'I'm an ambulance driver at Station 75, not far from the Tower of London.'

'I've served plenty of ambulance drivers from the mobile WVS canteen I work in,' Maude said. 'Perhaps we've met before in the middle of a raid.'

'You run a mobile canteen!' Bella smiled at her. 'Us ambulance crew are mighty grateful for hot cups of tea from WVS vans; they help keep us going while we wait for casualties to be dug out. This parcel packing's a great deal calmer than being out in the middle of an air raid, I rather enjoy it.'

'We've had a few near misses out in the van. But we don't let that stop us going out, though thankfully there haven't been any raids for quite a while now, and long may it continue.' Maude added the last item into her box. 'Look! They all fit! I've done it.'

'Well done, it's just a matter of thinking what will fit where and with what,' Bella said. 'The more you pack the better and quicker you'll get.'

They fell into silence for a few moments, listening to the music playing on the wireless as they packed. It was the *Music While You Work* programme and the notes of the theatre organ made a jolly backdrop to the packing centre, with many of the packers humming along to the tune.

'Have you been told about the next-of-kin parcels that can be sent to POWs?' Bella asked.

Maude shook her head. 'Not yet, the letter said they'd be sending me more information about where I could write to my son and send him things; I suppose it will be in that.'

'You can send him a parcel every three months. They're very strict about what you can and can't send — there are lists of things that you're allowed to put in the parcel and another of things that are banned. You'll get extra coupons to buy him some clothes to send. My mother and I knit my brother socks and put in anything that he's asked for, like pyjamas, pencils and boot laces. We even sent him his mouth organ.'

'But people must add other things their POW might like; after all, they wouldn't know what's inside the parcel once it's wrapped up?' Maude asked.

'Oh, they find out. Every parcel is opened and checked before it's sent off,' Bella explained. 'Connie, whose house I live in, works at the next-of-kin parcels centre in Finsbury Circus; she told me that each parcel is opened and its contents carefully checked for banned items because the Germans will only allow the POWs to have certain things sent and if they get other things it could put them in danger.'

Maude shook her head. 'Well, I wouldn't want to put my son in any danger. I'll be sticking to the list.'

'I'm sure he will appreciate anything you can send him.'

13

Winnie loved it when Mac telephoned her; hearing his voice made him feel so much closer, but she never knew when he would call, his job making it impossible for him to promise to telephone at a certain time or day. This meant that when he did, like tonight, before she left for her overnight shift at Station 75, it made it all the sweeter.

'How's your new attendant getting on?' Mac asked.

'Fine, Rose is a quick learner and even better, she's a lovely person, and an enormous improvement on Hooky! I'm very happy to be teamed up with her.'

'Which lucky person has got Hooky now?' Mac asked.

'Whoever the boss feels like sending her out with, but fortunately we haven't had many call-outs lately.' Winnie sat down on the third step from the bottom of the stairs, to where the telephone wire just reached. 'What have you been doing today?'

'We had to dig out a five hundred pounder, it dropped on farmland, probably jettisoned by a bomber on the way home, but it was hard going because of all the rain. The hole kept filling up with water, which made it tricky to see what we were doing but — '

'On second thoughts,' Winnie interrupted,

feeling queasy at the image of Mac digging for a bomb in a hole filled with water, 'it's probably best that I don't know.'

Mac laughed. 'You did ask. Well, apart from that we had a good game of darts, cleaned out the back of the truck and got the rota for our Christmas leave.'

Mention of Christmas leave made Winnie's heart pick up its pace. She was desperate to know whether Mac would be coming home for Christmas. 'What did it say? Are you coming home?'

The pause before Mac replied told Winnie everything. He knew how much she had been hoping he'd be given some leave, but clearly he hadn't. Tears of disappointment stung her eyes.

'I'm really sorry, Winnie, they gave leave to men who have been in the squad a lot longer than me and who have got children at home.' Mac sighed. 'You know I would much rather be with you than on duty, but it's the way it's got to be. We'll have other Christmases together.'

'It's all right, I do understand,' Winnie said, trying to keep her voice upbeat as tears slowly trickled down her cheeks. She dashed them away with the back of the hand; crying wasn't going to change anything, and she shouldn't waste precious telephone time with Mac being upset, there would be time enough for that later. 'I'll be working Christmas Day as well, so if you had been here you could've come to Station 75 and spent the day with me there.'

'I would have liked that, I do miss the crew there, they really are a good bunch of people.'

'We miss you too, it's not the same without you there. I still expect you to walk into the common room but you're not — 'Winnie's voice cracked and she stopped talking. 'I'm sorry.'

'It's all right, I know it's not easy for you,' Mac said. 'And I promise I'll get home just as soon as I can . . . ' He paused, and Winnie could hear another man's voice in the background. 'I'm going to have to go, there's a queue for the telephone. Look after yourself.'

'And you. Be careful, Mac.'

'I always am, and you be careful, too. I — ' Mac's voice was cut off and replaced with a humming sound.

Winnie stared at the telephone receiver for a few moments before replacing it. Then she leaned her elbows forward on to her knees, put her head in her hands and cried. She knew there were thousands of wives who wouldn't be spending Christmas with their husbands again this year and she really had no cause to make such a fuss, but it didn't dampen the feeling of sheer disappointment that filled her. She just wanted to see Mac again. It wasn't about Christmas — that was irrelevant — she missed him terribly every single day and wanted to see him, be with him, it was as simple as that. But Mac's life was ruled by the army now and their needs came first, she just had to accept that.

'Winnie! Are you all right?' Bella called as she ran down the stairs towards her and plonked herself down on the same step.

Winnie sat up and wiped away her tears with the back of her hand. 'Just feeling sorry for myself, that's all. I'm fine really.' She did her best to smile but it felt more like a grimace.

Bella put her arm around Winnie's shoulders. 'What's upset you? I heard the telephone ring; it wasn't your mother, was it?'

Winnie shook her head. 'Thankfully, no.' She paused. 'It was Mac and it was absolutely wonderful to talk to him, but he won't . . . ' Tears welled up in her eyes again and she swallowed hard to try and push them down. 'He hasn't been granted any leave over Christmas.' A few tears escaped and ran down her face. 'I'm being frightfully silly. He's in the army and I can't expect him to be here whenever I want.' She stood up and looked down at her friend, still perched on the stair. 'Come on, we need to get ready for work.'

Bella stood up. 'It's all right to be upset and disappointed, you know.' She linked her arm through Winnie's. 'I know how much you miss him and would like to have spent your first married Christmas together. It's the war; it's keeping so many people apart who want to be together.'

Winnie nodded. 'I know, I just need to demonstrate some stiff upper lip and get on with it, I'm not the only wife who won't be spending Christmas with her husband this year.'

'Maybe he'll get some leave again soon,' Bella said.

Winnie shrugged. 'He only had some a couple of weeks ago, so it could be months before he gets more. I just have to accept that it's the way it will be while he's in the army and there's a war on. I must be grateful that he's only in Colchester and not in some far-off place where I wouldn't have a hope of seeing him even if he did get some leave.' Winnie clamped a hand over her mouth and felt her cheeks grow warm. 'Oh, Bella, listen to me feeling sorry for myself when you haven't seen your brother for ages and haven't a clue when you'll see him again while this war still rumbles on. I'm so sorry.'

'It's fine, Winnie. I'm just glad Walter's out of the fighting. He might be in a prisoner of war camp, but he's far safer in there than battling the enemy in the desert.'

'And you're doing what you can to help him with the Red Cross parcels — who knows, he might get one that you've packed!'

'Perhaps, I like to think that when I'm packing them, but whoever gets the parcels, I know it will be a big comfort to them.' Bella glanced at her watch. 'Come on, we really do need to get a move on or else we'll be late getting to Station 75.'

14

The canteen of the London Hospital was quiet, with just a few groups of nurses huddled over much-needed cups of tea. Frankie and Alastair headed for a table over at the far side where they could be as alone as was possible. Having to snatch time together made it extremely precious and neither of them wanted to share it chatting with any of Alastair's colleagues. He was already halfway through his shift, whereas Frankie had yet to start hers, calling in to see him on her way to Station 75.

'I'm afraid I'm working on Christmas Day,' Alastair said in his beautiful Scottish accent as he sat down at a table opposite Frankie. He reached over and took her hand. 'They gave out the new roster today. I'm sorry.'

Frankie smiled. 'It's all right, I'll be working too; I'm on the day shift from eight to eight.'

'Perhaps we can meet after you've finished?'

'Yes, I'd like that. I ain't going to be in a hurry to go 'ome. I'm glad I'll be at Station 75 that day 'cos Christmas ain't going to be the same at home this year.' Frankie sighed. 'I thought last Christmas was odd with Stanley evacuated to the countryside, but this one . . . ' She took a deep breath. 'Well, with Grandad gone, it'll be awful. I don't want to spend the day with Ivy any more than she probably wants to spend it with me.'

'What about your new lodger, Rose?'

'She's Jewish, so she wouldn't normally be celebratin' it. Anyway, I'd rather be at Station 75 with my friends and no doubt we'll do somethin' fun; we sang songs and carols around the piano last year.'

'You know you could always come and sing carols here with some of your fellow ambulance crew. The patients stuck in hospital over Christmas would be delighted to see some new faces and be entertained.'

Frankie took a sip of tea, considering Alastair's suggestion. There were some good singers at Station 75; Sparky had an especially fine voice.

'What do you think?' Alastair said.

She nodded, smiling. 'You know, I think it's actually a very good idea. We will need to practise but I'm sure quite a few crew members would be willin' to join in. We'd 'ave to come after our shift, though; Station Officer Steele wouldn't let us leave the station in case there was a raid and we were needed to go out to incidents.'

'That's fine, come after work on Christmas Eve.'

'I'll look forward to it; Christmas needs cheerin' up.' She sighed.

'It's changed so much because of the war and so many people who should be 'ere are now gone.'

'And found, too, don't forget,' Alastair said.

Frankie frowned.

'Your mother, sisters and brother,' he reminded her.

Frankie shrugged. 'My mother asked me to go

there for Christmas but I can't because I'm workin'.'

Alastair looked at her and his striking blue eyes meeting hers.

'Would you have gone if you weren't?'

'No!'

'Why not?'

Frankie fiddled with a teaspoon. 'I ain't sure I'd want to. I don't know how I feel about her still — if I can even forgive her over what she did.'

'It's going to take time, but don't give up on her yet. Remember you had twenty years of believing she was dead; it's going to take more than a few months to get used to the idea of her being alive.'

'I know, but part of me thinks that I ought to be able to feel the same way about her that I did Grandad and Gran, but I don't. I like her but . . . ' Frankie shook her head and sighed.

Alastair squeezed her hand. 'You might in time. Don't worry about it because it hasn't been very long and you've only seen her twice and written letters. It takes time to build up a proper relationship, especially after what happened.'

'Is that your medical opinion, then?'

Alastair laughed. 'No, it's my personal opinion because I love you, Frankie, and care about how you feel.'

She smiled at him. 'Then I'd best take your advice, hadn't I?'

15

'Carol singing! What an absolutely wonderful idea,' Winnie said. Frankie had just told her about Alastair's idea to go carol singing at the London Hospital and she felt her spirits rise for the first time since Mac had told her that he wouldn't be home for Christmas. 'Can I help you organise it?'

'Yes, that would be a big 'elp.' Frankie stamped her feet as the temperature had plunged to just above freezing and it was hard to keep warm while they were outside in the courtyard taking their turn at picket duty, guarding Station 75's garages with their precious supply of petrol. 'I'm goin' to ask Rose if she'll play her violin.'

'We must get Sparky to join in; he's got such a marvellous voice. Remember how he and the boss entertained us last Christmas Day when we were on duty?'

'Yes, it was quite a surprise! I 'ad no idea he could sing so well. Do you think Station Officer Steele would join in too?' Frankie asked.

'I'll ask her,' said Winnie. 'She played the piano last year, but we can hardly take that with us to the London, can we?'

'No, but she could play for us while we practise, and we're goin' to need a lot of practice if we want to put on a good performance for the patients.'

'We've got a week before Christmas Eve, that's

enough time to practise and make our performance as good as we can get it.' Winnie tucked her arm through Frankie's. 'It will be jolly good fun and help cheer me up. I feel better already just talking about it!'

'Why do you need cheerin' up? Are you all right?'

'I had a telephone call from Mac earlier; he told me that he won't be home for Christmas after all. You know I was hoping he would be but . . . ' She sighed. 'I was rather upset about it, but it can't be helped, there's a war on and I'm luckier than many wives because Mac's only in Colchester and not thousands of miles away where it's impossible for him to ever get home. So, it's chin up for now, and concentrating on going carol singing at the London will help enormously.'

'I'm sorry you won't get to see him, but Bella and I will 'elp you keep your chin up, stop you from going all maudlin on us like we promised you on your wedding day. If 'elping me organise the carol singing makes you feel better then you can be in charge of the singers and I'll organise the musicians.'

'And between us we'll do a magnificent job. The patients at the London are in for a real treat!' Winnie said, hugging Frankie's arm. 'The Station 75 carol singers will be quite the sensation!'

★   ★   ★

Back up in the common room after they'd finished their picket duty, Winnie warmed her

90

hands around a mug of tea and homed in on her first potential carol singer.

'Sparky, how would you like to cheer up patients stuck in hospital over Christmas?'

He raised an eyebrow and looked at her quizzically. 'Aye, aye, you're on the prowl.'

Winnie pretended to look hurt. 'If that's your attitude, I won't bother asking you, then.' She turned to walk away.

'Wait, what do you want to ask me?'

Winnie turned back and smiled at him. 'I'm helping Frankie organise a group of carol singers from the Station to go and sing to patients at the London Hospital on Christmas Eve, and I wondered if you'd come and sing with us. You have such a magnificent voice it would really make a huge difference for us.'

'Well, if you put it like that, I can 'ardly refuse,' said Sparky.

'We'll need to practise beforehand if we're going to put on a good performance.'

'Well, we've got an entire week to perfect our singing, and it will give us something to do in the evenings while we're on shift. I'll draw up a timetable for rehearsals.'

With Sparky on board, Winnie had no problem in persuading most of the other crew members to sign up for the carol singing. Frankie had spoken to Rose, who was happy to play her violin while they sang, but there was one last person Winnie wanted to ask — Station Officer Steele. Knocking on the boss's door, Winnie waited for her to invite her in, something Winnie wouldn't usually do, but going by Station

Officer Steele's recent mood, she thought it wise.

'Yes, Winnie.' The boss looked up from the pile of paperwork on her desk.

'I just wanted to ask you something,' said Winnie, advancing into the office. 'Frankie and I are organising a group of crew members to go carol singing at the London Hospital on Christmas Eve after our shift ends, and I wondered if you would like to join in. We could really use your piano-playing skills to help us practise this week. Rose is going to accompany us on her violin at the hospital.'

Station Officer Steele tapped her pen on the piece of paper she'd been writing on for a few moments before turning to look Winnie straight in the eye. 'No, not this time.'

Winnie stared at her, not quite believing what she had just heard. The boss had seemed out of sorts just lately, but Winnie had never expected her to actually say no, remembering all too clearly how much fun Station Officer Steele had had playing the piano last Christmas while Sparky sang. 'Do you mind me asking why?' The older woman sighed and took off her glasses, pinching the bridge of her nose between her fingers, before replying. 'I'm just not in the mood right now, Winnie. I can't raise much Christmas cheer and I don't want to spoil it for anyone. You'd be far better off without me.'

'You're worried about your sister,' Winnie said sympathetically. Part of her wanted to try to persuade Station Officer Steele to join in anyway, the way she would've done if it had been one of her friends or other crew members, as taking part might help cheer her up. However, instinct told her that on this occasion if she tried to persuade the boss it might backfire on her. She had to respect that this was what the woman wanted. 'I understand, but if you change your mind you'd be most welcome to join us and we'd be very glad of your help playing the piano.'

'There are several others who can play the piano for you; I'm hardly the only one at Station 75 who can play.' She put her glasses back on and turned back to her work, clearly dismissing Winnie without further discussion.

Back in the common room, Winnie sat down next to Frankie, who was busy writing out a list of carols that they could sing.

'Will the boss play the piano for us?' Frankie asked.

Winnie shook her head, leaned closer to her friend and spoke in a quiet voice. 'No, I'm afraid she doesn't want to join in, she's worried about her sister and not feeling very festive. I hope she might change her mind, but we'll just have to wait and see.'

'Fair enough,' said Frankie. 'She would if she could, you know the boss. I'll ask one of the others to play the piano for us while we rehearse.'

'When shall we start?' asked Winnie.

'Why not tonight, if everyone is willing? Just a couple of carols to get us in the mood and then we'll have to practise every night up until Christmas Eve if we're going to be ready on time.'

Winnie stood up. 'Right, I'll rally the troops then and we can get started!'

93

16

Station Officer Violet Steele stared at the words printed in bold across the front of the *Daily Herald* spread out on her desk before her. The headline read: 'Singapore: Churchill's pledge to defend it'. The words felt like a balm to her after weeks of worry about her sister Lily and her family. If Churchill had pledged to defend Singapore then everything would be all right.

Taking a deep breath, she sat back in her chair, closed her eyes and finally let herself relax, the weight of worry sliding off her shoulders. Sitting still and silent, the sounds from out in the common room filtered into her office, the beautiful lyrics and music of the crew's rendition of 'Silent Night', as they did their final practice for tonight's carol singing at the London Hospital after the shift. Winnie had wanted her to join in, but she'd said no, because the weight of worry had stamped out any sense of Christmas cheer, but now that worry was lifted and she could enjoy listening to the Christmas carols.

'Cup of cocoa, boss?' Frankie said, standing in the doorway a short while later with a tray of mugs in her hands, while they were taking a break from singing.

'Yes please, that would be lovely.'

Frankie came in and put a mug of cocoa down on her desk, her gaze falling on the newspaper headlines. 'That's good news.'

Station Officer Steele smiled. 'The best, I feel much happier now.'

'You look it, if you don't mind me saying. Just in time for Christmas, too.' Frankie turned to go and then looked back. 'Don't suppose you'd like to come carol singing at the hospital with us tonight after all?'

'I haven't practised.'

'But you know all the carols and we're going to do a bit more after our break, you could join in then. We'd be pleased to have you.'

'I'm not sure.'

'It would be good to have our Station Officer with us, the patients would appreciate it.' Frankie smiled. 'I think you'd enjoy it, too. Singing always makes me feel 'appy and Christmas carols are lovely to sing.'

The boss held up her hand. 'Very well, I'll come and join in the rest of the practice and come to the hospital with you all. I'll just join in standing at the back, all right?'

Frankie nodded and smiled. 'You're the boss. I'm glad you're going to come with us.'

Station Officer Steele stayed in her office until the first notes of 'While Shepherds Watched Their Flocks by Night' were played on the piano, signalling the start of the practice. She quietly slipped into the common room, which was trimmed up for Christmas, with newspaper paper-chains hung in swathes across the ceiling, and where Sparky's improvised Christmas tree made out of wire, was draped with baubles and ornaments that she'd brought in from home. It looked very festive and added to the happy atmosphere. Joining the back row of singers, she started to sing the words she knew so well.

Her arrival didn't go unnoticed, however. Paterson, who worked as Sparky's attendant, spotted her from his seat at the piano where he was playing the accompanying music. He smiled at her and, when they'd sung the whole carol, he stood up and beckoned her to take his seat at the piano. She shook her head, but Paterson's movement had alerted other crew members to their boss's arrival and their welcoming smiles made her glad that she'd joined in at last.

'Come and play,' Paterson said. 'You're much better than I am.'

'Go on!' Sparky called. 'He's done his best for us but, like the man said, you're a much better player.'

Station Officer Steele smiled and nodded, then made her way over to the piano and sat down with a flourish, wriggling her fingers to warm them up and sending the crew members into a chorus of laughter. 'What should I play?'

' "O Little Town of Bethlehem",' Frankie called to her.

She looked at Rose who stood the other side of the piano, her violin ready in her hands, and nodded to her. 'One, two, three . . . ' And then she began to play the opening bars, with Rose joining in on the violin and the rest of the crew beginning to sing at the appropriate point. The combination of music and voices was quite lovely, and she lost herself in the joy of playing.

After they'd gone through their entire

repertoire of carols, it was time for another break and a much-needed cup of tea to wet throats that had become parched from so much singing.

'I'm glad you decided to come and join in,' Winnie said, coming up to the piano while the others got a drink. 'Do you mind me asking, what made you change your mind?'

'Frankie and Churchill.'

Winnie frowned. 'How?'

'Frankie made me see that as Station Officer I really should be with you tonight, and now Churchill's made his pledge to make sure that Singapore's defended I feel so much better, more in the mood to be festive.' She smiled. 'And I always enjoy a good sing-song.'

Winnie smiled back at her. 'I'm jolly glad you've joined us; it will be good fun at the hospital and I'm sure the patients will enjoy our singing.'

17

The last time Frankie had been on one of the wards in the London Hospital she'd been there as a patient, put there by an exploding landmine while she and Bella were attending an incident during the last raid on London. Walking through the doors of that same ward sent a shiver down her spine, and although the Christmas decorations strung across the room made the place look a bit different, the smell and familiar layout of beds whisked her straight back to the days she'd spent in here in May.

It wasn't just the memory of her injuries that spooked her, it was remembering that this was where her life had irrevocably altered, going from her normality with her grandad alive and her future secure, to her life tilting on its axis. When Alastair had told her that her grandad had been killed it had started a chain of unexpected events. His death had been terrible enough, but finding out that her mother was still alive had shifted everything that she'd grown up believing, and she was still struggling to come to terms with what had become her new life. Being here on the ward again brought it all back, the utter despair when Alastair had broken the news and the prospect of a bleak future without her grandad, followed by the shock of finding out about her mother. Frankie had a sudden urge to flee.

'Frankie, what's wrong?' Bella's voice startled her. 'You've gone very pale.'

Her friend's kind voice and the touch of her hand on Frankie's arm made her focus on what was happening right now. She was here to sing carols to the patients stuck in hospital over Christmas, stranded away from their homes and families. Now wasn't the time to dwell on memories of things that had already happened, things she had no power to alter. 'I'm fine, just remembering this was the ward I was in.'

Bella nodded sympathetically. 'I didn't realise. I wasn't allowed to come to visit you here, Connie and Station Officer Steele kept me confined at home.' Her brown eyes met Frankie's. 'Thank goodness we're both better now.'

'We were lucky we survived that landmine. Plenty don't when those things go off.'

Aware that the other crew members had formed themselves into a vaguely semicircular group facing the patients, she stamped down all thoughts of her time in here and what had happened afterwards, focusing instead on the here and now because she had a job to do. 'Ready, everyone, it's time to sing.'

Along with the rest of the crew, Frankie looked to where Station Officer Steele stood: Winnie had asked her to act as a conductor since she had no piano to play.

'Ready? One, two, three,' the boss said softly and Rose started to play the opening bars of 'Once in Royal David's City'.

As Frankie began to sing, the words of the

familiar carol were comforting, bringing with them the warm glow that she associated with them from so many Christmases past, starting at school when the advent of carol singing heralded the approach of Christmas and with it the delicious, bubbling excitement that children feel so vividly. It soothed and calmed her, the anxiety she'd felt on entering the ward melting away.

Other voices joined in with Station 75's crew as nurses and patients sang along too. It was beautiful and Rose's violin playing added a sweetness to the sound that swelled and filled the ward.

They were about to sing their last carol, 'Silent Night', when Frankie felt a gentle touch on her arm and turned to see Alastair.

'I'm on my break,' he whispered. 'I thought I'd come and join in.'

'You're very welcome.' She linked her arm through his, and together they joined in with the words of the beautiful, haunting carol, Alastair's rich baritone adding to the mix of voices that filled the ward.

As the last notes died away, everyone stood in silence for a few moments before Sparky called out, 'Merry Christmas, everyone!' and the ward erupted in applause from the patients and nurses.

'Merry Christmas, Frankie,' Alastair said, leaning close and kissing her cheek.

★　★　★

It was after midnight by the time Frankie climbed into her bed. She'd gone to the hospital canteen with Alastair and some of Station 75's carol singers for a much-needed cup of tea after their performance. It had been a lovely way to end the day with people she liked. Now, back at home, with the exception of Rose, she no longer had anyone here whom she wanted to spend Christmas Day with and was glad that in a matter of hours she would be back on duty at Station 75 where she would be with her friends and everyone would do their best to enjoy themselves.

Her eyes strayed to the parcel that her mother had sent her. She had put it on her chest of drawers ready to open in the morning, but it was already Christmas Day now, so, throwing back the covers, Frankie went over to fetch it and quickly climbed back in bed again, pulling the covers up over her to keep warm. She folded back the brown paper carefully to reveal a soft, hand-knitted leaf-green cardigan with a Fair Isle pattern of reds and golds worked into it across the chest. It was quite beautiful and the perfect colours to complement her auburn hair and pale skin. She quickly put it on and once more climbed out of bed to look at her reflection in the mirror that stood on top of her chest of drawers. The cardigan fitted her perfectly. Her mother must have put hours of work into making it for her ... The thought brought tears to Frankie's eyes. Christmas suddenly felt a whole lot better than it had a few minutes ago: she might not have the family here that she once had, but she did have her mother in her life again and had gained two sisters and a brother as well.

Getting back into bed, she kept the cardigan on and, hugging her arms around its soft warmth, she soon drifted off to sleep.

18

Christmas had come and gone, and the old year turned into the new. Now, in mid-January of 1942, with its freezing days and nights, Bella was grateful that the enemy hadn't returned to bomb London and the night shifts at Station 75 were still calm and quiet. Carrying a mug of cocoa for the boss, she knocked on the office door and waited for the older woman to beckon her in.

'Thank you, Bella. Do sit down; I've got something to show you.' Station Officer Steele reached into her handbag and pulled out a piece of paper. 'My brother sent me this cutting from a Scottish newspaper.' She handed it to her.

Bella read through the short piece, which reported on a fund-raising concert put on by the crew members of an ambulance station to raise money for the Red Cross prisoners of war fund.

'Well, what do you think?' the boss asked when Bella had finished reading.

'It's very good; every penny given to the Red Cross helps,' Bella said.

'Indeed, but what about the idea of a concert run by the ambulance station?'

'It was a very good way to raise funds; I'm sure the people taking part and the audience would have enjoyed it very much.'

'That's what I thought. We could do one, too.'

Bella stared at her. 'What, Station 75?'

Station Officer Steele nodded. 'Yes, and more precisely, you.'

'Me!'

'I'll help, but I think this would be just the sort of thing you'd be good at organising, Bella. We've got enough talented crew members to put on a good show and raise even more money for the POW fund.'

'But I don't know the first thing about putting on a concert,' Bella protested. 'I wouldn't know where to start.'

'My dear Bella, I'm not asking you to do this alone but I think it would be a good thing for you to do and what's more you'd do an excellent job.' Station Officer Steele looked at her with her shrewd, brown eyes warm behind her glasses. 'You miss writing for the paper, don't you?'

Bella nodded.

'Exactly, so I thought organising a concert would help fill the gap. You're a very capable young woman.'

'I'm not sure; I need to think about it.'

'Look, let's talk it through now and see if it would work — if it looks like it would be impossible, then we'll forget it.' Station Officer Steele picked up a pen. 'Right, let's think about what we need to organise.'

'Somewhere to hold a concert for a start: Station 75 isn't a suitable venue. We'd need somewhere much bigger where you can fit more people in and perhaps with a stage as well . . . A church, perhaps, or a school hall.'

'Excellent thinking.' The boss wrote it down. 'And what sort of acts might we have?'

104

'Singing, Sparky's got such a good voice, he'd be a real asset, and Rose could play her violin.' She paused, thinking about what entertainment shows she herself enjoyed listening to on the wireless. 'Perhaps some of the crew could act out funny sketches or tell jokes.'

'We would need to make sure they're good enough for people to pay money to see,' the boss said. 'We'd have to hold auditions.'

'Some of the crew from the other shift might want to take part, too,' Bella suggested. 'They'll have to be told about it, we'd need to put up a notice or something and — ' She stopped talking and looked at Station Officer Steele, who was smiling broadly at her.

'You know, I think we already have our answer, Bella, don't you, providing we can find somewhere to hold the concert? So, will you do it with me?'

Did she want the responsibility of putting on a concert, organising auditions and acts, finding a venue and selling tickets to raise money to help prisoners of war, to help her brother even? There was no question that the idea of raising money was a good one, the more the Red Cross got, the more they could help, but could she do it? A feeling of self-doubt gnawed at her, just as it had done when she'd been asked to write for the paper, but then when she'd doubted herself she'd just ignored it and gone ahead and had done well. There was no reason why she shouldn't do this and succeed, and at least this time she wouldn't be doing it alone, Station Officer Steele would be helping her too. Their decision was indeed made.

'Yes, I will.' Bella smiled at her boss. 'I think putting on a concert is a good idea, and it will give the crew something to think about, challenge them, and we'll be helping the Red Cross at the same time.'

'Excellent. I'm so glad you're on board with this, Bella. I think the first thing to do is find a venue, then advertise the concert to crew members and get them to sign up for auditions. So, if I find a venue, you can get on with finding us some acts?'

Bella was sitting at the table in the common room drafting a notice about the concert, when she became aware of someone standing behind her, peering over her shoulder. She quickly turned around to see Sparky, who raised his eyebrows at her.

'Are we having a concert?' he asked. 'Here?'

'Not exactly here at Station 75, it's not big enough, so it'll be in a school hall or somewhere. Station Officer Steele and I are hoping crew members will take part,' Bella explained. 'They can do any sort of suitable act: singing, juggling, dancing or performing sketches. It's to raise money for a good cause.'

'What?'

'The Red Cross prisoners of war fund.'

'Then count me in, I'll sing for you,' Sparky said.

'Thank you, Sparky, I hoped you would. I'll write your name on the list then, shall I? Though I should warn you, we'll have to hold auditions and to make it fair on the others, you'll have to

106

take part in them as well but I don't think there'll be any doubt that you'll get chosen to be in the concert.'

Sparky nodded. 'I'll do what's needed, so I'd best get some practice in.' He went off, humming a tune to himself and smiling.

Having Sparky on board was an excellent start, Bella thought, as she returned to working on her notice. By the time she finished it and pinned it up on the notice-board ready for people to sign up their names and chosen act, Sparky had spread the word around the crew members, and the common room was full of talk about what people might do.

'Sparky told us you are putting on a concert, Bella!' Winnie came rushing up to Bella, her cheeks red from the cold where she and Frankie had been outside on picket duty for the past hour.

'That's right, Station Officer Steele and I are organising it and we're hoping crew members will put on acts. Anyone interested in auditioning needs to sign their name on the notice.' She pointed to the noticeboard where several other crew members were already crowding around to read what Bella had put up.

Winnie nodded and stood quietly, thinking for a moment. 'I'd like to do something, but I'm not sure what. I can't play an instrument like Rose or sing very well at all — it was all right singing carols with everybody else, but no one wants to hear me sing on my own, they'd demand their money back!' She frowned. 'If only I could think of something . . . '

'Perhaps you could do a funny sketch with someone?' Bella paused as she spotted Frankie heading their way. 'Frankie, you'd make a good double act with Winnie.'

'What's that?' Frankie said.

'It is true what Sparky told us about the concert,' Winnie said.

'Bella's looking for acts and suggested we do a funny sketch together.'

'Perhaps something like they do on the wireless, only — live — you'd have to act it out,' Bella said.

'Me?' Frankie asked.

'Yes, you,' Bella and Winnie chorused, turned to look at each other, then laughed.

'I'm sure we can come up with something funny,' Winnie said.

'It's all for a good cause.'

'You'd have to pass an audition too,' Bella warned them.

'There you go, Frankie, they're having some quality control, so if we are truly awful we won't be in it. Will you do it with me? Please?' she asked. 'It'll be jolly good fun.'

'Go on, I'll give it a go, though I ain't promising to be a wonderful actor or comedian.'

'Splendid.' Winnie linked her arm through Frankie's. 'Come on, let's go and have a good think about what we might do.'

As Bella watched her friends go and sit down on the sofa to talk about their act amid the general hum of excited chatter from other crew members crowding around the noticeboard, she felt a warm glow of satisfaction. She was glad that Station Officer Steele had suggested they should put on a concert and that she'd agreed to help organise it. It would help fill the void left by her writing job because she really did miss it very much.

19

Despite wearing wool gloves, Frankie's fingers were numb from the frosty cold by the time she and Rose turned into Matlock Street a little before half past eight in the morning after finishing their overnight shift at Station 75. Bumping her bicycle over the cobbles towards home, she spotted someone hammering on the front door of number 25. It was Josie's oldest boy, ten-year-old Arthur.

'Arthur! What's wrong?' she shouted, her breath coming out in puffs in the cold air.

Hearing her voice, the boy turned and a look of relief washed over his face before he quickly ran to meet them.

'It's me mum — she's 'aving the baby and the midwife's already out at another delivery. Can you come and help her?'

Frankie swiftly dismounted from her bicycle and put a hand on his shoulder. 'We'll come straight away, go and tell your mother we're comin'.'

'Thanks.' Arthur rushed off to number 5.

'Will you come with me, Rose?' Frankie asked. 'It would be useful to have another pair of 'ands.'

'Yes, but I don't know how to deliver a baby.' Rose looked worried.

'Nor do I, but I've seen it done and we can't leave Josie on her own. With any luck the midwife will soon be 'ere.'

After stowing their bicycles at home, they hurried back down the street towards Josie's house, Frankie's mind recalling the night in Aldwych Underground when she'd watched Alastair deliver a baby girl during an air raid. He'd been so calm and had known exactly what to do, but then he'd had training and experience whereas she . . . Well, she was just an ambulance driver who normally took people to hospital to get help. Watching a baby being delivered by someone who knew what they were doing was a whole lot different than doing it yourself. She just hoped that the midwife would arrive in plenty of time to do what was needed, but until then, Josie needed her to be there and she couldn't let her friend down.

'She's in the bedroom,' Arthur said, opening the front door wide for them to come in and ushering them towards the stairs. 'You go up; I've got to keep an eye on the others.' He nodded to the kitchen door where two small faces were peeping through a crack watching them.

'We'll go up, you look after your sisters,' Frankie said. 'Have you made them some breakfast?'

Arthur nodded. 'Some toast and dripping.'

'Good lad.' Frankie smiled at him, then made her way up the stairs, heading for the front bedroom where she could hear groaning coming from.

Pausing outside the door, she glanced at Rose, who had followed quietly behind. The young woman looked worried.

'Are you sure you're all right?' Frankie asked.

Rose nodded and squared her shoulders, doing her best to appear more at ease.

Frankie tapped on the door. 'Josie, we're 'ere.'

'Thank Gawd,' Josie called. 'Come in.'

Frankie wasn't sure what to expect when she opened the door and went in, but the sight of Josie pacing up and down was a relief. She was dressed in her long white nightgown, her swollen belly straining at the front. She looked much as she normally would except for the sheen of sweat on her forehead, which Frankie thought was probably more due to the fact that she was in labour than the heat that the small coal fire in the grate was giving out.

'What do you need me to do?' Frankie asked, trying to sound calm although she felt far from that inside.

'Just be 'ere.' Josie nodded towards the bed, which was covered with brown paper and a clean sheet, and there was a pile of clean towels and sheets ready on the chest of drawers next to the bed.

'It's all ready. I don't think I'll be long now. Each baby I 'ave has come quicker than the one before — it's all the practice, I suppose. I — '

Her face grimaced and she leaned forwards, her hands braced on the iron bedstead at the foot of the bed, her breath coming in slow, steady puffs as her body was racked in pain.

Instinctively, Frankie put her hand on Josie's back, rubbing it while her friend waited for the pain to subside.

'Oh, that was a strong one.' Josie stood up and rubbed at her belly.

112

'Rose, can you go and boil some water and bring it up in a basin with some soap, please?' Frankie asked.

Rose nodded, glad of a job that she could easily do.

'Send Arthur and the girls next door to Freda as well, will yer?'

Josie added, 'Best they're out of the 'ouse now you're here.' Her face scrunched in pain. 'Here we go again.'

Frankie glanced at her watch, remembering how Alastair had timed the contractions of the woman in the Aldwych Underground station. 'Are the pains coming closer together?'

Josie nodded, leaning against the bedstead again until the pain had passed.

'I ain't never delivered a baby before, Josie, I don't really know what to do,' Frankie said. 'You're goin' to have to tell me what I need to do.'

'It's all right, ducks, I pop my babies out, but I need someone 'ere to catch it and wrap it up for me; you can do that, can't you?'

'Of course I can.' Frankie tried to sound more confident than she felt.

'Good, 'cos this one's coming soon.' Josie waddled over to the bed and heaved herself on to it. 'I can feel it comin'.'

Rose came in with the hot water and soap and at the sight of Josie looking like she was about to give birth, her face paled.

'Thanks, Rose, just put it on the chest of drawers and I'll wash my hands.' Frankie carefully washed and dried her hands. 'Can you

113

hold some towels near the fire to warm them, then we can wrap the baby in them when it comes?'

Rose took some off the pile and stood near the fire to warm them, her back to Josie who was puffing like a train, her face red as she started to bear down.

'It's comin', are you ready?' Josie's voice was strained.

Frankie grabbed one of the warmed towels out of Rose's hand and knelt down beside the bed, positioning herself ready to catch Josie's baby. 'I can see the head, it's got dark hair.'

Josie nodded but didn't say anything, her face screwing up as another contraction hit.

It happened fast, the baby's head was out and then the rest of it shortly after, slipping and sliding into the warm towel that Frankie held ready.

'It's a little girl, Josie!' Frankie's voice caught in her throat. She'd been completely terrified that something would go wrong, the baby would be stuck and she wouldn't know what to do, but Josie had guided her.

Frankie quickly wrapped the baby in the towel as it looked at her with big eyes, not crying and seemingly content with its sudden entry into a new world. 'What should I do about the cord?'

'You'll need to clamp it with — ' Josie began but stopped as the door opened and the midwife walked in.

'Looks like I'm too late,' the midwife said, putting her bag down.

'No, you're just in time, I don't know 'ow to

cut the cord or what to do next,' Frankie said.

'Don't worry, I can see to all that,' the midwife said.

Frankie was grateful that she'd turned up when she did and was able to cut the cord and then deliver the placenta while she had the far easier job of swaddling the baby in a clean, warm towel and presenting her to Josie to cuddle.

★　★　★

'Thank you, ducks,' Josie said, leaning back against the pillows a little later on when the midwife had gone, satisfied that all was well. 'I appreciate you being here to 'elp me.'

'I didn't really do much,' Frankie said. 'You did all the 'ard work.' She took a sip of the tea that Rose had made them all. 'I was scared, you know.'

'You did well. Perhaps you might want to think about trainin' as a midwife?' Josie suggested.

'Me?' Frankie shook her head. 'No, I think drivin' ambulances is definitely preferable to delivering babies for me.'

'What are you going to call her?' Rose asked.

'Well, we thought if it was a girl we'd call her after my husband's grandmother, so she'll be Flora.' Josie looked down at her new daughter, a look of love on her face.

'That's a lovely name,' Frankie said.

'I like it, too,' Rose said. 'I was very scared to see her born, but . . . '

She smiled at them both. 'I am glad I was here.'

Frankie held up her mug. 'Welcome to Matlock Street, Flora.'

20

Winnie shivered as she approached the Dorchester. It wasn't due to the cold January afternoon but because of what had happened the last time she'd been here when she'd come with Mac to meet her mother just before their wedding, in the vain hope that she would approve of their match. The encounter hadn't gone well and the memory of how unpleasant and cruel her mother had been to Mac still lingered in Winnie's memory.

Walking in, the familiar sounds of the soft piano music, the muted hum of conversation and the chink of cutlery on bone china took her right back to that last meeting with her mother, making her want to turn tail and run. Today wasn't going to be like that, though, she reminded herself; the member of her family whom she was meeting was utterly different and far more pleasant to spend time with. He'd invited her to meet him for afternoon tea as there was something he wanted to ask her advice about, and that, Winnie thought, was most unusual.

Harry was already seated at a table in the middle of the room and he stood up as she approached the table.

'There you are, old girl,' he said, smiling at her as she leaned close to kiss his scarred face. 'I was beginning to think you were going to stand me up.'

Winnie glanced at her watch as she sat down at the table. 'Sorry, but I'm only five minutes late.'

'You wouldn't dare do that if I were Mother, though, would you?'

'No, but if you were Mother then I wouldn't be coming here at all. The thought of taking tea with her isn't very appealing after what happened last time we met here.' Winnie's relationship with her mother was still very strained and she had seen very little of her since her wedding last July. In spite of her mother saying that she would not be attending, she had surprised Winnie by turning up with her father, although the pair of them had sat at the very back of the church and disappeared again afterwards, not attending the reception at Connie's house. It had been Harry's persuading them to change their minds that had made them come, but for the briefest of time possible. 'Whereas you, dear brother, are much more understanding and . . . ' She smiled at him. 'Much better company.'

Harry laughed as he opened a silver cigarette holder, took out a cigarette and lit it, blowing smoke up into the air. 'I shall have to make sure I'm splendid company then.'

'You usually are, I . . . ' Winnie paused as the waitress arrived to take their order.

'Afternoon tea for two, please,' Harry said.

When the waitress had gone Winnie looked at her brother, studying his face for signs of how he felt. The shiny, scarred skin looked much better now than it had done after he'd been burnt when the Spitfire he was piloting was shot down, but it was still clearly disfigured, and inevitably it attracted stares from people when they first saw him. The waitress had stared just now, although she'd clearly tried not to, but she wasn't the only person in the room who was looking at Harry's injuries. Winnie had noticed several customers casting looks at him and she had stared resolutely back at them, making it quite obvious that she knew what they were doing.

'You know you don't have to protect me,' Harry said. 'The look you just gave the woman sitting over there by the potted fern was enough to turn her to stone if you only had the power.' He smiled, the shiny skin around his mouth stretching as far as it could.

'Well, she's jolly lucky I don't go over there and pour a cup of tea right over her head! Doesn't she know that it's rude to stare?'

'Calm down, old girl. They might not have seen someone who's been fried before, it's not like East Grinstead here; there they are so used to seeing us chaps around the town they don't take much notice of how we look. I'm not going to worry about what people think of my face, I've been through enough without bothering about that — if they have a problem with how I look then it's theirs and not mine.' He nodded towards a woman at the next table who'd been sneaking glances at him. She blushed and quickly looked away.

'They ought to be ashamed of themselves; after all, you got burnt defending this country and its people. If people like you hadn't been up

119

there risking your lives, then our streets might be pounding to the sound of marching German soldiers now.' Winnie bristled. 'You know, I feel like standing up and telling everyone what happened to you and what you did for them.'

Harry reached across the table and patted her arm. 'Forget it, I don't mind attracting attention; I used to get it for being such a handsome chap and now I get it for my battle scars.' He shrugged. 'You know I always liked plenty of attention.'

The waitress appeared with a tray of tea things and quickly put them on the table, this time taking care to avoid looking directly at Harry.

In spite of what her brother has just said, Winnie couldn't help feeling angry on his behalf. 'If you're wondering what happened to my brother here,' she said, in a voice loud enough to be heard not only by the waitress but by those sitting at the tables around them, 'he was burned when his Spitfire was hit by an enemy fighter during the Battle of Britain — while he was defending our country.'

The waitress stared at her for a few moments, her face flushing crimson. 'I'm sorry about what happened to you, sir,' she said in a small voice, turning to Harry. 'If it weren't for men like you, who knows what might have happened to us all by now.'

Harry nodded. 'Thank you.'

The waitress bobbed a quick curtsy and then scuttled away.

'You shouldn't have done that,' Harry said. 'The poor girl was mortified.'

120

Winnie picked up the teapot and poured them both a cup of tea. 'It needed saying and it wasn't just that poor girl but everyone else in here; they need to understand what men like you have sacrificed for this country. I didn't do it just for you, Harry — it was for the other men they might come across in the future who bear the scars of battle. None of you deserve to be looked at like some curiosity.' She smiled. 'Right, are you going to tell me what this tea is all about? You said you wanted to ask my advice about something.'

Harry took a sandwich off the stand and bit into it, chewing slowly before answering. 'Mr McIndoe's happy with my face now; he's signed me off for the time being. I won't be going back on to Ward Three again.'

'That's wonderful.' Winnie raised her cup of tea in salute. 'To Mr McIndoe, the most talented and marvellous surgeon.'

Harry clinked his cup against hers and took a sip of tea. 'Well, in one respect it is marvellous, but there's a downside to it, too. I'll miss the other fellows and . . . ' His grey eyes met hers. 'Meredith.'

'Ah, Meredith, the pretty Welsh nurse with the beautiful sing-song voice and gorgeous eyes.'

Harry nodded. 'The thing is, I've rather gone and fallen in love with her and, surprisingly, she with me, so she tells me, and I would like to marry her and spend the rest of my life with her. She's an absolutely wonderful woman and I adore her.'

Winnie stared at her brother for a few

moments, completely lost for words. She knew he was sweet on Meredith but never expected him to want to marry her. He'd never been the kind of chap who wanted to settle down before; he had lots of girls chasing him but had never stayed with one for long, always preferring to have fun, but with no strings attached. However, that was before he'd been shot down and badly burned, and since then, Harry had undergone a transformation not only in his physical appearance, but in his character too; he'd become more serious and thoughtful. It had been Harry who'd made her see sense last year when she had stupidly broken up with Mac over his joining bomb disposal. If he hadn't helped her see how foolish she was being, she may never have asked Mac to forgive her and they wouldn't be married now. He'd have left Station 75 and she probably would never have seen him again. The mere thought made Winnie shudder.

'That's utterly wonderful. Have you asked her?'

'No.' Harry looked down at the pristine white tablecloth.

'Why not?' she asked.

He sighed. 'Because I don't want to make a fool of myself when she says no.' He looked up at her, his grey eyes meeting hers. 'I'm not the best catch any more, am I? Look at my hands.' He held them up and Winnie's heart squeezed at the sight of his poor fingers, which were curled inwards because of the burns; they were functional, but he couldn't straighten his fingers properly any more. His hands would never again work as they once had. 'And I'm no matinee idol to look at either.'

Winnie narrowed her eyes. 'Are you feeling sorry for yourself? Because if you are you can snap out of it right now. You are alive and kicking, which is more than can be said for a lot of your pals from your squadron. Remember Peter?' Harry's best friend had been shot down and killed just a few weeks before Harry. 'Peter wasn't so lucky.'

Harry held up his hand. 'Of course I do; you don't need to tell me I'm lucky to still be here when so many chaps I knew bought it. All I'm saying is Meredith could do a great deal better than me.'

'Does she think that?'

Harry shrugged. 'I haven't asked her.'

Well, you shouldn't presume to know how Meredith feels. If, as you say, she's told you that she loves you and you've spent plenty of time together so she's had a chance to get to know you well, then she might actually say yes to marrying you if you give her the chance.'

'Do you really think she might?'

'She might, or she might not, but you won't know unless you ask her, will you?'

'I suppose not.'

'Just do it, Harry. You're brave enough to fly into battle, so you can do this. The worst it can be is if she says no and the best is she'll become your wife.' Winnie took a slice of cake from the stand and bit into it.

'Please don't tell anyone about this, will you?

Not even Connie. If it goes wrong, I'd rather they didn't know.'

'Very well, if that's what you want. I'm just glad you're going to do as I suggested.'

'You can be quite bossy at times, do you know that?'

She nodded, smiling. 'And so can you. I'm just returning the favour from when you made me see sense over Mac and his decision to join bomb disposal.'

'All right, you've convinced me, old girl. I'll ask Meredith and hope she says yes, and if not, I can scurry away to my new posting and she won't ever have to see me again.'

'Do you know what you're going to do?' Winnie frowned.

'They're not sending you flying again, are they?'

Harry smiled at her. 'Loose lips sink ships. I'm not at liberty to tell you, you'll just have to wait and see.'

'Well, I jolly well hope not, I don't need any more worry, I've got enough worrying to do already over Mac.'

'How is he? Does he enjoy working bomb disposal?' Harry asked.

'He's fine, he enjoys the camaraderie of working with other men and I think the job itself, but he doesn't talk about it much to me — I'd rather not know, to be honest. The more I know, the more I worry.'

'At least there have been no more raids on London, so less unexploded bombs to defuse.'

'There are still enough.' Winnie sighed.

'Enemy bombers still drop them on other places and sometimes on the way back from their target just to get rid of them; they land in fields and still have to be dealt with. So long as this war carries on there will be no shortage of bombs that need dealing with.'

21

'How many potential acts have you got?' Connie asked, as she chopped carrots by the sink.

'More than we need,' Bella said. 'But that's a good thing because we can pick the best ones.' She was sitting at the kitchen table with bits of paper spread out on it as she worked out the final arrangements for tonight's auditions, which were taking place at Station 75 at the start of the shift.

'Better to have too many than not enough,' Connie said. 'There are bound to be some that aren't up to scratch and if you're asking people to pay money to see the concert then the acts need to be worth seeing. Sometimes people can have an inflated opinion of what they can do!'

'That's what Station Officer Steele says and thankfully she's going to be helping me weed out the poorer acts.'

Connie tipped the carrots into the saucepan. 'So, what have you got on offer for tonight?'

'Enough variety to grace a West End stage.' Bella picked up the sheet she'd pinned up on the noticeboard in the common room where crew members had written down their names and acts on offer. 'Well, we've a good selection of singers, some tap dancers, a comedian, a variety of musical instruments to be played, poetry reading, funny sketches and some magic tricks.'

'Winnie's doing a funny sketch, isn't she?'

'Yes, she's teamed up with Frankie and Sparky but I have no idea what they're actually planning on doing; they won't let me see it but I know they've been rehearsing it as much as they can.'

'I hope they pass the audition so I get to see it,' Connie said, her fingers deftly peeling a potato.

'Well, they'll only get through if it's good enough; there'll be no favouritism just because they're my friends.' Bella laughed. 'The boss will make sure of that. Once we've sorted out the acts we've got a few weeks to rehearse and sort out the running order so we're ready for the concert on the twenty-first of February. Let's just hope the bombers keep away that night.'

'If they do return, you'll just have to do what they do in the theatres: stop and go to the shelter.'

'Well, there's a shelter not far from the church hall where we're holding the concert, so if needs be we can all go there.'

'Try not to worry about it, Bella, it's out of our control whether the bombers come back or not, don't let it spoil what will be a lovely evening and think about what good it will do raising money for the Red Cross parcels,' Connie said. 'Afterwards you can write and tell Walter all about the concert and he'll be able to tell other POWs what we're doing to make money to help them.'

'I will, he'll be glad to hear it. Right, which act to audition first?' She looked down at the list. 'It has to be crew members from the day shift so they can get off home as soon as possible; we can

127

audition our shift after them. So, Connie, who should go first: the tap dancers, magic tricks, comedian or juggler?

'Tap dancers, I think, it's an energetic dance and they'll be tired after a twelve-hour shift, so let them do their bit first and then they can get off home,' Connie suggested.

Between them they worked out a running order for the auditions, making sure it was a mixture of acts, no similar performances leading on from another to give everyone a fair shot and make it interesting for those watching, and especially her and Station Officer Steele.

Bella was satisfied with the plan and clearing up her bits of paper when Winnie burst in through the outside door with Trixie following close on her heels. 'The queues at the shops get worse every time I go.' She dumped the shopping basket down on the table. 'I couldn't get any decent meat, I'm afraid, Connie, just some scrag end of mutton, but it will have to do.'

'No matter, it'll make a stew and we should be grateful for what we can get . . . ' Connie paused and smiled. 'Don't you know there's a war on?'

'All too well.' Winnie pulled out a chair and sat down at the table, her eyes coming to rest on Bella's pile of paper. 'What have you been up to?'

'Just working out the running order for tonight's auditions,' Bella said.

'Let's see. When's our act on?' Winnie asked.

Bella stood up, clutching the papers to her chest. 'You'll find out when everyone else does.'

'But . . . Oh, go on, Bella, tell me,' Winnie

said. 'It would be good to know so I can prepare myself.'

'No, I can't tell you,' Bella said. 'I'm sorry, but I really can't.'

'Go on, I won't say anything to anyone,' Winnie pleaded.

Connie frowned. 'Nice try, Winnie, but you needn't worry; Bella has very carefully worked out a running order so that everyone has a fair chance. It wouldn't be fair if you then had prior knowledge, would it?'

Winnie's cheeks grew pink. 'No, I suppose not. I'm sorry, Bella, I shouldn't have asked and you are quite right to say no.' She paused and then grinned. 'But you are going to be amazed at our act; it's so funny we've been in stitches working it out.'

Bella grinned. 'Yes, I've heard you laughing away in the back of the garages while you practised, but you need to impress Station Officer Steele with it as well as yourselves. She might not find it so funny.'

'Oh, I think she will,' Winnie said. 'I hope she does.'

'Well, we will soon find out, won't we?' Bella said.

22

'Oh, Danny-boy, the pipes, the pipes are calling, from glen to glen, and down the mountain side . . . '

The common room was absolutely silent except for Sparky's beautiful singing voice, accompanied by Rose on the violin. What was it about that song? Bella thought, swallowing the lump that had formed in her throat. She had no Irish relations that she knew of, but it still stirred something in her. She glanced around at everyone else, watching transfixed as Sparky sang; they were equally moved by the haunting melody and plaintive words, which made this act a certainty for the concert.

As Sparky sang the last line and the notes of Rose's violin faded away, the watching crew members burst into loud applause and whistles of appreciation. Clapping loudly herself, Station Officer Steele turned to Bella and nodded her head, her meaning crystal clear: Sparky had most definitely passed his audition and was on track for being a star turn of the show. Bella put a tick against his name on her list of potential acts.

So far tonight, other definites for the concert were the comedian, the magician and the tap dancers, who'd incorporated a funny routine into their dance, accompanied by fast and furious music from the old silent films; they'd had everyone laughing and clapping along. The juggler hadn't done so well, dropping her balls several times, which may well have been through nerves but had earned her act a question mark — Bella and Station Officer Steele would have to talk about that later on when they decided the final outcome of the auditions.

Looking at her list, Bella smiled as she read the next act to go on, Winnie's mysterious sketch — finally the secret of what they'd been rehearsing would be revealed.

'Winnie, Frankie and Sparky, you're next,' Bella called out.

'We'll just be a moment; we need to put something on,' Winnie said, jumping up from where she'd been sitting. She, Frankie and Sparky hurried out of the common room.

'What act are they doing?' the boss asked.

I have no idea; it's supposed to be funny, though.'

Station Officer Steele raised her eyebrows. 'Well, we shall see.'

A couple of minutes later Winnie and Frankie returned. Winnie was now dressed in a crossover, wrap-around, paisley-print apron and Frankie in a dull-looking skirt and cardigan which made her look drab.

They strode to the area set up as a stage and mimed playing trumpets while making trumpet sounds and then broke into song. 'It's that man again, it's that man again . . . ' they began, the familiar theme song from the popular *ITMA* radio show, which most people at Station 75 listened to in the common room. The show followed the adventures of the main character,

131

Tommy Handley, as he did a series of bizarre jobs, accompanied by some entertaining friends.

'So that's what they're going to do,' Bella whispered to the boss.

After they'd finished their introductory song, Frankie stepped offstage, leaving Winnie looking at the audience. 'Have you seen the boss?' she said, her voice mimicking the accent of Mrs Mopp, one of the *ITMA* characters. 'Only I've volunteered for the Ambulance Service and he told me to report for duty at Station 75 where he's taken over as Station Officer.'

Bella glanced at Station Officer Steele, who was smiling as she watched the performance.

Sparky stepped on to the stage area having quietly returned to the common room. He'd changed into a suit, and looked far smarter than he usually did.

'Ah, Mrs Mopp, the sweetheart of the scrub,' Sparky said, mimicking the voice and tone of Tommy Handley.

'Oh, sir, I'm ever so excited you're the new Station Officer, am I going to get my new uniform?'

'Uniform!' Sparky said, scratching his head. 'There isn't one, you'll have to wear the blackouts.' The room erupted into laughter. 'Do you know your first aid?'

'Oh, yes, sir, I've been practising on Mona, bandaged her head right up so she couldn't talk!' Winnie said.

'That must have been a blessed relief.'

'Am I going to drive an ambulance?' Winnie asked.

132

'Can you drive?' Sparky asked.

'No, sir, but I can clean. Can I do you now, sir?' Winnie said, repeating Mrs Mopp's famous catchphrase.

'Well, there are always ambulances to clean so you'll never be short of work here, Mrs Mopp.'

Everyone laughed and clapped at this remark.

'Oh, lovely, sir. I'll get right to it. TTFN.' Winnie bobbed a curtsy and exited stage left.

'Thank goodness the old blower's kept quiet this shift, no one calling out for help,' Sparky said. 'It's hard to get the staff these days.'

'Mr Handley.' Frankie stepped on to the stage. 'Did I hear you've got a call-out for me to go to? I'm ready and able.' She spoke in the dreary voice of Mona Lott, another *ITMA* character.

'No, not at the moment, the bombers have kept away,' Sparky said.

'I'm on alert, ready for action at a moment's notice,' Frankie said, she smiled, but her face only managed a slight twitching of her lips compared to her usual happy look. 'It's being so cheerful as keeps me going.'

Again, the watching crew members laughed, hearing Mona Lott's catchphrase from Frankie.

The banter between Sparky and Frankie, in character as Tommy Handley and Mona Lott, carried on for a few minutes more and then Winnie returned and the three of them took a bow to much clapping and cheering.

'Is that a yes?' Bella asked as the clapping faded. 'It's gone down well.'

'Absolutely.' Station Officer Steele smiled. 'I enjoyed it very much.'

'Good.' Bella put a tick by their names on her list and checked who was going next.

23

'Who's it from?' Winnie asked, looking at the package Connie had just handed her. She and Bella had recently arrived home from their shift at Station 75, and she'd just sat down on the sofa in the drawing room, enjoying the warmth of the fire burning in the large, marble-surround fireplace. She'd been looking forward to a sit-down and a soothing mug of cocoa before bed. There hadn't been any incidents to attend, but Station Officer Steele had kept the crews busy doing a thorough clean of the premises — garages, staff rooms, ambulances, anything that could be cleaned had been, and everyone had been relieved when eight o'clock had finally come around and they could go home to rest. Winnie certainly hadn't expected to find a package waiting for her.

'I don't know,' Connie said, 'it was delivered this afternoon.'

'Open it and find out,' Bella urged from the other end of the sofa where she was cuddled up with Trixie on her lap, the little dog enjoying her silky ears being stroked. 'It might be from Mac.'

Winnie opened it, taking care not to rip the paper wrapping so it could be used again, and inside was a slim box. She eased off the lid and gasped at the contents.

'What is it?' Connie got up from her armchair opposite and came over for a closer look.

135

'Not sure.' Winnie picked up the soft material and shook it out; it fell in swathes of blue, teal and aquamarine swirls. It was beautiful.

'It's a scarf,' Connie said. She stroked it. 'Silk. Well, it really is gorgeous and the perfect colours for you to wear.'

'Who sent it?' Bella asked. 'Is there a note or something?'

Winnie looked in the bottom of the box where a folded piece of writing paper was tucked inside. She took it out, unfolded it and read the note.

Dearest sister,
Meredith said yes! This is to say thank you for your advice because without it I don't think I would have dared ask her and I could have missed out on the best thing to ever happen to me. We're planning to marry in April, a quiet wedding, no fuss.
Your loving brother,
Harry.

'It's from Harry,' Winnie explained. 'It's a thank-you present for convincing him to ask the beautiful Welsh nurse on Ward Three to marry him.' She smiled. 'She said yes!'

'Oh, that's splendid news!' Connie clapped her hands. 'I knew he was sweet on her from what you said, but I didn't know he was that serious.'

'He talked to me about it when I met him for afternoon tea last week; he wasn't sure she'd want to marry a man like him,' Winnie said.

136

'Why ever not?' Connie asked.

'Because of his injuries,' Winnie said.

'It's what a person is like on the inside that matters,' Bella said.

'Exactly!' Connie agreed.

'He asked me not to tell anyone in case she said no, but I'm so glad Meredith said yes.' She tied the scarf around her neck and stood up to look at her reflection in the large mirror above the fireplace. 'It does look good, doesn't it?'

'This calls for a celebration,' Connie said, going over to her drinks cabinet and looking inside. 'A tiny tot of sherry, I think.'

With their drinks poured, Connie held up her glass. 'A toast: to Harry and his future wife; may they have a long and very happy life together.'

'To Harry and Meredith,' Winnie and Bella chorused, clinking their glasses against Connie's.

'So when's the wedding?' Bella asked.

'It says sometime in April, see.' Winnie handed her the letter.

'But it will be a small one.'

'I wonder if your mother will go.' Connie swirled the sherry around in her glass. 'Has she met Meredith?'

'No!' Winnie said. 'Harry has more sense than to even tell our mother about her, you know how she would react.' She sighed. 'Remember how utterly beastly she was to Mac before we got married? She hasn't seen him since our wedding, thank goodness, and she certainly never asks after him on the few occasions that we talk.'

'What's Meredith's family like?' Bella asked.

'If they're anything like she is, then absolutely

lovely, but her father's a miner so Mother wouldn't consider her to be from the right sort of background to marry Harry.'

'Perhaps your mother might have mellowed and appreciate that her children can make up their own minds who they marry?' Connie suggested, a smile playing at the corner of her mouth.

'That's like saying a leopard can change its spots, Connie,' Winnie said. 'That will never happen and my mother will never approve of Harry marrying a miner's daughter. I just hope he has the sense to make sure they don't meet until the deed is done, and even then, well . . . ' She shrugged.

'Harry knows what she's like and I'm sure he'll do what's right to protect his future wife,' Connie reassured her. 'I'm so happy for him.'

'So am I.' Winnie smiled. 'Meredith is exactly what my brother needs.'

24

'She's grown since I last saw her.' Frankie stroked baby Flora's soft, downy cheek. 'And that was only a couple of days ago.'

'And so she should have with the amount she feeds!' Josie said, patting her ample bosom.

'She's lost that squashed-up, new baby look she 'ad when she was first born.' Frankie gazed down at the baby girl who was cradled in the crook of her arm, fast asleep, her rosebud mouth making gentle sucking movements in her sleep. 'She's a little beauty.'

'Ain't she just? The others are besotted with her. If they didn't 'ave to go to school they'd be with her all the time. I ain't complaining, though, it's a big 'elp to me having them look out for her while I get on with my jobs between feeds.'

Ever since Josie's baby had been born three weeks ago, Frankie had popped in to see her neighbour whenever she could. She was both fascinated and enthralled by the baby, amazed at her tiny fingers with their shell-like nails and how perfectly formed she was and yet completely dependent on her mother. Frankie had no experience of babies and she was thoroughly enjoying getting to know Josie's little girl. Despite Flora not being her child or even any relation to her, Frankie felt a strong bond with her. She didn't know if that came from being there when she was born or from spending precious time with her since then, watching her grow and change, perhaps both. If she had to put a name to it, she was growing to love this tiny child and if need be she would care for her like a mother.

The thought surprised Frankie, she had never felt any maternal instinct before, but little Flora had awoken something in her.

'You all right?' Josie poured hot water into the brown earthenware teapot. 'Only you looked very serious.'

Frankie looked up at Josie and smiled. 'Oh, just thinkin' about the wonder of a new baby.' She paused. 'It's amazing how somethin' so small can wiggle its way under your skin and make you care for it.'

Josie laughed. 'Sounds like your maternal instinct is wakin' up.'

Frankie shrugged. 'How do you manage with four children? I mean, 'ow do you love them all?'

'Oh, that's easy, a mother's heart has room to love each child, there's more in there every time a new one comes along. If I 'ad another twenty children my heart would have room and would love them all.' She suddenly looked worried. 'Though I ain't planning on having any more. Little miss here was an unexpected present from my Bill's last leave.' She grinned. 'We'll be more careful next time.' Josie came over and looked down at Flora, who was still fast asleep. 'I wouldn't be without her now, though.'

The look of love on Josie's face as she bent down and took hold of Flora's tiny hand sent a sudden dart of hurt slicing through Frankie. Had her mother once looked at her like that? But she couldn't have, a voice whispered in her mind, because she'd left her and let her grow up thinking she was an orphan. Frankie looked away as tears stung her eyes and she swallowed to ease the ache in her throat.

'Here's a cup of tea and then you can tell me what's botherin' you.' Josie's voice brought her attention back to the present.

'There ain't nothing wrong with me.' Frankie's voice sounded odd to her own ears.

'I ain't daft, ducks, I can see you're upset about somethin'.' Josie put her hand on Frankie's shoulder. 'I only want to help you.'

Sitting with a cup of tea each, Josie looked at Frankie, her eyes searching her face. 'Right, what's the matter?'

'I'm just being silly, there ain't nothing wrong, really.' Frankie tried hard to make her voice light and happy. 'It's just sittin' here with you and Flora, I can see how much you love her and I just wondered if . . . ' Her voice wavered and she paused to collect herself. 'I wondered if my mother was ever the same with me.' She shook her head and shrugged. 'But she couldn't have been, otherwise she wouldn't 'ave left me like she did, would she?'

Frankie looked down at Flora who slept on, oblivious to anything except her milky dreams.

Josie reached across from her chair and touched Frankie's arm.

'Of course she felt the same about you.'

'But she left me!' Frankie looked at her friend,

tears smarting her eyes. 'She let me grow up thinkin' she was dead!'

'I know she did, and leavin' you to think you were an orphan weren't right.' Josie pursed her lips. 'But she did care for you, I know she did. She may have done something stupid, breakin' off all contact with you, and from what you've told me she regrets that, but she did love you.'

'Well, she 'ad a funny way of showing it.'

'I know she cared for you.' Josie's eyes held Frankie's for a few moments. 'I know that because she left you with your grandparents, she didn't just abandon you in a children's 'ome. She left you where she knew you'd be very well cared for and loved. And she did look out for you from a distance, keepin' in touch with your grandparents. She thought it was the best thing for you and her at the time.'

Frankie shrugged. 'Would you do that too?'

Josie sighed. 'My circumstances are very different to your mother's back then, but if I 'ad to do something to benefit my child at the sacrifice to myself then I would. I sent my other three to be evacuated at the start of the war, remember? I 'ad no idea where they were going or who would be lookin' after them. It were awful but I had to do it for their sake. And you did it to Stanley, too.'

Frankie nodded, recalling how hard it had been to make the decision to send Stanley away to the safety of the countryside to protect him during the Blitz. And unlike Josie's children, who'd been brought home again after the bombing had stopped last summer, Frankie was adamant that Stanley should stay where he was until the war was over and it was completely safe for him to return.

'I'd say your mother made the ultimate sacrifice for you and your grandparents. To do that she must 'ave loved you very much,' Josie went on. 'And you can tell that because she had to protect 'erself, cutting herself off from you.'

'I could never do that to any child of mine,' Frankie said. 'That's if I ever have one.'

Josie took a sip of her tea. 'None of us knows what we might do if the need arose; there but for the grace of God go I.' She raised her eyebrows to look at Frankie. 'I know you've found it 'ard to understand what your mother did, but speaking as a mother, I 'onestly think she sacrificed her happiness for you and your grandparents. So, give her a chance, ducks. Forgive her.'

Frankie looked down at Flora. As she stroked her little starfish hand, the baby stirred and grasped hold of one of Frankie's fingers tightly and then with a gentle sigh she slipped back into sleep, her grip loosening slightly. Perhaps it was time to start thinking of it from her mother's perspective, to appreciate how hard it must have been for her to leave her daughter and have no contact with her other than a yearly letter and photo sent from her grandparents. Up until now, she had only looked at it from her own point of view, fuelled with anger and hurt. Was it time to forgive her mother for what happened, to understand that she did what she thought was right at the time? To appreciate that, in fact, her mother had made a huge sacrifice? She did like her as a person, but had so far held back, not letting herself think of her in any way that might allow them to grow closer, and develop a stronger bond.

'Watcha thinking?' Josie asked.

'That perhaps you're right, Josie. I understand more how she must have felt, and what she did for me at the expense of herself.'

'Can you forgive her?'

Frankie nodded. The hard, ice-like lump of anger that she'd carried inside her since she'd found out that her mother was still alive felt as if it was softening and melting away, leaving nothing but a growing understanding of her mother's actions and, more importantly, a willingness to build a bond with her.

'Good.' Josie patted Frankie's hand. ' 'Cos I'm sure she is as proud as punch to have a daughter like you. Your grandad would be pleased you've found her and are gettin' on well.'

Flora started to stir, making little grunting noises, and then opened her blue eyes wide and stared up at Frankie for a few moments before taking a deep breath and opening her mouth wide to cry, taking more hearty lungs full of air to fuel her continuing wails.

'Time for a feed!' Josie 'said, reaching out her arms to take back the crying baby.

25

The door to Station Officer Steele's office was closed. Usually the boss left it open unless she was giving someone a dressing-down in there, but looking through the glass window in the door, Bella could see that she was quite alone, sitting at her desk, her shoulders slumped as she stared at something on it.

Bella tapped on the door and without waiting for an answer went in because something was clearly wrong with the older woman. 'Sorry to disturb you, only we said we'd go over the final arrangements for the concert.'

Station Officer Steele didn't respond, she just carried on staring at what Bella could now see was a copy of today's *Daily Herald* with its headline shouting out in dark, bold type: 'Singapore Army Hits Back and Holds On'.

'Station Officer Steele,' Bella said, gently putting her hand on the boss's shoulder.

'What?' The boss started in her chair, putting a hand to her chest. She looked up at Bella, glaring at her through her horn-rimmed glasses. 'You made me jump, what on earth are you doing creeping up on me like that? Haven't you heard of knocking?'

'I did knock but you were miles away. Is everything all right?' Bella asked.

'No, everything's not all right with this blasted war on and Singapore hanging by a thread.' The boss jabbed her finger at the map of Singapore on the front of the newspaper, where more than half the island was shaded in to show the portion now held by the Japanese compared with the smaller area still held by Allied forces. She hung her head and sighed deeply, her whole body looking defeated. Then taking a deep breath, she sat up straight and looked Bella directly in the eye. 'I'm sorry, I shouldn't have spoken to you like that; it was extremely unprofessional of me and downright rude. Please accept my apologies.'

Bella smiled at her. 'It's fine. I understand how you must be feeling seeing it there in black and white. Do you know where your sister might be now?'

The boss shook her head. 'I have no idea where Lily and her family are now. All I can do is hope that they are in here somewhere.' She put her finger on the area of the diagram representing the safe area still held by Allied troops. 'Wherever they are, Lily must be terrified about what's going on and what's going to happen next.'

'Remember Churchill's promised to defend Singapore,' Bella said.

Station Officer Steele shook her head. 'In that case the Japanese should never have been able to get on the island, should they? And now . . . they've taken over more than half of it and I don't think they'll stop till they've got the lot. And there's not a thing I can do to help my sister from here, not a single thing — ' Her voice cracked and she bit her bottom lip, her eyes

146

bright behind her glasses.

Bella put her hand on the older woman's arm. From looking at the newspaper reports and listening to the news on the wireless, things certainly looked grim for Singapore and all the people there. Churchill had made his pledge, but it hadn't stopped the Japanese, who had moved with surprising swiftness down through Malaya to Singapore and breached the island itself. Station Officer Steele's sister would have been trapped unless she'd managed to escape.

'Your sister might have already left, they'd have known the Japanese were coming and decided to evacuate, go to . . . Australia or somewhere safe.'

Station Officer Steele shrugged. 'I hope so, I really do. There's no way of knowing what's happened till I hear from her and I just have to wait . . . and hope.' She frowned. 'There's a lot of hoping going on around the world right now, people desperate to hear that their loved ones are safe . . . You went through it when your brother was missing.'

Bella nodded. 'And it turned out all right. I hope it will for you, too. I know I felt helpless not knowing and there was nothing I could do to ease that feeling or find him. I just had to wait and try to be patient, but it wasn't easy.'

'And that's what I must do: wait and try to be patient.' Station Officer Steele did her best to smile but although her lips moved it wasn't reflected in her eyes. 'Well, what was it you came to see me about?'

'The final arrangements for the concert next week.'

147

'Sit down and we'll go through it.'

Bella sat down on the chair beside the boss's desk. 'First, are you happy with all the acts we've decided on?' She handed over a piece of paper detailing the acts and running order that they'd already agreed.

The boss read it through and then nodded. 'Yes, I think we've got a good variety of acts that will hopefully entertain our audience — providing we get one, that is.'

'Don't worry, we will! We've got crew from Station 75 to begin with and I've taken posters advertising the concert to nearby ambulance stations — Stations 77 in Bishopsgate, 78 in Smithfield and 74 in Upper Thames Street. I've put up a poster at the Red Cross packing centre where I volunteer, and Maude who I work with there has been telling all her friends and putting up more posters. Connie's done the same at the next-of-kin centre. Sparky's taken some to nearby shops and ARP posts. Hopefully, out of them we'll get a good crowd in to watch and raise money.'

'Jolly good. It sounds as though you've covered a wide area and people who'd be interested in seeing our ambulance crews perform.' She paused for a moment, fiddling with a pen on her desk. 'I'm glad we're doing this, Bella, it's giving me something else to focus on.'

'It'll be good, I'm sure of it. Everyone's looking forward to the concert, either performing in it or watching,' Bella said. 'Let's just hope next Saturday night isn't the one the bombers choose to come back on.'

Station Officer Steele raised her eyebrows. 'Now who's being pessimistic? It will be fine. Station 75 will put on a concert that the audience will love and talk about for days afterwards.' She smiled. 'Who knows, the producers of the West End shows might come knocking on our door begging us to grace their stages.'

Bella laughed. 'Wouldn't Winnie just love that?'

'Indeed, but as my Deputy Station Officer her loyalty would have to remain to Station 75.'

'We're all loyal to this place and all who work here,' Bella said.

'So, remember I am always here to talk to if you want, I understand what you're feeling.'

Station Officer Steele nodded. 'Thank you, Bella. I know you are and I'll do my best to stay positive while I wait to hear. It wouldn't do to crumble now, would it, not when there's an ambulance station to run and people like Sparky and Winnie to keep in check?'

26

There were two envelopes waiting on the doormat of 25 Matlock Street when Frankie and Rose arrived home after working the night shift. Stooping down to pick them up, Frankie saw that one was for Rose, all the way from America, and the other for her in handwriting that she recognised — her mother's.

'This one's for you, Rose.'

'From my parents?' Rose took the envelope from Frankie, a hopeful look on her face which dimmed slightly when she saw who it was from. 'Not this time. It's from my Uncle Julius.'

'Your parents will write when they can, I'm sure of it,' Frankie said, linking her arm through Rose's. 'You don't hear from them because letters ain't getting through from Austria now, not because they don't want to send them.'

Rose nodded. 'I know, but whenever I see letters on the mat I can't help being hopeful.' She sighed. 'I am happy to hear from my uncle, though.'

They went through to the kitchen, Frankie stopping in the doorway at the sight of the mess on the table: dirty plates and cups, evidence of Ivy's meal from last night and her breakfast this morning. 'I wish for once we didn't have to come 'ome to this . . . ' She threw out her hand wide.

'It's all right, I'll soon clear it away and wash up the dishes,' Rose said, picking up a dirty cup

150

and plate and putting them by the sink.

'No, Rose! Don't,' Frankie said. 'I know you would, but really don't start clearin' up after Ivy because she'll let you and it will never end. Just clear them off the table and pile them up by the sink and I'll make sure she washes them up tonight when she gets 'ome from work. What you can do is put the kettle on while I go and feed the hens.'

Outside, Frankie threw corn down to the hens and checked they had plenty of clean water, trying her best not to let Ivy's slatternly habits get to her. She hated coming home to a mess but no matter how many times she'd told Ivy to clear up after herself, the older woman did nothing unless Frankie was there to make her. It was so wearing to have to keep at her to just do the basic tasks of keeping the house in order. At least working shifts she didn't see much of Ivy herself, only the mess she left behind, and the mess didn't say anything or scowl at her, Frankie thought.

Back inside, she gratefully warmed her hands around the cup of tea that Rose had made her. 'How's your uncle and his family?' She nodded towards Rose's letter, which now lay on the cleared table in front of Rose.

'He and my aunt are well, and he says that my cousins are expecting to be drafted any day now. They're keen to do something to fight Hitler, they want to fly bombers or fighters.'

'Did they leave Austria before Hitler took over?' Frankie asked.

'No, they were born in America. My Uncle

151

Julius, he's my father's brother, went there when he was a young man and he married an American and now has a business there. He's done well for himself and my father always said he'd like to go there like him one day, but he never did.'

'Have they heard from your parents?'

Rose shook her head. 'Nothing. They are worried, too.' She finished her tea and stood up. 'It's my turn to go shopping; I'll see what I can get for our rations today.'

Frankie and Rose took it in turns to cook their main meals, pooling their rations to help them go further and sharing the task of shopping, which involved a lot of queueing these days.

'I'll go and get the tin and give you some money.' Frankie ran up to her bedroom. She had taken to hiding the tin in which she and Rose put their housekeeping money under a loose floorboard for fear of Ivy pilfering from it. She couldn't be sure, but several times it had had less money in it than there should have been when they'd kept it downstairs in the kitchen dresser. Of course, when she'd challenged Ivy over it she had denied taking any, but Frankie hadn't believed her — the way the woman spent money she was bound to run out before payday and had probably helped herself a little to keep herself going.

Downstairs, Frankie handed over some money to Rose. 'See what the butcher's got; we could do with a nice warming stew today.'

Rose smiled. 'With dumplings.'

'Yes, please.' Frankie laughed. 'As long as you

make them, yours always come out much lighter and fluffier than mine.'

When Rose had gone, Frankie started on the cleaning jobs, taking out the mats and throwing them over the clothes line in the garden and giving them a good whack with the broom. That done, she went indoors and swept the floors. Bending down to sweep the pile of dirt into the dustpan, she felt a crackling sound in her dungarees pocket and remembered her own letter, which she'd put in there earlier before getting distracted by Ivy's mess.

She pulled it out and sat down on a chair to read it. As usual there were two letters inside, one from her mother and the other from her youngest sister, Eve.

She read the one from Eve first.

Dear Frankie,
Lizzie has been sent to train as a barrage balloon operator! I don't know if it's a good idea to have her in charge of such great big things floating around the sky. Mother says that perhaps the WAAFs have changed her and anyway she won't be in charge of the balloon herself, she'll just be one of the women pulling on the ropes and have to do what she's told.
We've had the first of the lambs born this week, a pair of twins that are doing well. Have you been to see the little baby you helped deliver lately?
Write soon.
Your loving sister,
Eve

So, Lizzie, her other sister, was training to work on the barrage balloons. Frankie often saw the crews at work at different sites around London, and it looked like a tough job, hauling the great silver beast around. From what little she knew of Lizzie, she would find it a demanding role, but the WAAF must think she was suitable for it or they would never have put her forward to train.

She moved on to her mother's letter. As always, the sight of her real name, Stella, gave her a jolt as mostly she was known as Frankie these days.

Dear Stella
I hope you're well. We're all fine and busy on the farm as usual. How is your neighbour and her new baby Flora? It must have been quite a shock to you to have to help deliver the baby and I think you did marvellously well. It's nice to hear of babies still being born in Matlock Street, you were born there yourself, in the back bedroom of number 25, with your grandmother and a neighbour helping to deliver you.

Frankie stopped reading for a moment. This was the first she'd ever heard of her birth apart from knowing that she was born in this house; her gran had never talked about it or about when she was a baby. She read on, eager to find out more.

You were the most beautiful baby, with big blue eyes that used to look up into mine as I fed you. Your father adored you, he came home on his last leave in August 1918 when you were six

154

months old, and thought you the best thing, he carried you around in his arms. I can still remember the way he looked at you, so amazed. I'm grateful that he got to see you before he died, it was just two weeks after he went back that I got the telegram to say he'd been killed.

Frankie's eyes filled with tears for the father she had no memory of.

It wasn't long after that, in the autumn, that I caught the Spanish flu and nearly died from it and your gran and grandad took over and looked after you.
By the time I'd recovered my strength after being back in Suffolk with my family you were sitting up and turning into a proper little person and your grandparents doted on you.

And that had been the point at which her mother had decided to leave Frankie with her grandparents and disappear from her life, leaving her daughter to think she was an orphan. Frankie had come a long way to forgiving her mother and understanding what she'd done and why, but part of her would always smart at what she had done. She read on.

You'll enjoy watching little Flora grow up and change.
Must finish now so Eve can go and put this in the post.
With my love
Your mother

Frankie leaned back in her chair and considered what she'd just read. It brought up more questions that she'd like answered: what had her father been like? How did he die? How had her parents met? All things she'd wondered for so long, but her grandparents had rarely spoken about their son, probably because they found his death so hard to bear. Perhaps now she could start to get answers to these questions; her mother could tell her and by filling in the gaps in Frankie's history she could help to heal the wounds of the past.

27

Since the air raids had stopped last May, and they no longer had to spend hours in the shelter or out at incidents, the crew members of Station 75 had taken to gathering in the common room to listen to the nine o'clock news when they were on the evening shift. Most of the crew who weren't outside on picket duty congregated there to hear the latest news about what was happening in the war both at home and abroad. Tonight, 15 February, was no different. Glancing at her watch, Station Officer Steele saw that it was almost nine o'clock, so she left the pile of paperwork she'd been working her way through and went to stand in the doorway of her office where she'd be able to hear the news when it started. Casting her eyes around the common room, she saw the crew members were occupied as they usually were at this time, some sewing or knitting, others drinking tea or reading. Sparky, Winnie, Frankie, Bella and Rose were playing a lively game of cards.

Spotting her, Sparky stood up from the armchair he'd been sitting in. 'Do you want come and sit down, boss?'

She shook her head. 'No, I'm fine here, but thank you.'

Sparky bowed his head and sat down again to resume his game of cards with the others.

As the announcer on the wireless introduced

the nine o'clock news the room fell silent, everyone listening intently. Station Officer Steele planned to listen to the summary of headlines and then would retreat back to her office and the pile of forms that needed dealing with, but when the newsreader introduced the Prime Minister, her chest tightened. Something had happened, something that required Winston Churchill to speak to the nation and to all the places his speech would be broadcast across the world. The atmosphere of the room seemed to change, the air almost crackling with anticipation as every crew member strained to hear what he had to say.

'Tonight, I speak to you at home . . . ' his familiar voice began. 'I speak to you under the shadow of a heavy and far-reaching military defeat . . . Singapore has fallen all the Malay Peninsula has been overrun . . . '

Station Officer Violet Steele felt as if her blood had instantly frozen and lay still and icy hard within her, she slumped back against the door frame. *Singapore has fallen.* Churchill's words echoed around inside her head and it took all her control not to cry out. What had happened to Lily? And George? And the girls? She suddenly became aware of hands holding her up on either side of her. Sparky and Winnie were supporting her and gently led her back into her office and lowered her on to her chair beside her desk. Frankie hurried in with a blanket and wrapped it around her shoulders.

'Bella's making some sweet tea for the shock,' Frankie said.

158

'I . . . ' she began, trying to form the words that skittered around her mind into a coherent sentence. 'Singapore . . . my sister.'

Winnie took hold of her hand and rubbed it in between hers. 'It's an utter beast. How could this have happened?'

'I think they underestimated the Japs,' Sparky said. 'And Singapore's the price for it.'

'Sparky!' Winnie hissed at him. 'Go and check everything's all right out there, will you? We'll look after the boss.'

Violet Steele felt a wet nose nudge at her other hand, then a soft silky head rub against it. Trixie. Bending down she scooped up the little dog, settled her on her lap and wrapped her arms around her. Trixie leaned against her chest, resting her head so that her liquid brown eyes gazed up into her face. It was as if she'd come to give comfort, not through words but just through being there with her and focusing on her, sensing her pain and worry.

Station Officer Steele didn't know how long the two of them sat there like that; she was vaguely aware of the young women in the room, but she just needed a little time to process what she'd heard and deal with the shock of hearing those three words which carried with them so much despair — *Singapore has fallen*. Had her parents heard it too, her brother? They would all be feeling like her. She'd have to telephone them.

'Here's some tea, I've put three sugars in it.' Bella's voice broke into her thoughts. 'Here we are, boss; you need to drink this — it will help with the shock.' Bella placed the cup on the desk beside her and then crouched down in front of her. 'I'm so sorry this has happened.'

She nodded and looked up to see that Winnie and Frankie were gazing at her with worried expressions on their faces.

'Is there anything else we can get you?' Frankie asked.

'Something to eat, perhaps?'

She shook her head. 'No, thank you.'

'Perhaps we should take you home?' Winnie suggested.

'No!' What would she do there but sit and brood? It was best she stayed here and carried on with her work, but not for a few minutes; she just needed to take it in. 'I'm staying here to do my job, but I'd like to be on my own if you don't mind. I'll keep Trixie with me.'

'We'll be in the common room; if you need anything just call us.'

Bella gently touched her arm, then stood up and ushered Winnie and Frankie out, quietly closing the door behind them.

Left with just Trixie, Station Officer Steele let out the sob that had been building up inside her, bowing her head over the little dog and letting her tears run freely down her face.

Where was Lily? Was she still alive? Had she survived the fighting in Singapore? And the girls, Grace and Helena? What about George, her brother-in-law, his RAF base would certainly have been under attack?

Never had she felt so utterly helpless. She'd been looking after Lily one way or another since

160

she'd been born, a surprise addition to their family. She'd been fourteen then and had often taken on the role of looking after her baby sister, mothering her; and that sense of responsibility for Lily had never left her, not even as her sister grew up and had children of her own. Station Officer Steele still had a strong urge to protect her sister and, in turn, her nieces, but she couldn't. They were thousands of miles away and she had no idea if they were safe or had been captured by the invading Japanese army. If they had been captured, what would they do to them? Keep them prisoners of war or . . .

Thoughts whirled around her mind, tormenting her with more questions that she couldn't answer and possible scenarios, none of which was good. What could she do to help her sister? The answer was nothing yet, she was too far away. All she could do was wait until she heard news of them, good or . . . bad. She didn't like feeling so useless and unable to fix the problem, she was used to being in charge and able to sort out issues that cropped up, but this . . . It was utterly out of her control; she could only accept the situation and wait, be patient and hope. She realised, too, that her feelings were nothing compared with what Lily and her family must be going through, they were the ones in the midst of the invasion, not her.

Taking in a deep breath she sat up straight; behaving like this wasn't going to get her anywhere, she had to stop it and get her work done, she had an ambulance station to run and if the bombers came back tonight she couldn't afford to be less than ready to do what was necessary. She took a sip of the tea Bella had brought her, its sweetness jarring to her unaccustomed taste buds, but the warmth of the liquid was soothing.

Stroking Trixie's butter-soft ears, she felt herself slowly begin to relax a little, the tightness in her shoulders easing slightly. There were plenty of people like her all over the world who were anxiously waiting, utterly helpless to do anything, and there was nothing for it but to keep calm and carry on like the posters said.

Finishing her tea, she sought solace in the repetitive task of processing the pile of paperwork waiting on her desk, still keeping Trixie on her lap, the little dog seeming quite happy as she curled herself into a ball and fell asleep, still providing a warm, comforting weight on her lap.

Station Officer Steele had no idea how much time passed, only judging it by the gradual diminishing of the pile of paperwork as she worked her way through it, signing things where necessary. When she'd almost finished a gentle tapping on her office door made her glance at her watch — it was almost eleven o'clock.

'Come in,' she called.

It was Rose who came in, carrying a mug. 'We thought you might like a cup of cocoa.' She looked uncertain but was doing her best to smile.

'Yes, thank you.' Rose put the mug down on her desk and turned to go. 'Wait! Why don't you get yourself a mug and come and join me?'

Rose nodded. 'All right, I would like that, thank you.'

Waiting for Rose to come back, Station Officer Steele moved Trixie, who had woken up, on to the blanket she kept folded up on the floor for the little dog to sleep on, and with a gentle sigh, Trixie quickly dropped off to sleep again.

'Shut the door and come and sit down,' she said when Rose returned with her own mug of cocoa.

'Are you feeling better?' Rose asked, once she'd sat down, nursing her mug between her hands as if to warm them.

'Yes, it was a shock to hear those words . . . ' She paused before she made herself say them. ' "Singapore has fallen." I'd hoped that our troops would fight off the Japanese, but it seems it was impossible. Now the whole island is overrun and they've been invaded by another power.' She took a sip of cocoa, letting the comforting chocolaty taste linger in her mouth before she swallowed it.

'They knew they were coming, so your sister and her family may well have fled to safety. Hopefully they are far away from Singapore now.' Rose paused, her face looking pensive. 'When people know trouble is coming they often try to get away if they can. Even if her husband couldn't leave, he might have sent them away; that's what my family did to me.'

Station Officer Steele reached out and touched Rose's arm. The young woman knew only too well what it was like to have your country over-run. 'This must bring back memories of when

163

the Nazis took over in Austria.'

Rose nodded. 'Though I think more people were pleased to see the Nazis arrive in Austria than perhaps the Japanese in Singapore. The Nazis were cheered on by huge crowds when they paraded through the streets of Vienna. Changes for the worse started right after the Anschluss, lots of Jewish people wanted to leave, some even committed suicide rather than live with the new regime. We became outcasts in our own country; people who used to be my friends crossed the road to avoid me.' She fell silent, pain etched on her face.

'It's no wonder your parents sent you to safety on the Kindertransport. I'm glad they did.'

'I suppose I am one of the lucky ones, but my parents didn't escape before the borders were closed.' Rose sighed. 'I truly hope your sister got away before the Japanese arrived.'

'So do I,' Station Officer Steele said. 'Because if she didn't I fear for what might happen to her.'

28

Station Officer Steele put the telephone receiver back on its cradle and quickly recorded the job on a chit of paper as she'd done many times before. The familiarity of it was soothing and she was in dire need of any scrap that she could find. Now, three days on since the fall of Singapore and with still no word from her sister, it was hard to remain positive. She was doing her best to keep busy and distract herself and now this call was a perfect chance to do just that.

She went out to the common room where some crew members were having their afternoon break. Rose was sitting at the table writing what looked like a letter.

'Rose, could you go and find Winnie, Frankie and Bella and tell them to come up to my office, and you with them, please?'

'Of course.' Rose put her letter in her pocket and went off to find the others, returning with them a short while later.

'Winnie, I'm leaving you in charge this afternoon while I'm out, you know the routines and if any calls come in, you can deal with them.'

Winnie nodded. 'All right. Where's the meeting? Do you need someone to drive you there?'

'No, there's no meeting, I'm going out to a call with Bella, Frankie and Rose.' She paused for a moment, noticing the looks of astonishment

165

on the young women's faces. 'I'll team up with Bella, and if you don't mind,' she looked at Bella, 'I'd like to drive. Frankie, you and Rose can pair up for this job.'

'What are we doing?' Frankie asked.

'We're going to meet an ambulance train at Liverpool Street station. There'll be ambulances there from other stations as well. Our job is to collect wounded men returned from North Africa and take them to Queen Alexandra's Military Hospital.' She glanced at her watch. 'The train's due in at two o'clock, so we'll need to leave in ten minutes' time.'

Winnie stayed behind in the office after the others had gone down to the garages to get ready. 'I've never known you go out to a call before.'

'I'm quite capable of it, I can assure you; I have all the training and plenty of experience driving ambulances in the Great War. Besides, I just felt like doing something different.'

'Have you heard anything about your sister?' Winnie asked, her grey eyes meeting hers.

'No, so I'm keeping busy and distracting myself as much as I can.' She walked to the doorway and paused. 'Keep within earshot of the telephone, won't you?'

'Yes, I know what I'm doing.'

'I know, otherwise I wouldn't leave you in charge of my precious Station 75, would I?' Station Officer Steele smiled and then headed downstairs to meet Bella.

★　★　★

'Can I ask you something?' Bella said.

'Yes.' Station Officer Steele drove the ambulance under the archway leading out to the Minories and she turned left. 'Is anything wrong?'

'No. I was just wondering why you're coming out to this job, that's all. I can't recall you going out in the ambulances before now, not even in the Blitz, because you had to stay at the station and keep control of the rest of us and where we went. So why now?'

'I felt like a change.' She glanced at the young woman before returning her attention to the road ahead. 'And I'm trying to distract myself from thinking about my sister too much. Since there's nothing I can do to help her from here, then I would like to help those that I can, like the servicemen coming back today.' She slowed the ambulance as they approached the junction with Aldgate Street. 'We sometimes used to take men to the ambulance trains when I was in France; it will be nice to see them come off at the other end this time.'

'I think it's a good idea; one of the best parts of this job is getting out and about, and you're usually stuck in the office dealing with paperwork,' Bella said. 'Perhaps you should go out on more jobs in the future, too.'

She shrugged. 'Who knows, but today it feels the right thing to do.'

'The concert's coming up on Saturday, that'll keep your mind occupied. Everything's ready for it now, we just have to hope people will turn up to see it.'

'I'm sure they will, and if not, then we'll have to go out on the streets and pull people in to watch.'

They parked outside Liverpool Street station behind a row of ambulances from other stations, with Frankie and Rose pulling up behind them.

'Right, let's go and welcome our boys home,' Station Officer Steele said as they all hurried into the station, which as usual was busy and noisy, with people hurrying this way and that, and the tang of soot and steam from the trains tainting the air.

Reaching the correct platform, she saw that the ambulance train had just arrived, and medical orderlies were carrying men off on stretchers and lying them down in rows along the platform. The arrival of the men was causing quite a stir with passengers disembarking the train from other carriages and stopping to look at what was happening.

'Nice welcoming smiles, everyone,' Station Officer Steele said to her crew members as they approached. 'Remember, these men have been through a lot. Talk to them. Make them smile.'

She was glad to see the young women doing just that and bent down to speak to some servicemen herself. 'Welcome home!' She smiled at the two men lying side by side. 'Is it good to be back?'

'It's smashing,' a soldier said. 'Been dreaming of coming back to Blighty and I'm finally here.'

'It's good to see you.' She noticed that he was missing a leg and had an identity label tied to his remaining big toe. 'We'll soon get you to the

Queen Alexandra's and you can have a cup of tea, if you'd like one.'

'Can a duck swim?' the other soldier said. From the way his eyes stared into space she could see that he was blind. It was hard seeing these young men so terribly wounded, with injuries that would affect them for the rest of their lives. She had to take heart from the fact that they were cheerful in spite of what had happened to them and were clearly very glad to be back in England.

She laughed. 'But at least that tea should be free of sand. I understand the tea where you've been can be a little gritty.'

'Not just the tea, the food as well,' the first soldier said. 'It'll be bliss to eat food that don't go crunch when it shouldn't.'

★   ★   ★

With four soldiers in the back of the ambulance and Bella in there to keep an eye on them on the journey to hospital, Station Officer Steele put the ambulance into gear and pulled smoothly away from the kerb, aware of how any jolting movement could cause pain for the injured men. She concentrated hard on keeping her movements smooth, taking care to brake gently, smiling as she heard laughter coming from the back of the ambulance as the men chatted to Bella, their spirits not defeated by what they'd been through. If they could cope with what had happened to them, then it put her waiting and worrying in perspective. It might needle her that

169

she didn't know what was happening to her sister, but others with far greater problems managed to keep going, and she had to do the same. She still had an ambulance station to run, with crew members to care for, and to do that job properly she needed to be cheerful and positive, like the men who were laughing in the back.

29

Bella took a last look around the hall to check that everything was ready — the chairs were set out in rows and a table had been put up near the little kitchen at the side of the hall to sell cups of tea from in the interval. Crew members taking part in the concert had helped set up the hall and were now buzzing with nerves and excitement, ready to do the concert.

'All set?' Station Officer Steele asked.

'I think so; all we need are people to sit in the seats and no air raid tonight,' Bella said.

'It will be fine,' the boss said. 'Everything will work out perfectly, you'll see. All the acts are practised to perfection.'

'I do hope so.' Bella sighed. 'We've all put such a lot of work into the concert; if it fails it will be awful.'

'It's going to be wonderful,' Winnie said, coming up behind her and throwing her arm around Bella's shoulders. 'It's a night out for a good cause and I'm sure we'll get loads of people coming along, the price of the ticket is worth it just to see our *ITMA* act!' Station Officer Steele laughed. 'I love your confidence, Winnie. It should be a good evening's entertainment and if there aren't enough people then we'll just have to go out and round up an audience in the local pubs.'

'Connie's coming, and Frankie's Alastair,'

Winnie said. 'So that's two already. There'll be a lot of Station 75 crew and crews from other ambulance stations. It'll be a great success.'

'I hope so.' Bella glanced at her watch. 'It's time to open the doors and get this concert off to a start.'

'The first of many,' Winnie said.

'Let's just get this one done first, shall we?' Bella threw back over her shoulder as she headed for the door.

★   ★   ★

With all the seats taken and people standing at the back of the hall, Bella's worry about no one coming had thankfully proven ill-founded and had blown away like mist off the Thames. They had a full house and the audience were looking expectant and eager for the show to begin. Bella glanced at Station Officer Steele, who was sitting at the piano to one side of the raised platform that acted as a stage. She nodded back and began to play the piano, the music quickly bringing a hush to the audience.

With her heart drumming hard in her chest, Bella stepped up on to the platform and looked out at the audience, feeling every one of their eyes on her, which made her legs shake. Just as she was about to speak, the door at the back of the hall opened and to her surprise and delight, James walked in. He was supposed to be working and had said he wouldn't be able to come. He looked directly at her and smiled broadly, which gave her a welcome shot of

172

confidence. She could do this.

'Good evening, ladies and gentleman, and welcome to Station 75's fund-raising concert for the Red Cross's prisoners of war parcel fund.' Her voice sounded wobbly, but she was determined to go on. Station Officer Steele had offered to do the introduction but Bella had been adamant that she had to do it herself because the concert and what it was for were very important to her. 'Thank you all for coming tonight and helping to raise money to send parcels to our men in camps. Those parcels are a lifeline to the men, giving them food, clothing and things that we take for granted at home. They also tell the men that they are not forgotten and give them a great deal of joy. I know that for a fact because my brother is a POW and he's told me so. Now, without further ado, please welcome our first act: Cleggy.'

The audience started to clap loudly and someone whistled a piercing note from the back row. Relieved to have said her piece, Bella retreated to her chair positioned by the stage where she could keep a check on the running order that she and the boss had carefully worked out, mixing the acts so that each one complemented the next, and would hopefully provide an entertaining mix. Sitting down, Bella realised that she was still shaking, but she was happy that she'd done what she needed to do and now it was up to the different acts to do their best.

Cleggy worked on the alternate shift from Bella and she'd only seen him in passing as the

173

crews changed shifts, but after he'd auditioned and practised for the show she'd come to realise that he was a very funny man. His wry look at life working at an ambulance station and the war in general was having the audience in stitches. He told some jokes but also chatted to them about things he'd seen and done and it was a great start to the concert. The mix of acts was going down well and by the time it was Sparky's turn to sing 'Danny Boy' just before the interval, Bella was finally beginning to relax and enjoy the concert. Sparky's fabulously strong voice, accompanied by Rose on the violin, almost seemed to lift the roof off the hall and entranced the audience. As he sang the final words and the sweet notes of the violin died away there were quite a few people wiping the tears from their eyes.

★   ★   ★

'You came!' Bella said as James found her in the interval. 'I thought you had to work.'

'I managed to swap shifts. I wasn't sure if I could till this morning so I couldn't tell you.' He took hold of her hand. 'I wanted to come and see your hard work paying off.'

'I'm really glad you're here,' Bella said. 'You'll be able to see Winnie's act, see how good she is at playing the fool.'

James raised his eyebrows. 'She needs no encouragement.'

'It's going brilliantly,' Connie said, coming to join them. 'You should be very proud of what

174

you've achieved here.'

Bella shrugged. 'It's very much a team effort.'

'Well, it wouldn't have come together without you and Station Officer Steele organising it. The money raised will help send out more parcels.' She nodded towards the nearby table where Maude, who Bella worked with at the packing centre, was demonstrating packing POW parcels, which was drawing a lot of interest from members of the audience who were out of their seats and having a cup of tea.

'How do you fit all that in there?' one woman asked.

'Carefully and with practice,' Maude said. 'It's packed in tightly to use up as much space as possible and any gaps are stuffed with paper clippings or straw to stop the tins and packets rolling around in transit.'

'You know a lot about it,' the woman said.

'I volunteer at a packing centre,' Maude said. 'They're always looking for more volunteers if you're interested. Come along and join in.'

★ ★ ★

The grand finale of the concert was to be Winnie, Frankie and Sparky's *ITMA* act, which had proven so popular with the other cast members that some of them had stepped in to help and the theme song introduction was now sung by other crew members accompanied by Station Officer Steele on the piano. Winnie, Frankie and Sparky had enhanced their costumes and now had props like a mop and bucket for Winnie's Mrs Mopp character. The audience lapped it up, roaring with laughter as they did their act. It was a brilliant way to end the show.

30

A bitter March wind was whipping around the streets, needling its way into any slight gap in Station Officer Steele's clothing as she hurried along, carrying her basket of shopping. She couldn't help wondering if the basket's contents had been worth the time she'd spent queuing to get them. Turning into her street she stopped still at the sight of a telegram boy standing on the steps of the house where she had her flat. Did he have a telegram for her? With her heart beating fast she half ran, half walked towards him, her legs seeming to move of their own accord.

As she reached the bottom of the steps leading up to the front door, the boy turned to look at her. 'Do you live 'ere?' he asked. She nodded.

'Are you Miss Steele?'

Her legs suddenly felt as if the bones inside them had dissolved and she grabbed at the metal railings at the side of the steps. 'Yes, I am,' she managed, her voice sounding strangely hollow to her ears.

'Telegram for you, miss.' The boy held it out to her and she stared at it for a moment before taking it from him. 'Thank you.' He touched the brim of his hat and left quietly, no doubt glad to get away, his job being one that so often brought bad and unwanted news to people.

Part of her wanted to rip the envelope open there and then to find out what it contained, but the more measured side of her insisted she wait until she was in the privacy of her own home where if, as she feared, this telegram brought bad news, she could deal with it far better than out in the street.

Climbing up the stairs to her upper-floor flat, her mind sorted through who it could be from. It was unlikely to be from her parents or brother as they would telephone. It had to be news of her sister . . . news which she'd been desperate for since before the fall of Singapore some weeks ago now.

Once inside she threw off her coat and hat and put the telegram in the middle of the kitchen table, then she sat down and stared at it. She should prepare herself for what it might contain. She'd gone through so many different scenarios of what might have happened to Lily and the girls, spending hours in the depths of the night worrying about where they were or even if they were still alive . . . She snatched up the telegram and tore off the envelope, pausing just long enough to take a deep breath before she opened the single sheet of paper and read it.

GIRLS AND I SAFE IN SOUTH AFRICA AWAITING NEWS OF GEORGE WHO STAYED IN SINGAPORE STOP LILY

Station Officer Steele hugged the telegram to her. Lily and the girls were alive and safe, thousands of miles away from Singapore. They'd got away. She closed her eyes and sent up a silent prayer of thanks. But what about her brother-in-law who had stayed in Singapore? What had happened to him? Had he been captured by the Japanese or had he escaped too? And if he had, would he find his way to Lily and the girls in South Africa? Would they stay there for the duration or try to get back to England and face the dangers of the Atlantic?

She shivered. The telegram had thrown up more questions than it answered, but at least for now she knew that Lily, Helena and Grace had escaped from Singapore and were safe. That was much to be thankful for.

31

The queue ahead of them edged forwards slowly as people were admitted for today's concert, the numbers being carefully counted up to the allotted amount allowed.

'Do you think we'll get in?' Frankie asked. They'd been standing waiting for the past forty-five minutes and she was starting to shiver with cold despite her warm, wool coat, beret, scarf and gloves. Waiting around outside in the cold March weather wasn't pleasant and if it all turned out to be for nothing it would be bitterly disappointing.

'We're getting nearer the door.' Alastair patted her hand, which was linked through his arm.

They'd almost reached the portico entrance and inched their way across the tiled floor. Would they do it? Frankie wondered. She desperately hoped so; it was so rare for her and Alastair to have enough time off work at the same time so that they could go to one of the concerts at the National Gallery. Fortune was on their side this time, however, as they were waved through the door, the man standing by it counting each person that passed.

Frankie turned to Alastair and smiled. 'We're in.' Looking back over her shoulder, she saw that they'd just made it, though, as only a handful of people passed through behind them before the door was closed and all those left outside would have to go home disappointed. The concerts were so popular there was no guarantee of getting in — tickets couldn't be bought, the only way to attend was to stand and queue and hope that you were one of the lucky ones. And today they were.

Down in the basement where the concerts took place, Alastair bought a penny programme and they sat down in the few remaining seats near the back.

'What are they playin' today? Is it Myra Hess?' Frankie asked, looking at the programme.

'It is, and she will be playing Mozart piano concertos.' He smiled at her. 'We're going to enjoy this.'

Frankie linked her arm through his and settled back in her seat to enjoy the music. Just as before, when Alastair had brought her here on their very first outing together, the music entranced her; she closed her eyes and was spirited away from the damp, cold basement, drifting off on the rise and fall of notes. It was quite beautiful and although the concert lasted an hour, it only felt like minutes before it ended and the basement echoed with the thunderous applause of people who'd been whisked away from life for a short while.

'Did you enjoy it?' Alastair asked as they stood up to leave.

'I loved it. I wish we could come every week.' Frankie smiled at him.

'So do I. Shall we get something to eat?'

'Yes, I'm 'ungry after listening to the music.'

They made their way to the gallery's canteen,

which had been opened up to provide hot meals, and were soon tucking into shepherd's pie and cabbage, followed by spotted dick and custard, which helped to warm them up again.

'How's Mac doing?' Alastair asked when he'd finished.

'He's fine; he enjoys bein' in the bomb squad, though Winnie still wishes he wasn't as she doesn't get to see much of 'im,' Frankie said, scooping up a last spoonful of custard.

'He doesn't regret leaving Station 75?'

Frankie shook her head. 'Not as far as I know. Winnie ain't said anything and I haven't actually seen Mac myself for months now.' She frowned. 'Even if he didn't like it he's in the army now, he volunteered and soldiers can't just leave if they decide they don't like it.'

Alastair fiddled about with the spoon resting in his empty bowl.

'Frankie . . . I'm thinking of joining up.'

She stared at him for a few moments. 'What? Why on earth would you want to go and do that? You're a doctor, for heaven's sake; there are plenty of people in London who need your 'elp and if the bombs start falling again . . . Well, you don't need me to tell you how much you'll be needed then.'

He shrugged. 'I know that but I feel I'd be more use working as a doctor in the Royal Army Medical Corp . . . ' He paused and reached across the table to take hold of her hand. 'It would be doing something directly to help the war effort and fight against the Nazis.'

'You are already 'elping the war effort!'

182

Frankie snatched her hand out of his. 'You patch up people who've been blown up! That's doing your bit and you're there lookin' after people who are keeping the home front going, day after day.' She shook her head. 'I can't believe you are seriously considering it; they'd send you off abroad to God knows where.'

'I know, probably where the fighting is, or just behind the lines where they bring the injured to. I've been thinking a lot about this, Frankie. It's not an easy decision to make and I haven't made up my mind; I just wanted to see what you thought.'

Frankie dropped her spoon into her bowl with a clatter and folded her arms, staring hard at him. 'I've told you what I think, Alastair: you are needed 'ere.' She sighed. 'I want you here.'

'I know.' Alastair reached his hand out to her again and after a moment's pause she took hold of it. 'I don't want to upset you; you've had a heck of a lot of that in the past year.'

'Then don't go. It's as simple as that,' Frankie, said, looking him straight in the eyes.

32

There were some jobs at Station 75, Bella thought, that she found very soothing and this one, the rhythmic sweeping of the garage floor amidst the smell of oil mixed with diesel and dust, allowed her mind to drift away while she worked. Today it had settled on the fund-raising concert a few weeks ago, which had been such fun and a great success, and in spite of all the hard work it had entailed, she really missed it. Like her writing for the newspaper, it had given her something else to focus on and challenged her in different ways; now it was gone she felt slightly adrift.

The mournful wail of the air-raid siren suddenly started up, making Bella jump, its eerie rise and fall echoing out over the rooftops of London as it warned everyone to scurry to safety.

'Here we go again!' Sparky pulled his head out from under the bonnet of the ambulance he was working on. 'Come on, everyone to the shelter, double quick.'

Bella followed Sparky and other crew members to the brick shelter built in the courtyard of Station 75; they'd had to run to it a few times over the past week when the siren had gone off. Yesterday it had gone off three times but so far none of them had turned out to be anything more than daylight nuisance raids, with no bombs dropped, just enemy planes passing overhead. 'We're in and out of 'ere like bleedin' yo-yos just lately,' Sparky said, holding the door of the shelter open and ushering everyone in ahead of him.

'Is everyone out of the garages?' Station Officer Steele asked, hurrying towards them.

'Yes, everyone's in 'ere that was working in the garages.' Sparky followed the boss into the shelter. 'Is this another false alarm?'

'We'll have to wait and see.' Station Officer Steele sat down in her usual position by the table where the telephone sat ready to relay any calls for aid that came their way. 'We're prepared for incidents if there's bombing and that's all that matters. Do sit down, Sparky, there's precious little room in here without you pacing about like a bear in a cage.'

The crew members laughed and Sparky rolled his eyes and sat down next to his crew mate Paterson.

'What's got into 'im?' Frankie whispered to Bella, who had found a space next to her friends.

Bella shrugged. 'I don't know, we've grown used to not having air raids and then the siren going off so much in the past few days is bound to put people on edge. It's been all right so far but our luck might run out at any time and the bombers will be back and we all know what that's like. I dread having to return to that again.'

Frankie tucked her arm through Bella's. 'I know, let's 'ope this is another false alarm, eh?'

When the all-clear sounded twenty minutes later the sense of relief in the shelter was so thick it could almost be seen, Bella thought. It was another false alarm; it would cause worry and disruption to people's lives, but at least that was preferable to bombs dropping, so they should be thankful.

'Thank Gawd for that.' Sparky sprang to his feet and was first out of the shelter, opening the door so that the light of a grey March day filtered in.

'Back to work then, everyone,' Station Officer Steele called.

'Bella, could you come up to my office? There's something I want to speak to you about. I'll meet you there in five minutes.'

Bella nodded.

'What's that about?' Winnie asked as they walked across the courtyard.

Bella shrugged. 'I've no idea.'

'You haven't done anything you shouldn't, have you?' Winnie asked.

'Of course she ain't,' Frankie said. 'Perhaps the boss wants to put on another concert?'

'We could do another sketch.' Winnie beamed. 'This time we could — '

'Hold on, Winnie, before you go getting carried away,' Bella said. 'Let's just see what the boss wants first. She probably wants to ask me to do some job like cleaning out the cupboards in the women's rest room or something. I promise I'll tell you as soon as I know, that's if I'm allowed and it's not some top-secret mission.' She caught Frankie's eye and winked at her.

'The boss might want to send Bella out on some undercover ambulance business. Perhaps

186

she wants her to infiltrate a rival station and find out their tips for cleanin' their ambulances to a brilliant shine,' Frankie said, her face a picture of seriousness.

'But we're your friends, you might need our help . . .' Winnie began and then looked at both of them and started to laugh. 'You beasts, you're having me on.'

'Well, you should be more patient, Winnie,' Frankie said. 'Bella will tell us what it's about all in good time. Now you and I 'ave to finish cleaning those windows or we'll have the boss after us for slackin'.' Frankie hooked her arm through Winnie's and steered her towards the spot where they'd left their buckets and cloths when the air-raid siren went off. 'We'll see you in a bit, Bella. Good luck!'

'Thank you.' Bella watched her friends for a few moments as they went back to work and then hurried upstairs to the boss's office.

'You must be wondering what this is about,' Station Officer Steele said, motioning for Bella to sit down on the chair she always kept beside her desk.

'Yes.' Bella smiled. 'And I'm not the only one.'

The boss laughed. 'Indeed, I saw Winnie was quizzing you when I left the shelter.'

'Frankie told her you were going to send me on an undercover mission to another ambulance station.'

Station Officer Steele raised her eyebrows. 'Sadly not on this occasion but . . .' She paused while she opened her desk drawer and took out a pile of what looked like booklets, which she put on her desk. 'But I do have something from several other ambulance stations that I think might interest you. Here.' She took a booklet from the pile and handed it to her.

Bella stared at what the boss had given her. The cover was designed with stylish writing proclaiming the title, *Four Times*, and the date, 3 April 1941.

'That one's from Station 4, hence the name, it's from last year but perfectly illustrates what can be done; and there are these, too.' The boss handed her two more booklets, each one different to the first. 'This one, *Moore's Almanac* from Station 12 in Hammersmith, and this one, *C18*, from Station C18, again both old copies but still worth a read.'

'What are they?' Bella asked.

Station Officer Steele looked at her for a few moments and then laughed. 'These are ambulance station magazines, written by crew members, published and sold for . . . ' She pointed to the cover of one of the magazines where it showed the price. 'Two pence. They were talking about them at the meeting of Station Officers I went to the other day. I'd not heard of them before and they kindly said they'd send me some copies . . . ' She paused for a moment and smiled at Bella. 'I rather thought it might be a good idea to have a Station 75 magazine and you, with your writing experience, are the perfect person to write some of it and act as editor. What do you think?'

'What sort of things would go in it?' Bella asked, dodging the boss's question before she

188

knew what she might be letting herself in for.

'All sorts of things; look through these and see what you think.' Station Officer Steele stood up. 'I'll go and make us some tea.'

Left on her own, Bella looked through the three different magazines; each had a different style and contained a wide variety of things, from editorial pieces to poems, cartoons and articles, even advertisements. There seemed to be something for everyone to enjoy, and what made each magazine special was it had been compiled from the work of a variety of crew members, each showing off their particular strengths and talents, be it artwork or writing funny poems or articles.

The more she read, the more she liked the idea of creating something similar for Station 75. There was a whole wealth of talent amongst the crew and it would be fun to put something together. The concert had been wonderful but it had been a fleeting moment in time, whereas publishing a magazine would make something more permanent and there could be more than one edition.

'Well, what do you think?' Station Officer Steele asked when she returned with two mugs of tea. 'Will you do it?'

'Yes, I'd love to.' Bella held up her mug of tea to toast the launch of a new writing venture. 'Here's to Station 75's very own magazine.'

The boss gently chinked her mug against Bella's. 'I look forward to reading the first edition.'

★ ★ ★

189

'Well, what did the boss want?' Winnie burst out, leaping up from the armchair she'd been sitting on when Bella walked into the common room.

'I thought you two were supposed to be cleaning windows.' Bella looked at her friends.

'We're just takin' a break,' Frankie said. 'Winnie couldn't concentrate and do the job properly so we thought it best to 'ave a breather and pop up to the common room and wait for you to come out of the boss's office.'

'So go on, tell us?' Winnie urged her.

'It's good news, very good news . . .' Bella sat down in Winnie's vacated chair, her friend perching on the arm beside her. 'The boss showed me these.' She held out the magazines she'd been given. 'She's asked me to organise something similar for Station 75.' She smiled at them both. 'I've got a new writing job.'

'That's absolutely marvellous.' Winnie patted Bella's shoulder.

'Exactly what will you be writing?'

'A Station 75 magazine, something like these.' She passed a magazine each to Winnie and Frankie and they started to flick through them. 'I won't be writing it all myself, most of it will be done by other crew members and I'll organise it all into a magazine and do editorial. What do you think?'

'It's perfect for you.' Frankie smiled at her. 'You've missed writing for the paper, 'aven't you? Of all the people here, you're the one who's most capable of doing somethin' like this.'

'Exactly,' Winnie confirmed.

'I'm going to need help, but there are a lot of

190

talented people at this station and together we can make something to be proud of Frankie, I hope you'll do some illustrations and cartoons for it for a start.'

Frankie nodded. 'I'd love to.'

'Winnie, perhaps you could write some funny anecdotes — you're never short of amusing tales to tell.'

Winnie laughed. 'I'll take that as a compliment. I'm sure I can think of something.'

'I need to have a good look through these magazines and make a list of possible ideas for pieces to include and then I'll put up a notice to encourage crew members to write something for our magazine.'

'What are you going to call it?' Winnie asked.

'I'm not sure yet, it will have to be something suitable for our station. I'll have to think about it, but if you've got any suggestions let me know.' She paused, her mind racing with different ideas. 'It's going to be fun putting this together.'

'This could be the start of a whole new career for you, Bella,' Winnie said. 'Today the Station 75 magazine, next you'll be working on *The Times* newspaper.'

Bella pulled a face and laughed. 'Let's just get this up and running first.'

33

Winnie shook out the blanket with a flick of her wrists and deftly folded it into a neat square before placing it on top of the pile of already folded blankets.

'I asked Mac if he's dug up any bombs on the moon and he said yes, they flew up there and back on a winged horse,' she said, picking up another blanket from the pile she and Frankie were sorting through.

'Hmm.' Frankie nodded, slowly folding her own blanket.

Winnie grabbed it out of her hands. 'You haven't been listening to a word I've been saying, have you?' She frowned. 'What's going on, Frankie? Something's bothering you.' She put her arm through her friend's and steered her over to sit on the pile of mattresses stacked on top of each other at the side of Station 75's women's rest room.

'What's wrong?' Winnie asked, sitting down beside Frankie.

'You look awfully peaky this morning, are you unwell?'

'No, I'm fine it's just . . . ' Frankie sighed, leaning forwards on her knees, wringing her hands together. 'Alastair told me that he's thinkin' of joining the Royal Army Medical Corp — thinks he'll be more use there than at the London.'

'Utter rot! Ordinary people need a doctor just as much as the army does,' Winnie said. 'That's no reason to join up.'

'I know, but because the raids have stopped for the moment, he thinks he should be doin' more for the war effort.'

Winnie threw her arm around Frankie's shoulders. 'He sounds like Mac did when he signed up for bomb disposal — only he'd already done it by the time he told me. Alastair hasn't joined up already, has he?'

Frankie shook her head. 'He says he's only thinkin' about it.'

'Well, that's something, I suppose. You don't want him to, do you?'

'No! But if he wants to go, I can't stop 'im.'

'No, you can't. It's up to them, but it doesn't make it any easier for the women that love them, does it?' Winnie sighed. 'I hope he doesn't go, Frankie, but if he does then you'll have to accept it. If you love them, let them go and all that.'

Frankie sat up and leaned her head against Winnie's. 'I know, I just don't want him to go. It's not because I won't see him, it's just that if he's here in London he'll be safer than where the fightin' is.'

'Will he? Are any of us going to be safe if the bombers come back? He could be sent to work in some army hospital out in the country-side . . . '

'Or behind the front line,' Frankie added darkly.

'Look, I know this sounds awfully trite, but try not to worry about it, Frankie. Alastair might

193

never do it, and even if he does it might not be as bad as you imagine. This beastly war rules our lives and sometimes we just have to accept things and make the best of them. Keep your chin up and don't let what might happen tomorrow spoil your today.'

'Thank you, Winnie.' Frankie smiled at her. 'You are such a tonic.'

'My wisdom is hard won — remember those awful weeks I had when Mac and I were apart after he told me he'd joined bomb disposal. They were wasted days; we were both miserable apart when we should have been happy together and making the most of the time we had left in the Ambulance Service.'

'You did get back together again in the end.'

'Yes, and I'm grateful every day that we did and that Mac is now my husband. We — ' Winnie stopped as the door opened and Bella walked in.

'The boss wants — ' She halted, looking at them. 'Are you all right?'

'Yes, Frankie was feeling a bit down, that's all.' Winnie quickly explained about Alastair.

'I do hope he doesn't join up; we still need good doctors here,' Bella said. 'Come on, Station Officer Steele wants everyone in the common room, she's got an important announcement to make, apparently.'

'What about?' Winnie stood up. 'She hasn't said anything to me.'

'I don't know.' Bella opened the door for the three of them.

'There's only one way to find out.'

Winnie perched on the arm of the sofa, looking around at the entire crew who were gathered in the common room. There was much speculation going on about what the boss was going to announce.

'Perhaps the war's over,' Sparky said excitedly, 'and we can go 'ome and get back to normal life.'

'In your dreams, I'm afraid,' someone shouted back at him.

'Hitler ain't beaten just yet.'

Winnie bitterly wished he was. She'd been racking her brains trying to think through what the announcement might be. The boss hadn't hinted at anything when Winnie had been going through her Deputy Station Officer work with her. Was she leaving, was that it? Her heart sank at the thought, Station 75 without Station Officer Steele would be like a ship without a rudder.

'Here she comes.' Bella nudged Winnie's elbow.

The room fell silent as Station Officer Steele emerged from her office and walked over to stand by the window from where she could see everyone in their various places — sitting on chairs, perched on the edges of tables or simply standing, politely waiting.

The boss looked around at them, her keen brown eyes behind her owlish, horn-rimmed glasses, surveying the crowd, clearly checking everyone was there.

'Thank you all for coming in here. I'm sure you're wondering what this is about, what announcement I have to make.' She paused, but nobody spoke or made daft comments as they usually would. Winnie quickly glanced around at her fellow crew members: everyone had their eyes on the boss, their faces expectant as they waited to hear what she had to say.

'It has been decided,' Station Officer Steele continued, 'that London Auxiliary Ambulance Stations are to change to working on a twenty-four hours on, and twenty-four hours off rota, working nine a.m. to nine a.m.' She paused once more, letting the news sink in and for the comments that the news had sparked to die down. 'This is obviously quite a change, but nothing we can't deal with efficiently. Remember we changed from eight-hour shifts to the current twelve-hour system. Twenty-four-hour shifts will be no more difficult and will, I think, be better. I will be putting a new work rota in place to ensure all the jobs are set out for each day so that Station 75 can keep running as smoothly as it does now.'

'Hear, hear!' Sparky shouted.

Station Officer Steele smiled at him. 'Thank you, Sparky. I knew I could count on you. There are some other important changes I must tell you about. Firstly, as crew members will be on duty for twenty-four hours at a time, it has been decided that each ambulance station will have a cook and meals will be provided on site.'

'Things are looking up!' someone shouted.

'As long as it ain't you who's doing the cooking!' Sparky called out and everyone laughed.

'I will be employing a proper cook,' the boss went on, 'but I will also need a crew member to act as a catering auxiliary, helping the cook with the meals and doing food shopping rather than working on the ambulances, so if anyone has any particular cooking skills and experience and would be interested in the post, come and see me. And finally,' she paused again, 'I have saved this piece of news for last as I know it's been longed for . . . ' Winnie could see the boss was desperate to tell them, barely concealing her smile. 'At last, after far too long a wait, we are going to be getting our uniforms — they will all be arriving shortly. I — '

Station Officer Steele's words were drowned out by the huge cheer that erupted in the crowded room. Winnie could hardly believe it — after being in the Ambulance Service for over two and a half years they were finally going to have their own uniform.

'That's marvellous,' Bella said, throwing her arms around Winnie's shoulders and hugging her tight.

'About bleedin' time!' they heard Sparky shouting above the hubbub.

'Indeed,' Station Officer Steele called out, waving her hands to quieten the delighted crews. 'I take it from your response that you are as happy as I am. Our uniforms are long overdue and I know it has been a sore point with many of you,' her eyes met Winnie's as she said this, 'as the other Civil Defence services have had theirs for years. So,' she smiled around at the assembled crew, 'things are changing at Station

197

75, but I have no doubt that my crew will be just as excellent at their jobs, all the while looking even smarter in their new uniforms.'

Someone started to clap loudly and it rapidly spread to the rest of the crew. As Winnie joined in, she caught Frankie's eye and her friend grinned at her, looking much happier than she had a short while ago. Perhaps the changes at Station 75 would help Frankie if her worries did come true and Alastair did join up.

34

There were so many bits of paper spread out on the large desk in Connie's library that Bella couldn't actually see its wooden top. They were all part of the makings of the station's magazine, which was coming together nicely now. There'd been a positive response to her notice and many crew members had submitted something to put in it, so there was a good mixture of features to choose from. Sparky had surprised her by writing a humorous article based on the routines of life at Station 75 — he really was a man of many talents.

Bella was working out the best order in which to use the pieces, wanting a balance of light and more serious features throughout the pages to make it a pleasant read. She was so engrossed in what she was doing that she wasn't aware that anyone had come into the library until someone bent down and kissed her cheek, making her jump.

'Oh!' She looked up and was delighted to see James smiling at her. She leapt to her feet and threw her arms around him. 'What are you doing here?' she said, hugging him tightly. 'What a wonderful surprise!' She loosened her arms and looked up at him.

'It's good to see you.'

'And you.' James kissed her. 'I had to come to London for a meeting and thought I'd grab the chance to see my favourite girl while I'm here.'

'Well, I'm glad you did. How long have you got?'

'Only a few hours, I've got to get the last train back to Bletchley.'

'Let's make the most of it then. Shall we go out somewhere?' Bella asked.

James shook his head. 'Let's just stay here and be together. What's this?' He picked up a piece of paper from the desk.

'This,' Bella said, throwing her arms wide, 'is the makings of Station 75's magazine; I told you about it in my letter.'

'Show me.'

'Sit down, then. Right, this is the cover that Frankie drew.' She pointed to the clever design of an ambulance with the name of the magazine on the side just as a shop might advertise its name on the side of its delivery vans. 'She did several different ideas, styles and layouts but we liked this one best.'

'It's very eye-catching, and I like the name, 'Seventy-five Blitz & Pieces' — it's quirky, different and fun,' James said. 'Who thought of that?'

'Your dear sister. We had several options and put it to the vote of all crew members and this one won by a long way. It appealed to their sense of fun, I think.'

'It must be taking up a lot of your time,' James said.

Bella shrugged. 'I don't mind, I'm enjoying it very much and now we're working twenty-four-hour shifts I've got longer blocks of time to work on it when I'm not at Station 75.'

'Or at the Red Cross packing centre.'

Bella nodded. 'Or there, but I like being busy and you know I love writing.' She reached out and took hold of his hand. 'But I'm not too busy doing it to spend proper time with you now I've got you here. Come on.' She stood up and pulled James to his feet.

'Let's leave this and go and make some tea and snuggle up on the sofa in the drawing room where it's much more comfortable.'

James raised his eyebrows. 'That sounds like a good idea.'

'And before you ask, Connie's out at a Red Cross meeting and Winnie has gone to the pictures with Frankie and Rose.'

'Didn't you want to go?'

'I've already seen Gone With the Wind twice, this'll be the third time they've been to see it.' Bella smiled. 'I'm glad I didn't go, or I'd have missed you — and you, James, are far better than Rhett Butler any day.'

35

'The stew was quite delicious, thank you,' Station Officer Steele said.

Mrs Sally Connelly, Station 75's new cook, bobbed her head of grey curls in response. 'I'm glad you liked it, there weren't any left over so that were a good sign.'

'You have everything you need in here?' She looked around at the kitchen, which was now the catering hub for the station, producing three meals a day to feed the hungry crew.

'Aye.' Sally wiped her hands dry on a cloth. 'But my catering auxiliary needs to work a bit faster to get through all the washing-up.' She swivelled her eyes to the sink, where Hooky was working her way through a pile of dirty plates from lunch.

Station Officer Steele could see that Hooky had heard Sally's comment from the way her shoulders suddenly tensed.

'She did volunteer to take this job,' she said. 'I'll speak to her.' She went over to stand beside Hooky who carried on washing up, albeit very slowly. 'Sally is concerned that you're not working fast enough when there's a lot to get through, Hooky. Are you sure this is what you want to do? There were other crew members who volunteered for this job if you don't think it's right for you after all.' She'd been very surprised when Hooky had come rushing up to her after she had announced the need for someone to help the new cook. 'You can always go back to working as an attendant on the ambulances, I wouldn't mind.'

'No!' Hooky splashed her hand in the soapy water, sending a splat over the side of the sink and on to the floor. 'I really want to stay doing this; I don't want to go back to going out in the ambulances, I didn't like it. I'm not very good with blood and . . . ' She shivered. 'Seeing people hurt and . . . '

Station Officer Steele frowned. 'Why on earth did you sign up to the Ambulance Service in the first place, then?'

Hooky shrugged. 'I thought it sounded glamorous and romantic but it's not.'

'It's certainly neither of those. But why didn't you leave if you felt that way?'

'I never got around to it because I didn't know what I'd have to do instead; I could have ended up in a munitions factory.' Hooky pulled a face. 'And then they passed the rule saying ambulance crew couldn't leave and I knew I was stuck here for the duration, so when you wanted a volunteer to help Cook . . . ' Hooky did her best to smile. 'Please don't make me go back on the ambulances; I promise I'll work harder.' She started washing up again at a noticeably faster pace than before.

'Very well, I'll keep you on as Cook's assistant for now but if you can't keep up with the work I'll have no option but to replace you with another crew member. Understand?'

Hooky nodded. 'Thank you.'

Station Officer Steele patted the young woman's shoulder and then turned back to Sally, who was sitting at the table writing.

'I thought we'd have these meals for the next week, providing I can get the ingredients.' Sally pushed the piece of paper over for her to see.

She read through the list of hearty meals worthy of any good home cooking. 'They look jolly good, Sally, thank you. Don't forget there are the vegetables from the allotment, too. Just tell me what you need each day and I can send someone down to pick them for you.'

'That allotment's a real help,' Sally said.

'I'm — ' The boss stopped as Frankie came hurrying into the kitchen.

'Sorry to disturb you, boss, only there's a delivery come for you and the driver ain't accepting anyone else's signature for it except for the Station Officer's,' Frankie said.

'What is it?'

Frankie shrugged. 'He won't say, he's a bit of a bad-tempered so-and-so.'

'All right, I'm coming now. Thank you, Sally. Keep me informed if you need anything or have any problems.'

'Aye, I will.' Sally nodded.

'What do you think is being delivered?' Frankie asked as they went down the stairs to the courtyard.

'It could be . . . But I was told they wouldn't be here till next week.'

'What?' Frankie asked.

'Our uniforms.'

Frankie's eyes widened. 'Really?'

204

'It might not be them, so keep quiet about it.'

Outside in the courtyard the delivery driver was leaning against the van smoking a cigarette, a surly look on his face.

'I'm Station Officer Steele,' she said with a look that made him stand up straight. 'What have you brought?'

He pulled a delivery book out of his jacket pocket and opened it.

'According to this, it's uniforms.'

'I wasn't expecting them until next week,' she said.

'I'll take them away again, should I?' he said.

'Absolutely not! We've waited long enough for them. Where do you want me to sign?'

With her signature on the delivery book, the driver went around to the back of his truck to unload.

'Sparky, can you organise a team and bring the boxes up to the women's rest room, please? And Frankie, can you find Bella and come and help me set up in there, please?'

'Will do, boss,' Sparky said. 'About bleedin' time we had a proper uniform.'

'Precisely, and if we all work together on this you will do by the end of the day,' she said. Being able to issue her crews with their uniforms would be a real morale boost to them. She knew a lot of them felt that their job was more about keeping the ambulances clean and ready to go rather than rescuing casualties now. They'd gone from one extreme to the other, from being out in air raids with bombs falling and dealing with terrible injuries to day after day of quiet routine.

'What do you want us to do with them?' Frankie asked as she opened the last box to reveal pairs of black trousers folded neatly inside.

Station Officer Steele surveyed the open boxes on the floor of the women's rest room. 'I think the best thing to do is to arrange the different garments in a row on the table, then crew members can pick up what they need in an ordered fashion. If we start at this end,' she said, moving to one end of the long trestle table that they had already set up ready to use, 'with the shirts, then trousers, skirts and finally tunics. Ties and badges can be given out last.'

'What about different sizes?' Bella asked.

Station Officer Steele took a tunic out of the box and shook it out. 'It's more a question of small, medium or large — there's no fine tailoring gone into these, though they look fairly smart.' She rather liked the shiny buttons down the front of the tunic, and crew members wearing uniforms rather than their own odd assortment of clothes would look much better.

'They could do with being altered,' Frankie said, picking up another tunic and holding it against herself. 'A few darts and some hemming to fit would make all the difference.'

'Well, your uniform will look good then.' Bella held up a pair of trousers to her waist; they were far too long, the bottom of each leg flapping on to the floor.

'I'll alter yours for you,' Frankie offered. 'And yours, too, boss.'

Frankie smiled at her. 'If you'd like me to, that is.'

'I most certainly would. You've given me an idea, Frankie,' she said. 'How would you like to work as Station 75's official tailor for a while, just until any uniforms that need altering are dealt with? You'd be relieved of other duties and we could set you up in here to work. If we're going to wear uniforms at last then we want them to fit well. What do you think, Frankie? I know you would do an excellent job.'

'It would be easy enough using a sewing machine, and I've got my gran's at home,' Frankie said.

'You could take a car and go and fetch it, that's if you'd like the job?'

Frankie nodded. 'I'd love to do it.'

'Excellent. Thank you, Frankie. Right, let's get these uniforms set out and then we can start issuing them.'

The table was piled with uniforms all neatly folded and ready to give out when the door burst open and Winnie came rushing in, closely followed by Trixie and Rose.

'I heard the uniforms have arrived!' Winnie's eyes fell on the piles of clothes on the table. 'When are we getting them?'

Station Officer Steele smiled at Winnie, who had felt the lack of uniform so deeply, often bemoaning the fact that the other Civil Defence sections had already been given theirs. It was a pity that Winnie and Rose had been out on a job taking the station's dirty laundry to be cleaned and collecting the clean in return, on the very

207

day the uniforms were finally delivered. 'Well . . . '

'Can we get them today?' Winnie asked, as eager as any small child on Christmas morning.

'How about, as you've argued the case for our uniform for so long, you can be the first to get yours?' she said.

'Really?' Winnie's creamy skin flushed pink. 'But what about you? You're the boss, and Frankie, Bella and Rose are here and they need theirs too.'

'And they will get them.'

'Come here, Winnie.' Bella linked her arm through Winnie's and pulled her over to the table. She selected a suitably sized white shirt and put it into her friend's arms, followed by trousers, a skirt and finally a tunic.

Station Officer Steele waited for Winnie at the end of the table and presented her with her tie and selected the appropriate badges to sew on to the tunic.

'There's the Ambulance Service badge for the top of your sleeves, the Civil Defence insignia for your left top pocket, and the London badge for below that, and two stripes for your sleeve for being Deputy Station Officer. They'll all need sewing on.'

'Thank you very much!' Winnie beamed at her. 'I'm going to put them on straight away.' She hurried over to the other side of the room and began getting undressed.

'Winnie, what are you doin'?' Frankie said.

'Getting changed.' Winnie was now down to her silk undergarments. 'When you've been to boarding school it's no good being a shrinking violet, it's only us in here anyway, there are no men around,' she said, putting on her white shirt, and buttoning it up, then adding her tie.

Station Officer Steele caught Bella's eye and she raised her eyebrows. 'Let's get the rest of us kitted out, shall we, and then we can see what needs doing before we call in the rest of the crew to get their uniform.'

Following Winnie's example, they all changed into their new uniforms and stood looking around at each other.

'Don't we look different?' Frankie said. 'It's really strange all of us bein' in the same clothes.'

'I think you all look extremely smart.' Station Officer Steele smoothed down the front of her tunic and checked that her belt was buckled correctly. 'We just need to sew on our badges and then everything will be in place.'

'You'll need bringin' in here.' Frankie pointed to the side of her tunic. 'And your sleeves are a little too long.' She gently folded the end of one of Station Officer Steele's sleeves under. 'There, that's better.'

'I think you are going to be kept busy altering our uniforms, Frankie, but then we'll be the best turned-out ambulance station in London.'

'Come on, let's go and show the others,' Winnie said, smiling broadly, her pillar-box-red lipstick standing out even more against her black uniform. 'We'll give them a fashion parade.'

'Very well, a quick one — there's lots to be done if we want everyone kitted out this afternoon,' she said. 'And then Frankie can take a car and go and fetch her sewing machine so that she can set up in here as Station 75's tailor!'

The look on the other crew members' faces as they paraded around Station 75 was priceless, Station Officer Steele thought. Everyone knew the uniforms were coming but to actually see their fellow crew members wearing them was a special moment.

'Blimey!' Sparky said, casting his newspaper aside to have a closer look as they walked into the common room. For once he was lost for words.

Suddenly seeing people who you were used to working with all dressed alike was rather strange but also unifying. Station Officer Steele liked it very much; it added to the sense of them all working towards a common goal — keeping Station 75 running like clockwork. With the bombing ceased for the time being she'd sensed a slight drifting of purpose in some crew members, a subtle slacking off. Getting a uniform would hopefully help refocus everyone on their jobs, though perhaps they needed a tighter rein to keep them in check because Station 75 still had to be ready to jump into action at a moment's notice. She needed to consider if the crew needed something else to keep them going.

36

The April sunshine was doing its best to warm the London streets, but the chill wind whipping along the pavements was keeping people well wrapped up in their coats, scarves and gloves. Winnie hurried home, with Trixie trotting happily at her heels. They'd been on a long walk in Regent's Park, making the most of Station 75's new shift system. Winnie rather liked having a whole twenty-four hours off before having to return to work, as opposed to having to squeeze things into her twelve hours off. It felt a positive luxury to have an entire day to herself.

Scooting around Russell Square she turned in to Bedford Place and as she walked the final few yards towards home, she noticed a familiar figure coming towards her from the other end of the street, looking smart in his RAF great coat and cap. It was her brother, Harry, and walking beside him, her arm linked with his, was Meredith, his fiancée.

Trixie had spotted him too and set off, streaking down the pavement to greet him and dancing around his legs as Harry bent down to pat her ears. The little dog was still ecstatic about his arrival when Winnie reached him.

'Well, this is a lovely surprise,' she said, kissing her brother and then Meredith on the cheek. 'It's jolly nice to see you both. Come on, I'm sure you could do with something warm to drink, it's perishing out here.'

Settled in the drawing room with a match put to the fire in honour of the visitors, Winnie sat back in her armchair and smiled across at Harry. 'Go on then, you look like the proverbial cat that got the cream; do tell what's making you so happy.'

Harry glanced at Meredith, who was sat close beside him on the sofa. 'I thought my eagle-eyed sister would have spotted it by now.' He held up Meredith's left hand and Winnie saw the elegant band of gold shining on her fourth finger.

'You're married!' Winnie exclaimed. 'Congratulations!' She rushed over to Meredith and pulled her to her feet, embracing her. 'Thank you, Meredith, for being brave enough to marry my brother, and welcome to our family!'

'Thank you,' Meredith said, smiling, her cheeks dimpling prettily. 'It's a joy to be married to Harry.' She gazed down at her husband, her eyes full of love for him.

'So, when did you get married?' Winnie said after returning to her chair, followed by Trixie, who jumped up on to her lap and settled down, leaning against her mistress. 'I thought you were planning a quiet wedding?'

'We had a very quiet wedding, in East Grinstead, just us, one of Meredith's fellow nurses and one of my fellow Ward Three patients as witnesses. That was it, we didn't want any fuss.'

'When was it?'

'Four days ago; we just got back from our honeymoon,' Harry said. 'We brought the

212

wedding forward because I've been posted to my new job and have to report for duty next Monday, so we got a special licence and did the deed.'

'They've passed you fit for duty, then?' Winnie frowned, the thought of having to worry about Harry flying again filling her stomach with lead. 'But surely you're not going to be flying Spitfires, are you? You've done more than enough, Harry; it's someone else's turn.'

'It's fine, old girl. They've posted me fit for my new job but not for piloting Spits any more.' Harry sighed and held up one of his hands, which still bore the damage of the fire, his fingers curled inwards at an unnatural angle. 'I couldn't control a kite properly with these any more, wouldn't be safe to fly.' He shrugged. 'It's a damn shame, but I know the doctors are right when they say you need to be completely fit to fly — when you've got a Messerschmitt bearing down right on top of you, you can't afford for your fingers not to work properly.'

'What are you going to be doing?' Winnie asked.

'I'm going to be a fighter controller instead. Still involved in the action but this time from the ground.' Harry reached for Meredith's hand. 'We're heading off to our new posting tomorrow.'

'Where is it?'

Harry laughed. 'You know I can't tell you that. Let's just say if you head north, you're going in the right direction.'

'You'll have left Ward Three then, Meredith?' Winnie asked.

'Will you get another nursing posting where you're going?'

'I hope so,' Meredith said, her sing-song Welsh accent sounding delightful. 'At a nearby hospital or perhaps on the base. There's always a call for more nurses, especially now. I don't mind where I work as long as we're together.' She smiled at Harry and he threw his arm around her, hugging her closer to him.

Watching the pair of them so in love and at ease with each other was lovely to see after all her brother had been through. His experiences had changed Harry, for the better in some ways, Winnie thought. He might not look as handsome as he once did, his face now marred by shiny, pinkish scars and his nose a different shape to what it used to be after having to be rebuilt, but his character was much nicer. He was far more open and loving than he used to be. Meeting Meredith and marrying her had to be one of the best things that had ever happened to him and it clearly made them both very happy.

Winnie felt glad for them both. She only wished that she and Mac could be together, too. Since Mac had joined the bomb squad, they'd only had snatched moments together. It was hard to be apart and she missed him dreadfully, but she knew she mustn't let that taint her joy for her brother and new sister-in-law's happiness.

'I'm sure they'll miss you on Ward Three,' Winnie said.

'I'll miss them too,' Meredith replied. 'It's an exceptional place, but I want to be with my husband. He needs me, and I need him.'

'Are you going to visit Mother before you go north?' Winnie asked.

Harry shook his head. 'No time, I'm afraid; and I haven't told her we're married yet either.'

Winnie's eyes met her brother's. 'Ah.' Winnie understood why her brother hadn't told their mother before the wedding. She would have been against the match, would have told him that Meredith wasn't good enough, didn't come from the right sort of background. Winnie had heard her say the same about Mac before they'd married. It hadn't stopped her, of course, but it saddened her how snobbish, unkind and utterly unsupportive her mother had been.

'You are going to, though?'

'I'll telephone her once we get to our new home. Then there's no chance of her coming to London to see us before we leave, you know what she's like.'

'A wise move,' Winnie said. 'Harry has told you about our mother, hasn't he? How, er . . . beastly she can be if she doesn't like something.'

'Oh yes!' Meredith smiled. 'He told me how she behaved towards your husband before you got married. I've told Harry I can deal with people like her, it wouldn't upset me.'

'I don't doubt that you can, but it's not pleasant to see her being unkind to the people you love. Mac and I had a showdown with her in the Dorchester.' Winnie sighed, recalling her mother's unyielding attitude, her ramrod-straight back and the way she had hidden them away at a table behind the potted palms so no one would see her daughter and the lower-class man whom she wanted to marry. Her plan to persuade Winnie not to do so hadn't worked. 'Harry only wants to protect you from that, the same way I did for Mac.'

'How is Mac?' Harry asked.

'Fine, as far as I know. I haven't seen him since December; he hasn't been able to get any leave, not even a forty-eight-hour pass. He telephones when he can, and writes, but I'm getting rather impatient to see him. If he can't get to me then I might have to go to him if I ever want to see him. Now we're on twenty-four-hour shifts I can do that much more easily.'

'Then do, he's only in Colchester; if he can't come to you, then go to him. If you want something, old girl, you don't usually let anything stop you. What are you waiting for?'

Winnie stared at Harry for a few moments and then nodded firmly. 'Very well then, I will.'

37

'Do keep still, Winnie! If you keep movin' around I'll end up jabbing a pin in you by accident.' Frankie stopped pinning a dart to improve the fit of her friend's uniform jacket.

'I'm doing my best!' Winnie said, wriggling her shoulders and arms to relieve the tension. 'You know I'm not the most patient of people.'

'I know. Look, if you'd rather I do your uniform another day I don't mind, there are plenty of others who want theirs altered.'

'No, no, I need it done today.' Winnie touched Frankie's arm.

'I'm sorry, I promise I'll stand as still as I possibly can. I really do need my uniform sorted out today because I want to look my best for tomorrow.' She took a deep breath and resumed her previous position. 'See, I'm ready.'

Frankie frowned. 'Why tomorrow? What's the hurry?'

'I'm going to see Mac; I want him to see me in my uniform.'

'Ah, I see.' Frankie smiled at her. 'In that case, I'd better get on with it. Keep still, I'll be as quick as I can.'

She started pinning again, using her expertise to make the jacket a more flattering shape for Winnie's willowy figure. 'I'm sure Mac will think you look very smart.'

'I do hope so. I'm going to surprise him; he

doesn't know I'm going.'

'Is that wise? He might not be there when you get there.'

'I'm prepared to risk it. I'm utterly fed up of not seeing him. I want to surprise him, and if I telephone to check if he's there then it won't be a surprise, will it?'

She stopped talking as the door of the women's rest room, which was currently doubling up as Frankie's sewing room, opened and Rose came in. 'Station Officer Steele wants everyone in the common room for a meeting at two o'clock.'

'What for?' Frankie asked.

'I don't know, I'm just the messenger,' Rose replied.

'Another of the boss's great meetings,' Winnie said. 'What's she going to announce this time, I wonder?'

'Thanks for telling us, Rose, we'll be there,' Frankie said. 'Right, we've got a quarter of an hour before then, let's get the fit of this jacket sorted out then I can sew it up later.'

★   ★   ★

The crew that were gathered in the common room a short while later looked a lot smarter than the last time they'd met there a week ago now they were wearing their uniforms rather than their own mismatched clothing.

'As we're now on twenty-four-hour shifts,' Station Officer Steele began once the chatter had died down, 'I've worked out programmes of work to ensure the smooth and efficient running of Station 75. I want to keep this station running like clockwork so if . . . ' She paused. 'More likely *when* the bombing starts again we are ready for action.' She held up two sheets of typed paper. 'First is the daily programme of work, commencing at nine a.m. sharp with the change of shift, and detailing the scheduled times of different jobs, meals, et cetera. I'm not going to read this one out, I'll pin it on the board and leave it to you to familiarise yourselves with it.' She laid the two sheets of paper on the nearby table and held up another. 'This is the weekly programme of jobs that will run in addition to the daily job rota, it details specific jobs for the day, such as the first aid lectures and the stirrup pump drill. Again, you'll need to ensure you familiarise yourself with this.'

'Cor blimey! Ain't this all going a bit far, boss?' Sparky called out. 'We've managed perfectly well without being timetabled moment by moment before. It sounds more like the bleedin' army than the Ambulance Service.'

'On the contrary, I think it is more necessary than ever before to keep this station in perfect working order and ready for action at all times.' The boss's voice had a steely edge to it.

Winnie looked at Frankie, who raised an eyebrow back at her. Station Officer Steele had always run Station 75 with great skill and had never needed any regimented timetables before now; were they really as necessary as she claimed? Winnie wondered. Weren't they more likely to put the backs up of some crew members

219

like Sparky who liked to be more free and easy but still got the job done well?

'Well, I ain't convinced we need it.' Sparky looked positively mutinous, sitting in the armchair with his arms firmly folded.

'We can discuss this further in my office if you wish,' the boss said coolly. She surveyed the assembled crew members, her brown eyes shrewd behind her glasses, looking to see if anyone else wanted to say something, but everyone sensibly, remained silent. 'Right, moving on, the new twenty-four-hour regime allows time for crew members to have leave of about two hours from the station to attend vocational classes or carry out voluntary work, I have a list of possible activities you can sign up for, which will also be put on the board for you to look at. Once you have made your selections, I'll work out a timetable for you to attend them, as I need to ensure I have enough staff on site at all times in case of an emergency. So, lots of new things to take in and put into action.' The boss smiled. 'I do hope you'll *all* do your best to cooperate with the new system and will take advantage of the educational and voluntary opportunities. Winnie, would you kindly pin up those sheets on the board for me?' She gathered the pieces of paper together and passed them to Winnie. 'Any questions or problems regarding the new system should be brought to me.' Station Officer Steele waited for a moment, looking around at them, then with a nod of her head, she turned on her well-polished heels and went back into her office.

The moment the boss's door had closed behind her the common room erupted into chatter as crew members voiced their various opinions on the new regime, with Sparky clearly not the least bit happy about what had happened.

'Let's have a look at that timetable, Winnie,' he said.

'You can read it off the board like everyone else,' Winnie said, going over to the wall where notices were pinned up.

Taking care to place each sheet of paper in the right order, she pinned them up, her eyes skimming the detailed instructions for each day as she did so. The boss had clearly invested a lot of thought and effort into this, but was it really necessary?

'I like the sound of the voluntary work,' Frankie said from behind her. 'What's on offer?'

'Quick, have a look before everyone crowds around to read these,' Winnie whispered, pulling her friend's arm and propelling her to where she had a clear view of the notices.

'Ooh, helping in daytime nurseries!' Frankie said excitedly, reading from the list. 'I like the sound of that, it would be fun!'

'Or you could try a vocational class — typing and shorthand or leatherwork and glove-making,' Winnie added. 'But I like the idea of doing some voluntary work, I ought to do something more for the war effort.' She read through the list of options, and one stood out to her immediately — helping at the American Eagle Club — that sounded like real fun and would be very different from working at Station 75.

'Come on, out of the way, let everyone else have a gander,' Sparky said from behind Winnie.

'Go on then, Sparky.' Winnie stepped back and watched as the other crew members surged forward to get a good look at the new timetables.

'It's like the bleedin' army!' Sparky said, sounding appalled.

'Half past ten do this, eleven o'clock do that.'

'It's not all bad, Sparky,' Frankie said. 'We've got a chance to go off and do classes or voluntary work.'

'You could try dressmaking!' his attendant, Paterson, said, slapping Sparky on the shoulder.

'Very funny,' Sparky muttered, not taking his eyes off the list.

Winnie hoped Station Officer Steele's changes wouldn't spoil the happy atmosphere of Station 75. The boss hadn't seemed herself for some time; Winnie knew she was worried about her sister and her family, so perhaps this was her way of coping — being in control of everything she could to make up for feeling so helpless about her sister's situation.

38

The earlier clamour over the rota had died down by the evening and now crew members were occupying themselves in various ways, some knitting or sewing, reading or playing cards or simply listening to the wireless. One or two had dozed off in their armchairs.

Bella had been thinking all day about which option she'd like to sign up for. The typing and shorthand course sounded perfect, she'd learn valuable skills that would help her with the station magazine and could come in very useful for getting a job after the war, because she wasn't going back to doing what she'd done before. Her days of being a housemaid were well and truly over.

Standing by the noticeboard, she read through what the others had signed up for. Frankie was volunteering at a day nursery, Winnie and Rose at the American Eagle Club. Sparky, despite his earlier protestations about the new regime, had put his name down for the leatherwork classes. Pulling a pencil out of her dungarees pocket, Bella wrote her name by the typing and shorthand class.

'What have you picked?' Rose said, coming up beside her and looking at where she had written her name. 'Ah, typing and shorthand.'

'It'll come in useful and I'm already doing some voluntary work packing Red Cross parcels for prisoners of war.'

'Frankie told me your brother is a prisoner of war,' Rose said sympathetically.

'Yes, that's right; Walter's in a prisoner of war camp in Italy and that's why I do it — I know how much getting parcels means to the POWs. And it feels like I'm doing something to help people like my brother.'

'That's why I signed up for the American Club canteen,' Rose said. 'I have American cousins who have just been drafted so I'll be helping people like them.'

'Do you hear from them much?' Bella asked.

Rose nodded. 'Not my cousins directly, but my uncle writes to me every week. Now I don't hear from my parents any more he's the only family I have contact with until I meet them again.'

Bella put her hand on Rose's arm. 'I hope you'll hear from your parents soon; don't give up hope.'

'I never will,' Rose said, a look of determination on her face. 'Do you hear from your brother much?'

'Walter's never been the most regular of correspondents, I've always sent him far more letters than he sends me, but I know that he appreciates getting them. Now he's a POW, his letter-writing opportunities are more limited, but he writes when he can. And at least he's out of the fighting and that's a huge relief.'

'My uncle worries about what's going to happen to my cousins once their training's done. He doesn't know where they'll be sent — they could be sent to fight the Japanese in the Pacific.'

'Or the Germans,' Bella said. 'They might be sent here; there are plenty of American servicemen arriving in the country now.'

'Oh, I hope so, if they come to England we might be able to meet each other, I've never seen them, only photographs.'

Bella crossed her fingers. 'Let's hope they come here then so you can meet your cousins. I'm sure they'll be very proud of the way you've coped with coming to live in a new country and now working for the Ambulance Service.'

Rose shrugged. 'I was still a schoolgirl when I left Austria.'

'Exactly, you've had to grow up a lot since then and changed into a young woman with a responsible job.'

Rose looked worried. 'I'm not sure that I will be able to do it properly now, though.'

'What do you mean?'

Rose looked around and then leaned closer to Bella and whispered, 'The new rota, it's so exact, what if I can't do the job in the time given, will Station Officer Steele make me leave?'

Bella put her arm through Rose's. 'I wouldn't worry about it. I know there was a lot of fuss over it this morning but it'll all sort itself out, the boss is just trying to keep us organised and her timetable will only work if things are a bit flexible. In my experience it's best to wait and see what happens, there'll probably be a few problems, but it'll get sorted out and will carry on as usual.' She pulled Rose's arm. 'Come on, let's go and make some cocoa.'

39

Winnie stared out of the carriage window at the passing countryside. The sun was shining warmly and spring finally seemed to have arrived, but all she was interested in was urging the train to go faster so she could get to Colchester that much sooner and then to Mac. She'd caught the crowded train from Liverpool Street station, going straight there from Station 75 after her shift had ended at nine o'clock that morning, sending Trixie home with Bella. Winnie knew she was taking a chance just going to see Mac like this, but she was utterly fed up with not seeing him because he couldn't get leave. If he couldn't come to her, then she had no choice but to go to him.

She missed Mac desperately and sometimes still expected to see him at Station 75 and then when she realised he wasn't there, it made the pain of their separation all the sharper. It was worth taking a chance to go and see him, even though she knew that there was a good possibility he wouldn't be there, he could be out on a call, digging up a bomb . . . But waiting around for him to come home wasn't getting her anywhere and she wasn't going to let something like that stand in her way. It was worth the risk.

Finally arriving at Colchester station she asked directions and made her way to the school that the bomb disposal squad had taken over after the children had been evacuated; this was where Mac now lived. Standing outside on the pavement she looked at it and hoped that her husband was somewhere inside and that it would only be a matter of minutes before she could see him again. Winnie knew her turning up out of the blue was highly irregular and his commanding officer might not be so keen to let her see him, it was the army after all and far stricter than Station 75, but she wasn't going to let it stop her.

She smoothed her honey-blonde hair and then marched in through the school gates and up to the front door, which was piled around with sandbags like so many buildings now, to where a soldier stood on guard.

'Good morning,' Winnie said cheerfully, turning a beaming smile on him. 'I wonder if I could see my husband, please, Sapper William McCartney?'

'Sorry, missis, we don't allow visitors in here, this is an army depot,' the guard said. 'It's the rules.'

Rules. Winnie wanted to snap back that in her book rules were made to be broken, but this was the army she was dealing with and if she kicked up a fuss then she could easily find herself frogmarched off to the nearest police station.

She nodded. 'I understand, but could you at least go in and tell him I'm here and perhaps he could come out? I wouldn't have to set foot in your depot.'

'I would if I could, but I can't leave my post or I'll be in trouble.'

The guard looked sympathetic. 'I'll tell Mac you were here, though.'

'Is he here? Not out on a call?'

'Yes, he's here.'

Winnie stared at the doorway behind the guard. She could just make a run for it, push past him and get in, but how far would she get? It would definitely get her in trouble and perhaps Mac as well. Coming all the way here and falling at the last hurdle was infuriating, and something she'd not had much experience of before. She usually found a way around things, but it looked like this time she was beaten. Sudden tears of frustration stung her eyes.

'All right, please tell him I was here and that I tried to see him.'

'I'm sorry I can't let you in or go and fetch him for you, missis, I really am, but rules is rules.'

'I know.' Winnie sighed. 'I just wanted to see him.'

'You're ambulance crew?' the guard asked.

'Yes. Well, thank you anyway.' Winnie was about to go but stopped as the guard suddenly spotted someone approaching, sprang to attention and saluted. Winnie turned and saw an officer walking towards them.

'What's this, is someone hurt?' the officer asked, taking note of Winnie's uniform. 'I didn't see an ambulance.'

'There's no one hurt, sir?' The guard dropped his salute. 'This lady here came to see her husband, but I've told her that unfortunately she can't because of the rules.'

'And who might your husband be?' the officer asked.

'Sapper William McCartney — Mac. I just wanted to see him as it's been so long since he was last home. I came straight here from London after my shift finished.'

'Mac's one of my men; did he know you were coming?'

'No, I took a chance and it seems that it was rather foolish of me.'

She sighed. 'I'm sorry to have disturbed you.'

'I'm sure Mac would be utterly delighted to see you.' He thought for a moment then turned to address the guard. 'Go and find Mac, will you, Evans? Tell him he's got a visitor.'

'Yes, sir.' The guard stamped his army boots and went in to the building.

'Thank you, I do appreciate this, I know I shouldn't have just turned up like this but . . . ' Winnie sighed. 'It's hard not seeing him, I worry about him.'

'I'm glad to help. If my wife found out I'd turned away a fellow chap's wife who'd come all this way to see him, then I would well and truly be in the dog house.' The officer took off his peaked cap and ran his hand through his hair. 'I know how hard it is for you wives.'

Winnie nodded. 'And for lots of wives out there, too, worrying and waiting has become part of marriage these days. I try to keep busy as that helps.'

'So where are you stationed?' the officer asked.

'Station 75, just north of the Tower of London,' Winnie said.

'You must have seen a lot of bombing, then.'

'We were out in the thick of it, but thankfully it's been quiet for a while now and long may it last.'

They chatted for a few minutes until the door opened and Mac came out, his eyes wide with surprise at the sight of Winnie.

'Winnie!' he said before quickly recovering himself and stamping his foot and saluting the officer. 'Sir.'

'Ah, Mac, your charming wife has come all this way to see you on a surprise visit and since all is quiet for the time being, why don't you take her over to the cafe there for an hour or so? I'll send for you if you're needed.'

'Thank you, sir. I appreciate that,' Mac said.

'And so do I,' Winnie added. 'You can tell your wife about this, she'll be delighted with you.'

'I will indeed. Off you go and enjoy your time together.' The officer touched the brim of his cap in salute to them and went inside.

'Come on, what are we waiting for?' Winnie grabbed Mac's hand and pulled him towards the gate and once they were out of sight of the guard who'd returned to his post, she threw her arms around Mac and hugged him tightly, then kissed him thoroughly.

'It's good to see you,' Mac said, pulling apart slightly and looking at her. 'You look smashing in your uniform. Mind you, you look good whatever you wear.'

'Why thank you. We're rather proud of our uniforms now we've got them.' Winnie reached out and cupped his cheek. 'I miss you, Mac, and

I couldn't bear another day not seeing you. I had to come here and find you, though I nearly didn't. If your officer hadn't come along when he did I'd have been slinking back to the station now.'

Mac laughed. 'You're lucky I am here, I could have been out on a call.'

'I know I was taking a risk, but it was worth it for the chance of seeing you. And it's paid off.'

He smiled at her. 'You don't let anything stand in your way when you want something, do you?'

'I try not to but the army's rules stumped me. I did consider barging past the guard and running in to find you, but thought I might end up in big trouble if I did.'

'You are quite incorrigible, Winnie, but I do love you and I'm delighted you're here.' Mac put his arm around her shoulders. 'Come on, let's go to the cafe and make the most of this precious hour.'

Sitting in the cafe across the road from the depot, Winnie grasped Mac's hand, wanting to hold on to him while she could.

'How are things at Station 75?' Mac asked.

'The boss's new rota is causing a bit of a stir; it's planned out almost to the minute with who should be doing what and when.' She pulled a face. 'I don't like it and nor do many of the crew. I don't know why she had to go and change things.' Winnie frowned. 'The station ran perfectly well before we had it.'

'The boss must have her reasons. When are you starting your voluntary work at the American Eagle Club?'

'Next week. I'm looking forward to it: a chance to escape from the dreaded rota of Station 75! Rose is hoping she might meet someone there that knows her American uncle or cousins.'

The precious hour passed by as they talked and laughed and enjoyed being together again. Winnie was conscious of their limited time ticking down and that soon Mac would have to report back, but even that was curtailed when the door of the cafe burst open and another sapper rushed in.

'Mac, we've got to go!'

'All right, I'm coming.' Mac stood up. 'I'm sorry, I'm going to have to go.' He reached out and pulled Winnie to her feet and kissed her. 'I'm glad you came, I really am.'

Winnie grabbed hold of his hand and followed him out of the door. 'Be careful, Mac.'

'I always am. I love you.'

'I love you, too.'

Mac gave her one last kiss and hugged her fiercely before running across the road back to the depot, leaving her standing there. She watched him until he disappeared inside the building and, for once in her life, Winnie didn't know what to do; she wanted to stamp her feet and yell out that they should still have at least fifteen minutes left together, but what good would that do? He had a job to do and when the call came he had to go, just like they did at Station 75. The war didn't stop so husbands and wives could spend precious time together.

There was nothing for it but to go back to

Colchester station and back to London, but she wasn't going anywhere until she'd waved Mac off, hungry for any fleeting glimpse of him that she could get before she left. She crossed the road and stood outside the school gates that led into the playground, where she could see men climbing into the back of one of the army lorries with its distinctive red-painted mudguards, which declared they were bomb disposal to all who saw them. Mac was among them, changed out of his khaki uniform now and dressed in the denims they wore for digging out the bombs. One of his fellow sappers spotted her and must have called to Mac because he leaned out of the back of the canvas-covered truck and waved to her. She smiled at him and waved back, flinging her arm high in a wide arc above her head.

An army car drove out first, driven by the officer she'd spoken to earlier; he, too, smiled and raised his hand to her. Next came the lorry and Winnie's heart was thudding hard as it swung out past her and turned to follow the officer in the car — there in the back, standing in the middle and hanging on to the side was Mac. He smiled at her and blew a kiss, much to the amusement of his fellow sappers who cheered and joined in as he waved to her. Winnie laughed and waved back, ignoring the stinging in her eyes; she didn't want to send him off with tears. She kept waving, her eyes glued to the figure in the middle of the lorry, until it turned left, and Mac was gone.

Winnie dropped her hand to her side and stared after the lorry, letting the tears run

233

unchecked down her face. Watching Mac drive away had left a heavy feeling in her stomach. Before, she had only been able to imagine what it looked like when he went off to deal with a UXB, but now she knew the reality. The image of him in the back of the lorry packed with all the equipment needed — the tools, wheelbarrows, sandbags — as well as Mac's fellow sappers was imprinted on her mind.

Winnie sighed. Had she been too impulsive coming here to see him? Should she have thought it through properly beforehand? Probably, but nothing would have changed her desire to see Mac; what was done was done now, and she had to live with the consequences. Seeing him, even for such a short time, had been wonderful and that's what she had to hold on to.

★　★　★

Back home in Bedford Place that evening, Winnie paced up and down the black and white tiled hall of Connie's house. Should she telephone Mac's bomb depot or not? She hadn't heard from him and had no idea if he'd come back or not from the call-out she'd waved him off to. It was over nine hours ago now and she was worried. Normally she'd have had no idea when he was out digging up a bomb, but today she'd seen him go, known he was at risk, and it worried her dreadfully. It was far worse than the general worry she had for him.

'Are you still out here watching the telephone?' Bella asked, coming out of the drawing room. 'Why don't you just telephone and ask? Mac doesn't normally ring you every time he gets back from a job and he probably wouldn't think to do so this time. If it's worrying you that much, just do it, Winnie.' Bella touched her arm and went down the stairs to the kitchen in the basement.

Bella was right, Winnie thought, Mac probably wouldn't think to telephone, so she should just put her mind at ease. She grabbed the telephone receiver and gave the operator the number she needed.

'Hello,' Winnie said when the other end was answered. 'Can I speak to Mac, Sapper William McCartney, please?'

'Hold on, I'll find out if he's back,' the man's voice said.

The telephone receiver at the other end was put down and she could hear army-boot footsteps, a door opening and muffled voices followed by approaching footsteps again and the receiver being picked up.

'Mac?' she said.

'He's not back yet, I'm afraid. Can I take a message?'

Icy cold fingers trickled down Winnie's spine. 'Shouldn't he have been back by now?'

'There's no telling; depends if they have to work around the clock to get the job done. Is there a message for him?'

'Yes, just tell him his wife telephoned.'

'Will do, goodbye.'

Why isn't he back? Winnie thought, replacing the receiver. Had something gone wrong? She was more worried than ever now and there wasn't a thing she could do to fix it. All she could do was wait and she wasn't very good at that.

40

Frankie was nervous. Why on earth she'd volunteered for this job she didn't know. At the time it had seemed like a good idea but now she was actually here and about to enter a world she knew nothing about, she wanted to turn around, run all the way back to Station 75 and tell the boss she'd made a terrible mistake. But she couldn't, for starters people were expecting her to help today and every Tuesday afternoon from now on. She'd feel bad if she let them down and Station Officer Steele wouldn't be happy either. Bracing herself, she took a deep breath and pushed open the outside door of the day nursery.

Inside, the nursery was surprisingly quiet. She'd expected it to be noisy, with babies crying and children playing, but instead there was an air of calm and as the matron showed her around she saw why — the children were napping.

'These children are between two and five years old,' Matron explained in a whisper, as they looked over the room where children were lying fast asleep on little canvas beds, their small forms snuggled up under blankets. She'd already told Frankie that the nursery was divided into two parts — the toddler nursery that they were standing in now and the baby nursery for those from six months to two years.

'You'll be helping out in the baby nursery where an extra pair of hands will be most welcome — it's this way.'

Frankie's stomach dropped at the thought of having to help with babies. She'd held little Flora often enough but not done any of the actual caring for her — changing nappies, feeding her. Sitting holding her didn't require much skill, as all she had to do was sit there. Following Matron through to another room where again children were napping, she wanted to explain that she really didn't think she would be much use.

'The babies spend most of their time in their cots.' Matron waved her hand to where cots were lined up against the wall and where some nursery nurses were checking their charges, looking so calm and efficient in their uniforms with pristine white aprons. 'But the older children,' she pointed to the other side of the room where more small, low canvas beds were lined up with sleeping children on them, 'those who can crawl and walk, enjoy playing with toys and that's what I'd like you to help with. Building wooden blocks, reading them stories, that sort of thing.' Matron smiled. 'I hope you'll enjoy it very much, the children are delightful.'

Frankie smiled back at her, grateful that she wasn't going to be responsible for taking care of babies. Reading stories and building blocks with the older children, now that sounded straightforward enough; perhaps this wouldn't be so bad after all.

Matron glanced at her watch. 'Nap time is almost up, so if you'd like to spread a blanket out on the floor over in that corner and get some toys out of the cupboard there, then you'll soon have some children to entertain.'

Once she'd arranged her area with a selection of toys spread out on an army blanket on the floor, Frankie sat and waited for her first children to wake up — they were beginning to stir in the little beds, clearly used to the routines of the nursery.

Looking around her, she saw how everything was set up to care for the children in their charge, with small nursery-sized tables and chairs where the children would eat their meals. Many of the toys were home-made since new ones were now scarce in the shops. She'd picked some lovely hand puppets made from old socks out of the cupboard for the children to play with, all carefully sewn with stitched eyes or bits added to make ears, noses or even tongues.

'This is Gracie,' a nursery nurse said, putting a little girl down on the blanket near Frankie. 'She's eighteen months old.'

The little girl had rosy cheeks from her sleep and had her thumb firmly stuck in her mouth; she looked at Frankie with huge brown eyes.

'And this is Robert,' another nursery nurse said, sitting him down beside Gracie. 'He's just turned one and is still crawling, but watch him because he's fast and can soon disappear. Try and keep him with you here on the blanket.'

'Hello.' Frankie smiled at both children, who were unconcerned by her being new and were already reaching for the toys that she'd put out.

'Enjoy yourself and if you need anything just call us,' the older nursery nurse said, before rushing off to deal with other children that were waking up.

Looking down at her new charges, she smiled at them. 'I'm Frankie.' Gracie and Robert ignored her and carried on with what they were doing. Robert had picked up a sock puppet and had started to suck it and Gracie was pushing a block around, her thumb still firmly stuck in her mouth.

'What shall we play?' Frankie tried again. But the two children didn't respond. Robert had pushed himself on to his hands and knees and was crawling around the blanket.

'How about building something?' She picked up some more wooden blocks and began to stack them into a house shape, which caught Gracie's attention, and the little girl joined in, handing Frankie more blocks to add. Frankie had almost finished a second layer of bricks when she realised that Robert wasn't on the blanket. She turned and saw him crawling determinedly towards the cots, going surprisingly fast.

Leaping to her feet, Frankie hurried after him and scooped him up, his little legs pumping in the air as he yelled in surprise.

'Come on, back to the blanket with you.'

'Told you he was quick,' one of the nursery nurses said, smiling at her as Frankie returned to the blanket where, thankfully, Gracie still sat adding more bricks on to the pile.

Clearly looking after two children wasn't simple, she needed to do something that would keep them both occupied. Reaching over to the pile of toys she selected a sock puppet and put it on and then started to play around, making it tap Gracie on the shoulder and then hide away when she looked. Robert was transfixed and then started to chuckle, a delightful gurgling sound that she couldn't help joining in with.

Pulling another sock puppet on to her other hand, she started to make up a little story with them, adding funny voices and sometimes hiding one behind her back so that the children had to point to where it was. The game kept them enthralled and Robert didn't try to escape again.

After that they played with some little tin cars and some wooden animals and finally Frankie read them a story, with Robert crawling into her lap and Gracie leaning against her, putting her podgy hand on Frankie's arm. It was a lovely end to what had turned into a fun but exhausting afternoon.

'You've done very well,' Matron said as Frankie handed Gracie and Robert back into the care of the nursery nurses who had set up the little tables with a drink of milk for the children. 'Did you enjoy it?'

'I did, though it's a lot more tiring than I'd expected,' Frankie said. 'You've got to keep watch on them all the time.'

Matron nodded her head. 'Indeed, but you did well to keep them occupied. So next Tuesday at the same time, then?'

Frankie smiled. 'I'll be here.'

41

Winnie worked the rake back and forth, reducing the crumbly soil to a fine tilth ready to sow some rows of carrots and beetroot. Normally, this sort of work would have a soothing effect on her, but not today; she still felt as out of sorts as she had when she'd woken up this morning, and in fact ever since she'd watched Mac drive off to dig up an unexploded bomb yesterday, her hopes for spending time with him disappearing like water down a plughole. She hadn't heard a thing from him since and that worried her more than usual. Had he come back from dealing with it, or were they still working on it . . . or . . . ? Stop it! She wasn't going to let herself think about the alternative or she'd turn herself into a nervous wreck. Going to see him yesterday was supposed to have been a joyful occasion, a chance to spend some precious time together, but it had backfired on her spectacularly and now she felt worse than before.

'Winnie, is it ready to sow the seeds?' Rose's voice brought Winnie's thoughts back to what she should be focusing on: the planting of seeds at Station 75's allotment in the dry moat of the Tower of London.

She looked down at where she'd been working and was satisfied that she'd prepared the soil well. 'I'll mark out a line and you can plant the seeds if you like, a couple of rows of carrots and then the same of beetroot and we can sow some more in a few weeks.' Winnie used the corner of her rake to make a shallow trench across the width of the vegetable bed for Rose to plant the seeds in. 'I'll mark the ends of the rows with sticks so we know where we've planted them.'

With the seeds successfully sown and covered over with soil, all they had left to do was to cut a couple of spring cabbages to take back for Mrs Connelly to cook for the crew members later on.

'Come on, let's have a sit-down in the sunshine,' Winnie said, making her way over to the boundary wall of the Tower. 'We'll cut the cabbages just before we go back so they'll be fresh.'

'But shouldn't we be getting back to Station 75?' Rose asked, following her.

'A ten-minute break soaking up some spring sunshine will do us good.' Winnie settled herself down and leaned back against the wall. Trixie, who'd been sniffing around the allotment, came over to join them and sat down beside her, resting her head on her mistress's lap and promptly falling asleep. 'I wish I could drop off as easily as she does.' She stroked the little dog's silky ears, aware of knots of tension that had settled in her shoulders yesterday and hadn't shifted.

'This is lovely,' Rose said, settling down beside her. 'I like to think of all the history that has passed by here, all the things these old stones have seen, imagine what stories they could tell.'

'Mac told me Queen Elizabeth the First was imprisoned in the Tower before she became queen. He loves history and with him being a teacher he's taught me a lot more about it than I ever learned at school he — ' She stopped as a sudden wave of angst gripped her.

'Winnie?' Rose looked worried. 'Are you all right? You have gone very pale.'

Winnie sighed. 'I am and I'm not.'

'Are you ill?'

'No, just worried about Mac. You know I went to see him yesterday but I'm afraid that it's made things worse rather than better.'

'Wasn't he pleased to see you?' Rose asked.

'Oh yes, he was surprised but he was as pleased to see me as I was him, and everything was going swimmingly till a beastly UXB needed digging up and defusing and he had to rush off with the rest of the bomb disposal chaps. Watching him go — ' She stopped again, her throat painful with emotion. 'Well, before I didn't know how it actually looked, I could imagine it, though I tried not to, but now . . . I know what happens and can picture it as it is. Ignorance was bliss compared to knowing the reality. Actually, as much as I wanted to see Mac, it might have been better for me if I hadn't gone charging off to see him and then had to witness him rushing off like that to do his job.'

'You can't unsee it again,' Rose said sympathetically.

'Exactly. I thought I was doing the right thing and it was absolutely wonderful to see him.' She smiled, remembering how marvellous it felt to hold him in her arms again and just be together. 'You know, this is where Mac asked me to marry him, down here at the allotment.'

Rose smiled at her. 'That is a good memory to have here.'

'Yes.' Winnie nodded. 'It is. I need to hold on to that and try not to dwell on worrying, though it isn't always easy, is it?'

'No.' Rose sighed. 'I worry every day for my family.'

Winnie reached out and patted Rose's arm. 'When you love people it's natural, and with everything that's going on in this ghastly war there are so many more things to worry about than normal.'

★   ★   ★

Arriving back at Station 75 a short while later, Rose went to put the tools away in the garage, while Winnie, with a spring cabbage tucked under each arm, headed for the kitchen. She met Station Officer Steele coming through the door out to the courtyard.

'They look good cabbages,' the boss said. 'I'm sure Mrs Connelly will be delighted with them.' She started to walk across the courtyard towards the garages but then turned back. 'Winnie, did you finish the inventory of the stores early?'

'No, I haven't done it yet; I'm going to start on it right after I've delivered these to the kitchen. I thought it best to go to the allotment while the weather was good and do the inventory later.' Winnie didn't add that she'd thought working at the allotment might be better for her mood than the tedious job of checking lists against the station's stores.

'It's on the rota for you to do that job between eleven and twelve, and now it's . . . ' The boss glanced at her watch. 'It's ten past twelve and you haven't even started it yet.'

The small amount of good feeling that she'd gained from sitting in the sunshine and talking to Rose instantly evaporated and Winnie started to bristle. 'Does it really matter if I do it now? It will still get done.'

Station Officer Steele's eyes narrowed behind her owlish spectacles. 'I'm trying to run an ambulance station here, Winnie, one that should be ready to respond to a call at a moment's notice, and to do that, jobs need to be done and everything must be in perfect working order. The rota is there to make sure that happens. Imagine if all the crew members took your attitude and did things when they felt like it, where would that leave us?'

Winnie was aware that other crew members who were working on the ambulances and within earshot were listening to them whilst trying to look as though they were doing their jobs. 'It's only checking the stores, not preparing an ambulance; what difference does an hour make either way?'

'Those stores provide essential equipment for the ambulances. I expect you to stick to the rota and do the job you have been *told* to do and as *Deputy Station Officer* you should be setting an example to the others!'

'Don't you think you are taking this rota business too far? We never had such a rigid

246

timetable before and we managed just fine, and that was through the thick of the Blitz.' Winnie shook her head. 'It's ridiculous that there can't be a bit of leeway.'

Station Officer Steele's brown eyes glinted. 'Take those cabbages to the kitchen and I'll see you in my office.' She turned on her heels and marched back inside, letting the door slam behind her. Winnie sighed. She was in for it now.

'You all right?' Sparky came over to her, wiping his oily hands on a rag. 'You know the boss has got a bee in her bonnet about that bleedin' rota and you've just gone and stirred up the whole damn beehive.'

'Thanks for that, Sparky. I didn't mean to, but honestly, does it really matter when a job is done, especially one like that? I was just about to start it anyway.'

Sparky shrugged. 'According to the boss, it does. Good luck up there, you might well need it.'

'Look after Trixie for me, will you? I don't want her being upset if things get a bit heated and shouty up there; and I think they might, the way I feel right now.'

Sparky raised his eyebrows. 'You want to watch yourself, Winnie. Don't go looking for trouble.' He bent down and picked up Trixie who as usual was close by her mistress.

Winnie shrugged. 'I'll try to behave, Sparky. But honestly, it's ridiculous worrying about a stupid rota when there are much more important things to worry over.'

By the time Winnie had delivered the cabbages

247

and made her way to the boss's office her temper was bubbling away beneath the surface like lava in a volcano. After the day she'd had yesterday and the worrying over Mac, it wasn't going to take much for her to blow up. This wasn't a good time to face Station Officer Steele but the boss had ordered her there and she had no choice but to go.

Knocking on the office door she tried to dampen down the fizzing feeling running through her body. She breathed deeply and waited for the boss to call her to come in.

But instead the door was pulled open by a stony-faced Station Officer Steele, who motioned for her to come in.

'Sit down, Winnie.'

The boss remained standing and started to pace up and down the small office for a few moments, her lips set in a thin line, before she stopped and turned to face Winnie, her hands on her hips.

'I am doing my best to not immediately demote you, Winnie. I expected better from my Deputy, you are supposed to help and support me, not question my orders and *especially* not in front of other crew members.'

'Even if I don't agree with them?' The words were out of Winnie's mouth before her brain could filter them for appropriateness. She stood up to stand face to face with the boss. 'Because I don't! I think this whole rota business is ridiculous in so many ways. Have a list of daily jobs, weekly jobs, that's absolutely fine, but to nit-pick and have a minute-by-minute timetable with no flexibility on jobs that aren't essential is utterly ludicrous.' She threw her arms wide in exasperation. 'It's just putting crew members' backs up. Mine included!'

Station Officer Steele didn't say a word. Her silence seemed to fill the room and it was worse than if she'd retaliated straight back. Part of Winnie wanted to say something funny to defuse the situation but the stubborn part of her wasn't going to budge an inch, and if she got demoted then so be it.

When the boss did speak her voice was quiet and clipped. 'All I am trying to do is run Station 75 efficiently so that we can respond when we're needed. I am not trying to be a tyrant.'

Her quiet tone was like a slap in the face to Winnie; she would rather the boss had shouted at her. 'I know, but is it worth worrying about things like exactly when a non-essential job gets done when there's so much other stuff going on and things to worry about?'

'Such as?' Station Officer Steele's shrewd eyes held Winnie's.

Winnie felt her cheeks grow warm. 'Well, our families and friends and . . . husbands.'

'Ah, Mac.' The boss nodded. 'I might have known.'

Winnie folded her arms. 'Known what?'

'Sit down, Winnie.' The older woman pulled out the chair at her desk and sat down in it and waited until Winnie was seated too. 'What happened yesterday when you went to see Mac? You didn't have a falling-out, did you? Is that what all this is about?'

249

'How did you know I went to see Mac?'

'As I've told you before, there is very little that goes on at Station 75 that I don't know about.' The boss paused. 'Sparky told me, actually.'

Winnie rolled her eyes. 'No, we didn't have a falling-out, he was very pleased to see me, actually, and what time we had together was lovely.'

'So what's got you into this mood then?'

'A call came in of a UXB and Mac had to rush off to deal with it.' Winnie sighed. 'I watched him go.'

'I see. And it's haunting you now you know more about what goes on?'

Winnie nodded.

'Is that why you went to the allotment instead of doing what was on the rota? I know you love it down there.'

'Yes.' Winnie sighed and looked down at her clasped hands. She suddenly realised that her bad mood was softening like a pricked balloon. 'I felt bloody-minded and needed to do something that might help.'

'You should have come and talked to me about it before charging off and causing havoc with my rota . . . ' Winnie looked up at the boss and was surprised to see her smiling at her. 'I am always here to talk to, you know; better that than do something you'll regret.'

'Are you going to demote me, then?' Winnie asked.

'Do you think I should?'

Winnie shrugged. 'I was rude to you and I apologise for that, but I do think there ought to be a bit of leeway in the rota on non-essential jobs that don't have to be done by a specific time.'

Station Officer Steele raised her eyebrows. 'Indeed. Well, I take your point.' She paused for a few moments. 'One of the reasons I worked out the rota was to keep me busy — you know, stop me from worrying so much about my sister before I knew that she'd escaped from Singapore. I still worry about her but at least she's safer in South Africa than she was in the Far East.'

'You just swapped one worry for another,' Winnie said.

'Exactly.' The boss looked thoughtful. 'You are a fine member of this ambulance station, Winnie, and I'm not going to demote you, but I *am* going to give you an official warning. Any more behaviour like this morning's and you will no longer be my Deputy. Is that understood?'

Winnie nodded — the boss was being fair and she deserved it.

'Our job is important and we need to conduct ourselves in a professional manner, regardless of what we have going on in our personal lives. We all have our problems, Winnie, and we must not let them affect our work, especially in our positions when we have the responsibility of the crew and running the station smoothly.' Station Officer Steele sighed. 'But I'm not immune to taking constructive criticism so I'm going to ease up a bit on the rota on non-essential timed jobs. I think perhaps I was being a bit too . . . well, dictatorial, and the last thing I want to do is put the crew's backs up. But I am going to say to you that in future, if you're given a job to do which for any reason you don't agree with, then come and see me immediately, do not take it into your own hands to change things without my say-so. Understand?'

'Yes. Thank you.' Winnie smiled. 'I'm glad you're going to ease up on the rota; all the crew will be happy about that.'

'Right, there's a stores cupboard that needs checking.' Station Officer Steele smiled. 'And by the time you've got that done it should be time for lunch, I think. We'll see what Mrs Connelly has done with those cabbages.'

Winnie stood up and made for the door before the boss could change her mind.

'Oh, Winnie, I know it's easier to say than do, but try not to worry too much about Mac. He's no fool and he won't take risks. He wants to come home to you as much as you want him to.'

42

'How about if this goes here?' Bella said, putting a recipe for carrot cake from Sparky's wife on the left of the mock-up page of *Seventy-five Blitz & Pieces*. 'And then this can go here.' She moved a cartoon that Frankie had drawn of Mrs Connelly busy at work in the kitchen preparing a meal while hungry crew members peered through the door at her.

Frankie nodded. 'Yes, I think that works well.'

The pair of them were sitting at the large table in the common room, busy working on the first edition of the station magazine. All the finished pieces were typed up and ready to go, their job now was to arrange them ready for printing, making the magazine look good with a variety of interesting things on each page.

It had taken nearly two months to get this far after Bella had agreed to take charge of producing a magazine, partly because she was having to fit it around her work here and her voluntary work at the Red Cross parcel packing centre, and partly because she had to allow time for crew members to write their pieces or do drawings or whatever they were contributing to *Seventy-five Blitz & Pieces*. It was a far cry from the deadlines she'd grown used to writing to for *The War Illustrated*, but it was rather nice to work at a more leisurely pace and not have the time pressure imposed by a fortnightly printing of the magazine.

'Any chance of a sneak peek?' Sparky said, coming over to see what they were doing.

Frankie put her arms out, leaning on the table to cover up what they'd been working on. 'No! You'll have to wait the same as everyone else.'

'Well, 'ow much longer, then?' he asked.

'Providing we can get this finished tonight,' Bella said pointedly, 'then we'll be going to the printers tomorrow and then the magazine will be for sale soon after.'

'Reserve me a copy, won't yer?' Sparky said. 'Want to see me words in print and my missis her recipe.'

'We certainly will.' Bella smiled at him.

Sparky nodded and leaned over Frankie's shoulder to see if he could see anything.

'Sparky! Clear off so we can get this finished or you won't be gettin' your copy any time soon.' Frankie glared at him. 'Hop it!'

He held up his hands in surrender. 'All right, I'm goin'; it's only 'cos I'm looking forward to it, that's all.'

Frankie sighed. 'Well, leave us alone to get on with it then.'

'I'm goin'.' Sparky grinned and finally left them in peace.

Bella started to laugh.

'What's so funny?' Frankie sat up and straightened out the paper she'd shielded from Sparky's prying eyes.

'You defending and protecting the magazine.'

'After all the work we've put in, we don't want

254

him seein' it and telling everyone what's in there, do we?'

'No, of course not. Well, at least we know we've sold one copy,' Bella said. 'I'm a bit worried we won't sell many more.'

Frankie frowned. 'I think we will — everyone who's put something in it will want a copy and the rest of the crew who haven't will want one to see what they've been up to. Friends and family might buy one — Connie, for instance, though I know Ivy won't bother. We could even try to sell some at other ambulance stations.'

'I hope so; if we print enough for every crew member and a few extra it should be enough.'

'What about another issue after this one?' Frankie said. 'Will you do one?'

Bella shrugged. 'Perhaps. I've enjoyed doing this and it's been nice to not have to write to a deadline. I do miss writing but not the struggling sometimes to think of something new and interesting to write about. If the magazine's popular we can perhaps think of doing another one, maybe quarterly so there's no rush, and we can enjoy the process.'

'We ain't no competition to Fleet Street then?' Frankie smiled.

'But it's good to do something our way and with our people. I think they're goin' to like *Seventy-five Blitz and Pieces*.'

43

The sound of Ivy's raucous laughter met Frankie as she opened the door of 25 Matlock Street. She'd spent most of Saturday morning in queues shopping for food, but the number of things she'd got in the shopping basket didn't warrant the amount of time it had taken for her to get them. Still, at least with her and Rose combining their rations it helped to stretch things a little further when it came to making meals.

Ivy's laughter came again and this time it was joined by a deep chuckle that was most definitely not Rose's. Not that Frankie had ever seen Ivy and Rose laugh together; they generally avoided each other as much as possible. Someone was here: a man. Frankie was instantly on alert. Who was it and why were they here?

Pausing by the kitchen door, Frankie listened to voices talking inside before she went in, there was definitely a man in there and from the sound of his voice he wasn't English.

Opening the door, she marched into the kitchen and stopped at the sight of an American soldier sprawled in one of the armchairs. Ivy was perched on his lap, her hair coming down out of the waves and rolls she favoured and her lipstick smudged over the edges ofher lips. Her skirt was riding up, revealing her thighs.

'Well, hello there,' the man drawled in an

American accent. 'And who is this, Ivy — your daughter?'

Ivy staggered to her feet, her unsteadiness betraying her drunken state before Frankie took in the empty bottle of gin and glasses on the table. 'She ain't no daughter of mine.' Her words came out slurred.

'Gee, she's a beauty, whoever she is.' The American rose to his feet and swaying slightly held out his hand to Frankie. 'Pleased to meet you, miss.'

Frankie plonked her shopping basket down on the table and ignored his hand. 'I'm Ivy's step-*granddaughter*.'

'Granddaughter!' The American looked stunned and grabbed at Ivy's arm. 'Are you old enough to be a grandma?' He started to laugh. 'Gee, I ain't never dated a grandma before.'

'You should go,' Frankie said. 'Now!'

The American looked at Ivy, who opened her mouth to speak and swayed, before grabbing the back of the chair and slumping down into it. 'We was only having a good time. I don't mean no harm, miss.'

'I'm sure you don't, but it's time you were leavin'.' Frankie went to the kitchen door and stood by it, waiting for him to move.

'So long, Ivy,' he paused. 'Grandma.'

Ivy glared at him. 'Bugger off.' She leaned against the back of the chair and closed her eyes.

The American looked hurt. 'Don't worry, I'm going. Who wants to date a grandma? You shouldn't go around picking up guys at your age, you said you were thirty.'

Frankie bit back a laugh. 'And then some. You should be more careful in future who you . . . date.'

'I sure will, just wait till the guys hear I landed myself a grandma,' the American said as he lumbered out of the room and followed Frankie to the front door. 'If you wanna go on a date, I'd be real happy to show you a good time.' He swayed towards Frankie who side-stepped him and opened the front door.

'I'll give it a miss. Goodbye.' She closed the door behind him and leaned back against it with a sigh. What had Ivy been up to? From the state of her, she and the American had gone well past the holding-hands stage, if they'd even bothered with that. Had she no dignity or decency? What would her grandad have thought? Frankie took a deep breath and went back to the kitchen, preparing for battle.

'What the hell are you playin' at, Ivy? He was young enough to have been your son.'

Ivy's icy blue eyes snapped open. 'I was just havin' a bit of fun, that's all, until you came home and spoiled it all.'

'What would Grandad have said? He'd have been disgusted the way you're carryin' on, have you no shame?'

'He's dead, in case you hadn't noticed, and I ain't. I ain't going to sit around moping cause he's gone; none of us know how long we've got. I'm goin' to enjoy my life and if I want to go out with a Yank I will.' She smiled, her smudged lipstick making it look more frightening than friendly. 'Look what he gave me.' She stretched

258

out one leg and smoothed her hand along her stocking.

'Helped me put it on an all.' She giggled.

'He's not coming back here.'

Ivy shrugged. 'There's plenty more Yanks around who want to show a lady a good time. He ain't the only one. And you can't tell me what to do or stop me havin' fun with them. I bet you don't know how to have a good time with that Scottish fella of yours.' Frankie stared at the woman whose behaviour still had the power to surprise her. It was awful enough having to live with her, but this — having a swipe at her relationship with Alastair — was a new low. She knew Ivy was trying to goad her into a full-blown row, deflecting her from what she'd just done, but she wasn't going to take the bait. 'You're right, I can't stop you seeing them, but I'm not havin' you bringing them back here.'

'You can't stop me — ' Ivy began.

'If you want to stay livin' here then you won't, Ivy! I'm not going to put up with you bringing strange men home and behaving like some tart. If you carry on like that I'm leaving. Remember, if I leave you can't afford the rent and you'll lose the house. And I can go at any time; I've got somewhere to go to, have you?'

Ivy ignored her question and stood up, grabbing hold of the table to steady herself. 'I'm going to lay down.'

'I mean it, Ivy. You should know better than to behave like that and I ain't going to put up with it.'

The only response Ivy made was to slam the

kitchen door hard, making the plates on the dresser rattle, before she stomped up the stairs and repeated the door slamming with her bedroom door.

Frankie sighed and sat down at the table, resting her head in her hands. She was glad that Rose hadn't been here to witness that — she'd gone to try to get into a concert at the National Gallery after hearing about Frankie and Alastair's last visit there.

Living with Ivy was always difficult, yet somehow the impossible woman still found ways to make it worse, pushing at the boundaries and horrifying Frankie with her irresponsible behaviour. It would have appalled her grandad and made it so much harder for Frankie to live with the woman and fulfil the promise she'd made to him. How much longer could she go on putting up with Ivy's behaviour? When would she reach the point of saying no more? Would Ivy do as she'd told her and not bring any more men back here? Frankie wasn't here all the time — the new twenty-four-hour shifts she was working would give Ivy ample opportunity to bring men home.

What would happen if Ivy got caught out and ended up in the family way? She was still young enough to have a baby. At forty she'd been fifteen years younger than Grandad and when she was dressed up with her hair done and face painted she passed for younger. It was no wonder the Yank had fallen for her.

What a mess, Frankie thought. Things would be so much better if Ivy just left — she'd be able to live her life as she saw fit and Frankie wouldn't have the bother of her. But that was unlikely to happen unless her step-grandmother got a much better offer, because she was clinging on to a home at 25 Matlock Street and wouldn't give it up easily.

44

Walking in through the door of the American Eagle Club on Charing Cross Road, under the Stars and Stripes flag that was flown over the entrance, Winnie always felt as if she were stepping into somewhere out of the ordinary and slightly removed from the everyday life of London. She didn't know if it was the Americans' accent, their different uniforms or their mannerisms, but it was as if they brought a part of their country with them. It wasn't only the Americans that frequented the club — all Allied servicemen were welcome there.

Since she and Rose had started volunteering at the club on Wednesday afternoons, they'd done a variety of jobs depending on what help was needed. Last week they'd been making up beds, but today she was put to work serving at the coffee bar while Rose had been asked to go and help with sewing, as there were often servicemen who needed buttons sewn on.

'There we are.' She smiled at the two Americans standing the other side of the bar as she handed them their cups of steaming coffee.

'Thank you, ma'am,' they said together.

'Is this your first visit to London?' Winnie asked. She always liked to have a chat with the men if they weren't too busy.

'It sure is,' the taller of the two said. 'It's a swell place.'

'It certainly is, in spite of all the bomb damage. Thankfully there are still plenty of beautiful buildings standing. Where have you been so far?'

'We only just arrived,' the shorter man said. 'We're planning on having a good look round.'

'Did you know you can get a free ticket for a show from the information desk here?' she said;

'No, that sounds good; we should get one and see a show,' the shorter serviceman said.

'I hope you enjoy it and the rest of your stay in London.' Winnie smiled warmly at them and went to serve another serviceman who'd just arrived at the bar.

The afternoon flew by as she served coffee and the occasional cup of tea, and it was almost time to leave when Rose came hurrying into the coffee bar.

'You've got to come and see this before we go, Winnie,' Rose said.

'What's going on?' Winnie said, following her out of the room and up the stairs to the upper floor. 'What is it?'

Rose smiled at her. 'You'll see, just be very quiet when we go in.' She led the way to the door of one of the larger rooms, opened it quietly and slipped inside.

Winnie followed her and was surprised to see what was going on inside. The room was set out with rows of chairs, each one occupied by a serviceman, and others were standing around the outside, all of them watching what was going on at the front of the room. A tall radio microphone was set up and men were taking it in turns to

263

speak into it, sending messages home.

Standing quietly at the back of the room, Winnie listened as the announcer introduced the next man who walked up to the microphone.

'Sergeant Dan Johanson, where are you from?'

'Chicago, Illinois,' Dan Johanson said.

'Go ahead and send your message home,' the announcer said.

'I'd like to say hello to my folks. I enjoy getting all your letters and look forward to that can of peanut butter you promised to send.' The audience laughed, no doubt many of them missing peanut butter too. 'Happy Birthday to Jack. It's not so bad here, the British treat us well and we had hamburgers today.' The room erupted into cheers and clapping, Winnie and Rose joining in, as Dan finished his message and the next man stood up to take his turn.

They watched a few more men speaking their messages to their family and friends back home before it was time for them to head off to work at Station 75. Seeing the men having their contact with home, no matter how distant and fleeting, touched Winnie, it reinforced her feeling that the Eagle Club was a special place and she was glad that she had the chance to come there and help.

45

'How are we going to sell these?' Bella asked. 'Do you think the best way is to go around and ask each crew member if they want one?'

Frankie stopping untying the string that was bound around one of the piles of magazines that they'd just fetched from the printers. 'There's only one way to do it, ain't there, and that's the proper way like all good newspaper sellers — we'll shout about it.'

'Ah . . . I don't know if we should, not here. It's not like it's in the street, is it?'

'It'll only be for a few minutes just to attract the crews' attention and get them buying the magazine. I'll do it if you'd rather not.' Frankie smiled. 'I'd enjoy it.'

Bella nodded. 'All right then, you do what needs to be done and I'll be ready to collect the money.'

They waited until break time, when many of the crew were sitting outside in the courtyard drinking their tea in the beautiful May sunshine, before launching their sales pitch.

'Ready?' Frankie asked before they opened the door to go outside into the courtyard, both with a pile of magazines in their arms and Bella with a tin to collect the money in.

'Yes, but I'm nervous, too,' Bella said.

Frankie frowned. 'Why?'

'In case they won't like it.'

'It's a great magazine, Bella. I'm proud to have been involved and have my drawings in there. The rest of the crew are going to love it too. You'll see. 'Ere goes, then.' Frankie took a deep breath, opened the door and walked out shouting, 'Roll up, roll up, get your *Seventy-five Blitz and Pieces* here.'

Bella stood in the doorway, watching her friend as she marched across the courtyard, her voice as loud and clear as any East End market trader.

'Come on, line up properly,' Frankie shouted as Bella joined her in the courtyard, 'or you won't get your copy.'

Bella was stunned to see how keen the crew members were to get their hands on a magazine — they abandoned their deckchairs in the sun and hurried to buy their copies, crowding around them until Frankie had to shout for some order.

'Put your three pence in the tin,' Bella said, holding out a copy to Paterson, who had managed to get to the front of the queue.

'I've been looking forward to this. Is my poem in there?' Paterson asked, dropping his money into the tin with a satisfying clinking.

'Yes, it's a very good one and sums up working at Station 75 perfectly,' Bella said, 'and it's very funny too.' Paterson was quite the poet, his humorous poems a delight to read or hear — his last one had gone down well at the concert.

'Roll up, roll up; get your station magazine 'ere!' Frankie shouted again. She nudged Bella's arm and nodded to the upstairs common-room windows where Winnie, Rose and other crew members had gathered to see what was going on. 'See, it attracts attention.'

Bella laughed. 'You're a natural at it.'

It didn't take long to sell the magazines they'd brought with them, as other crew members came down from the common room to buy their own copies, including Station Officer Steele.

Bella was thrilled to see how much interest and excitement *Seventy-five Blitz & Pieces* was generating, with exclamations of delight as people saw the pieces they'd written in print, or were laughing at something funny in there like problem page letters.

'Well, what do you think?' Frankie linked her arm through Bella's. 'I told you they'd love it.'

Bella smiled. 'I know you did and I'm very happy to say that you were quite right. This shift's crew have all bought a copy and there's enough left for the other shift to get tomorrow. I think we can honestly say this has been a great success.'

'Indeed, it has,' Station Officer Steele said, coming over to them.

'You have done an excellent job.' She flicked through the magazine. 'You should both be very proud of what you've achieved. I hope that this is the first edition — that there'll be more?'

Bella glanced at Frankie, who nodded. 'We were thinking of producing one quarterly.'

'Excellent idea, I look forward to it. Now if you'll excuse me, I'm going to start reading this while I have my cup of tea.' She smiled at them, turned on her well-polished heels and went inside.

'See! Praise indeed,' Frankie said.

46

It was after nine o'clock on a beautiful June evening, and with all the ambulance preparations and general duties done, many of the crew members were sitting outside enjoying the warmth. Some were down in the courtyard in front of the garages, but Frankie, Winnie, Bella and Rose had gone up on to the flat roof of Station 75 where they could enjoy the view out towards the Tower of London, Tower Bridge, the River Thames and beyond.

'Do you remember we were sitting up here the night of the first raid of the Blitz?' Winnie asked, leaning back against the chimney stack that poked up through the roof. 'We saw the bombers coming up the river like swarms of black flies.'

'Don't remind me.' Frankie looked up from the drawing she was doing. She sometimes dreamed of that night, hearing the drone of the approaching bombers in her sleep and the dull thud of bombs dropping as they came closer.

'It's part of our history now,' Winnie said. 'Something to tell our grandchildren in years to come.'

Bella stopped writing in her notebook; she'd been practising the shorthand she was learning on her course. 'You trying to tell us something, Winnie? You're not . . . in the family way, are you?'

'Absolutely not!' Winnie laughed. 'Seeing as I

see so little of Mac it would be impossible. Not that I wouldn't like children one day, but not now, in the middle of wartime; and, besides I'd have to leave Station 75 and I wouldn't want to do that.'

'Your mother would be delighted,' Bella said. 'She'd have you go and live with her and she could boss you around and — '

'Stop, stop, no more.' Winnie held up her hands. 'You're supposed to be my friend, so don't torment me.'

Bella pulled a sad face. 'I'm sorry; I didn't mean to upset you.'

'Would your mother not like to have grandchildren?' Rose asked.

'I'm not really sure, to be honest.' Winnie frowned. 'It's not something we've ever discussed. You see, my mother is rather . . . ' She paused.

'What Winnie is tryin' to say is that her mother's a difficult woman,' Frankie said. 'And that's an understatement.'

'Is she like Ivy?' Rose asked.

Frankie laughed. 'Only in that they are both difficult women, but they are very different types of people: Winnie's mother is far grander than Ivy.'

'Can you imagine if the two of them met?' Winnie said. 'That would — ' She stopped as a sudden, loud explosion echoed out across the rooftops.

'What on earth . . . ?' Frankie leapt to her feet and looked around, spotting a plume of smoke mushrooming several hundred feet up into the

269

air to the south of the river. 'Look!' She pointed towards it.

'What was it?' Bella said. She and the others were on their feet, staring at the smoke.

'Sounded like a bomb but the siren hasn't gone off.' Shielding her hand above her eyes, Winnie scanned the blue sky. 'There's no sign of any bombers.'

'What's goin' on?' a voice called from the courtyard below.

Frankie walked nearer to the edge of the roof. Looking down, she could see Sparky standing in the middle of the courtyard below.

'What the bleedin' hell was that?' he shouted up at her.

'Looks like an explosion south of the river,' Frankie called back.

Sparky shrugged. 'Well, we ain't had an air raid. Made me jump out of me skin.'

'I don't know what it is,' she called back to him. 'Go back to your game of cards.'

Sparky put his hand up in salute and re-joined the other crew members he'd been playing with.

'What do you think it was?' Bella asked as Frankie sat down again and picked up her sketchpad to continue with her drawing.

'I don't know. I know what it sounded like, but there ain't been no bombers dropping bombs tonight — we'd have seen and heard them sittin' up here. Perhaps it was a gas main blowing up or something.'

They settled down again to an uneasy silence, each wondering what had happened for such a loud explosion to echo out across the rooftops, from time to time glancing over to where there was still a cloud of smoke and dust hanging in the air south of the river.

A few minutes later, a loud piercing whistle from the courtyard broke their quiet reverie and had Frankie walking over to near the edge of the roof to see what was going on.

'Boss wants all you four in her office double quick,' Sparky called up. 'There's a call-out.'

She waved to him and made her way back to where the others were sitting. 'We've got to go; boss is sendin' us out on a call.'

'What, all of us?' Winnie asked.

'Yes.' Frankie held out her hand and pulled Winnie to her feet.

'So much for spending our evening enjoying this gorgeous sunshine,' Winnie said.

★   ★   ★

'I understand you've been up on the roof,' Station Officer Steele said a few minutes later when the four of them were gathered in her office.

'That's right, very nice it was up there too,' Winnie said. 'Beautiful in the sunshine, we — ' She stopped as Bella nudged her arm.

'Yes, well, a call's come in from out of our area. You may well have seen the cause of it,' the boss said, 'and heard it. I certainly did in here.'

'What was it?' Frankie said. 'We heard an explosion and saw smoke coming from south of the river.'

'There's been an explosion in Gurney Street,

Elephant and Castle, that's all I know, and they've called for ambulances to attend from other areas.'

'Must be bad.' Bella glanced at Frankie.

'Where's Gurney Street?' Winnie asked.

'Here.' Station Officer Steele pointed to the large street map of London pinned to her wall, which they referred to whenever they were sent out of their own area. 'You'll need to go across Tower Bridge, along Tower Bridge Road to here,' she traced their route with her finger, 'then right into New Kent Road and Gurney Street is here, the sixth street along on your left.' She handed Bella and Rose a chit each with the address of the incident on. 'I don't know what's happened, so be careful. Remember to keep your steel helmets on at all times.'

★   ★   ★

Driving across Tower Bridge felt very odd, Frankie thought, as they rarely went out to calls south of the river because it was out of the designated area that Station 75 served. The fact that they had been called showed that whatever they were going to was big and had resulted in a lot of casualties.

'I'm uneasy about this,' Bella said as they turned right on to the New Kent Road, their ambulance following Winnie's along the route. 'I don't usually feel like this going to an incident, but this feels odd, no siren or air raid, just a sudden, loud explosion. What do you think it was?'

272

'I don't know.' Frankie shrugged. She looked up at the sky over the area they were heading towards; it was tinged with a grey dustiness that obscured the blue, the smoke and dust lingering above it and not spreading far yet as it was such a still evening. 'We'll soon find out.'

Turning into Gurney Street, they were directed where to go by a policemen, and pulled up behind Winnie in a line of ambulances parked along the pavement in front of a line of tall, four-storey houses.

Winnie and Rose had already jumped out of their ambulance and were unloading a stretcher from the back. Winnie waved at them and pointed further down the street where, with some craning of their necks, they could see that the row of houses suddenly stopped and was replaced with a huge pile of rubble and debris that spilled out over the pavement.

'Look at that!' Bella said. 'What caused it?'

'I don't know, but from the size of it there must be a lot of people hurt.' Frankie touched Bella's arm. 'Come on, it's going to be a busy shift after all.'

Frankie had lost count of the number of incidents she'd attended since starting at Station 75, many of them out in the thick of the bombing, but this one tonight was odd. There was no raid in progress, there'd been no warning and yet something had happened here for houses to disintegrate into rubble, filling the air with the smell of dust, plaster and brick, which tickled the back of Frankie's throat. There was a strange air of disbelief on the faces of people they passed as she and Bella hurried to collect their first casualty. The street was busy, not just with the usual rescue workers and ARP wardens, but with normal people who lived in the street.

'Over 'ere,' a woman called to them from where she was kneeling down next to an unconscious, dust-covered man. 'It's me husband, he was outside.'

Frankie and Bella crouched down beside him and, with practised ease, quickly assessed the situation and the man's injuries.

'We'll need to splint his legs together,' Bella said, taking bandages out of her pack to tie his ankles together.

'What's his name?' Frankie asked the woman as Bella got to work.

'Jim. Jim Webster. I'm Eileen, his wife,' the woman said. 'Can't believe, it, there weren't no warning or nothin'. Whole block of flats gone and the houses.' She waved her hand towards the mountain of rubble where steel girders stuck out like bones and where rescue workers were desperately searching for survivors, many digging in the debris with their bare hands. 'I'd just gone indoors to make a cup of tea, we were outside talkin' to the neighbours, enjoying the lovely evening . . . ' Eileen looked at Frankie, her eyes wide with shock.

Frankie could imagine the scene, one that would have been played out in many streets across London on such a warm Saturday night, neighbours coming out of their houses to chatter on their doorsteps while their children played in the street. They did it in Matlock Street, often bringing out chairs to sit on and cups of tea; it was always a lovely time. She reached out and patted Eileen's arm. 'We'll soon get Jim to hospital; they'll look after him there.' She quickly wrote his name and details of the incident on to a label and secured it to his jacket for the hospital to use.

She and Bella were gently lifting him on to their stretcher when another woman came rushing up to Eileen, wringing her hands.

''Ave you seen my Stan and Vera? They were out playin' and I can't find 'em.'

'No, love, but I'll help you look.' Eileen kissed Jim's forehead and stood up. 'You'll look after 'im?

'Of course we will,' Bella said, tucking blankets around him and then securing him on to the stretcher with the straps.

'This is bad,' Frankie whispered to Bella as she made the final checks before they got ready to lift the stretcher. 'The street would 'ave been busy, with people . . . children out playing . . . '

Bella nodded. 'At least in an air raid they're safely tucked away in shelters. Whatever happened here caught everyone unawares.'

As soon as they'd filled the four stretchers in their ambulance, Frankie drove them to Guy's Hospital, part of the steady flow of ambulances that were ferrying the injured to hospital before returning to collect more. There was little time to dwell on what had happened there, the priority being to get the injured to hospital.

A little after two o'clock in the morning, Frankie and Bella returned to Gurney Street for the fourth time, the street now lit up with floodlights which had been brought in to help with the rescue efforts. Looking for a place to park, they spotted Sparky and Paterson loading up a casualty into their ambulance.

'What are they doing here?' Bella asked.

'Perhaps they put in a call for more help.' Frankie pulled up alongside them and opened her window. 'Did they send for reinforcements?'

Sparky jumped out of the back and came over to them. 'Nope, the boss sent us to replace you two. Winnie and Rose have already gone back to Station 75 and been replaced by Taylor and Pip, so go back to base and get some rest.'

'But — ' Frankie began.

'Just go, Frankie, the boss ain't daft, she knows how to make best use of her crews — better to send fresh ones to take over than keep you going till you drop. It ain't as if there's been any other call-outs tonight, just this one.'

Bella tugged at Frankie's arm. 'Come on; let's do as we're told.'

Frankie sighed. 'All right.' Now she thought about it she was beginning to feel tired, too tired to argue with Sparky and Bella or question the boss's orders. 'We'll see you back at the station, Sparky.'

47

Winnie's eyes felt gritty. She didn't know if it was from lack of sleep or the dusty air at the incident on Gurney Street. After being recalled to Station 75 she'd managed to get a few hours' sleep but it had been fitful and she'd found it hard to stop thinking about what she'd seen there and the niggling thought of what had happened to cause so much devastation.

'Here, get this down you.' Frankie put a mug of tea on the table in front of Winnie and sat down opposite her, leaning her elbow on the table, chin in her hand.

'Thanks. If you don't mind me saying, you look awful.' Winnie wrapped her hands around the mug and let its warmth seep in to her fingers. Her hands felt strangely cold considering it was looking like another beautiful summer's day outside.

'You ain't looking so great yourself,' Frankie batted back at her, her face breaking into a smile, making her look better, though it was going to take a bath to get the dust out of her auburn hair and her uniform needed a good brushing-down and wash.

'Didn't sleep well and . . . ' Winnie shrugged her shoulders. 'Something about that call-out . . . ' She shook her head.

'You as well.' Bella sat down next to her, putting a plate of toast on the table and motioning for them to help themselves.

Winnie took a slice. 'What do you mean?'

'Well, it was odd last night, we've been to a lot of incidents, but that one was strange, there was nothing to warn anyone — they were just going about their usual business on a warm summer's evening and boom . . . buildings coming down . . .'

'At least in an air raid, you get some warnin',' Frankie said, helping herself to a slice of toast.

'And they would 'ave been warned and evacuated if they'd known they'd got a UXB laying there,' Sparky said, coming into the common room out of Station Officer Steele's office.

'You're back!' Bella said.

'Just signed off the job.' Sparky nodded at the plate of toast. 'Got any spare?'

Bella handed the plate to him and he wiped his dusty hands on his dusty trousers before taking a slice. 'Ta.'

'What do you mean a UXB?' Winnie said, her stomach knotting.

'Is that what it was?'

Sparky nodded, his mouth full of toast.

'That explains a lot,' Frankie said. 'It must have been there for months. We ain't had a raid since last May, that's over a year ago, so it's been layin' there for at least a year, maybe longer.'

'That's what they reckon caused it,' Sparky went on. 'It must have fallen in the basement of one of the buildings and no one knew about it.'

'What made it blow up?' Winnie asked, the thought of the bomb lying there undetected, biding its time, waiting to suddenly explode, making icy fingers creep down her spine. Since Mac had joined the bomb disposal, any mention of UXBs always unnerved her, but they'd all been ones that were known about, not ones like the bomb in Gurney Street that had sinisterly lain there waiting while people went about their lives all around it until one day it exploded.

'They ain't sure; could have been a number of things, according to the rescue workers — changes in temperature or vibrations from traffic. They won't know for sure, only that it finally blew up and took a whole block of flats and some houses down with it.' Sparky sighed. 'They're still diggin' in the rubble for any more survivors.'

'How many people are still unaccounted for?' Bella asked.

Sparky shrugged. 'I don't know but a lot of them are children. They were out playin' in the street, it being such a lovely Saturday night . . . '

'But they'll keep looking for them, keep diggin',' Frankie said.

'Course they will.' Sparky nodded and rubbed his hand over his dusty eyes. He looked tired.

'It's not fair, bombs going off in air raids is bad enough, but to lie there like an insidious monster and blow up when little children are out playing with no warning, it's . . . ' Winnie shook her head.

'War ain't fair, you should know that by now,' Sparky said.

Winnie stood up. 'You don't need to remind me, Sparky. I've seen enough to know that. Our shift's almost over so I'm going to go and do what I can to help in Gurney Street. Bella, will you take Trixie home with you?'

'No!' Bella stood up. 'I won't, because I'm coming with you.'

'And me!' Frankie stood up too and came around the table, linking her arm through Winnie's. 'We're both comin' with you.'

Winnie smiled at her good friends, glad that they were coming with her, because for all her bravado and determination there was a prickle of fear of what she might be getting into nudging at her, but with Bella and Frankie beside her she'd be able to face anything.

'What about Trixie?' Frankie said. 'We can't take her there; she might be in the way or get hurt.'

'I'll look after her.' Rose had just come into the room having been asleep in the women's rest room and must have heard the last part of their conversation. 'I'll take her back to your house for you if you want.'

'Thank you, I appreciate that. Connie will be there.' Winnie smiled at her. 'Will you tell her what I'm doing?'

Rose nodded. 'Shall I then come to Gurney Street and help?'

'No, you go home and see to the 'ens for me; they'll need food and water and I know Ivy won't bother herself with them,' Frankie said quickly. 'I'll be back as soon as I can.'

'But you could — ' Winnie stopped as Frankie nudged her arm and gave her a slight shake of her head. Clearly, she didn't want Rose to go, no doubt wanting to protect her from what they might see. Frankie had become like a big sister to her since she'd gone to live with her at Matlock Street.

'Could what?' Rose asked.

'Have something ready for Frankie to eat when she gets home,' Winnie said, thinking quickly.

Rose nodded.

★　★　★

Back in Gurney Street, this time arriving on their bicycles, daylight showed the full horror of what had happened. The blast had punched a hole in the row of four-storey houses and toppled a neighbouring block of flats, making a crater more than twenty feet deep, and one hundred and twenty feet across. It was filled with large lumps of mortar and brick, with steel girders and wooden beams sticking at odd angles out of the thick, powdery, pulverised brick.

The site of devastation was filled with activity, as the Civil Defence's rescue workers painstakingly dug in the rubble looking for any signs of survivors or the bodies of those who hadn't survived. They carefully probed the wreckage, searching for gaps where someone might be sheltering, and cleared away debris that had been sorted through. Cranes had been brought in to shift rubble that had been removed and lorries stood ready to cart it away. They were doing all they could to find the missing.

'Have you seen a little boy, dark hair and blue

eyes, about this high?' A woman with red-rimmed eyes grabbed hold of Winnie's arm as they walked towards the crater. 'He's my son Jack, have you seen him?'

'No, I'm so sorry, I haven't; we've only just arrived to help.' Winnie touched the woman's arm. 'I hope you find him.'

She nodded and looked around for someone else to ask and spotting another new face rushed off to ask them.

Winnie glanced at Bella and Frankie, who both looked as shocked as she felt.

'Don't mind her,' an ARP warden who'd watched what had happened said as they approached him, to see what they could do to help. 'The poor woman's desperate.' He sighed. 'There's a lot of missing children; one family lost four out of their five children last night. They found the four of them all dead together just a little while ago. Poor little things were only out playing together . . . '

'We were here on duty last night and have come back to help,' Frankie explained.

'We want to do what we can,' Winnie added.

The warden nodded. 'Well, they won't let you go digging in the rubble, that's the rescue's job, they know what they're doing, but they'd be glad of a hand getting rid of the rubble. Come on, this way.'

A few minutes later, they'd been organised into part of the chain of people passing the baskets of removed rubble to the crane bucket ready to be lifted to the lorry and taken away. Winnie and Frankie were at the end of the chain, and as Bella and the man opposite her handed the basket to them, they grabbed hold of the handles and tipped the contents into the crane bucket then passed the basket back again to be refilled. It was filthy work, the powdery dust flying up in the air and covering them, getting into their hair and irritating their noses as they tipped, but neither woman cared, they were just happy to be doing something to help.

'Quiet please!' a rescue worker suddenly called out through a loud speaker and immediately everyone stopped what they were doing and fell silent. 'Can you hear me? If you can tap, three times like this: tap . . . tap . . . tap.'

Everyone listened, and you could almost feel them willing a response from under the rubble. But there was nothing. Winnie looked at Frankie, whose blue eyes were full of hope.

'If you can't tap, say 'Ah',' the rescue worker tried again. There was a long pause as they all waited. He repeated it several times and they stood still and silent, hoping and hoping. But there was no response. 'Thank you, carry on.'

Winnie felt a huge pang of disappointment as they all set to work again. She'd seen the rescue workers searching in the rubble many times before but this time being part of the work and the fact that it had been caused by an undetected UXB going off with no warning heightened her desire to find people alive in there. How much greater that must be for the families of those who were missing, like that poor woman who was desperately looking for her son?

'Winnie!' Frankie's voice brought her attention back to the moment and she grabbed hold of the full basket being passed to them and upended it, tipping the rubble into the crane bucket and sending dust swirling up into the air.

A short while later, a shout went up that someone had been found and once again everyone fell silent, waiting and hoping. From where they stood, Winnie could just make out what the rescuers had found: a hand. She watched as they carefully dug down, excavating the rest of the person and it soon became clear that this was a body and not someone who had survived. As they freed it, lifting it up on to a stretcher, Winnie's throat tightened — it was a child.

Frankie reached out and touched Winnie's arm, clearly feeling the same way.

As the small body was carried to a waiting ambulance, all the rescue workers bowed their heads. Then it was back to work, back to digging and painstakingly searching for anyone else, hoping they might have been luckier than that poor child.

By two o'clock, Winnie's arm muscles were aching and she felt so tired. The day had grown warm and they had removed their tunics and worked in their shirts; the back of hers was stuck to her skin as she was hot and sweaty, and her hair stuck to the back of her neck under her steel helmet but still the work went on. They'd only had a couple of short breaks for something to eat and drink from the WVS van, which had arrived to serve those helping with the rescue, but there was still a mountain of rubble to be moved and people unaccounted for.

'I'm going to have to go home soon,' Frankie said a short while later as they emptied another basket out and passed it back down the line. 'I'm just about all in and I'm goin' to need to clean my uniform before tomorrow's shift.' She looked down at her shirt, which was soiled and dusty and a far cry from the neat, clean outfit that Station Officer Steele expected them to come to work in.

'Me too,' Bella said. 'I don't want to leave but we need to think about tomorrow's shift and be ready for that, and . . . I'm tired, we didn't get much sleep last night through being here.'

Winnie was tired, hot, dirty and aching but her stubborn streak wasn't willing to let her be the first to admit it or to allow her to give in to it. 'There's still so much to move. I'm not going home yet.'

'But you ain't responsible for doing it all, missis. It'll take days to search through all this and clear it up,' said the man who was working opposite Bella in the chain. 'You've done a fine job, and it was good of you all to come here and help, but you need to be ready for your next shift as well.'

'You two go home, I'm going to stay a while longer,' Winnie said.

'Winnie!' Bella and Frankie chorused.

'You're due back at Station 75 in the morning and you need to get yourself cleaned up and get some sleep in the meantime,' Bella said. 'What use will you be as an ambulance driver if you're

285

too tired to do your job properly? And the boss will not be happy if you turn up looking like that.' She nodded at Winnie's uniform, which was just as filthy as her own.

'But there's still so much to do here.' Winnie threw her arm wide. 'I know,' Bella said. 'And it's going to take days to clear it out. We can't do it all and we mustn't neglect our proper job — we need to be ready for it.'

'You can't do everythin', Winnie. Even if that stubborn streak of yours makes you think you can.' Frankie looked at her, her hands on her hips. 'Think sensibly about it.'

'I know, but I just want to stay a bit longer. You two go home and I'll be along in a while.'

Bella glared at her and shook her head as she and the man passed on another full basket. 'We're not going to shift you on this, are we?'

'No.' Winnie worked with Frankie to tip a full basket into the crane bucket, sending up another cloud of brick and plaster dust.

Bella sighed. 'If that's what you want to do, we can't stop you.'

'Look, I'll be fine; don't worry.' Winnie smiled at her friends as they stepped out of the line ready to leave. 'Go home and get cleaned up and I'll see you later.'

48

Arriving back in Bedford Place and bumping her bicycle down the steps to the basement of Connie's house, all Bella could think about was how soon she could get into a warm bath and soak away the aches in her muscles. But as soon as she walked into the kitchen those thoughts were swept away at the sight of the man sitting at the table talking to Connie with Trixie sitting on his lap. The little dog launched herself on to the floor and rushed over to joyfully greet her.

'Mac!' She stood stunned, staring at him for a few moments as she patted Trixie. 'I didn't know you were coming home.'

He smiled at her. 'Hello, Bella, I've got a week off. I only found out yesterday; I thought I'd surprise Winnie.' He frowned. 'Where is she?'

'Still helping in Gurney Street, working in a chain getting rid of the excavated rubble.'

'Rose told me what happened last night when she brought Trixie home,' Connie said. 'Do they know more about what caused it?'

'Only that it was an unexploded bomb, it brought down a block of flats and some houses with it. It was such a lovely evening, people were outside in the street enjoying it when the bomb exploded,' Bella said. 'A lot of children have been killed and they're still looking for missing people in the rubble.'

'That's terrible,' Connie said, shaking her head.

'Why didn't Winnie come home with you?' Mac asked.

'Because she wanted to stay longer. Frankie and I had had enough, we were both exhausted and needed to leave, and we tried to persuade Winnie to go home too but she was determined to keep going . . . ' She shrugged. 'You know Winnie — once she gets an idea in her head, she won't budge.'

Mac stood up. 'Can I borrow your bicycle, Bella? I'm going to go and bring her home.'

'Help yourself. Hopefully she'll listen to you, Mac.'

'I'll pick her up and carry her away from there if necessary. I'll see you later.' He went out of the kitchen and headed for the outside door.

'Right,' Connie said, looking at Bella. 'You need to get out of those dirty clothes and have a bath. If you leave your uniform outside the bathroom door I can see to it and then you can have something to eat and get some sleep. Come on.' Connie linked her arm through Bella's and led her upstairs to the bathroom.

Bella didn't argue, the thought of all those three things — the bath, food and then sleep — sounded perfect.

Winnie wiped the sweat off her forehead with the arm of her shirt, leaving a damp streak in the dust-covered cloth. Another twenty-five baskets, she told herself, and then she'd consider calling it a day. Her muscles were aching and she was bone tired, but there was still so much to be done and —

A movement at the corner of her eye made her turn her head and the sight of a soldier walking towards her jolted her, he looked like Mac . . . She must be overdoing it if she had started to have hallucinations. She shook her head and closed her eyes for a few moments before looking again. This time the soldier had moved closer and he was looking directly at her.

'Winnie, you need to come home.'

She stared at him, the familiar voice registering in her tired brain. It was him, it really was! Her heart leapt at the sight of him. 'Mac! What are you doing here?'

'I've come to take you home.' He held out his hand to her. 'Come on.'

The man who was working opposite Winnie nodded. 'Go on, missis; you've more than done your bit 'ere.'

Winnie was about to protest but the man patted her on her shoulder and then propelled her towards Mac.

Now she'd finally let herself stop, waves of exhaustion hit her and she was grateful when Mac put his arms around her and hugged her tightly. She leaned against him, breathing in his gorgeous familiar smell.

'I did think I might have to carry you away from here if you refused to come home,' he whispered in her ear. 'I would have done as well.'

She stepped back and looked at him, smiling. 'If you'd come half an hour ago, you may well have had to, but I've got to admit I'm exhausted now. I'm ready to come home.' She paused for a minute, looking at his face, enjoying seeing it again. 'Anyway, what are you doing in London? How did you know I was here?'

'I've got some leave. A whole week off.' Mac smiled at her.

'A week!' Winnie beamed back at him. 'That's absolutely, marvellously wonderful.'

'I wanted to surprise you so I went straight to Connie's house and discovered you'd come here and then Bella came home alone when you refused to leave, so I had to come and get you.'

'I'm so pleased to see you.' Winnie's eyes filled with tears. Being with Mac was the best medicine of all and right now she needed that.

'It's good to see you, too.' Mac kissed her tenderly. 'Come on, let's go home.' He put his arm around her and together they walked away from the bomb site back to where they'd left their bicycles.

★　★　★

'Are you awake?'

Winnie struggled to open her eyes, taking a few moments to remember what had happened, and then as her mind recalled that Mac was here, was home and right there beside her, a warm glow enveloped her and her stomach flipped with happiness. Snapping her eyes open, she smiled at Mac who was lying beside her, looking at her with a smile on his face.

'You look so beautiful in your sleep.' He reached out and pushed a strand of hair off her face. 'And you're not so bad when you're awake either.'

'Is that right?' Winnie grabbed hold of his hand. 'I'm so glad you're here, Mac; I kept thinking of you while I was helping at Gurney Street. I never appreciated what a UXB can do before, what havoc it can bring, and that one had laid there for at least a year, no one knew it was there till it blew up.' Her eyes filled with tears. 'It made me understand why you do what you do now, to stop what happened in Gurney Street happening more often.'

'It was bad luck that UXB was never found and defused. If it came down in the last big raid it's no wonder it was missed, it was bad that night and if it fell in a basement where no one found it . . . ' He shrugged. 'Thankfully we don't get many like that.'

Winnie nodded. 'You came home at just the right time, Mac.' She reached out and put her arms around him. 'I'm going to enjoy every second I have with you here.'

49

Frankie dabbed some furniture polish along the length of one of the stretcher runners in the back of her and Bella's ambulance, smoothing it along with a rag to ensure that each bit was covered. Then she rubbed it to a shine, creating a smooth, slippery surface for the stretchers to slide in and out on. She tested it with her finger, gliding it along the metal surface and, satisfied that it was ready, she moved on to do the same to the next one.

Outside, someone started to sing 'There'll be bluebirds over the white cliffs of Dover', the song that Vera Lynn had made so popular. Other crew members who were working on their own ambulances joined in, including Bella, who was perched on the back of their ambulance between the open doors, polishing the buckles on the straps of each stretcher. The beautiful June sunshine made everyone cheerful and glad to be working outside, making the most of it, and she could hear it in their voices.

'Tomorrow, just you wait and see,' Frankie sang along, enjoying the sound of so many voices in harmony. She loved moments like this, when everyone enjoyed themselves while they worked; it gave a wonderful sense of camaraderie amongst the station's crew.

Reaching the end of the song, she looked up from her work and was shocked to see who was standing near Bella, looking in at her through the open doors of the ambulance: Station Officer Steele and Alastair.

'Alastair!' she said. 'What are you doing here?'

'He's come to speak to you, Frankie,' the boss said. 'Why don't you take your break now?'

Frankie jumped out of the ambulance. 'What's going on? What's wrong?'

'Take as long as you need.' Station Officer Steele nodded and headed back to her office.

Frankie looked at Bella, who shrugged, clearly as puzzled as she was.

'Alastair, what's goin' on?'

'Come on, let's go for a walk down by the river.' Alastair took her hand and led her out of Station 75, aware of the looks from the other crew members.

They hadn't gone very far when Frankie recovered from the surprise of Alastair's sudden arrival and the boss's instruction to take a break. She stopped in the middle of the pavement. 'What the hell is going on, Alastair?' She folded her arms. 'Why's the boss involved? And why are you takin' me off for a walk?'

Alastair turned to face her. 'I asked Station Officer Steele if I could talk to you while you were on duty. She said yes and suggested we go for a walk away from the station so we could speak in private.'

Frankie's suspicions were instantly raised. Something was going on here and she had the strongest feeling that she wasn't going to like it. 'What have you come to see me for?'

'Let's just get down by the river where we can talk.' He took hold of her hand again.

'But why not just tell me now?' Frankie protested.

'I will as soon as we get there. I promise.'

She frowned at him, wondering what this was about, different scenarios of what Alastair might want to talk about running through her mind as they walked down past the Tower of London towards the bank of the River Thames.

'Right, spit it out, then,' Frankie said as soon as they reached the river. 'What do you want to tell me? Or should I just guess?' She paused, looking at him, noticing that his blue eyes looked more anxious than she'd ever seen them, even in the middle of an air raid. 'You've joined up, 'aven't you?'

He shook his head and a wave of relief washed through her.

'What is it then?'

'I haven't joined up . . . yet.'

That last word was heaped with meaning, and her stomach plummeted into her shoes. 'But you're going to, ain't you?'

Alastair nodded and took both of her hands in his. 'Yes, Frankie, and I'm sorry because I know you don't want me to, but I feel so strongly that I have to do it. I haven't signed up yet, I wanted to tell you first before I did, not just present you with a done deed.'

'When are you going to do it, then?'

'This afternoon; I'm going straight to the recruiting office after I leave here.'

Tears stung Frankie's eyes. 'I feel like shoutin'

294

at you, Alastair Munro, that you're a bloody fool.' She hung her head, aware that her heart was beating fast as if in protest at what he was going to do.

'Frankie.' Alastair gently touched her face and she looked up at him. His face looked strained and his eyes searched hers. 'Leaving you is going to be the hardest thing about this. If you feel . . . ' He paused and looked away at the river for a moment before looking back, his eyes holding hers. 'If you feel that you'd rather not wait for me, break things off, then I'd understand.'

She stared at him. 'Why would I do that?'

'Winnie did when Mac told her he was joining the bomb disposal squad.'

'But I ain't Winnie.' She smiled at him, tears swimming in her eyes, making his face blur. 'I don't want you to go because I love you, but I ain't goin' to break up with you just because you're joining the army. I'll just 'ave to wait for you to come back again, won't I?'

A look of relief washed over Alastair's face. 'I thought you'd tell me to clear off.'

'I'd never do that to you.'

He kissed her and then folded her into a tight embrace and they stood holding on to each other for a few minutes, oblivious to anyone else around.

'Station Officer Steele was right,' he said finally, stepping back and putting his arm around her waist as they turned and looked out over the diamond-glinting river where tug boats were working their way upstream.

'Right about what?' Frankie asked.

'She said you'd understand.'

She frowned. 'You told her about joining up?'

'I had to tell her why I wanted to speak to one of her crew in the middle of their shift. She suggested I bring you down here so we could talk without one of the others overhearing. She's a good boss.'

'Yes, she is.'

★   ★   ★

Back at Station 75, after Alastair had left to go to the recruiting office, Frankie found herself frogmarched up to the flat roof by Winnie and Bella, who had made her a cup of sweet tea.

'Drink that up and then tell us what's going on,' Winnie said, sitting down cross-legged beside her friend and leaning her elbows on her knees, her chin in her hands.

'Give her some time, Winnie, this isn't an interrogation,' Bella said, kneeling down next to her. 'Take your time, Frankie.'

'The boss said you'd need some sweet tea when you got back.' Winnie narrowed her grey eyes against the bright sunlight. 'Sweet tea's what we usually give for shock.'

Frankie shook her head and smiled at her friend. 'You're wasted in the Ambulance Service, Winnie, they could use you to interrogate prisoners — they'd be beggin' you to let them tell you everything they know.'

'Come on, spill the beans, as they say; do tell us what's going on. We're desperate to know and . . . ' She reached out and touched Frankie's arm. 'Well, we want to help you if we can.'

Frankie sighed and took a deep breath. 'Alastair's gone to join up. He — ' She couldn't say any more, her throat suddenly thickening and tears filling her eyes.

Bella moved closer and put her arm around Frankie's shoulders.

'What does he want to go and do that for?' Winnie said, throwing her arms in the air. 'They'll send him abroad, they're bound to.'

'Winnie!' Bella said. 'He's a brave man because he could have spent the war working at the London.'

'I know.' Frankie sniffed and wiped at her tears with a handkerchief. 'I wish he would, but he wants to do more.'

'You haven't broken off with him, have you?' Winnie asked.

Frankie shook her head. 'He was worried that I would, but I could never do that, I'll just 'ave to wait for him and hope that he comes back.'

'That's two of us with our men off in the army,' Winnie said. 'Thankfully, you won't have to worry about James joining up, Bella: his job is most definitely for the duration. They wouldn't let him leave, though doing paperwork isn't the most exciting way to spend the war. Still, at least it is relatively safe, and for that I'm grateful, both as James's sister and for you, Bella.'

Bella nodded. 'So am I.' She leaned her head against Frankie's. 'We'll look out for you, Frankie, cheer you up and jolly you along when you feel down and are missing him, just like you and I do to Winnie when she goes all mopey over missing Mac.'

Winnie rolled her eyes. 'I don't get all mopey, well, not much, I try not to anyway but sometimes . . . ' She shrugged. 'Bella's right, Frankie, we're with you and together we'll get through this.'

'Thank you.' Frankie smiled at her wonderful friends. 'I know you are and I appreciate it, I don't know what I'd do without you two.'

50

A week had passed since Alastair had signed up to join the RAMC and Frankie was still trying to accept what he'd done. This morning would finally make it real, however, because Alastair was leaving London to begin his training. Frankie had seen him last night when he'd come to visit her at Station 75 while she'd been on duty and they'd said their goodbyes, having decided that it was best if she didn't go to see him off at the station. Only now she'd changed her mind and wanted to see him again, to be with him till the last moment possible.

'You all right, Frankie?' Bella asked as they went to collect their bicycles at the end of the shift at nine o'clock that morning.

She shrugged. 'I've changed my mind; I'm goin' to see Alastair off at Waterloo. I've got to grab the chance to see him before he goes.'

Bella put her hand on Frankie's arm. 'Are you sure? I thought you'd both agreed it was less upsetting that way.'

'What's less upsetting?' Winnie asked, coming up behind them.

'I'm goin' to see Alastair off,' Frankie said. 'I've changed my mind.'

'I don't blame you,' Winnie said.

'But it'll be more upsetting for you,' Bella said.

'It's upsetting for Frankie already, Bella, and if she wants to seize the opportunity to see Alastair while she can then she should. I would if it was me, and I do when Mac comes home. I go with him to the station even though it makes me . . . ' Winnie pulled a face. 'Cry!' She bent down and scooped Trixie up and put her in the basket on the front of her bicycle.

'Do you want me to come with you?' Bella asked.

'No, but thanks for offering, Bella. I'll be all right; it'll be sad but it's more important to me that I get to see him again before he goes than how I'll feel when he's gone.' Frankie glanced at her watch. 'I'd better go, or I'll miss him.'

'I think you're doing the right thing.' Winnie smiled at her. 'Just try to hold back your tears until the train's gone so the last he sees of you is a smile.'

Frankie nodded. 'I'll try.'

★ ★ ★

Waterloo station was busy, so many people on the move and many of them servicemen or women in their uniforms with kitbags. That would be Alastair soon, Frankie thought, weaving her way through the crowds to where she could see the display showing which platform the train that stopped at Aldershot left from. Platform two. Now all she had to do was find Alastair.

It looked like he wasn't the only one heading to Aldershot to join the army: there were quite a few other men heading towards platform two and its waiting train, all of them in their civilian clothes and carrying suitcases. There was no sign of Alastair. Could he already be on the train? Frankie glanced at her watch: there were ten minutes to go before it was due to leave.

She hurried along the platform, peering in at the compartments, which were filling up fast. None of them had Alastair in. Had he changed his mind? But he couldn't, once you signed up and were passed medically fit, that was it and you were in for the duration, there was no changing your mind.

She turned to retrace her steps and stopped suddenly at the sight of Alastair rushing on to the platform.

'Alastair!' she shouted and ran towards him.

He looked shocked and then started to smile, opening his arms wide.

'I had to see you again,' she said as he folded her into his arms. 'I know we said goodbye yesterday, but I had a change of heart.'

'Good.' Alastair looked at her, studying her face intently.

'What are you doing?'

'Drinking you in so I can remember every little detail until I next see you.'

'You've got your photograph of me, ain't you?'

He nodded. 'This is an added extra.'

The guard shouted from the far end of the train nearest the engine and started to work his way along, slamming any open doors in preparation for the train's departure.

Frankie swallowed against the lump that had lodged in her throat.

'I'd better get on.' Alastair wrapped her in a

fierce hug and then kissed her. 'Look after yourself, Frankie; write to me.'

She nodded. 'You be careful.'

He grinned. 'I will and I'll come back and see you just as soon as I get leave, that's a promise.'

'I'll hold you to that.' Her voice came out odd and she was struggling to hold back tears but she remembered what Winnie had said about sending him off with a smile. With the greatest effort she made her face smile even though her heart felt like it was cracking.

'I'm glad you came.' Alastair touched her face and then picked up his suitcase and climbed on board, slamming the train door shut behind him and then sticking his head out of the window.

Frankie reached out her hand to him and he took hold of it. Then, too soon, the guard gave a piercing blast on his whistle, waving his green flag, the engine responded with belches of smoke chuffing out of its chimney and slowly the train began to glide along the platform. Frankie walked alongside it, still holding Alastair's hand, but then she had to let go and she watched as he waved and kept waving out of the window until the train snaked its way out of the station and his hand was lost from view and she was left stranded on the platform.

Now she could cry, Frankie thought. And she did.

51

'How would you like a trip out into the countryside?' Station Officer Steele asked.

Bella glanced at Frankie and Winnie, who, like her, had been summoned into the boss's office. 'What do you mean?' she asked. 'Well, I've had a job come in that involves a rather longer call-out than usual. You'll need to stay out overnight so it will be longer than your usual twenty-four-hour shift, but you can take the extra time off your next shift.'

Bella caught Winnie's eye, her friend raising her eyebrows in surprise.

'Where do you want us to go?' Winnie asked.

'The job is to take a mother and her new baby out to the East End Maternity Hospital's maternity home in the countryside; the baby needs special care.' The boss paused for a moment and then went on. 'It's at Tyringham Hall in Buckinghamshire.' The boss smiled at Bella. 'You'd stay there overnight and then bring back some mothers and their babies who've been staying there and are now ready to come home. I rather thought you all might enjoy it — a chance to get out of London and visit Buckinghamshire.'

'I'd be very happy to go,' Bella said. The thought of going back to her home county and out in the countryside on such a beautiful June day, when the trees would be in full leaf and the wildflowers blooming, was enchanting.

'Absolutely,' Winnie agreed. 'I'm missing Mac terribly now he's gone back to his unit, this job will cheer me up no end.'

'Frankie, are you happy to go?' the boss asked.

'Yes, it'll make a nice change,' Frankie said. Bella was relieved that Frankie had said yes; for a moment she thought she'd turn the offer down as she'd been much quieter than usual since Alastair had left to join the army. She and Winnie were worried about her.

'I'm sending the three of you because I think an extra person will be useful: one of you will need to ride in the back with your patients, the other two can navigate and drive. Who does what you can organise between yourselves and take turns doing each job.'

'We can make a real trip of it,' Winnie said, linking her arm through Frankie's.

'Remember, your first priority is to your patients,' Station Officer Steele said sternly. Then she smiled. 'You'll need to go home and get your overnight things, and as you're picking up the mother and baby from the London, I suggest you go to Frankie's house in Stepney first, then collect your patients, then call in at Winnie's and Bella's en route, only stopping briefly, though — you won't need more than your night things.'

'What's the best way to go?' Bella asked. 'I've only ever travelled back and forth from Buckinghamshire on the train.'

'Well, if you get as much help as you can from this,' the boss said, going over to the large map pinned on her office wall, 'it will get you out of

London and then you'll have to find your way as best you can.'

Bella looked at Winnie, who raised her eyebrows. With signposts taken down it wasn't going to be easy.

'If you don't know the way, you'll just have to ask. You're very capable young women and I have every faith in you.' Station Officer Steele smiled at them. 'Enjoy the trip. Oh, and Mrs Connelly has packed you up some food to take with you as you'll miss your lunch here; remember to collect it from the kitchen before you go.'

Once they'd written down directions as far as they could from the map, and collected the food and drink from the kitchen, they made their way to the garages.

'Who wants to drive first?' Bella asked. 'And who's navigating and who's going to ride in the back once we pick up the mother and baby?'

'I'll ride in the back,' Frankie volunteered. 'I'm more used to babies with helpin' at the nursery and seeing Josie's little Flora.'

'Thank you,' Winnie said. 'I'm not very experienced with babies. Do you want to drive or navigate, Bella?'

'I'll drive and if we get lost I can blame you.' Bella laughed at the face Winnie pulled in response.

'I will do my best, and if in doubt then we'll stop and ask the way,' Winnie said, picking Trixie up and putting her in the front of the ambulance.

Once they'd been to Frankie's home to collect

her overnight things, then stopped at the London to pick up the mother and baby — a tiny little girl who weighed just under five pounds and was well swaddled in blankets to keep her warm — followed by a quick stop at Connie's house, Winnie was able to navigate them north-west out of the city and out into the countryside towards Buckinghamshire.

'Look at the green; it's so fresh and clean-looking,' Bella said as she drove along. She was thoroughly enjoying being out in the countryside again. It felt like a balm to her eyes after the drab buildings she was used to seeing in London.

'It's beautiful.' Winnie sighed happily. 'And such a glorious day to be out here. It was good of the boss to send us.' She lowered her voice. 'Do you think she thought we needed it?'

Bella glanced at her friend and nodded.

'We should make the most of being out here, don't you think?'

'What do you mean?'

'Well, think about it, Bella. We couldn't have been sent to a better place, could we? Who lives in Buckinghamshire? Your mother, Stanley and James! While we're there we can go and visit them.' Winnie beamed at her. 'It will be absolutely marvellous.'

'The boss is sending us to the maternity hospital, not gadding off around the county,' Bella reminded her.

'Yes, but she didn't say we couldn't, did she? Look, once we've delivered our patients to the hospital then we're done until tomorrow

306

morning, so we should make the most of being there. Your mother's home and Bletchley aren't far away at all; it would be a terrible shame if we didn't take the chance to see our families. I'm sure Frankie would love to see Stanley.'

'Well . . . ' Bella was sorely tempted, she hadn't been home to see her mother since her week's annual leave last autumn and she would dearly love to see her.

'It would do Frankie good to see Stanley,' Winnie whispered.

'It's just what she needs right now.'

'Ask her,' Bella said.

'All right.' Winnie tapped on the back of the cab to get Frankie's attention. 'How would you like to go and see Stanley?' she called through, then explained her plan to Frankie.

'I'd love to,' Frankie called back.

'See.' Winnie grinned. 'Let's make the most of this trip, Bella. We don't get chances like this every day and imagine your mother's and James's faces when we turn up on a surprise visit.'

Bella looked at her friend and nodded. 'All right then, you've convinced me.'

They managed the journey to Tyringham Hall well; when they weren't certain of which way to go they stopped and asked directions in towns and villages on the way. With the signposts taken down, sometimes it was impossible to know which way to go in a town so the only thing to do was ask.

'Look at that!' Bella peered out of the windscreen as she drove them up the drive to the front of Tyringham Hall. 'This is a bit different from the East End.'

The house was grand, with a porticoed entrance and a dome on top, rather like a miniature version of the one crowning St Paul's Cathedral back in London. The East End mothers who came here to have their babies, or to recuperate afterwards, must be astonished to find themselves in such surroundings after the bombed-out streets of their home town.

'Come on, let's get mother and baby safely inside,' Winnie said as Bella parked outside the front, 'then we can go and see your mother and Stanley first, and then James later on, if he's at home.'

★　★　★

'Why's there an ambulance 'ere? Is someone hurt? What's — ' Stanley had arrived home from school and burst into the kitchen of Linden House where Bella's mother worked as the cook, words failing him as he caught sight of Frankie, Winnie and Bella sitting around the kitchen table drinking tea.

Frankie stood up. 'Hello, Stanley. The ambulance is ours, and it's all right, no one's hurt.' She quickly crossed the kitchen and threw her arms around him, noticing as she hugged him that he'd grown since she'd seen him the previous year.

'I didn't know you were comin',' Stanley said when she loosened her arms and stepped back to have a proper look at him.

'Nor did I till this morning. We had to bring a mother and baby out to Tyringham Hall maternity hospital and we're not going back to London till tomorrow and so we thought we'd come and pay you visit.'

Stanley grinned. 'It's a nice surprise. Do you want to come out and see the garden? I've got my own patch now.'

'Yes, I'd like that.' Frankie looked at Bella and Winnie, who were both smiling at her.

'While you do that, I'm going to help Mother with Walter's next-of-kin parcel,' Bella said. 'We need to pack it all up and make sure it's not over the weight limit.'

'Can I come out in the garden?' Winnie asked.

Stanley nodded. 'Are you Winnie?'

'That's me. And this is Trixie.' Winnie stood up, holding the squiggling little dog who'd been sitting on her lap and who was desperate to say hello to Stanley. 'We haven't met before, but I've heard about you from Frankie.'

'You saved Trixie after she was dug out from a bombed-out house, didn't you?' Stanley stroked Trixie's ears, laughing as she contorted her head to lick his hands.

'She came to live with me after that and work at Station 75 as well,' Winnie said. 'She's taken a shine to you.'

'Come on, then, let's go and see what you've been up to in the garden,' Frankie said, putting her arm around Stanley's shoulders. 'And Trixie can have a good run around as well.'

★ ★ ★

309

'Your Stanley is quite the most delightful young man,' Winnie said as she steered the ambulance down the drive of Linden House, while Frankie and Bella waved out of the passenger window to Stanley and Bella's mother, who had come out to see them off.

'I know,' said Frankie, sitting back in her seat as the house disappeared from view. 'I'm really glad we came here, seein' him today was lovely.'

'Just what you needed, eh?' Bella said, holding Trixie in her arms where she sat in the middle, sharing the passenger seat with Frankie.

Frankie nodded. 'Cheered me up no end. It was lovely for you to see your mother, too, Bella.'

'Good, that was the whole idea,' Winnie said, throwing a glance at her. 'I know you've been feeling blue, so this trip coming along was perfect timing. God bless Station Officer Steele!'

'Do you think the boss planned this?' Bella asked.

Winnie shrugged. 'Who knows? But it seems a bit of a coincidence: she could have chosen any of the crew to go, but she chose us, all of us with connections in Buckinghamshire, not far from Tyringham Hall.'

'She didn't tell us to go visitin', though, did she?' Frankie said.

Winnie laughed. 'No, but she didn't say not to, and we do have this time to spare; it's only common sense to make the most of it, don't you think? Good for morale, and all that. Our next visit's just going to build on that even more. By the time we get back to Station 75 we'll feel like we've had a holiday.'

Frankie and Bella both laughed.

'You are quite incorrigible, Winnie, did you know that?' Bella said.

'Now you come to mention it, I have been told that before,' Winnie said. 'I suppose it must be true.' She turned to them and smiled broadly. 'Nothing ventured, nothing gained, eh?'

★ ★ ★

Winnie knocked on the door of the house in Bletchley where James was billeted, hoping that he was at home. There was a chance that he'd be at work but as they were in the area, it was definitely worth visiting just in case.

The door was opened by a woman wearing a crossover apron. 'Yes?' She looked Winnie up and down, clearly taking in her Ambulance Service uniform.

'Hello, I've come to see James Churchill; is he at home?' Winnie asked, smiling at her.

The woman folded her arms. 'I don't approve of women callers, my lodgers know that.'

'I'm his sister.' Winnie felt herself starting to bristle at the woman's attitude and had to rein herself in. 'I'm in the area for my work and was hoping that I might see my brother.'

'Well, he's not here.'

Winnie felt a pang of disappointment. She knew there had been no guarantees, he worked shift work the same as they did, so it would be chance whether he was at home or work. 'Right, would you tell him I called?'

She turned and was halfway down the path to

the gate when the woman called out. 'He's gone to the pub.'

Winnie spun round and smiled at her. 'Where?'

'First one you come to that way.' The woman pointed to the left.

'Thank you.' Winnie beamed at her and hurried back to the parked ambulance where Frankie and Bella were waiting.

'Come on, he's in the pub.' She leaned in through the open window. 'Let's go and give my brother a surprise.'

Inside the pub, which was noisy and thronged with men and women, someone was bashing out a song on an out-of-tune piano. Winnie eventually managed to spot her brother sitting at a table with another man, engrossed in a game of chess. She marched up to him. 'Hello, James.'

At the sound of her voice he looked up and the surprised expression on his face was quickly replaced with a broad smile. 'Winnie, what are you doing here?'

'I've come to see you, and I've brought someone who you might be pleased to see.' She stood aside so that he could see Bella and Frankie and from the look of delight on James's face she knew was right to push at the boundaries and come here.

With everyone found a chair and bought a drink, they settled down at the table, the game of chess forgotten and James's friend introduced as a colleague from work. James had, Winnie noticed, sat himself next to Bella and the pair of them were holding hands under the table. They made such a lovely couple and seeing them together lifted her heart. She had hopes that one day Bella would be more than just her good friend.

'So, what brings you to Bletchley?' James asked.

'Your sister's cunning ways,' Bella said. She explained about their job taking the mother and baby to the maternity hospital and their plans to go visiting family for the rest of the day.

'Well, I'm very glad you have,' James said. 'It's brightened up the day considerably.'

★ ★ ★

Station Officer Violet Steele ran her ambulance station like clockwork, but she knew when it was time to give a little bit of slack to her crews for their own good and from the look of Winnie, Frankie and Bella when they arrived for work on Wednesday afternoon they had made the most of it. The three of them looked happy and cheerful, the trip away seeming to have done them the power of good, especially Frankie, who had regained the spark to her eyes.

'How did the trip go?' she asked, perching on the arm of the sofa where the three of them sat during the tea break.

'Very well,' Bella said. 'The mother and baby were delivered safely to Tyringham Hall and four mothers and their babies brought home yesterday.'

'I'm glad to hear that; and did you make good use of your free time?' As she stroked Trixie's ears, she noticed a look pass between the young women and wondered what they would say.

'Absolutely,' Winnie said. 'We went visiting . . . ' Bella and Frankie both nudged Winnie, but she ignored them and went on. 'Since we were in the area and had time, we thought we'd go and see Bella's mother, Stanley and James.'

Winnie looked the boss straight in the eye, while Bella and Frankie looked worried and clearly expected Station Officer Steele to be angry, but she wasn't. Instead, she smiled at them. 'I'm glad to hear that. It looks as though it's done you all the world of good.' Bella and Frankie glanced at each other, looking relieved, while Winnie smiled back at her.

'I hoped you'd think that,' Winnie said. 'I thought we needed it.'

'Indeed. It's important to see your family when you can. I'm sure they'll have been surprised but pleased to see you.' She stood up. 'I appreciate your honesty.'

'Did you expect us to do that?' Winnie asked. 'You know about our families being in Buckinghamshire, not far from the maternity hospital.'

'I would have been rather disappointed if you hadn't taken the initiative and grabbed the chance to see them while you could.'

52

It was a beautiful summer's day, the sky a clear blue above Matlock Street, and Frankie was determined to make the most of the time off that the twenty-four hours on and off shifts gave her. Sitting out in the garden, taking a break after working on the vegetable patch that took up most of the back garden, even extending on to the roof of the Anderson shelter where she'd planted some lettuces in the layer of soil that her grandfather had covered it with, she took the letter out of her pocket that she'd been saving to read when she sat down for a breather. Frankie had grown so fond of getting these weekly letters from her mother, and now looked forward to hearing about what was going on with her family in Suffolk.

Reading through it, she enjoyed hearing about life on the farm and what her mother had been doing with the village Women's Institute. But the last paragraph of the letter disturbed her relaxed state of mind.

We haven't heard from Lizzie for several weeks now and I'm getting worried.

Frankie's sister had been posted to a barrage balloon site in London but had made no attempt to contact Frankie since she'd arrived.

Would you be able to go and see if she's all right? If you can, please tell her to write to me.

Frankie sighed; she'd only met Lizzie once when she'd gone to see her mother in Suffolk, and her sister had made no attempt to hide her hostility towards her. She probably wouldn't be happy to see Frankie turning up at her balloon site either, but clearly their mother was worried and Frankie had to do what she could to help. She knew only too well what it was to worry about someone you cared for — she'd done plenty of that over Stanley. There was nothing for it but to go and visit Lizzie and find out why she hadn't written home for weeks.

'Tea.' Rose came out into the garden with two mugs and handed one to Frankie. 'Are you done for today?'

'For now; I'll do some more later. I'm goin' to have to go and pay my sister a visit, apparently she ain't been writing home and my mother's worried.' Frankie nodded at the letter open on her lap.

'That's the one who works on the barrage balloons?' Rose took a sip of tea.

'Yes, she works on the site down by the War Museum. Do you want to come with me?'

Rose nodded. 'Yes, I'd like to see how they fly their balloons. I've seen them in the air but I don't know how they're connected to the ground.'

'Well, you'll find out and hopefully I can discover why Lizzie's not been writing 'ome.' Frankie smiled at Rose, glad that she was going

316

along with her as she wasn't looking forward to confronting her sister.

⋆ ⋆ ⋆

'Look, there it is; it's bigger than I thought,' Rose said as they turned into Lambeth Road and caught their first sight of the silver barrage balloon tethered to the ground in Geraldine Mary Harmsworth Park in front of the War Museum, which was now closed for the duration. It was glittering like a huge silver fish in the bright sunshine.

Riding their bicycles in through the gates of the park, they could see some WAAFS, all dressed in blue overalls, busy tending to their balloon. Up close they could see the many ropes dangling from the balloon, tethering it to concrete blocks; there was a lorry with a winch on the back ready to get the balloon sky-borne and another lorry packed with gas cylinders lying on their sides ready to top it up.

Leaving their bicycles leaning against a wall, Frankie and Rose made their way over to the nearest WAAF, who was busy cleaning the winch, the smell of the diesel oil she was using to do it hitting them yards before they reached her.

Seeing them approach, the WAAF stopped what she was doing and smiled at them. 'You come for a look at the balloon?' she asked in a Geordie accent.

'No, I'm lookin' for my sister, she works here,' Frankie explained.

'Right, we get a lot of locals come and have a

317

look. What's your sister's name?'

'Lizzie Jacobs.'

'She's over in the tent brewing up, I think, or she should be,' the WAAF said. 'I'm gasping for a cuppa. Go and have a look and tell her Vee's ready for her tea.'

'Thanks.' Frankie and Rose headed towards the bell tent but before they got there a figure emerged carrying a tray of mugs. It was Lizzie. She too was wearing blue overalls, her dark brown hair rolled up to regulation length above her collar and a beret on her head. She looked different from the last time Frankie had seen her, more grown-up and responsible-looking.

Lizzie spotted them and her step faltered but she managed not to spill the tea. She scowled before quickly rearranging her face into a more neutral expression, but not one that welcomed her sister.

'What are you doing here?'

'Hello, Lizzie,' Frankie said, doing her best to sound friendly.

'Where's the tea?' Vee shouted from the winch. 'Get the tea round done first, Lizzie, and then you can talk to your sister all you want.'

Lizzie looked relieved and hurried off to give out the mugs of tea to the other girls who had stopped what they were doing and were sitting themselves down on the grass to enjoy the sunshine while they had their tea.

'She didn't look very pleased to see you,' Rose said quietly.

'I know. It must be a bit of a shock me turnin' up like this, I suppose. That, combined with her dislike of me, ain't the best of starts.' Frankie shrugged. 'I won't keep her long, I just need to find out why she ain't sent letters home and tell her she needs to, then we can be on our way. Why don't you go and talk to some of the WAAFs if you like, ask them about their job?'

Rose smiled. 'Yes, I would like that.'

Frankie watched as Rose joined a group sitting on the grass and was soon talking to them and joining in their laughter about something.

'Why are you here?' Lizzie hissed as she marched up to Frankie, now she'd distributed all the tea. She was scowling again and made no attempt to hide her annoyance at Frankie's sudden visit.

'I'm 'ere because of Mother, mine *and* yours.' Frankie saw Lizzie wince as she spoke of *their* mother, something that linked them together. 'She sent me a letter sayin' she ain't heard from you for weeks and she's worried about you. She asked me to come and see why you ain't written to her and to tell you to write.'

'Well, you've told me, so you can go.' Lizzie folded her arms across her chest. 'I'll write to her tonight.'

'Why haven't you been writin'?' Frankie asked.

Lizzie narrowed her eyes. 'Because I've been busy. I have to work twenty-four-hour shifts, you know.'

'So do I: twenty-four hours on and twenty-four hours off. I write to her when I've got twenty-four hours off duty. You could too.'

'I need to catch up on my sleep.'

'Not for all that time, surely?'

319

'And I do other things.'

'Such as?' Frankie asked.

'None of your business.' Lizzie glared at her. 'Right, you've passed on the message, so you can go now.'

Frankie shrugged and smiled at her sister. 'Very well. Goodbye, Lizzie.'

Her sister didn't bother to reply, she just turned on her heels and Frankie watched as she stalked over to the bell tent and went inside. Clearly Lizzie's attitude towards her hadn't improved since their first meeting; joining the WAAFs hadn't given her any more sense of compassion towards Frankie.

Her job done, it was time to go home and get on with what she wanted to be doing instead of chasing halfway across London to see a rude and ungrateful sister.

53

As Frankie built the bricks into a tower again, one-year-old Robert sat patiently by her side on the army rug spread out on the floor. The moment she finished, he gave her a big grin and reached over and pushed it with his pudgy hand, sending the wooden blocks tumbling to the floor and making him burst into a fit of giggles.

'Gain,' Robert said, when he'd calmed down, his large blue eyes looking at Frankie.

'Don't you want to have a go at building them up yourself?' she asked.

He shook his head, picked up a brick and handed it to her.

'All right, then, one last time and then we'll have a go at playing something else.' Once again, she started to build the tower, smiling to herself at how much delight small children found in the simplest of things.

Since she'd started to do voluntary work here at the day nursery, her eyes had been opened to the world of young children. Having no siblings of her own, she didn't have the experience of seeing how they observed the world. Stanley had already been six when he'd come to live with her family, so much more used to the world and past the stage the children were at here in the nursery, when they were discovering so much for themselves and still enthralled in the tiny, overlooked things of life.

'Nearly there,' Frankie said, making a play of placing the last few bricks on to the top of the tower. 'Just this one to go.' She held out the red, wooden brick to Robert. 'Do you want to put it on top?'

He shook his head.

'But I need some help, just put your hand on mine and help me.'

Robert put his hand on top of hers and she placed the brick on top of the tower. 'There, thank you.'

Once again Robert pushed it over and dissolved into gurgling laughs as the bricks tumbled to the ground. His giggle made her laugh, too, its sound deliciously infectious.

Catching her breath as she calmed down, Frankie became aware that someone had joined them and was crouching down at the edge of the blanket. It was the black army boots that she spotted first and she quickly looked up to see who was there.

'Alastair!' Frankie stared at him, taking in his army uniform which still seemed so odd on him. It wasn't the first time she'd seen him in it as he'd been back on a short forty-eight-hour leave after finishing basic training and before he started his next army course.

'I'll take Robert,' one of the nursery nurses said, bending down and scooping up the little boy who was staring at Alastair. 'Matron said it's fine for you to leave a little early today, seeing as you have a visitor.' She winked at Frankie as she stood up with Robert in her arms.

Alastair reached out his hand to her and

pulled her to her feet.

'Hello, Frankie, you look rather shocked.'

She nodded. 'I am.' She smiled at him. 'But it's good to see you.'

'You too, I can see you've become rather good at building towers with wooden blocks.'

'I've had lots of practice.' She linked her arm through his and together they walked out through the nursery, where she noticed Alastair was getting many glances and not just from the children who always quickly spotted anyone different who came in.

Matron was near the door. 'We'll see you next week, Frankie. It was good to meet you, Dr Munro. I hope all goes well for you.'

'Thank you,' Alastair said. 'I appreciate you letting me steal Frankie away.'

Matron bowed her head. 'My pleasure.'

'What was that all about?' Frankie asked when they were outside. Alastair stopped walking and turned to face her. 'I may as well tell you now, I'm on embarkation leave. I told Matron so that she knew why I'd had the cheek to come looking for you. She saw my RAMC badge and asked what I did but at least she let you leave a little early.' His bright blue eyes held hers. 'I want to spend as much time as I can with you before I have to go.'

Frankie knew it was a strong possibility that he'd be sent abroad but she'd harboured a hope that he'd be posted to one of the military hospitals in England instead. She knew it was unlikely — working in casualty had given him lots of experience of dealing with emergencies and made him perfect for the job of a doctor in a field hospital near the fighting. Even so, the news that he was going was like a heavy weight dropping into her stomach.

'How long have you got?'

'Forty-eight hours. I need to report back by midday on Thursday.' Frankie sighed. 'I'm workin' today and won't be finished till nine o'clock in the morning.'

'Station Officer Steele has given you the afternoon off, as long as you're back at Station 75 by six o'clock tonight.' She frowned.

'But how . . . ?'

'I went straight to Station 75 from Waterloo and saw your boss, told her what was going on and found out where you were. She insisted you take the time off.'

'Well . . . ' Frankie smiled. 'In that case, I better had then.' She glanced at her watch: it was just past three o'clock. 'We've got three precious hours, what would you like to do?'

'How about going to a pie and mash shop to start with, I'm hungry and could do with something tasty to eat, the food's not up to much in the army, and then we could have a walk, see where that takes us'

'All right then, but first I want a kiss!'

Alastair laughed. 'Most happy to oblige.'

★ ★ ★

After they'd been to the pie and mash shop they meandered their way through the streets of the East End, their arms around each other's waists, just enjoying being together. It was a soft, warm, September day, the sky blue with just the faintest wisps of high cloud, and they eventually found themselves down by the Tower of London, looking out over the river. This had become a favourite spot for many of Station 75's crew, but fortunately none of them was there now.

Leaning against the wall bordering the banks of the river, Frankie asked the question that had been preying on her mind since the moment Alastair told her he was on embarkation leave, but which she'd been afraid to ask for fear of what the answer might be.

'Where are they sending you?'

Alastair shrugged. 'You know I can't tell you that.'

'But you could give me a clue, couldn't you?'

'I could.' He paused. 'Let's just say I've been issued with light-coloured, cooler uniform.'

'The desert then? North Africa?'

He raised his eyebrows. 'Somewhere hot.'

'You won't be in the fightin', though, they don't send doctors to do that, you're needed to help the wounded.'

'Don't worry, we'll be in field hospitals behind the lines.'

Frankie nodded, biting her bottom lip as the reality of Alastair going to war grew ever closer. Him away training had been hard enough but at least she'd known he was still in England and not that far away from London, but in just a couple of days' time he'd be on his way to a distant country where the war was raging.

'I won't be taking any risks, I promise you,

325

because I want to come home to you.' He paused and gently touched her face. 'In fact, Frankie, when I come home again I'd like you to become my wife. Will you marry me, Frankie?'

She stared at him, completely taken by surprise, but very quickly the answer came winging its way to her lips, both from her heart and from her head.

'Yes!'

'You will?'

Frankie nodded. 'Yes, yes, yes.'

He pulled her into a tight embrace and leaning her head against his chest Frankie could hear his heart beating as fast as hers.

When they eventually pulled apart, Alastair felt in his tunic pocket and pulled out a red leather ring box. 'This was my grandmother's engagement ring, she left it for me for when I found the woman I'd like to marry one day . . . and I have.' He smiled. 'And I met her in a bombed-out Anderson shelter, do you remember?'

'Of course I do.' Frankie would never forget that day when she'd had to crawl into the shelter to look after the little boy when both his mother and his sister lay dead nearby, and how Alastair had come in to help. Then she'd met him for the second time at the London Hospital when she'd gone to visit the boy and take him his beloved toy that he'd dropped in the shelter and would need even more with his mother and sister gone. 'We'll be able to tell our children about how we met, one day.'

'I do hope so.' Alastair took the ring out of its

box and slipped it on to the third finger of her left hand. 'I was worried it wouldn't fit, but it's perfect, as if it was made for you.'

She looked at the ring on her finger; it was beautiful, a golden band with a ruby set in a circle of tiny diamonds, by far the nicest ring she had ever seen. 'It's beautiful. Thank you.'

'Thank you, Frankie, for agreeing to be my wife; I wasn't sure you'd agree — '

'Why ever not? I love you.'

'I know, but with me going away . . . '

'Now I know you'll want to come back.'

Alastair took her face in his hands, his eyes meeting hers.

'Always, Frankie; I'll always want to come home to you.'

54

'What will we do if she's said no?' Bella asked, holding up a large letter S, cut out of newspaper, to Winnie, who was standing on a chair to reach the beam that ran across the ceiling of the common room at Station 75.

'Do you think she will turn him down?' Winnie frowned. 'I would be very surprised; Frankie adores Alastair.'

'I know, but with him going off to war . . . ' Bella shrugged.

Winnie put her hand on her hip and looked at the letters she'd pinned up across the beam; there was just the S left to add to spell out 'Congratulations', part of her hastily put together party to celebrate Frankie and Alastair's engagement, but if they weren't . . . Had she gone headlong into doing something in typical Winnie style without thinking it through properly first?

As soon as Alastair had told her what he planned to do when he'd come here looking for Frankie earlier, the idea of a party had popped into her mind, but there hadn't been much time to get organised. She'd cobbled together the sign out of some of Sparky's old newspapers, the crew had been warned to hide ready for when they returned and jump out and surprise them, and Mrs Connelly had been persuaded to make some currant buns, which they'd have with some tea to celebrate. It wasn't going to be a magnificent occasion with champagne but what it lacked in finesse, it would make up for in wholehearted delight from all the crew to see Frankie and Alastair engaged . . . That's if they were.

'Well, we'll have to find out before they come up here,' Winnie said, thinking quickly. 'They're due back at six o'clock, so if one of us goes down to the courtyard and meets them there and finds out and another can wait by the window and watch for a signal. Thumbs up and everything is fine, thumbs down and the letters will have to be torn down quickly before they come up here and we'll just eat the buns for tea, no harm done.'

'Now you've said that, I do hope Frankie said yes,' Bella said.

'So do I, but best to be prepared either way.' Winnie pinned the letter S into place. 'How does that look?'

Bella stood back to check. 'It looks good.'

Winnie jumped down from the chair and went over beside her. 'It's just the ticket, shame we couldn't use some coloured paper or card but there's a war on . . . ' She smiled at Bella. 'So, who's going to waylay them and find out the truth?'

Bella laughed. 'You, this was all your idea.'

⋆   ⋆   ⋆

By the time six o'clock approached Winnie's stomach was somersaulting inside her. She desperately hoped that her friend had said yes, not because if she hadn't it would ruin her party plan, but because if she didn't she feared her friend might come to regret it later on when the harsh reality of Alastair being sent abroad hit home. There was no telling how long he would be gone for or what the future held, but if they had parted with that special bond between them, then Frankie would always have that come what may and not regret that she'd turned him down. And they were perfect for each other, too.

Positioning herself in the garages with a broom in her hand as if she was doing some work, but where she could see them as soon as they walked through the archway, she waited. She'd already checked that Bella was in position in the common-room window and was watching for a signal.

As soon as she saw them she knew the answer, the pair of them seemed to glow with happiness.

Stepping out of the garages as they approached she had a final check to make sure and saw the ring sparkling on Frankie's finger.

'Have you had a good time?' Winnie asked, putting one hand behind her back, her thumb sticking up to signal to Bella.

'The best.' Frankie beamed at her. 'Alastair and I are engaged.'

'Oh, that's absolutely marvellous. Congratulations!' Winnie threw her arms around her friend. 'I'm so happy for you, darling Frankie.' Then she did the same to Alastair. 'You are the loveliest couple.'

'Look, this was Alastair's grandmother's ring.' Frankie held up her left hand to show Winnie.

Winnie smiled at her. 'It's very beautiful. It's such a shame you've got to be here on duty instead of out celebrating. Come on, let's go and toast to your engagement in tea.'

Leading the way up to the common room, Winnie hoped that everyone was in place, hiding around the room to look like no one was there. They'd already practised it earlier so the crew members knew where to go when Frankie arrived back.

'It's quiet in here,' Frankie said when they went into the common room. 'Where is everyone?'

A mighty shout of 'Surprise' rang out as crew members popped up from their hiding places behind chairs and tables and out of cupboards, all of them delighted for Frankie. Station Officer Steele had joined in, stepping out from behind a cupboard door holding an excited Trixie in her arms, who was waggling her tail madly, picking up on the joyful atmosphere.

Frankie looked momentarily stunned, and then her face broke into a wide smile as she spotted 'Congratulations' pinned up on the beam. She turned to Winnie and laughed. 'Is this all your doing?'

'Well, me and a few others. We couldn't let this occasion pass without celebrating. No champers, I'm afraid, just tea, but Mrs Connelly's made some currant buns specially.'

Frankie's eyes filled with tears. 'Thank you; thank you, everyone.'

Alastair put his arm around Frankie. 'This is a lovely surprise, thank you.'

'Come on then, let the celebrations begin!' Winnie said.

With everyone sorted out with a cup of tea, Station Officer Steele tapped on her mug with a teaspoon until the room fell silent. 'I know I'm speaking on behalf of all of us here when I say how delighted we are that you are engaged and wish you a long and happy future together.'

'Hear, hear!' Sparky shouted.

'I know the coming months will be hard for you and I hope that having made this commitment to each other will bring you joy and comfort, and that in the not too distant future you'll be able to become husband and wife.' The boss raised her mug. 'To Frankie and Alastair.'

The rest of the crew joined in and Winnie found herself blinking back tears as she raised her mug in salute. It was so important to grab at moments of happiness like this to help bolster yourself against the harsh reality of whatever war threw at you. She hoped that when times were tough for Frankie worrying over Alastair, which was bound to happen, she'd look back and remember today and that it would help.

'Who's for a currant bun?' Sparky called out, offering the plate piled high with Mrs Connelly's delicious bready buns first to Frankie and Alastair.

'You were right,' Bella said quietly, coming to stand beside Winnie. 'I'm so glad she said yes.'

She linked her arm through Bella's. 'Me too.' The pair of them stood watching their friend and her fiancé accept congratulations from all the crew members. 'It's not going to be easy for her when he's gone.'

'We'll be there for her,' Bella said.

Winnie nodded. 'Absolutely.'

55

Station Officer Steele stared at the telegram in her hands. It brought good news, and bad, as well as stirring up a whole new raft of questions that floated around in her mind and which she could put no answers to.

COMING HOME STOP RECEIVED NEWS THAT GEORGE KILLED STOP LEAVING TOMORROW STOP LILY

She reread it for the tenth time since the telegram boy had delivered it to her flat a short while ago.

She sat down in an armchair and took a sip of the whisky that she'd poured herself. She was glad, so glad and relieved, that finally her sister Lily and the girls were coming home, but their return was tinged with sadness as her sister was now a widow. Where, when and how her poor brother-in-law George had died she didn't know — there was no clue in the three sentences in the telegram. Had he died in Singapore when the island had been overrun by the Japanese, or perhaps it had happened while he tried to escape? The answer to these questions would have to wait until her sister arrived back in the country. But how long would it be before they got back? How long did it take to sail from South Africa to England? Questions, questions;

questions! It would only be when Lily was home that she could know the whole story and finally be able to stop worrying about her sister.

Violet Steele took another sip of whisky, enjoying the warmth of the fiery liquid as she swallowed it, and allowed herself a glimmer of joy that Lily was coming home again. It had been two and half long years since she'd seen her sister and nieces and it would be wonderful to see them again, and once they were back she'd be able look out for them. Now Lily was a widow she'd need help and Violet Steele would be only too glad to help her sister as she had done since she'd been born. They could stay with her in the flat or perhaps they'd prefer to go and live with her mother and father down in Devon, at least they would be safer there from bombing.

Her mind started to run through all the things her sister would need to think about on her return to England. Where would the girls go to school? They'd have to get used to being in England after Singapore, they'd find it cold. Would they have suitable clothing? Probably not, as they'd have grown out of the clothes they had in England and only have ones suitable for the warmer climate. She'd have to see if she could buy some for them so that they'd have something warm to wear as soon as they got back. There was a lot to think about and do if she was going to be ready to help them when they arrived.

56

Frankie had never known time pass so quickly. Why was it when you didn't want something to end then it seemed to speed up and yet when you wanted something over with it dragged by?

Alastair's leave was almost up; he had to report back to his barracks by midday, in just four hours' time, and she had to be at work in a little over half an hour. Much as she wanted to go to see him off at Waterloo station as she had when he'd first left to join the RAMC, she couldn't because she had to go to work and they'd decided that it really was for the best if they said their goodbyes here in private and not in the middle of a busy station.

She and Alastair had stayed last night with Winnie at Connie's house as he no longer had a room in the doctors' home at the London Hospital and needed somewhere to stay. Frankie had stayed there, too, so they could make the most of every moment they had left together and she wouldn't have to waste time travelling to and from Stepney.

Yesterday they'd spent the day just being together and storing away images and memories of each other for when they were far apart. They'd walked in the park, enjoying the September sunshine, had afternoon tea and gone dancing at the Lyceum.

Now, eating breakfast in the kitchen, left on

their own by Winnie and Bella who'd already said goodbye to Alastair, the last minutes together were rushing by.

'You need to eat some toast at least,' Alastair said. 'Doctor's orders.' He reached his hand across the table and took hold of hers.

'I can't, no appetite.' Frankie tried her best to smile. 'Don't worry, I'll have somethin' later; Mrs Connelly makes sure we don't starve.'

'You will look after yourself, won't you?' His eyes held hers.

'Us ambulance girls need to keep fit and strong; the boss would soon be after me if I didn't.'

'I know, she's a good woman. She told me she'd look out for you, she always does.'

Frankie raised her eyebrows. 'And when was that?'

'When I came to find you the other day and told her what was going on.'

He glanced at his watch and sighed. 'I'm going to have to go.' He stood up and came around to her side of the table and pulled her into his arms when she stood up, hugging her tightly.

'I've changed my mind, I'm comin' to the station with you.' Her throat was aching so much she could hardly speak.

'No, not this time.' He loosened his arms and stepped back, putting a finger under her chin and gently raising her face so that their eyes met. 'We agreed. It's not that I don't want you to, I would love more time with you, anything I can have, but I couldn't leave you standing there on your own upset when I left. This way is best;

you've got Winnie and Bella here with you.'

She swallowed hard against the lump that had wedged itself firmly in her throat and nodded, not daring to speak.

'I love you, Frankie, so very much, and meeting you has been the best thing about coming to work in London.' He stopped and cleared his throat. 'I'm so happy that you want to be my wife and as soon as I get the chance to come home we'll get married, all right?'

Tears were blurring her eyes and she didn't try to stop them as they spilled over and slipped down her face. 'I love you, too.'

Alastair wiped her tears away with his thumb, kissed her and then enveloped her in a fierce hug, resting his chin on her head.

Frankie held on to him hard, not wanting to ever let him go, imprinting the feel of his arms around her into her memory. Slowly he loosened his grip and stepped back, taking a long, hard look at her before swiftly kissing her again and then striding over to the door where his bag was waiting.

Frankie ran over to him for one last kiss and then he was gone. She felt bereft and had to stop herself from running after him, even though every cell in her body was screaming out for her to do just that. She heard him shut the outside door and his army boots clumping up the steps to the pavement and then fade away. She stood stock-still, frozen, only aware of the blood rushing around her head, and an awful hollow feeling that had settled in her chest. She didn't know that her friends had come in to the room

338

until gentle hands took hold of her, pulling her into a warm hug as Winnie and Bella enveloped her in their arms. Then she began to cry. They didn't say anything, and for that she was grateful, they just continued to hold her and hand her a handkerchief until her tears dried up.

'Hot, sweet tea,' Winnie ordered eventually, guiding Frankie to sit down as Bella made the drink. 'You're going nowhere till you've had some.'

Frankie didn't argue and drank the tea silently when Bella gave it to her, grateful for the warmth and sweetness it provided.

'The worst bit's over now,' Bella said, taking hold of Frankie's hand. 'Saying goodbye is hard.'

'Absolutely,' Winnie agreed. 'It's utterly beastly, but saying hello again next time will be divine — keep that in mind now, Frankie, for when you next see Alastair. It will be heavenly.'

Bella laughed. 'We get the picture. How are you feeling now?'

'I'm all right.' She sighed. 'I'll be fine, honestly I will, thousands of other women have their fiancés overseas, we all have to just carry on, there ain't no other choice.'

'Exactly, chin up, old girl,' Winnie said. 'Now we'd better get a move on or we'll be late for work and the boss will be after us.'

'Thank you,' Frankie said, doing her best to smile.

'What for?' Winnie said.

'For being here and mopping up my tears.'

'That's what we do, it's what friends are for,' Bella said. 'And like you and I do for Winnie if she starts moping around, she and I will do the same for you; we'll pick you up and stop you feeling bad. We're all in this together.'

'Like the three musketeers,' Winnie said. 'One for all and all for one!'

'But without the swords and fighting,' Bella added with a grin.

⋆ ⋆ ⋆

The day looked how she felt, Frankie thought, looking up at the grey clouds scudding across the sky in the brisk wind — unsettled and gloomy. Inside the courtyard of Station 75 it was fairly sheltered from the wind, but there was a definite feeling of autumn in the air and she could feel the coolness on her wet hands as she washed the windscreen of her ambulance. She was glad to be doing this routine work today, keeping herself busy and helping to distract her from thinking about Alastair being gone.

'Frankie.' Rose's voice made her look around. 'I must tell you that I'm afraid Ivy and I had an argument this morning — she might say something about it when you see her tomorrow.'

'What 'appened? What was it about?' Frankie asked, instantly on alert at the news of Ivy arguing with Rose in her absence.

Rose looked uncomfortable. 'It was about you.'

'Me?'

'Ivy wanted to know where you were and what you were doing, but it's all right, I didn't tell her as you told me not to.'

'Thank you.' Frankie hadn't told Ivy anything about Alastair joining up or about him being posted overseas; she didn't trust her not to make some unkind or nasty remark about it. It was bad enough him going, without Ivy adding any of her barbed comments to how Frankie felt about it. 'I'm really sorry she was 'orrible to you; I know what she's like, how unkind she can be.'

Rose's blue eyes filled with tears. 'She threatened to throw me out on the street if I didn't tell her.'

'What?' Frankie's blood was fizzing around her body and she squeezed her hands into tight fists. 'She 'ad no right to say that at all. My name is on the rent book, not hers — I made sure of that after Grandad died. She shouldn't 'ave threatened you that way.'

'I didn't give in and tell her, though.' Rose managed a watery smile. 'She wasn't very happy about it.'

Frankie put her arm around Rose's shoulders. 'You 'ave no fear of losing your home. You can live at 25 Matlock Street for as long as you want to, and that's a promise.'

'Thank you, Frankie.'

'I'm going to be 'aving words with Ivy about this, she ain't going to get away with upsetting you.'

'It's all right, you don't need to, I'm fine, I know she can be unkind and say nasty things.'

'Yes, and don't I know it?' Frankie sighed. 'But it's none of her business where I was. She's always telling me she ain't doing anything for me, so she 'as no right to suddenly want to know

341

where I am and what I'm doing.'

'She definitely wanted to know this morning,' Rose said.

'Thank you for not tellin' her and I'm really sorry you got it in the neck for protecting me. I'll sort it out with her.' Frankie held up her hand. 'And don't worry, I can 'andle Ivy, I've had enough practice.'

Back at work on her ambulance, Frankie couldn't get what Ivy had done to Rose out of her mind. Threatening to throw her out was viciously unkind, especially knowing what Rose had been through, having to leave her home and family. Thinking about it made her so damn angry and coming on top of Alastair going away magnified her feelings. Ivy had to be sorted out. Frankie couldn't let her behaviour go unchecked and she wasn't prepared to wait until the end of this twenty-four-hour shift tomorrow to sort it out either. She'd go and find Ivy today, go in the dinner-time break to where her step-grandmother worked. That way she could deal with it sooner and Rose wouldn't have to witness it and Frankie risk the vile woman turning her venom towards poor, sweet Rose again.

★   ★   ★

Frankie had sought permission from Station Officer Steele to leave the station over the dinner-time break, telling her she had some urgent family business to deal with, and now she stood, arms folded across her chest, waiting for the doors of Cohen's garment factory to open and the women to spill outside for their break. She knew the routine well enough as she'd worked here before she'd joined the Ambulance Service.

At 12.30 on the dot, the door was flung open and the women poured out in twos and threes, finding somewhere to sit around the area and opening their packet or tins of sandwiches. Some of them recognised Frankie.

'You come back to join us again, 'ave yer, ducks?' one woman said.

'No, I'm just here to see Ivy,' Frankie answered.

'Well, you look smart in yer uniform,' the woman said. 'Ivy'll be along in a minute; the supervisor was just 'aving a word with her.' She raised her eyebrows as if to say that happened a lot.

A few more minutes passed, and Frankie was about to go in and find Ivy when she spotted her coming out through the door looking like thunder. Finding her step-granddaughter waiting for her did nothing to improve the look on her face.

'What are you doin' 'ere?' Ivy said, taking her cigarettes out of her handbag, putting one to her lips and lighting it.

'I've come to see you.' Frankie put her arm through Ivy's and steered her over to the far corner of the factory yard, out of earshot of the other women. 'I 'eard you've been asking where I was.'

Ivy's ice-blue eyes narrowed. 'Yeah, I don't

343

know what your grandad would 'ave said about you stoppin' out all night, and I know you weren't at work 'cos Rose was at 'ome.'

'No, I wasn't at work, but where I was is none of your business, Ivy.' Frankie looked her straight in the eye. 'And if I ever 'ear of you being unkind to Rose again I'll put your threat of throwing her out into action, only it won't be Rose made homeless, it'll be you!'

Ivy drew on her cigarette, her lipsticked lips puckering and wrinkling around it, and then blew out a stream of smoke upwards before smiling a cruel-looking smile that didn't reach her eyes.

'You can't do that.'

'Oh, can't I? It's *my* name on the rent book, not yours. I'm in charge of who lives in the 'ouse and if you can't behave like a decent human being then you're out!' Frankie glared at the other woman, her hands on her hips. 'This is your *final* warning; any more, bitchy, vicious unkindness from you and you're out. Got it?'

Frankie didn't bother to wait for a reply, she turned and walked away to where she'd left her bicycle, her heart drumming hard, but she felt a whole lot better for what she'd just done. She'd more than honoured her promise to her grandad to look out for Ivy; if it hadn't been for her often making up the rent, the vile woman would have had to leave 25 Matlock Street months ago. Ivy had pushed Frankie to the very limit this time and the next time she over-stepped the mark, she'd be out, and Frankie would be delighted to see her go.

57

'The boss wants you, and quick!'

Bella stopped sweeping out the back of the ambulance and looked at Rose, who'd just delivered the message. 'Why?'

'There's a telephone call for you. She said to be quick. I'll take over here for you, if you like.'

'No, it's all right; you've got your own work to do.' Bella jumped out of the ambulance. 'But thanks anyway.'

Hurrying to the office, she wondered who it could be telephoning. It was always a worry if someone rang here: was someone hurt, or worse?

Her worry must have shown on her face because the moment she reached the office doorway Station Officer Steele said, 'It's nothing to worry about, Bella — quite the opposite, in fact.' She handed her the telephone receiver and sat smiling at her.

'Hello? Bella said.

'Ah, Bella, it's Fred Dawson here from *The War Illustrated*.' Her stomach tightened, the last time she'd seen him she'd lost her writing job when he'd told her that they didn't want her to write about working for the Ambulance Service any more. 'I hear you've been writing a station magazine, it's very good to know you've kept up with your writing. I have another opportunity for you: we want to run a column looking at women's jobs for the war effort to help encourage those who aren't doing anything to join in. The editor and I thought of you . . . you being a woman . . . well, you'd see it from a . . . woman's point of view.' He paused for a breath and then went on. 'What you'd have to do is interview a variety of women doing different jobs, you'd write about one job per issue. What do you think?'

Bella was stunned. She'd given up all hope of ever being asked to write for them again, it was last December that she'd written her last piece and that was some eleven months ago now. The idea of writing about a different job each time sounded good, there would be no need to struggle to find something interesting to say as she'd done at the end of writing about the Ambulance Service, and she'd get to interview women about what they were doing. It would be fun and interesting.

'I'll do it! In fact, Mr Dawson, I would love to do it. Thank you very much for asking me.'

'I'm very glad you said yes, you're the perfect person for this job: you have a lovely writing voice and I know you'll do a good job. Your first column is due on December the first.'

'How many words?' Bella asked.

'Eight hundred, and a photograph as well. If you let me know where you go, I can send a photographer there to take some pictures. I'm glad to be working with you again, Bella. Cheerio.' He hung up.

'Well, that's a wonderful surprise, isn't it?' Station Officer Steele beamed at Bella. 'And a great opportunity. I was telling him about you writing for and running *Seventy-five Blitz and Pieces;* he was very impressed.'

'I'm surprised and delighted. I never thought I'd hear from him again.'

'You obviously made a good impression before and he did say he'd be in touch if anything suitable came up, and now it has. What are you going to write about first, any ideas?'

'A few, I'll need to think about it first, but in the meantime, I'd better get back to cleaning out the ambulance.'

'You can think about it while you work,' the boss said.

Bella smiled. 'I will be, don't worry.' Her mind was going to be toying with ideas for the rest of the day.

★   ★   ★

The next afternoon, Bella was working at the table in the basement kitchen of Connie's house, sheets of paper with possible ideas for her column spread out in front of her. Her mind had been whirling with possibilities ever since Mr Dawson had given her the job, and she was trying to work out which was the best one to start with.

'You look busy.' A voice made her start and she turned around to see James in the doorway.

She put a hand to her chest. 'Oh, you made me jump!' She leapt up and rushed over to throw her arms around him. 'What are you doing here?'

James hugged her back and then put his arm

around her and led her over to the table. 'I've got the day off and I thought I'd come up to London and see if you'd like to come out for tea before I have to catch the train back to Bletchley. What are you up to? You looked completely absorbed in it when I came in.'

'It's for my new job.' She'd told him about Mr Dawson's telephone call yesterday. 'I'm trying to work out what's the best one to do first. I want to make a good impression with readers and make sure the editor keeps the column going.'

James read the list of jobs that she'd written down. 'They're all good. You need to think about which ones are going to be easier to do than others: the Fire Service will be easy, there are plenty of fire stations around. Come on, let me take you out for tea and we can talk about it over tea and cake.'

'All right, then, thank you. Just give me time to put on something nice and we'll go out,' Bella said.

⋆ ⋆ ⋆

The Lyons Corner House they went to was warm and cosy inside after the cold walk through the darkening November afternoon, the tinkling of the piano making the atmosphere most inviting.

'What would you like?' James asked as Bella scanned the menu.

'Tea and scones, please,' Bella said.

'I'll have the same,' James said.

After the nippy had taken their order, James

348

reached out and took hold of Bella's hand across the table. 'Have you heard from your brother lately?'

'Yes, just the other day — one of his short letters, but he was all right. They'd had their Red Cross parcels, so he was happy about that. He said they were going to put on a concert, he was doing a turn with his mouth organ.'

'They put concerts on at work sometimes,' James said. 'They're always looking for people to do a turn or act in a play.'

'You should do something.'

James shook his head. 'Winnie's the exhibitionist in our family. I'll just go along and watch.'

'Do you like what you do?' Bella asked. 'It doesn't sound very interesting, if you don't mind me saying so, all that paperwork. Winnie says you're too clever to be doing that.'

He shrugged. 'It's what the powers that be put me in when I signed up.'

'What about after the war? Do you ever think about what you'd like to do then?'

'I'd rather like to carry on with my studies, go back to university and do some research.'

Bella smiled at him. 'I hope you do.'

'I don't think that will be for a while, though; the war's not over yet. What . . . ' He paused as the nippy returned with a tray of their tea things. 'What about you, what would you like to do after it's all over?'

'Not go back to being a housemaid, that's for sure,' Bella said, pouring them both a cup of tea. 'I'd rather like to train as a teacher if I can. I could always do secretarial work, I suppose, now

I know how to do shorthand and typing.'

'Or better still, work as a writer.' James spread some jam on his scone. 'Make use of your talent.'

'We'll see. Like you said, the war's not over yet so I'm not dwelling on what comes next. I need to deal with what's coming soon, and that's my new writing job for Mr Dawson. Come on, which women's job should be written about in my first article? Help me work it out, James. It needs to be a good one to attract the readers.'

58

'How long should it take to sail from South Africa to England?' Station Officer Steele suddenly asked.

Winnie looked at the boss and frowned. They were in the office going through some details of the running of Station 75 when she'd suddenly asked her the odd question. 'I beg your pardon?'

The boss repeated her question, adding, 'I thought my sister would have been here by now; it's been seven weeks since she sent me the telegram to say they were leaving the next day.'

'I'm not sure. Can't you get in touch with the shipping company to find out when her ship's due in?' Winnie said.

'I can't. I don't know what ship she was sailing on, she didn't say in her telegram.' The boss sighed. 'I'm worried something's happened to them and I have no idea and no way of finding out. It was bad enough when she was in Singapore, but I thought my worries were over when she said she was coming home.'

'I know it's hard but try not to worry,' Winnie said sympathetically. 'Sometimes journeys take longer than expected; there might have been delays.'

'I know, I'm just impatient to have her and the girls safely back in England.'

'Now that's an admission indeed, you being impatient!' Winnie smiled at her boss. 'I thought

I was the one who suffered from that.'

Station Officer Steele smiled. 'You are not the only one; it jumps out and bites us all from time to time, usually over something we long for so desperately.' She paused and took a deep breath. 'In the meantime, I have a station to run and something extra to organise and I'm going to need your help.'

'What is it?' she asked.

'Can you march, and more to the point can you teach marching?' Winnie frowned. 'Pardon?'

'Have you ever done any marching, Winnie? It's a simple enough question.'

'And it's a simple answer: no!' Winnie laughed. 'Why on earth have you asked me that?'

'As you may well be aware, we have Civil Defence Day coming up in a couple of weeks on November the fifteenth and the Ambulance Service have been asked to take part and march past the King and Queen. Well, our station has been chosen to take part to represent the service.' The boss looked pleased. 'It's an honour and we need to present a well-turned-out crew who can march perfectly.'

'But we're not the army,' Winnie said. One of the reasons she'd chosen to join the Ambulance Service instead of one of the services like the WAAFs or WRENS was her loathing of being told what to do, especially for what seemed like pointless things like marching up and down. Taking orders in the Ambulance Service had been difficult enough at times, but at least they didn't have all the rules that dominated the lives of those women in the services and once she was off duty, she was free to go home and do what she wanted.

'Indeed, we're not, but we will be in the parade with other Civil Defence groups who will be marching, and I don't want Station 75 to let the Ambulance Service down by putting on a poor show.'

'Fair enough, but why ask me if I can teach it?'

Station Officer Steele raised her eyebrows behind her owlish glasses. 'Because as my Deputy Station Officer, I'm putting you in charge of preparing the crew for the parade and that entails teaching them to march.'

'Me!' Winnie shook her head. 'That's ridiculous, if you don't mind me saying-so.'

'Not at all.' The boss paused. 'And that's precisely why I want you to do it. You need a challenge, Winnie, and this is a good one to push you out of your comfortable routine.'

Winnie frowned. 'I honestly think you're making a mistake here. I'll learn to march if I have to, but me teaching it to the rest of the crew is utterly crazy — the blind leading the blind. I don't know how to march so how can I teach it? Sparky would be a far better choice than me, he was in the army.'

'I've made my decision, Winnie. I'm putting you in charge. How you go about it is up to you, as long as the job is done. Just use your initiative, you're an intelligent woman.' She picked up her pen and started to write on the sheet of paper on her desk, clearly signalling that their conversation was at an end.

'What's the matter with you? You look like you lost a shilling and found a tanner,' said Sparky, looking up from the engine of an ambulance, where he was topping up a battery with distilled water.

'Rather that than what the boss has just ordered me to do,' Winnie said.

'Aye, aye, what's she want now?'

'To teach the crew to march for Civil Defence Day on the fifteenth; Station 75 has been chosen to represent the Ambulance Service.' She shrugged. 'And I haven't ever marched myself before, let alone taught anyone. She tells me I've got to use my initiative.'

'Well, you have, ain't you?' Sparky said, screwing the top back on the bottle of distilled water. 'You've come to the right place; I can teach you how to march, Winnie. It ain't difficult, even for you!'

She ignored his last remark. 'Would you?'

'Yes, I said I would. It'll be nice takin' part in the parade; my missis can come along and watch.'

'Thank you, Sparky, I really would appreciate your help.' She smiled at him. 'I did suggest to the boss that you taught the crew but she wouldn't have it.'

'Hang on, I'm only teaching you; you've got to teach the rest of them, not me.' Sparky grinned. 'This is going to be an interesting challenge.'

★ ★ ★

After an intensive lesson on how to march from Sparky, Winnie was feeling more optimistic about carrying out Station Officer Steele's order. Marching hadn't been that bad, she'd managed to march forward at a steady pace, her arms swinging backwards and forwards looking the part. Now, with the crew members gathered in the courtyard of Station 75, wrapped in warm clothes against the chill of the November day, all she had to do was pass on what she'd learned.

'Listen up, everyone, can you arrange yourself into rows of six?' She paused and looked at Sparky, who nodded his head in agreement and then took up his position in the front row as she'd asked him to do.

Once the crew were lined up in their rows it was obvious that they needed some readjustment before they could even begin marching — some people were closer together than others and the whole group looked a mess.

'You need to space yourselves out evenly. If you put your right arm out so that your knuckles touch your neighbour's shoulder,' she said, remembering what Sparky had told her, 'that's how far apart you need to be. Do that and we should have a tidier-looking crew.'

'This ain't the army,' someone shouted from the back row.

'I know that,' Winnie retorted. 'But we need to look smart to march past the King and Queen.'

With a great deal of shuffling and some more adjustment, Winnie was finally satisfied with the formation. Her lesson with Sparky had been much easier than this because she'd only had herself to think about; clearly teaching a group of twenty-four crew members to march in formation was going to be a lot harder.

'That's great, so the next thing we need to do is practise marching. On my command 'Forward' you need to put your weight into your right foot but not move, and when I say 'March' step your left foot forward and swing your arms in a natural motion opposite to your feet, so left foot forward and right arm forward. When I say 'Halt' you stop and come back to standing as you are now. Is that clear?'

'As mud,' the joker on the back row called again.

'You're doing all right, ignore 'im,' Sparky said, smiling at her encouragingly.

'Where are you goin' to be?' Frankie asked from her position in the second row in between Bella and Rose.

'I'll be marching along beside you, don't worry.' Winnie moved herself into position near the front row. 'Ready . . . Forward . . . March!' Winnie stepped forward and started to march just as Sparky had taught her and the rest of the front row moved off with reasonable ease, but the noise of laughing and comments of 'Get a move on or we'll march into you', from the rows near the back made Winnie turn round only to see a jam of bodies almost crashing into each other. The formation was skewing to the side as crew members were out of step with each other, their arms swinging out of time and looking more like windmills. The whole thing was a complete mess.

Winnie shouted, 'Halt!' and a movement in the window of the common room upstairs caught her eye. It was Station Officer Steele watching this disastrous attempt at teaching the crew to match.

'It's too many things to think about all at once,' Hooky complained.

Winnie started to bristle and would happily have given up but she couldn't — it was her responsibility to teach the crew to march and she would somehow, even if it took every drop of her very limited patience. Station Officer Steele had said it would be a challenge — she was absolutely right.

'All right, fair enough, let's just try the feet first. Get back in formation like we started with before. Reach out your right arm to touch your neighbour's shoulder.'

Thankfully, they managed to do that much quicker and better than the first time.

'Remember on the command of 'Forward' it's weight into your right foot but don't move and then when I say 'March' you step your left foot forward.'

'Which is my left foot?' someone shouted, and everyone laughed.

'Ready? Forward . . . March.' Winnie stood and watched rather than join in this time and there was some improvement but there was still a bit of crowding as some crew members were going faster than others. 'Halt! That was better, but you need to all go at the same speed. Sparky, can you march at the front to set the pace and the rest of you follow him, no slower, no faster.

Back in formation . . . '

After half an hour of practice, the crew were getting there: the formation was neater, the pace was steady and most of the crew were managing to get their arms swinging in the same direction at the same time.

'Let's call it a day,' Winnie said, her patience well and truly used up. 'You've done well, but we'll need some more practice sessions before the fifteenth.'

'You did all right,' Sparky said. 'It ain't easy and this lot ain't used to doing this sort of manoeuvre.'

'Why thank you, kind sir.' Winnie bobbed a curtsy. 'That is praise indeed. I could cheerfully have given up several times, and without you here to act as a role model it would have been utterly hopeless. Thank you, Sparky, I appreciate your help.'

'It was quite amusing.' He grinned. 'Made a change from sorting out ambulances.'

59

'I'll ride in the cab with you and Rose can walk in front,' Hooky said as they made their way down the stairs to the garage while Rose got the chit with the details of the call-out from Station Officer Steele.

Winnie halted and flung her arm across the narrow stairway to bar Hooky from going any further. It was only a matter of minutes since the boss had told her that Hooky was going out with them and already the woman was starting to infuriate her with her self-centred attitude. She could feel herself starting to bristle and the blood rushing around her head. It had been sheer bliss to not have to work closely with Hooky over the last months, but tonight's thick fog made it necessary to send out teams of three in each ambulance and Station Officer Steele was having to make use of all crew members — even Hooky, who usually worked in the kitchen.

Winnie took a deep breath before she turned back and looked at Hooky. 'Right, let's get this straight — you are coming out in my ambulance and I will be deciding who does what and when. Not you. Me!'

Hooky looked startled. 'Well . . . I was only making a suggestion; we'll both take turns, obviously.'

'Since this is the first time Rose will have been

out in thick fog like this, she's going to need to learn what to do, so she can ride in the cab with me to start with to see how it's done and you can walk ahead guiding us.'

Hooky pressed her lips into a thin line. She clearly wanted to challenge what Winnie had said but for once had the sense to keep silent.

'Come on, it's going to take long enough to get there without wasting any more time,' Winnie went on, and she hurried down the rest of the stairs to the outside door where Trixie stood waiting for them.

★   ★   ★

Even with Hooky walking ahead of them shining her torch along the kerb, Winnie found it hard to see more than a yard or two in front of the ambulance bonnet. Using the white-painted kerb as a guide to prevent her from straying across the road, she drove slowly along, no faster than walking pace, keeping Hooky and the kerb in sight, her left foot hovering over the brake in case she needed to stop suddenly.

'It's so thick; I've never seen fog like it,' Rose said, peering out of the front windscreen as she held Trixie on her lap.

'It's a real pea-souper,' Winnie said. 'Thick fog combined with the smoke from thousands of chimneys makes almost zero visibility and causes a lot of accidents because people can neither see where they're going nor be seen, which makes a lot of call-outs for us.'

Usually Station 75's call-outs were for air-raid

casualties, but tonight's dense fog — bringing an increase in accidents and longer time needed to get to and from calls — had overwhelmed the normal Ambulance Service and Auxiliary stations like theirs had been called in to help.

They made achingly slow progress and Winnie's left foot was cramping painfully from hovering over the brake by the time they reached their destination and she parked outside the terrace house they'd been sent to. Their arrival must have been looked for as the front door of the house was thrown open, light filtering out into the fog and turning it a milky green colour, and a woman hurried out, waving her arm at them.

'Hurry up, please,' the woman said as they climbed out of the ambulance. 'My daughter's in trouble and I don't know how much longer she can last.'

'I'll come straight in,' Winnie said. 'Rose, Hooky, you get the stretcher and bring it in.'

'Thank you.' The woman led Winnie into the front parlour, which had been set up with a bed on which lay a young woman writhing in agony, her swollen belly immediately showing what was going on. Winnie didn't like taking expectant mothers in the back of her ambulance, especially those in labour — she hadn't forgotten the last time she did when they'd narrowly missed a building falling down on them. But it wasn't just that, it was the fear of the baby being born and her not knowing what to do properly. She wasn't a midwife.

'She's been 'aving the pains since yesterday

and the doctor's been and said she needs to get to hospital, he's told me to call for an ambulance and had to go off to another delivery.'

It was obvious that the young woman needed to get to hospital and fast, but with the fog hampering how quickly she could go, it was going to be a long and anxious journey.

'It's all right, we'll get her there, don't worry.' Winnie smiled at the mother, doing her best to look more confident than she felt.

The young woman was soon in the back of the ambulance, attended to by Hooky, at Winnie's insistence, since she had some experience of transporting expectant mothers to hospital. So it was Rose's turn to act as guide.

'Keep your torch on the kerb and if for any reason you need to stop you need to signal to me before you do, wave your arm out to the side so I can see. I don't want to run you over. All right?'

Rose nodded. 'I can do this, Winnie, I will be fine. Rather this than in there.' She nodded to the back of the ambulance.

'Me too. Remind me sometime to tell you the tale of the last time Hooky and I took a mother in labour to hospital,' she said, before climbing into the cab and starting the engine. Rose moved into position in front of the ambulance, shining her torch on the kerb as she started to walk ahead, quickly disappearing into the gloom in only a few yards. Winnie put the ambulance in gear and gently pulled away to follow her.

They made painfully slow progress to the London Hospital, and a journey that would normally take a matter of ten minutes or so took four or five times as long. It wasn't helped by Hooky frequently hissing 'How much further?' or 'How long now?' through the grille in the back of the cab. Winnie desperately wanted to go faster but it would have been dangerous and downright foolish in the swirling fog that held the streets of the city in its creepy grasp.

As the gate posts of the hospital finally loomed up out of the fog, Winnie felt a huge sense of relief. The expectant mother, whose groans of agony had filtered through to the cab, would soon be helped, and Winnie hoped that her child could be born safely and live to tell the tale of its mother's journey through the fog.

60

Bella had experienced many different things since joining the ambulance service, but guiding an ambulance through such thick fog was the eeriest. The cold, dank mist that had settled over London on this chilly November Armistice Day had turned familiar streets into a spooky world where she could see only a yard or two in each direction, and the air was full of the smell of smoky chimneys.

For someone who had grown up in the countryside and had been used to being able to see far off into the distance, the streets of London had seemed cramped and crowded when she'd first arrived to work in the city. Slowly she'd grown used to only being able to see to the end of the street, but now, even that was gone, with the fog feeling like it was pressing down on her, blocking out the world. As darkness fell, it seemed to crowd around even closer, and Bella had to keep reminding herself that it was just tiny drops of water in the air and nothing more sinister and that up above it the stars would still be twinkling down on London. She shivered, pulling her scarf up higher around her neck.

Distances were hard to judge in the fog, and without being able to see across to the other side of the road and pick out familiar buildings as landmarks it was hard to tell exactly where they were until she was within a couple of yards of something and it loomed up out of the fog. The junction with Aldgate should be coming up soon, she thought, though how they were going to get across it safely in this, Bella wasn't sure. She was grateful that this call-out was to an incident at the Houndsditch and Bishopsgate junction and no further, for it was taking an awful lot longer than normal to make this journey. She hoped that whoever they were going to help could hang on till they got there.

Aldgate junction was thankfully under the direction of policemen, who were directing traffic using flaming torches which made bright globes of milky white light as they were waved around to keep the traffic moving safely, albeit at a snail's pace.

As she approached the far end of Houndsditch, Bella could gradually make out where the casualty was: a policeman and a small group of people seemed to be gathered around someone lying on the ground, their figures slowly growing clearer, coming into focus as if through a camera lens. Signalling with her arm outstretched that she was going to stop, Bella stepped out of the road and on to the pavement, and Frankie pulled over to park beside her.

'The casualty's over there,' Bella said, opening the passenger door of the ambulance where Pip, one of the volunteer crew members, sat beside Frankie — like all the other ambulances that had been sent out tonight, they were a crew of three instead of the usual two. 'I'll go and see what's happened while you get the stretcher out.'

'All right, we'll be there as quick as we can,' Frankie said.

As she always did when approaching a casualty, Bella started to look for clues for what had happened to them and what treatment they might need. Getting closer she could see it was a man and he wasn't moving so probably unconscious.

'You're here!' the policeman said, spotting her approaching.

'He's been hit by a bus, stepped out in front of it in the fog.'

'You can hardly see your hand in front of your face in this,' Bella said. 'Let's have a look at him. Hello, can you hear — ' She knelt down beside the man but her voice faltered when she saw his face — a dear face that she knew so well. James. It was as if she had suddenly been doused with a pail of icy water. What was he doing here? He should have been safe in Bletchley, not here. Not lying here hurt.

'Bella!' Frankie's voice startled her. 'Oh my God.' Frankie knelt down beside her. 'Let me do this, Bella.'

'No!' Bella reached out to take his pulse, but Frankie firmly took hold of her hand and pushed it away.

'I'll do it,' Frankie insisted. 'You keep talking to James; see if you can get 'im to come round.'

'Do you know this man?' the policeman asked.

Bella nodded. 'He's James Churchill.' She turned her attention back to James while Frankie started doing the checks to assess his injuries as much as she could. 'James, can you hear me? It's

366

Bella. Wake up, James. Can you open your eyes?'

There was no response.

'Frankie's here and we're going to take you to hospital so they can sort you out,' Bella said, gently stroking his face. He looked as if he were just asleep and could wake up at any moment.

'I can't feel any broken bones,' Frankie said a few minutes later.

'He might have hit his head when he landed on the ground and knocked himself out cold.'

'The bus that hit him weren't going fast, nothing is in this fog,' the policeman said, 'but it still caught him and the impact threw him down.'

'We need to get him to hospital so the doctors can see what the matter is. Maybe he'll just wake up on the way there.' Frankie put her hand on Bella's arm. 'Pip and I will carry him to the ambulance; you can watch over him in the back on the way to hospital, all right?'

Bella nodded, she would have insisted on watching over him on the journey to hospital if Frankie had suggested otherwise, but her friend understood the need for her to be with him, she had wanted the same when they'd taken her injured grandfather to hospital.

Once they were on the way, Bella knelt by James's side, holding on to his hand and willing him to wake up, to flicker his eyelids, anything, but he didn't. She kept a close watch on him, her torch giving off a dim light so that she could see him. Never had a journey to hospital taken so long, each minute was stretched out and the ambulance seemed to be barely moving along as they had to crawl at walking pace because of the fog.

'What were you doing there?' Bella asked him. 'Where were you going to? Had you been somewhere?' She racked her brains, trying to remember if James had said anything about coming to London the last time she'd spoken to him on the telephone a couple of days ago, but then sometimes he was sent there to a meeting at very short notice. That's what must have happened today; he'd be able to tell her when he woke up.

'You'll be fine once the doctors have checked you over, probably have a horrible headache for a day or two, but you're lucky no bones are broken.' She stroked his face and suddenly stilled, aware that no warm breath was coming out of his nose. He'd stopped breathing. Bella quickly felt for a pulse in his wrist, her fingers fumbling in her haste. She couldn't feel one. Her own pulse now rapidly drumming in her body, she tried his neck, but again there was nothing. Panic surging through her, she tore off the top of the blanket and put her head on his chest to listen for his heartbeat. It was silent.

The world seemed to freeze in that moment and her blood along with it. James was dead.

She opened her mouth to shout out, but no words came out, her mouth suddenly parched dry. She swallowed and tried again, this time managing a feeble, 'Frankie!' and she banged hard on the back of the cab to attract her attention.

'You all right, back there?' Frankie's voice

came through the grille.

'No!' This time her voice came out in a wail. 'Help!'

She felt the ambulance stop. 'I'm coming,' Frankie called.

Moments later the back of the ambulance was thrown open and Frankie climbed in, Pip standing in the doorway behind her.

'Bella, what's happened?'

'He's dead!' Bella was shaking, her whole body shuddering as if she were freezing cold.

Frankie felt for James's pulse, trying his wrist and then neck, just as Bella had done, and finally listening for his heartbeat, her solemn expression speaking volumes. She shook her head and put her arms around Bella and held her tightly.

'What happened?' Frankie said, when she loosened her arms but still holding on to Bella.

'He just stopped breathing. I was watching him like a hawk . . . and he just stopped. I don't know why . . . ' She started to cry, her body heaving with great sobs. 'What did I do wrong?'

'Nothing, you did nothing wrong!' Frankie looked her in the eye.

'He may have had internal injuries or a brain injury; it was nothing we could see. You did everything that any one of us would have done.' She blinked back her own tears. 'We're going to have to get him to the hospital all the same, you know the routine.'

Bella nodded.

'I'm going to have to drive and Pip will lead us through the fog. Do you want to sit in the cab with me?'

369

'No, I want to be here with him.'

'I understand. Shout for me to stop if you need me to, all right?' Frankie hugged her again in a fierce embrace and then climbed out of the ambulance and with a last look in at her, closed the door.

Bella knelt down beside James and took hold of his hand, stroking his hair with her other . . . She stayed in that position all the way to the London, glad that they were going so slowly as she didn't want the journey to end because this would be the last time they would be together and she didn't want to say goodbye to James, not now, not ever.

61

Frankie sat cross-legged beside the mattress where Bella lay, gently stroking her friend's hair and willing her to fall asleep so that she could find some fleeting peace from the torment she was suffering.

Returning to Station 75 a short while ago, Frankie had taken charge of Bella, bringing her inside and telling the boss what had happened. Station Officer Steele had been marvellous, swooping in like an angel and knowing just what to do, insisting that Bella go and rest after she'd drunk a cup of sweet tea for the shock. Now Bella lay in the quiet of the women's rest room, no nearer sleep than when she'd first come in here. She lay quite still, seemingly unaware that Frankie was there, her brown eyes staring up at the ceiling.

'Try to sleep,' Frankie said softly.

Bella looked at her and shook her head, tears pooling in her eyes and then spilling over and running down the sides of her face.

Frankie's heart squeezed at seeing her friend like this, but she understood only too well how she felt. When her grandad died it had felt as though her world had suddenly crumbled to dust. She was left floundering, trying to make sense of it and to accept that it was the new normal, even though it felt anything but right and all she'd wanted was to go back to how things were. How things should have been. People died at random, you never knew when, and war made that so much more likely. Only James hadn't been killed by war; his death, as a result of the fog, seemed so senseless, stupid and a terrible, terrible waste of a young life.

'It's all right; just do what you need to do, sleep if you want, stay awake.' She took hold of Bella's hand.

Bella nodded her head slightly and returned her gaze to the ceiling.

The door of the rest room opened, and Rose came in. The sight of her made Frankie's stomach clench — if she was here then Winnie was back, too.

'The boss sent me to fetch you,' Rose said. She looked at Bella and frowned. 'Are you ill, Bella?'

'I'll be back soon,' Frankie whispered to Bella and then stood up and went over to Rose. 'Can you stay with Bella for a bit, please?'

Rose nodded. 'Is she ill?'

'No.' Frankie leaned close to her and whispered what had happened.

Rose gasped. 'I'm so sorry.'

'I 'ave to go and speak to Winnie, so will you stay with Bella?'

'Yes, don't worry, I'll keep with her.'

Frankie patted Rose's shoulder and with a final glance back at Bella, who still lay staring at the ceiling, she headed for Station Officer Steele's office, dreading what she was going to find there. Hesitating outside the open door of the boss's office, Frankie looked in at Winnie who was signing off the job, looking quite normal, with Trixie waiting close by her mistress. Station Officer Steele looked up and saw her standing there and their eyes locked, the older woman looked like she was feeling the same way as Frankie, that she dreaded having to tell Winnie the news that would change her life for ever. Watching her friend now, moments before they had to tell her that her brother was dead, was painful. Frankie desperately wished James hadn't been hurt, hadn't died, and that there was no need for them to break the news to Winnie. If only they could let her go on being the happy person she looked now, but they had no choice, her brother was dead and she had to be told.

'Frankie! Come in,' Station Officer Steele said, beckoning her in.

Winnie spun around. 'You're back too. Isn't it dreadful out there? It takes so much longer to get to patients and then take them to hospital . . . ' She paused and frowned. 'Are you all right, Frankie? You look a bit peaky, if you don't mind me saying so.'

'Sit down, Winnie,' the boss said. 'If you can close the door, Frankie.'

Frankie did as she was told and then went to stand beside Winnie and took hold of her friend's hand.

'What's going on?' Winnie looked up at her, her grey eyes wide.

Station Officer Steele reached out her hand and put it on Winnie's arm. 'Winnie, I'm afraid I have some bad news for you.'

Winnie instantly stiffened and Trixie jumped

up on to her lap, leaning against her chest as if she sensed something was wrong.

'What's happened? Is it Mac? Has he been hurt?'

'No, it's not Mac,' Frankie said.

'I'm sorry to have to tell you that your brother James has died,' the boss said, her voice gentle.

'James!' Winnie stared at them. 'No, that can't be right.'

'I'm so sorry, but it is,' Frankie said. 'Bella and I were sent out to an incident to collect an injured pedestrian near Bishopsgate and Houndsditch and it was James. He was crossing the road and got 'it by a bus in the fog. He died on the way to hospital — ' Frankie's voice cracked.

Winnie shook her head and stood up. She began to pace around the office, holding Trixie in her arms. 'James should be at Bletchley, not here in London, there must be some mistake.'

'There's no mistake, Winnie. Bella and Frankie know James well and it was him,' Station Officer Steele said. She put her arm around Winnie and guided her towards a chair and sat her down again.

Winnie sat in silence for a few moments, her hands stroking Trixie's soft fur as the little dog leaned against her chest. As the news sank in, her shoulders began to shake and her body heaved with sobs.

Frankie knelt down beside her friend, put her arms around her and held on to her as she cried. It was several minutes before Winnie could speak. 'I don't understand what he was doing there. How was he injured?'

'We don't know why he was there, but Bella said he sometimes had to come to London for meetings. It was an accident, the fog out there is . . . You know how bad it is and he was crossing the road and couldn't see the bus and . . . it wasn't going fast, so the policeman said, but it threw him and he must have 'it his head when he landed.' Frankie glanced at Station Officer Steele, who nodded at her to go on. 'He was unconscious when we got there and had been since the accident, so they said. He just never regained consciousness and he . . . he died on the way to hospital. I think perhaps his brain was injured . . . '

'Of all of us, James should have been safe . . . ' Winnie's voice was hoarse. 'Harry nearly got himself killed flying around and I'm out in raids, but James should have been safe at Bletchley pushing his bits of paper around, not hit by a bus in the bloody fog.' Tears ran down her cheeks and her chin wobbled as she fought to control herself. 'It's utterly wrong, utterly bloody wrong.'

And such a waste of a life, Frankie thought. Ripples from James's untimely death would impact the lives of his family and friends and his beloved Bella for the, rest of their lives. The Armistice Day fog would never be forgotten by those who knew him.

62

Winnie stared out of her bedroom window at the street below her, Trixie glued to her side, leaning against her mistress's legs. People were walking past as if nothing had happened. Didn't they know James was dead? But then again, why should they? They wouldn't have known he existed, *had* existed, her mind corrected for her. It was odd that life was carrying on as if nothing had happened. But something had happened, because James had died and Winnie's life would never be the same again, it had shifted, almost as if it had suddenly taken a new unexpected path.

An unwanted path, too. She sighed as another wave of grief rolled in and hit her hard in the chest, making her gasp. She left her lookout post at the window to seek the comfort of her bed. Flinging herself down on it, she threw the silky eiderdown over her head and let herself cry in the welcome darkness, her tears soaking into her bedclothes. Trixie crawled in under the covers and moulded her body to Winnie's, giving comfort the best way she could.

★ ★ ★

'Winnie!' Someone was knocking on her bedroom door. Trixie stirred and jumped to the floor, her feet making soft thuds as she landed on the carpet. Winnie's brain was fuzzy as she tried to comprehend that someone was calling her; she must have fallen asleep. 'Winnie,' the voice came again, it was Connie.

Throwing back the cover, Winnie called out, 'Come in.'

Connie came in, her face pale, with dark rings under her eyes. 'Did I wake you? I'm sorry.' She bent over to pat Trixie, who was dancing around her legs in welcome, and then came and sat on the edge of the bed. 'Sleep is good if you can manage it.' She sighed. 'It's escaped me but I'm not worrying about it too much, going on the theory that eventually I'll get so tired I'll just fall asleep.'

Winnie leaned her head on her hand. 'I wasn't planning on it. Last thing I knew I was crying . . . ' She shrugged.

'Your mother's been on the telephone; she's going to call back at three o'clock. I told her you were sleeping and I wouldn't disturb you. I didn't actually know you were but I knew you were up here and needed some time on your own.'

'Thanks.' Her mother was the last person she wanted to talk to right now, but she knew she'd have to.

'I expect she wants to know what happened, as much as you can tell her,' Connie went on.

'I know. I'll tell her what I can, I don't want her quizzing Bella about it, she's upset enough as it is. Where is Bella?'

'In the library.'

'That's where she and James first met, beginning their relationship through their mutual love of books . . . ' Winnie swallowed against the lump that was forming in her throat.

'They made a lovely couple and I had hoped they'd get married.' Connie shook her head.

They sat in silence for a few minutes, both thinking of what could have been and what should have been.

'I'd better get up, it'll soon be three and I need to be prepared.' Winnie pushed herself up to sitting and swung her legs around to the edge of the bed. 'Though I don't know what I'm going to say.'

'Just tell her what you know, that's all you can do. She wants to know how it happened, to understand why.' Connie stood up. 'It's so hard when people die unexpectedly; knowing what happened can help make sense of it.'

'I'm not sure I'll ever understand or accept it.' Winnie ran a hand through her honey-blonde hair, which she hadn't bothered putting into its usual rolled-up style today.

At three o'clock precisely the telephone started to ring. Winnie stared at it from where she sat on the bottom of the stairs, waiting for several long seconds before she went and picked up the receiver.

'Margot, is that you?' Her mother's voice came down the line sounding exactly as it always did; there was no hint of hoarseness from crying.

'Yes, hello, Mother.'

'What happened to James?'

Winnie opened her mouth to speak but no words came out, tears pricked her eyes and her throat felt like it was constricting. Crying to her mother would not do. Not do at all. She swallowed hard and took a deep breath, fighting to dampen down her feelings.

'Margot?' Her mother's voice carried a hint of impatience that Winnie knew so well. Hearing that acted like an injection of fuel, making her start to bristle with annoyance at the way her mother could make her feel with just the tone of her voice.

'He was crossing the road in the thick fog and was hit by a bus; he must have hit his head when he fell.' She said it as simply as she could.

'And where precisely did this happen?'

'Near the junction of Bishopsgate and Houndsditch.'

'Your father and I couldn't understand why he was in London and not Bletchley, so your father has made enquiries via the War Office and James had been at a meeting in London.'

That confirmed what Winnie had suspected; her brother did sometimes come to London for meetings to do with his work. Where he'd been and where he was going when he was hit they would never know, but even if they did it would make no difference to the outcome. It wouldn't bring him back.

'I understand that two of your colleagues took him to hospital,' her mother said.

'Yes, they did all they could for him but he was too badly injured.' Winnie wasn't going to tell her who it was; she didn't want Frankie and especially Bella being interrogated by her mother.

'I see.' Her mother paused. 'We've arranged

the funeral for the fourteenth, at two o'clock, no point in delaying it. You will need to ask for leave from work.'

'There's no need, it's my twenty-four hours off duty.' Though she knew Station Officer Steele would have given her time off if it had been necessary.

'Good. And will your . . . husband be attending?'

Winnie was instantly alert at the tone of her mother's voice, the way she had almost struggled to get the word 'husband' out and not referred to Mac by name. 'If he can get leave, then he'll be there. Mac liked James very much, and James felt the same way about him.' She'd telephoned Mac's depot and managed to speak to him that morning and told him what had happened.

'I will see you on Thursday, Margot. Goodbye.' Her mother ended the call abruptly.

Winnie replaced the receiver, glad that it was over. She didn't know what she'd been expecting, but her mother didn't sound like she'd just lost one of her children — there'd been no emotion there, no warmth, no compassion. But that was how she was, Winnie should know by now not to expect anything more, not even in such extraordinary and utterly beastly circumstances.

63

'Do you think you should really be here today?' Station Officer Steele asked Winnie and Bella, the two of them having come into work as usual this morning. She'd invited them into her office to have a cup of tea with her and to talk. 'It would be quite understandable for you to have a few days off on compassionate leave.'

Winnie shook her head as she stroked Trixie's ears, the little dog sitting on her lap, staying close to her as if sensing her need for comfort. 'No, I'd rather be here, keep busy.'

'Same for me,' Bella said, the usual spark missing from her brown eyes.

They both looked pale and were naturally subdued after what had happened, but the boss understood their need to keep busy. Isn't it what she did herself?

'Very well, but if you do need to go home I will understand, just come and tell me.' She paused. 'Do you know when the funeral will be?'

'Tomorrow, at two o'clock,' Winnie said. 'My parents have arranged it at their village church near Oxford. We'll be off duty then so there's no need for us to have time off.' She glanced at Bella who nodded in agreement. 'We'll be able to get there and back the same day.'

'You could stay with your parents for a day or two afterwards if you wanted,' Station Officer Steele suggested.

'Absolutely not!' Winnie snapped and then sighed, holding up her hand. 'I'm sorry, that was rude of me. I don't think it would be a good idea and in fact I definitely don't want to. They are difficult enough at the best of times, but now . . . ' She shrugged.

'No need to apologise, Winnie; I understand.' She smiled sympathetically. 'Do you think the crew need another practice march today?'

'It won't do any harm; they've just about mastered marching, but I don't want them to slip with only two days to go before the big day.' Winnie looked relieved at having something else to focus on. 'I'll go and get everyone organised.' She stood up, with Trixie in her arms. 'Will you help me tell everyone, Bella?'

Bella nodded, got up and went to pick up the tray of tea things.

'No, leave those, I'll deal with them in a moment,' the boss said.

'Would you ask Frankie to come and see me, please?'

A few minutes later Frankie appeared in the office doorway. 'You wanted to see me, boss?'

'Yes, please come in; and close the door behind you, if you would.' She motioned for Frankie to sit down beside her desk.

'Do you think I should send Winnie and Bella home? I'm worried about them and surprised they've both come in today.'

'They want to keep busy — it helps. Let them stay, at least they're with friends here.'

She nodded. 'I hear that the funeral is

tomorrow afternoon; that's going to be hard for them both.'

'I know. I'm going with them to support them, especially Bella as Winnie will be with her family there,' Frankie said.

'That's good. They're both putting on a brave face at work, but a funeral is a different matter and I know that Winnie has . . . difficulties with her mother. It will be good for them both to have you there to support them.'

'I 'ope Winnie's mother don't go upsetting her,' Frankie said.

'Indeed. It's a terrible thing to have happened and an awful waste of a young life. If he'd died fighting or in a bomb blast it might somehow have felt more acceptable, but to be run over in the fog . . . ' She shook her head. 'Such a waste.'

'I know, I keep running through it in my mind seeing him laying there and Bella so shaken . . . ' Frankie shrugged. 'It's not right, but it is as it is and none of us can go back and change it, as much as we want to.'

Station Officer Steele nodded sympathetically. 'I know. Life is a strange thing. None of us can know the way it will twist and turn and sometimes the things that happen are hard to fathom out . . . The only way is to accept them, though that can be very difficult and take time.' She paused. 'We're going to have to keep a close eye on Winnie and Bella to help them deal with this.'

Frankie nodded. 'Only we mustn't let on to them that we are, especially Winnie.'

'Don't worry, a Station Officer can be as

subtle or as frank as we need to be.' She smiled. 'I keep a close eye on all my crew members. Sometimes I feel like a mother hen, but it's only because I care for you all and will do all I can to help you.'

'Including telling us off.' Frankie grinned.

'Oh, absolutely! And Winnie's had a good few of those in her time here.'

64

Bella stared at the coffin, finding it hard to believe that James was actually inside. She knew he was, of course, but it still felt unreal that he could be dead and that she would never see him again, never hold him in her arms or laugh with him or talk to him about books. He was gone. It wasn't right, it wasn't fair, but life wasn't fair and she knew that all too well. She shivered, and it wasn't just from the cold inside the church but from the sadness that flowed around her body like ice.

The church was packed with mourners but she and Frankie had managed to find seats halfway down the church at the aisle end of a pew. From there she could see Winnie and Connie sitting with the rest of the family in the front pews on the other side of the church. Harry was there, smart in his RAF uniform, his new wife Meredith beside him. On his other side sat Mr and Mrs Churchill, both of them sitting ramrod straight, staring at the altar.

Frankie nudged Bella's arm as the mourners suddenly stood up ready for the next hymn. She got to her feet as the organ launched into the opening bars of 'Jerusalem', while Frankie opened the hymn book to the appropriate page and linked her arm through Bella's, holding the book so that they could both see it.

Frankie leaned close and whispered in her ear.

'Are you all right?' Bella nodded. But she wasn't all right; it was as if she was in a dreamlike state, here in person but not fully conscious of what was going on. She'd been aware of the parson talking but hadn't taken in any of his words. As the mourners began to sing the familiar words of the song that she'd sung in church since childhood, Bella couldn't sing a single word, her throat was too painfully constricted with emotion and she was on the verge of breaking down into sobs. Hanging her head, she focused on taking slow, calming breaths while hot tears rolled down her face. Frankie glanced at her sympathetically, hugging her arm tighter, and sang louder for both of them.

The rest of the service passed in a daze. Bella was longing for it to be over and yet dreading it at the same time, because then James would truly be gone for ever, buried in the cold earth and out of reach. Following in the procession behind the parson, the coffin and mourners outside in the churchyard, where a blustery, icy wind was blowing the bare trees' branches around, and heavy clouds scudded across the sky, Bella thought the day suited the mood — cold, grey and sad.

★　★　★

Winnie wished that Mac was here to hold her hand and help her get through this, but his commanding officer had refused his request for compassionate leave to attend the funeral — even a measly few hours, just enough to get here and back again, had been turned down. She'd done a lot of wishing that hadn't come true in the past few days, some of which was impossible anyway, like having James miraculously come back to life, or for time to turn back and him never to have been out in the London fog.

Walking arm in arm with Connie in the procession behind the coffin to where James would be buried, she wanted to shout and scream that this wasn't right, it wasn't how things should be. James was young and clever and should have had his whole life before him and not be lying dead in a wooden box. Never had she wanted to do something so badly, but she couldn't, she mustn't. This was not the time or the place to express that sense of utterly hopeless loss, it would be disrespectful to James. Breathing deeply, she stuffed her free hand into her coat pocket and curled it into a tight fist, holding on to her emotions for now.

Reaching the prepared grave site, her parents, Harry and Meredith and she and Connie arranged themselves around the open grave. She tried to ignore the gaping hole in the ground where James would be buried, but her eyes were drawn to it and it was hard to comprehend that her brother would be laid to rest in there. It seemed so wrong, but it was the way of things; she should know from working at Station 75 how easily and quickly death can come. The parson began the final words of the service, and as the undertakers slowly lowered the coffin into the ground, Winnie bit hard on her bottom lip, her chin quivering in a vain attempt to stem her tears. She glanced at her mother who stood still, her face impassive and unreadable behind the black veil of her hat. To look at her it was impossible to believe that she was witnessing her son's burial. The lack of emotion broke Winnie and she let her tears fall unchecked. She didn't care who saw them because they were for James and he was worth crying for.

★ ★ ★

Frankie stood with Bella beside the large window looking out at the wintry garden with its smooth green lawn and flower beds that were in their dormant phase with only the bright stems of plants to brighten them up. It was very different from the back gardens of Stepney.

'Do you mind if I join you?' a sing-song Welsh voice asked.

Frankie looked around to see Meredith, Harry's wife.

'Please do.' Frankie moved to one side, making room for Meredith to look out of the window.

'Thank you. I'm Meredith, Harry's wife, and I know you are Bella and Frankie.' She smiled at them both. 'Harry told me.' She leaned closer. 'I hope you don't mind me joining you; only I thought you looked friendly and . . . ' She pulled a face. 'I feel a bit uncomfortable with some of Harry's family.'

Frankie glanced across the room where she could see Winnie's parents talking to some people over by the blazing fire, their whole manner stiff and formal. 'I know what you mean. We're hidin' over here too until it's time to go. I ain't sure where Winnie is.'

'Probably hiding somewhere else,' Bella said.

'This is the first time I've met Harry's parents, and I don't think they liked me,' Meredith said. 'His mother was quite cold but perhaps that's because of what's happened to his brother; it's not the best time to meet your husband's parents, is it?'

'If it's any help, she's like that normally and she didn't approve of me either, wanted me to let James go . . . ' Bella's voice wavered, her brown eyes filling with tears.

Frankie put her arm through Bella's.

'It was such a shock to hear about what happened,' Meredith said.

'Harry was distraught. I've never seen him so down, not even when he was in a lot of pain after his operations.' She glanced over at Harry, who was talking to a relative over by the fireplace. 'He's putting on a brave face now.'

'It's what they do: stiff upper lip,' Frankie said. 'Not sure I could do it myself.'

Meredith shook her head. 'No, me neither, if I feel it then I show it, that's what my family do.'

'Then you are a breath of fresh air into this one,' Bella said, wiping her eyes with a handkerchief. 'Harry's lucky to have you, Winnie thinks so.'

Meredith's cheeks grew pink. 'I think I'm lucky to have him, he's a lovely man.'

'Ah, here comes Winnie,' Frankie said, spotting her friend slipping in through the door and heading their way.

'It's time to go?' Winnie said. 'I need to get out of here before I explode. Connie's coming too; she's telephoned for a taxi to take us back to Oxford station, it should be here any minute.'

'Are you all right?' Meredith asked.

'No, not really, and if I have to spend any more time trying to be polite and avoiding my mother then I truly will burst into a torrent of shouting and screaming and I'd rather not.' She shrugged. 'It has been lovely to see you again, Meredith, and Harry, but that's been the only good thing about today. I hope you are happy together in your new home.'

Meredith smiled and nodded. 'Very happy.' She reached out and took both of Winnie's hands in hers. 'I'm so sorry about James, I really am.'

Winnie nodded, tears shining in her grey eyes.

Frankie saw Connie put her head around the door and beckon to them to come. 'Looks like it's time to go.'

As they drove down the drive on the first leg of their journey home, Frankie was glad that it was over, the funeral done as well as the awkward dealings with Winnie's parents. This was just part of the sad process of dealing with James's untimely death; picking up the pieces of their lives was going to take a lot longer for Winnie and Bella, but she would be there for them just as she had been today, and for as long as it would take.

65

There were times when Station 75 felt like a refuge, a place where things were usually the same, somewhere where she could forget what else was happening in her life and apply herself to her work, and today was one of them, Winnie thought, as she waited for the crew members to arrange themselves in formation ready to do a last practice march before they set off to take part in the morning's parade.

Yesterday had been like a bad dream and she wanted to forget it for a while. She would never, ever, forget James, and would always wish that he was still here, but she needed to let herself be distracted by other things for a while to give her mind a rest from the pain and grief, and today was going to give her a chance to do that. Station Officer Steele had asked her if she'd rather not take part under the circumstances, but Winnie had been adamant that she wanted to do this.

Taking her place beside Sparky in the front row, she took a deep breath and called out, 'Ready, forward, march,' her breath fogging in the cold air. Stepping forward in time with the rest of her row, she was aware that the row behind her was doing the same, everyone moving their legs and arms in unison, looking smart and doing Station 75 proud. It had taken several practices for them to achieve the perfection that the boss had asked for.

'And halt!' Winnie shouted as they reached the far wall of the courtyard and ran out of room. 'Well done, we're ready to go.'

The crew members started to talk amongst themselves but were suddenly silenced as church bells began to ring out across the city. The sweet, mellow sound brought a lump to Winnie's throat, and looking around at other crew members she could see that they were feeling the same way too. Pealing bells had once been a common sound but they hadn't been heard in London for more than two years and were only to be used to warn of an invasion. Today, they were ringing out to mark a new day of celebration — Civil Defence Day — which had been appointed by the King to honour the work of the Civil Defence services, the Ambulance Service included.

Lined up in their position in the parade later that morning, with Station Officer Steele at their side, Winnie thought it was almost as if the air was charged with national pride and devotion. The crew from Station 75 were a small part of the 1,500 Civil Defence workers that were taking part in the parade, coming not only from London but from all over the country.

They'd been organised into a chronological sequence of groups to mark the principal raids of the war so far, with them marching as part of the London contingent. There were groups from Dover, Coventry and the more recently bombed cities that had suffered attack during the Baedeker raids, such as Norwich, Bath and York. Each represented place carried a banner to show where they were from.

Everyone looked smart in their uniforms; some people were wearing the medals they'd been awarded for their work. Winnie was wearing her own George Medal, but only because Station Officer Steele had insisted on it. She was glad to have it but still regarded what she'd been awarded it for as nothing special, just part of the job, which any other crew member would have done in the same situation.

'Looks like they're off at the front,' Sparky said, nodding towards where they could see the front of the parade moving off, the men of the Anti-aircraft heading the parade, followed by a detachment from the RAF, then the Police and Fire Service, each in their different colour and style of uniform.

As the group of ARP wardens in front of them started to march, Winnie gave the order ready for Station 75 to move off smoothly. 'Ready, forward ... march.' And they were away, following on behind the ribbon of marching Civil Defence workers, which snaked its way through the streets towards St Paul's Cathedral.

With her body moving to a rhythm, her feet marching, arms swinging in time with the rest in her row, and hopefully with the others behind, Winnie glanced around at the crowds lining the street, who clapped and cheered as they went past. It was a cold, dull November day but the atmosphere generated by the parade and the onlookers was warm and glowing and Winnie was glad to be here.

Marching past St Paul's where the King and

Queen stood watching the parade, sheltered under a striped awning, the crew members turned their heads to the right in acknowledgement of the royal couple and Winnie could see the King saluting back to them. Then they were past, they'd done it, and were shepherded towards the doors of the cathedral where they were going to take part in a special service of commemoration.

'That went well; you did an excellent job with the crew,' Station Officer Steele said as they were ushered towards their seats.

'Thank you.' Winnie smiled at her. 'Sparky was a huge help; I couldn't have done it without him.'

'You used your initiative and the skills of crew members; that's good teamwork and that's what makes the crew of Station 75 so good at their job.' The boss touched Winnie's elbow. 'Are you all right?'

Winnie nodded. 'Yes, I'm fine, I'm in my favourite building of all so that's a big help.'

Station Officer Steele smiled. 'Ah, yes, you and St Paul's. Well, you'll have a chance to soak up its grand atmosphere before the service begins. Go and sit down, I want to check on Bella.'

Winnie did as she was told and found a seat in the section the ambulance crews were being directed to, glad of the chance to sit quietly on her own for a few minutes. She looked up at the soaring roof and felt a tingle run down her spine as she always did when she came in here. It was a place so big and grand that it made you feel small and insignificant; it had a way of making her calm down and she needed that now. All around her she could hear the muffled voices of people talking quietly but she felt apart from that, as if she were in a bubble of her own and it was soothing.

'Winnie!' Frankie's voice brought her back to the present a few minutes later as her friend sat down beside her, followed by Bella and Rose at the end of the row. 'Are you all right?'

She nodded. 'Just being still and soaking up St Paul's. You know me and this place . . . ' She shrugged, her eyes suddenly filling with tears-.Frankie nodded sympathetically. 'This is a good place for you to be today. Remember when we came in here pretendin' to have been called to an incident all because you wanted to see what bomb damage had been done?'

'I was sure they'd know we weren't really supposed to be here,' Bella added. 'But you were as cool as a cucumber, Winnie.'

Winnie remembered how determined she'd been to see what had happened to her beloved St Paul's and how her friends had come with her, risking getting into trouble themselves. They were always there for her, just as they had been yesterday, only poor Bella was grieving herself too. She reached out and took hold of Bella's hand. 'I'm glad you were with me, just like you were yesterday.'

Bella's eyes filled with tears and she looked down at their clasped hands.

'All for one and one for all,' Frankie said softly, putting her arms around Winnie and Bella's shoulders and squeezing them to her.

'Oy, you lot, here comes the King and Queen,' Sparky hissed from the row behind them. 'Look smart.'

Winnie sat upright and looked to the aisle where the royal couple walked past, the pair of them elegant and upright, the King wearing uniform and the Queen dressed in a blue suit with a diamond maple leaf brooch on her hat. The service was about to start, Winnie had to rein in her emotions and apply some stiff upper lip; there'd be time enough for tears later. James wouldn't want her crying now, she was here representing the Ambulance Service and she had to do that with dignity and nothing less. It was what Station Officer Steele would expect.

66

Bella's slice of toast lay cold and uneaten on her plate, as she stared into the bottom of her empty teacup, ignoring the chatter that was going on around her in the common room of Station 75. She'd even stopped paying attention to the conversation Winnie, Frankie and Rose were having as they sat beside her on the sofa and nearby armchair, her hand absent-mindedly stroking Trixie's head as the little dog leaned against her legs like a warm, comforting blanket.

'You should see what's in today's paper!' Sparky's sudden, loud voice made her jump, pulling her out of her stupor. She looked up and saw him hurrying over to the table, waving a newspaper in the air, getting everyone's attention. 'Come and 'ave a look.'

He made a great show of laying it down on the table, spreading it smooth with his hand and flicking through the pages till he found what he was looking for as crew members crowded round to see. Winnie, Frankie and Rose got up to see what it was, but Bella stayed where she was.

'That's us!' Frankie said.

'Look at that magnificent marching,' Winnie added. Other crew members were making remarks and there was a lot of excited chatter going on.

'Don't you want a look, Bella?' Station Officer Steele sat down beside her on the sofa.

Bella shrugged. 'I will in a bit.'

The boss nodded and sat quietly for a few moments, watching the crew members delighting in what they were seeing in Sparky's paper. 'I was wondering if you'd decided who you were going to interview for your first piece for the paper, though you may already have done it. Have you?'

'No.' Bella didn't want to be reminded about the article she'd agreed to write because she'd lost all interest in it.

'Do you know what you're going to do?' the older woman probed.

Memories of that last time she and James had been together before his accident flooded into her mind, when they'd talked and laughed as they'd come up with possible ideas for her new column. Tears stung Bella's eyes and her heart ached. She didn't want to do it now.

'Bella?' Station Officer Steele put her hand on Bella's arm. 'You need to do this. You're very good at it and you love it and . . . ' she paused. 'James wouldn't have wanted you to stop writing, would he?'

It was as if the boss had just poked at her open wound with a sharp stick and Bella glared her through tear-filled eyes, making the image of the older woman swim and distort. Swallowing against the hard lump that was filling her throat, she shook her head. The boss was right, though: James would never have wanted her to stop.

Station Officer Steele looked at her sympathetically. 'Well, I have an idea, if you don't already have something sorted out. You could go and talk to the WAAFs manning the barrage balloon where Frankie's sister works. She's been there, and it will be an easy one to start with. What do you think?'

'A barrage balloon crew were on my list to talk to.'

'Good. Frankie!' the boss called to her. 'Can you come here a moment, please?'

Frankie came over, her face looking concerned as she spotted Bella's face. She crouched down in front of her. 'Bella, are you all right?'

Bella nodded and did her best to smile.

'Would you take Bella to your sister's barrage balloon site, so she can interview the WAAFs for her column?' the boss asked.

'Yes, of course. I'm sure they'd be happy to talk to you, they're a nice bunch,' Frankie said. 'We can go tomorrow after we get off duty, if you like?'

'Splendid, and I'll look forward to seeing your piece in *The War Illustrated*, Bella.' The boss smiled and stood up. 'I'd better have a look at what Sparky's got everyone so excited about.'

Frankie sat down in the boss's vacated place next to Bella. 'Are you really all right, only you've been ever so quiet lately, since . . . James died?'

'I can't really believe he's gone. I know he is but the thought of never seeing him again . . . it's like a knife in my chest.' Bella's eyes welled up with tears again.

'I know.' Frankie leaned her head on Bella's shoulder. 'It's horrible when someone you love dies, it feels as if part of you has gone with them,

399

but it will get better with time, I promise you. You just have to keep goin', keep doing things, like your writin'. It'll help.'

Bella sighed, leaning her head against Frankie's. 'I know, but it's hard.'

'The deeper the love, the stronger the grief.' Frankie stood up and held out her hand to Bella. 'Come on, come and see your photo in the paper.'

'What?' Bella took hold of her friend's hand and stood up.

'You'll see.' Frankie led her over to the table where Sparky's newspaper was spread out.

Bella looked at the page with its title 'The day that will commemorate civilian valour and fortitude', under which were photographs showing different views of the Civil Defence Day march, and in one of them were the crew of Station 75 marching past the King and Queen. She could see them all: Station Officer Steele, Sparky, Winnie, Frankie, Rose and herself.

'Look at that magnificent marching,' Winnie said, pointing to the picture. 'Worth all the practising we did.'

'We did Station 75 proud,' Station Officer Steele said.

67

Frankie rubbed her gloved hands together to warm them up as the icy air was starting to make her fingers tingle. She was enjoying watching the WAAF barrage balloon crew demonstrating their work while the photographer, who'd been sent from *The War Illustrated*, took pictures to go with Bella's piece. The WAAFs seemed to be thoroughly enjoying themselves and were full of smiles and good cheer despite the freezing weather. Even Lizzie looked happy, Frankie thought.

'She doesn't look like you,' Winnie said quietly. She'd come along with them to support Bella and because she was nosy and wanted to see Frankie's sister.

'No, she's like her father . . . my stepfather,' Frankie said. 'My other sister looks like me and our mother, though.'

With the photographer finished and on his way to his next job, Bella started to interview the WAAFs, who had readily agreed to speak to her, happy to share their experience of working as members of a barrage balloon crew. It was good to see her friend looking happy; she'd lost her spark since James had died and this was the first time she'd seen the old Bella return.

'Watch out! Here she comes,' Winnie whispered as Lizzie left the rest of the WAAFs and came marching over to them. 'She doesn't look very welcoming.'

'I don't know why you're here. I write home every week, regular as clockwork, so there's no need to come checking up on me.' Lizzie glared at Frankie, her arms folded tightly across the front of her overalls.

'I'm glad to hear that, but I ain't here to see you. I brought Bella along to do the interview since I knew where the barrage balloon site was.' Frankie looked her sister straight in the eye. 'Does it matter?'

'Look, Stella or Frankie or whatever your name is, I don't want you coming here, all right? I'm happy here doing my job and I don't need you turning up, checking on me and interfering.'

'Now look here — ' Winnie began before Frankie nudged her hard in the arm to silence her. She could feel her friend bristling and didn't want this to turn into an argument, not when this was about being here to support Bella.

'I really didn't come here to see you, Lizzie, so don't go gettin' on your high horse,' Frankie said quietly. 'I don't know what I've done to upset you, but you've been off with me from when we first met. Why's that?'

Lizzie rolled her eyes. 'We don't need you in our family. We were perfectly all right before you turned up.'

'And I was perfectly fine until I found out my mother was still alive,' Frankie said. 'It ain't my fault our mother left me behind and didn't tell you about me. I don't want anythin' from you, Lizzie, and I ain't trying to steal your mother away, if that's what you're worried about.'

'I'm not,' Lizzie snapped.

From the furious look on Lizzie's face, Frankie knew she'd hit a nerve. Was her sister jealous of her? And yet she'd been the one who'd grown up with their mother, had years of her love and attention; whatever the case, Frankie's contact with her had clearly stirred up resentment in Lizzie.

'We don't 'ave to be the best of friends, but perhaps we should try to just get along with each other,' Frankie suggested.

Lizzie shook her head. 'I've got one sister, I don't need another one.'

'I'd be very glad to have Frankie as my sister,' Winnie said. 'You should count yourself lucky and stop being so stubborn and foolish.'

'It's none of your business!' Lizzie snapped. 'So keep out of it.'

Frankie looked at Winnie and shook her head, making it quite clear that she could deal with this; Winnie clamped her lips tightly shut, clearly having to keep a control on herself.

Frankie shrugged. 'Well I *am* your half-sister and you can't change that. But don't worry, Lizzie, I ain't going to come botherin' you here again.'

'Good.' Lizzie turned and marched off to join the other WAAFs who were clustered around Bella.

'She's jealous of you,' Winnie said. 'You should have let me speak.'

'No.' Frankie linked her hand through her friend's arm. 'I'm not bothered if she don't want to be friendly, honestly I'm not. After today I ain't got any plans to come here and see her again.'

'Well, she's a fool. I would be delighted if I found out you were my long-lost sister.'

'What's the saying? You can't choose your family but you can choose your friends; and you are my good friend, Winnie, far better than a grumpy, half-sister any day.'

'Did you get all the information you needed?' Frankie asked Bella as they all walked back to where they'd left their bicycles a short while later.

'Yes, they were very talkative and funny, told me all about their job and what it's like to work on the balloon site,' Bella said. 'I enjoyed it. Thanks for bringing me here.'

'I'm glad you liked it, you certainly looked like you were havin' a good time, even my surly sister was talking to you and laughin'.'

'Yes, she seemed nice.' Bella frowned. 'I noticed she was talking to you for a bit, how did that go?'

Winnie tutted. 'Let's just say she wasn't nice then.'

'I ain't worried, it's up to her. I don't need her to be my sister andI ain't comin' here to see her again.'

'It's a shame she's behaving that way. If you turned up saying you were my sister, I'd be pleased — you're a lovely person, Frankie.'

'That's exactly what I said.' Winnie smiled.

Frankie laughed.

'She might come around one day,' Bella said. 'Realise what a good sister you could be to her.'

Frankie shrugged. 'I'm not holding my breath. I've already got a difficult enough relation to deal with in Ivy, I don't need any more.'

'I've got an idea,' Winnie said as they collected their bicycles.

'It's not far from here, so why don't we go to Gurney Street, see what's happened there? I still think about it sometimes.'

Frankie and Bella looked at each other and nodded.

'All right then,' Frankie said, mounting her bicycle. 'You lead the way.'

★ ★ ★

Gurney Street looked completely different from the last time she was there, Frankie thought. There were no lorries lined up to take away rubble, no rescue workers frantically searching through crumpled buildings, no smell of plaster and brick dust in the air. No sense of desperation as the search for survivors was carried out. Life was carrying on as normal again, only with a massive gap now scarring the street where the UXB had exploded.

They dismounted their bicycles as they drew level with the gap and stood staring at it, not saying anything for a short while.

'I can still picture how it was here that night, and the next morning,' Bella said.

'Me too.' Frankie had seen plenty of bomb damage around London but this one seemed different, the yawning gap in the row of buildings and the memories of that night were an uncomfortable mix.

'Are you all right, Winnie?' Bella asked.

Frankie looked at her friend, who for once had remained silent since they'd arrived.

Winnie turned to them and nodded, her grey eyes bright with tears. 'It's strange to see it like this . . . ' She threw her arm wide towards the gap. 'Makes the damage look even bigger than when we last saw it . . . all the people who were in there or nearby when that bomb exploded . . . '

'I know.' Bella touched Winnie's arm. 'Come on, we should go home.'

Winnie nodded, not arguing like she had the last time they were here.

As they turned their bicycles around, Frankie noticed two people walking along the pavement towards them, the man leaning on a stick, the woman with her arm linked through his free one helping to support him. There was something familiar about them but before she could work out what, the woman called out to them.

'Hello, ducks, you were 'ere that night, weren't you? You took my Jim 'ere to hospital.'

Frankie suddenly remembered. He had been the first casualty they'd collected here. She smiled at them. 'That's right. Bella,' she pointed to her friend, 'and I took you to Guy's. How are you?'

'Not so bad,' Jim said. 'I lived when a lot of 'em didn't.' He threw a glance at the gap they'd just been staring at, which must remind the residents of Gurney Street of that night every time they looked at it.

406

'Thank you for what you did for 'im,' his wife said.

Frankie shrugged. 'I'm glad we could 'elp.'

'How are the other families here?' Winnie asked. 'So many lost their children.'

The woman sighed. 'They're carrying on, that's all they can do. We'll never forget them or what happened.'

They fell into silence for a few moments, everyone's eyes drawn to the gap again, each of them lost in thought and memory. Coming back to the scene of an incident wasn't something they usually did, Frankie thought, or meeting again someone that they'd taken to hospital, but she was glad they'd come back, pleased to see Jim healed and home again. Their job was all about getting the casualties to hospital, not about seeing what happened next. Gurney Street had broken all the usual rules — its unexpected, horrific explosion with no air raid and now their return and seeing Jim again. It helped to know that despite that awful night, life in Gurney Street was carrying on, but always with the memory of those who had been lost.

68

Christmas Eve wouldn't feel right without putting up a few decorations, Station Officer Violet Steele thought, as she hung some colourful glass baubles from the mantelpiece in her flat. She had no Christmas tree again this year and had taken most of her decorations to Station 75 to decorate the common room with, as that's where she would be spending Christmas Day, but she'd kept a few back to put up at home on Christmas Eve, even though she felt far from festive. She couldn't feel excited about the festivities when she was so worried about her sister; it was now over three months since she'd had the telegram from Lily telling her that she was coming home, but since then there'd been no word. Nothing. She had no idea where she was or what had happened to her. All she knew was that it shouldn't have taken that long to sail home from South Africa.

With her minimal decorations finished, she poured herself a small glass of the precious Scottish whisky that her brother Gerald had brought her on his last trip home from where he was posted in Scotland. Sitting back in an armchair, listening to music on the wireless, she sipped the fiery liquid, enjoying its peaty taste and the warmth it spread in her as it went down. She must have drifted off to sleep as she was woken by a loud knocking at her door. Glancing at the clock on the mantelpiece, she saw it was nearly ten o'clock. Who would be banging on her door at this time of night? It wouldn't be her brother come home on unexpected leave, he had a key and would let himself in.

Standing up, she straightened her skirt, smoothed down her ruffled hair and went to answer it. Opening the door, she was stunned and overwhelmed at the sight that greeted her, and when she opened her mouth to speak, no words came out.

'Hello, Violet,' her sister Lily said, and the two girls standing either side of her smiled at her shyly.

Recovering herself, Station Officer Steele threw her arms around the three of them and hugged them tightly, not caring that tears were running down her cheeks. They were alive, they were here, they were home.

Standing back to have a proper look at them, she noticed how tired and thin they were. 'Come in.' She looked around for their luggage, but there didn't seem to be any except for the small bag that her sister was carrying. 'Where are your things?'

'This is all we have.' Lily held up her bag. 'But we're here and home and that's all that matters.'

'Absolutely.' She ushered them into the flat. 'Are you hungry? I'll make you something to eat.'

Lily shook her head. 'Thank you, but there's no need; we had something to eat on the train. The girls just need to get to bed.'

'Yes, of course.' She wanted to ask her sister

what had happened, where they had been, why it had taken so long for them to come home, but the questions would have to wait. Her nieces looked like they were ready to fall asleep on their feet. 'The bed's made up in Gerald's room, it's a double so plenty of room for both of you.' She smiled at her nieces, Grace and Helena, who'd grown so much since she'd last seen them just before they'd sailed for Singapore three years ago.

'That will be fine, and I'll sleep in there too,' Lily said.

'Will there be room?'

'Yes, don't worry, we'll be perfectly fine; we've slept in a lot worse places than Gerald's comfy bed.'

'I'll fill up some hot-water bottles while you get them ready for bed.'

Once the girls were tucked up in bed, where they quickly fell asleep, cuddled up together, Violet made some tea and she and Lily sat down together for the first time in several years.

'Oh my, that tastes good.' Lily took a sip of tea and leaned back in her armchair, closing her eyes.

'Do you need to go to bed?'

Lily opened her eyes and smiled at her. 'Soon, but not yet. I'm sure you're itching to know what happened, aren't you? I can see it on your face.'

Violet laughed. 'You always did know what I was thinking. And yes, I do want to know, I've been terribly worried wondering where you were. After I got your telegram in September I've been waiting for you to come home but you

410

didn't, until now. What happened?'

'It's a long story.'

'Start at the beginning then: what happened in Singapore?'

'Air, raids started as the Japanese got closer and we knew we had to get out before they overran us. The order to leave came quickly and we could only take hand luggage with us, and, of course, George had to stay behind. I last saw him standing on the dock side . . . ' Lily's voice wavered and she paused for a few moments before going on. 'He promised to follow on as soon as he could. We sailed from Singapore under cover of darkness. The ship was full of women and children fleeing and praying that the ship wouldn't get bombed. Luckily for us it didn't and we were taken to Colombo, then on to South Africa, where we waited for George to join us — that was what we'd planned.'

'Where did you live?'

'We were billeted in hotels and the girls went to school while we waited. I didn't want them missing out on their education and it gave them something to do.' Lily sighed. 'And then I found out when another woman's husband arrived who'd been in Singapore with us that George had been killed in an air raid not long after we left, and all I wanted to do then was come home.'

Violet reached out and took her sister's hand. 'I'm so sorry about George.'

Lily nodded. 'I know. If only he'd come with us on the boat, but he had to stay and do his job.' She fell silent, looking into the fire where the coal embers were glowing orange and red.

'I got your telegram saying you were sailing the next day, I expected you back long before now, did you not get that boat?'

Violet looked at her. 'Yes, but I wish we hadn't. We sailed on the RMS *Laconia*. It was packed with servicemen from the Middle East and was carrying Italian prisoners of war as well. We stopped at Cape Town and went ashore and then carried on. On the fourth day out from Cape Town we were torpedoed by a German U-boat.'

Violet stared at her sister. She'd never imagined that this was why her sister hadn't come back; it had been too horrible to contemplate. 'Did the ship sink?'

Lily nodded. 'We were lucky to get on a lifeboat, but a lot of people didn't. The water was full of people, it was chaos . . . so awful.' She sighed. 'We had sixty people in a boat meant for thirty and we had to ration the water and the food. It was so hot in the day. After four days the U-boat that sank us appeared, it had been rounding up the lifeboats and they linked all the boats up in a daisy chain behind it and took all the women and children on board. We spent the night on a submarine, sleeping in German officers' bunks.'

'What happened next?'

'The next day we were put back in the boats and the submarine sent out messages that it had survivors and displayed the Red Cross flag, but it was attacked by an American bomber, two lifeboats were hit and the submarine had to dive to protect itself. They contacted a Vichy French warship, which came and picked us up and we were taken to Casablanca to an internment camp in the desert run by them. And that's where we've been until the Americans came and we were freed and brought back to England.'

'I never imagined any of that was happening to you. I had no idea where you were but to be shipwrecked and then imprisoned.' Violet's eyes stung with tears.

'We survived, Violet, we were very lucky, because many people on the *Laconia* didn't.' Lily yawned. 'I'm sorry, I'm tired.'

'You need to go to bed. I'll find you a nightdress and we can talk more in the morning.' Violet stood up and put out her hand to help her sister up. 'I'm so glad you're home.'

Lily smiled at her. 'Coming back is what kept me going. I wanted to bring my girls home.'

69

Before the war, Frankie would have hated the idea of having to work on Christmas Day — it was a day for spending with your family, enjoying each other's company and good food, but today she welcomed the prospect. Christmas Day 1942, the fourth one of the war, wouldn't be any fun at home in Matlock Street with Ivy, so she was relieved to be going to work a twenty-four-hour shift at Station 75.

Arriving at work with Rose, they left their bicycles at the back of the garages and went up to the common room ready for the morning briefing, when Station Officer Steele would give out the jobs for the day. With it being Christmas Day there would be some leeway, but as they were an operational ambulance station, all the vehicles needed to be ready to go at a moment's notice, and regardless of the day they would still need to be checked and prepared for action this morning.

'Merry Christmas!' Winnie called out to them as they entered the common room, which was looking festive with its newspaper paper-chains that the crew had made and the wire Christmas tree that Sparky had fashioned and which was hung with the boss's decorations.

'Merry Christmas to you, too,' Frankie said, going over to sit with Winnie and Bella, who were sitting on the sofa, waiting for their morning briefing.

It wasn't long before the boss appeared and Frankie was surprised at the transformation in her. She looked as if she were floating on air; she'd lost the haunted look that she'd worn like a cloak over the past few weeks. Something has happened, Frankie thought, and for the good.

Winnie nudged Frankie's elbow and nodded at the boss, clearly having noticed the change herself.

'Merry Christmas to you all,' Station Officer Steele said.

'Merry Christmas,' everyone chorused back.

'As usual we must be prepared for incidents, but I hope that we can still enjoy the day as well.' She paused for a moment. 'I must tell you that the most marvellous thing has happened: my sister and nieces have returned home, they turned up at my door last night. They're home and safe.' She smiled, the widest and happiest smile, that Frankie had ever seen her give.

A loud cheering and clapping erupted in the common room, the crew having all been aware of the boss's worry over her sister after the fall of Singapore.

'What took 'em so long?' Sparky called out.

Station Officer Steele raised her eyebrows. 'They were shipwrecked after being torpedoed by a German U-boat, adrift in a lifeboat for days, finally rescued and then imprisoned in an internment camp in the desert, that's why they took so long to come home.'

'Blimey!' Sparky said. 'It's a wonder they got 'ome at all.'

'Indeed, and I am very grateful that they did,' the boss said.

'Where are they now?' Winnie said.

'At my flat.'

'They should come here and 'ave Christmas dinner with us; we can celebrate their home-comin',' Frankie said.

Mrs Connelly was planning a feast for the crew. Bella's mother had sent two large cockerels for the meal, and Frankie had brought in some eggs to make decent Yorkshire puddings with. Other crew members had brought in what they could to add to the meal, some of them contributing rations the previous week to help Mrs Connelly make some Christmas puddings, adapting her recipe to include more carrot and apple rather than the usual dried fruits, which were in short supply now.

'Absolutely,' Winnie agreed. 'I could go over and pick them up in one of the cars.'

More cheering and shouts of 'Yes' and 'Go and get them' filled the common room and Station Officer Steele had to raise her hands in the air to finally quieten them down. 'It's very kind and generous of you but I'm not sure that we should use a car to fetch them.'

'You're the boss, you can decide that it's fine,' Sparky shouted.

'So, just do it and let Winnie go and fetch them here.'

Station Officer Steele smiled. 'Very well then, go and fetch them, but only after you've finished preparing your ambulance. Bella, if you'd go with Winnie, too. I'll telephone my sister and tell her they're invited to share Station 75's Christmas lunch.'

⋆ ⋆ ⋆

'Do you think this is enough?' Rose asked, her breath pluming in the cold air as she pointed at the pile of parsnips that she'd carefully dug up in Station 75's allotment down by the Tower of London.

'I'd dig up a few more — we've got extra people comin' with the boss's sister and nieces, and roast parsnips are always popular,' Frankie said, adding more carrots to the pile that she was carefully digging out of the soil, the leaves now too weak to pull them up with. Station Officer Steele had sent her and Rose down to the allotment to harvest the vegetables to go with Mrs Connelly's Christmas lunch. They had potatoes stored back at the station, but the parsnips, carrots and sprouts needed to be picked fresh.

'I'm looking forward to the meal.' Rose gently pushed her fork into the soil near the parsnips.

'Me too. It must be strange for you to be involved with Christmas celebrations.'

'I'm getting used to it; this is my fourth Christmas in England.' Rose smiled at Frankie. 'I like it.'

'Christmas has changed a lot since the war started, though. No proper Christmas puddings or cake. We ain't even got a proper Christmas tree at the station.' Frankie sighed. 'So many people not together for the day any more — or not around at all.' She was thinking of her grandparents, who used to love Christmas and made it such a joyous occasion, and Stanley, who was spending another festive season miles away from home in the safety of the countryside. And Alastair, who was somewhere in North Africa in the heat and sand. 'I'm glad we're workin' today. It'll be fun, we'll have a sing-song around the piano later on.'

'Will this be enough?' Rose asked, adding more parsnips to the pile.

Frankie nodded. 'Yes, that lot should satisfy the crew, even Sparky.' She knocked the soil off the last lot of carrots she'd dug up and threw them into the basket. 'We just need to pick the sprouts.'

Rose pulled a face. 'Horrible things.'

Frankie laughed. 'At least these ain't rationed. Come on, we need to pick them quickly and get the veg back to Mrs Connelly so she can get them ready.'

★ ★ ★

Christmas lunch was a huge success, the food was delicious and plentiful and a joyful sense of good cheer and camaraderie had filled the common room of Station 75. Now with all the clearing away, washing and drying up done by all the crew members helping — a case of many hands making light work — people had gathered around the piano in the common room ready for a sing-song, many of them still wearing the funny paper hats that Sparky had made for everyone

418

out of newspaper. Station Officer Steele was seated at the piano ready to play, and Sparky was going to lead the singing.

Everyone looked happy, Frankie thought. The boss's sister, who looked very much like her, only quite tanned after their time in the desert camp, and her two girls, Grace and Helena, had seemed delighted to come to see Station 75 and had thoroughly enjoyed their meal, joining in with the chatter and laughter. No one could guess from the look of them what they had been through. It was the same for all the crew members: there wasn't a person in the room who wasn't touched by the war in some way, and who hadn't seen or experienced what pain and unhappiness wartime brought in either their work or their personal life, or both. And yet they were carrying on, living their lives and making the most of today because who knew what tomorrow might bring.

Frankie linked her hands through Winnie's and Bella's arms, who were standing either side of her, as Station Officer Steele played the introduction of the first song, the notes filling the room with a sweet melody.

'Are you ready for this?' Frankie smiled at her friends as they both turned to her.

'Absolutely,' Winnie said.

Bella nodded, smiling back.

Frankie knew that they were both still hurting over James's untimely death and were doing their best to hide it. She couldn't ease their pain or take it away, but she was watching over them, she would be there for them when they needed

419

her. She had no idea what the future held for any of them and preferred not to dwell on the what-ifs because it was a waste of time. The only thing she could be certain of was that she would be beside Winnie and Bella and that would never, ever, change.

Acknowledgements

It takes many people to make a book and I'm very fortunate to have a brilliant team supporting me and working hard at Sphere to get Winnie, Frankie and Bella's story out into the world. Thank you to my editor Maddie West for her wonderful enthusiasm and guidance, and to Tamsyn Berryman, Clara Diaz, Amy Donegan, Bekki Guyatt and Alison Tulett for all they do to bring the book together and launch it into the world.

Thank you to my brilliant agent, Felicity Trew, for her support and care, and for championing my writing, especially on days when it feels like it's not going well.

My writing pals in the Romantic Novelists' Association and the Strictly Saga group are a brilliant support, so thank you all for your friendship and advice, and for lots of fun and laughter.

The Imperial War Museum has been a fantastic source of research and to have copies of real ambulance station magazines was so helpful.

It's wonderful to hear from readers and I enjoy finding out what you think of the East End Angels. Thank you for reading the book and taking time to leave reviews — they are all very much appreciated.

Thank you to Isobel for her typing and editing and to Tom for fixing my computer issues.

As always, thank you to David for your unwavering support.

We do hope that you have enjoyed reading this large print book.

Did you know that all of our titles are available for purchase?

We publish a wide range of high quality large print books including:
Romances, Mysteries, Classics
General Fiction
Non Fiction and Westerns

Special interest titles available in large print are:
The Little Oxford Dictionary
Music Book
Song Book
Hymn Book
Service Book

Also available from us courtesy of Oxford University Press:
Young Readers' Dictionary
(large print edition)
Young Readers' Thesaurus
(large print edition)

For further information or a free brochure, please contact us at:
Ulverscroft Large Print Books Ltd.,
The Green, Bradgate Road, Anstey,
Leicester, LE7 7FU, England.
Tel: (00 44) 0116 236 4325
Fax: (00 44) 0116 234 0205